DUST TO DUST

LILLIAN STEWART CARL

AN AUTHORS GUILD BACKINPRINT.COM EDITION

AN AUTHORS GUILD BACKINPRINT.COM EDITION

Published by iUniverse.com, Inc.

For information address:
iUniverse.com, Inc.
620 North 48th Street, Suite 201
Lincoln, NE 68504-3467
www.iuniverse.com

Originally published by Diamond Books

ISBN: 0-595-09446-5

Printed in the United States of America

For Patricia C. Wrede,
deo gratias

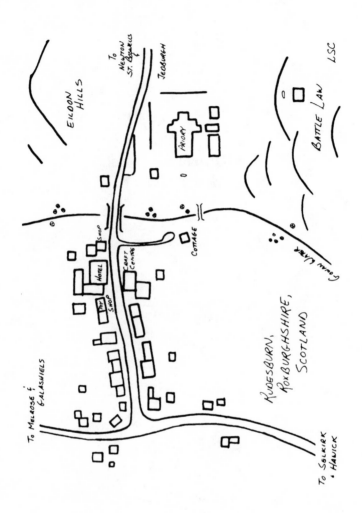

EILDON HILLS

To NEWTON ST. BOSWELLS &

JEDBURGH

PRIORY

BATTLE LAW

LSC

SHOP

COTTAGE

CRAFT CENTRE

HOTEL

POST SHOP

SHOP

GOVAN ESTATE

To MELROSE & GALASHIELS

RUDESBURN, ROXBURGHSHIRE, SCOTLAND

To SELKIRK & HAWICK

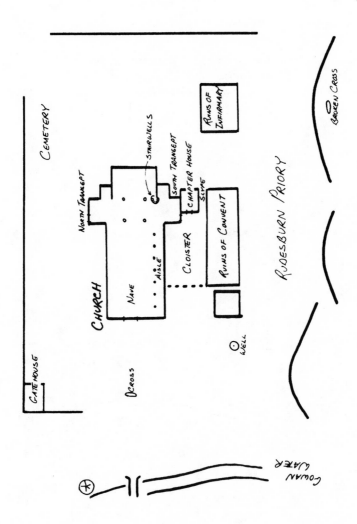

RUDESBURN PRIORY

For the reader's benefit, a glossary of Scottish slang has been provided at the back of the book.

Chapter One

REBECCA'S ANCESTORS HAD crossed the Atlantic from Scotland to America in steerage. For her, going back in an economy seat in a DC-10 was somewhat better. The torture lasted only during those few hours between New York and Europe.

She closed her eyes and tried to convince herself she was sleepy. The tendons in her neck and shoulders were tight with tension. With a sigh she opened her eyes. Her contact lenses felt like cockleburs against her pupils.

Beside her, Adele breathed tiny ladylike snores, deep in the sleep of a person with a clear conscience. Across the aisle, Dennis was a blanketed cocoon, his mouth open, his snores anything but delicate. The sleep of the—well no, Rebecca decided generously, not the dumb but the innocent. She had just met the two students, so it was premature to be passing judgment on either of them. She simply wasn't in a very generous mood. She'd slept only fitfully for a week, and here, so close to Scotland at last, she abandoned all hope of sleeping now. Her feelings ricocheted from anticipation to apprehension and back again.

Michael, Rebecca said silently, his name a kiss on her lips. Six months ago he'd asked her to return to Scotland with him. She'd replied that she couldn't; she didn't want to blame him if she never got her doctorate.

She'd submitted her dissertation at the beginning of June. It would be September before the degree she'd struggled toward these many years would be granted or denied. Now she was spending six weeks of those months shepherding a group of students to the excavations of Rudesburn Priory. The job didn't pay much, but it would be an important asset to her résumé, and she would once again be living and working with Michael.

If everything went well at the dig, maybe she could find a job and launch a career. Then they could afford to marry. If they wanted to marry. If she wanted to stay in Scotland.

An American professor of British history searching for a job in Edinburgh would give new meaning to the expression "coals to Newcastle." Of course Michael already had a job, a toehold on the career ladder, as a curator at the National Museums of Scotland.

If only she hadn't heard those rumors about the excavation—she so needed that excavation to be successful. . . . As if she didn't have enough to worry about without worrying over the dig itself. Body, mind and soul, love and money. She squirmed, her mind still trapped by random strands of thought. For a twenty-eight-year-old, she was feeling very immature.

Rebecca felt rather than heard the change in the timbre of the engines. She glanced at her watch which she'd set to Greenwich time while the plane was taxiing for take-off. Six a.m. The plane was scheduled to land at Prestwick at seven. To Rebecca's internal chronometer, as crumpled as her sweater and khaki pants, it was barely past midnight. But she'd grown very familiar with this wide-eyed weariness in the last few months.

She raised the blind on the window and peered out. Dawn. The sky was an impressionist painting, pale blue lavished with gold. Far below was a green coastline frilled with white breakers—Ireland. Ahead lay the peninsula of Kintyre, and Scotland. Rebecca's heart swelled; she was coming home, even though she'd been here only twice before.

The lights flickered on in the cabin, bringing groans of protest from the huddled masses wrapped like corpses after a battle. Adele stirred, brushed at her no-nonsense sheaf of gray hair, and looked up. "Are we almost there?"

"Terra firma Scotia is on the horizon."

"Good." Adele polished her glasses, adjusted her double-knit jacket, and applied her only concession to makeup, a bit of lip balm. Her pale blue eyes were as bright if she'd spent eight hours asleep in her own bed.

Rebecca was vaguely embarrassed at finding herself with a student twenty years older than she. But if Adele chose to go back to school after being widowed, more power to her. When the flight attendant came down the aisle doling out coffee and sweet rolls, Adele told her, "I don't drink caffeine or eat sugar. I'll just take some juice."

Across the aisle, Dennis wriggled against the confines of his seat, yawned, and asked Adele, "If you don't want your roll, can I have it?"

Rebecca drank her own cup of caffeine, wishing she could take it intravenously, and choked down the sugary flour and preservative patty the attendant optimistically called food. She picked up her purse, dug her toothbrush out of her carry-on bag, and eyed the line waiting for the lavatory.

Adele asked, "Your young man will be at the airport?"

"My young man?" Adele made it sound as if she and Michael had courted discreetly in the front parlor under the watchful eye of a chaperone. "He said he'd be there 'to collect me.' I can see myself chloroformed and poured into a bottle labeled 'American Historian.' "

"How appropriate, to study British history all your life and then find yourself a nice British boy."

"Yes." Rebecca scrambled into the aisle, adding to herself, *maybe just a little bit too appropriate*. What if she only loved him because of his accent? If he got laryngitis, the relationship would fall apart.

She hated the fluorescent light in airplane lavatories. Her complexion was tinted green, and the circles below her dark, faintly crazed eyes were purple bruises. Yesterday her brown hair had been combed into a tidy Princess Diana; now it was cowlicked from leaning against the seat, looking more like Bride of Frankenstein. Rebecca tried applying a little blush to the hollows in her cheeks. Michael's discerning eye would notice immediately that she'd lost weight she hadn't needed to lose. Well, it was his own fault she'd eaten soup and crackers for dinner so often. Transatlantic phone calls weren't cheap.

She squeezed her way down the aisle, picked up Dennis's napkin from the floor and gave it back to him. He gazed at her quizzically and stuffed it into the seat pocket. Despite his twenty or so years, she thought, Dennis was just like her ten-year-old nephew—not quite domesticated.

Adele was looking through the stack of books and papers with which Rebecca had tried to while away the night. "Have you ever been to Rudesburn?"

"No, I haven't. That's why I've been reading up on it." Rebecca packed the books away. "This one's a pretty good account of Scottish monasticism—did you know Rudesburn's one of the few medieval convents in the country? And this one on folk customs tells about the Lammas Fair, the August Borders Festival the village development group is reviving."

Adele indicated a third book, a paperback illustrated with a ghostly figure looming over a castle that owed more to Disney than to defense. "That one says the fair-goers should avoid the ruins of the priory because the ghost of a sixteenth-century prioress puts a curse on lovers."

So that's where I'm going with my lover, Rebecca thought. She shook her head. "There're a dozen versions of that story, applied to half the ruins in the country. Ghosties and ghoulies, clanking knights and spectral nuns, buried treasures and magical artifacts. Typical."

"But the priory might be haunted," Adele insisted. "Sometimes people can't make the transition into the other world; they stay behind because of an unresolved need. Guilt, or to guard something, or to avenge their murder."

Tell me about it. Rebecca quirked a brow at Adele. "Most of the time it's only legend."

"It wasn't legend at Dun Iain, was it?"

It was uncanny how the woman knew what she was thinking. Rebecca's other brow shot up. "The problems there were caused by human beings. I'm surprised you heard about it."

"When I heard from the University Archeological Network that you were going to be our instructor, I recognized your name. I live in Pittsburgh, we get the news from Ohio, and I was fascinated by what happened at Dun Iain last winter. Of course, if you don't want to talk about it . . ." She paused both discreetly and expectantly.

Rebecca turned back to her bag, wedging the sheaf of photocopies Michael had sent from the museum between the books. "I'd prefer not to, if you don't mind. It was . . ." She groped for a word, remembering moments of terror, of exhilaration, of farce, and settled on the innocuous. ". . . demanding." She was biting her lip. She stopped it, telling herself she had nothing to hide. What had begun as a straightforward job helping to catalog the artifacts in an old house had become a desperate struggle to save not only the house and artifacts, but also her life. And the life of her temperamental Scottish co-worker. Funny, how at first she and Michael had barely tolerated each other.

"I'm sorry," Adele said. "I'm not trying to pry. It's just that it's so seldom you get a parapsychological manifestation, a survival of consciousness, that can't be explained away."

"There were ghosts, or whatever you want to call them, at Dun Iain. But they went away—to wherever it is we all go eventually." Rebecca turned and looked out the window again, hoping Adele would take the hint. She'd known the older woman was studying religion, but she'd expected a more conventional one.

"Maybe there are vibrations of a life force at Rudesburn Priory," Adele said, so quietly Rebecca hardly heard her. "Some poor lost soul who needs help in finding the door to the other side."

Rebecca laid her forehead against the cold glass of the window. The plane was gliding over Ailsa Craig, the sharply pointed island puncturing the blue of the Irish Sea. Ahead was the coast of Scotland and a tiny white town nestled against the beach. The plane banked steeply to the left, and the early morning sunlight, diffused by gauzy cloud, glinted in Rebecca's eyes. Squinting, she looked down past the coping of the window like a poor woman looking greedily through the glass of a jewelry store. Streams and small lakes shone like diamond necklaces against green velvet hills that faded imperceptibly into blue horizon. Rebecca wondered if it were the magical light or her weariness that made land and sky seem so insubstantial, like the shimmering and yet distorted images of a dream.

The "Fasten Seat Belt" sign came on. Rebecca buckled up without taking her eyes from the window. As the plane lost altitude, the ground solidified. Gray stone fences and sheep like tiny cumulus clouds made patterns on that transcendent green. Then she saw a road, cars, light standards, and felt the thunk of the wheels hitting the runway.

Rebecca stepped out of the door of the plane onto the top of the staircase a few minutes later and inhaled the cool, moist wind. She herded Dennis and Adele into a long, low building and down a corridor into customs. The agent stamped their passports with a flourish, lingering over Rebecca's. "Reid—there's a good Scottish name. You've been here before, then? Well, welcome home to you."

Rebecca beamed at the man. He sounded like Michael. She and the students claimed their suitcases and passed through customs. Through wide automatic doors was the lobby: no Scottish vernacular architecture, not a portcullis in sight, just an expanse of linoleum dotted with plastic chairs and rent-a-car booths.

Rebecca's steps slowed. She looked around eagerly for a tall, lanky, jeans-and-sweatshirt-clad body. Michael had said he'd be here. He had called her last week to check on her arrival time and said, "It's damned expensive courtin' via trunk call, lass. You'd best be gettin' yoursel' ower here."

So we can have it out right and proper, Rebecca added to herself.

Dennis paused by a video game and looked suspiciously at his handful of British coins. Adele strolled over to the information booth and gazed at their display of maps. Rebecca kept on walking. Well, it was barely past seven. He'd had to drive the fifty miles from Edinburgh—maybe the traffic was bad. He'd said he'd be here. Her thoughts shifted painfully from worry to doubt.

Then any thought at all vanished as Michael's voice, his real voice, not an electronically transmitted facsimile, called her name.

She stopped dead, causing other travelers to bump into her back. He was standing in front of the window of the gift shop, his image repeated in the glass. No wonder she hadn't recognized him. It wasn't that he was wearing the intricate but nicely rational fisherman's sweater his mother had made for him; she'd seen that. Below the sweater he wore a kilt of blue-green tartan, complete with sporran and tall socks. Above the top of one peeped the black handle of the traditional small dagger, a sgian dubh.

She'd seen a photo of him in a kilt—he'd played in a pipe band. But this vision was up close and personal. Rebecca's cheeks flushed, and her eyes crossed. Michael, enjoying his effect, unleashed his most dazzling grin.

She flew into his arms. "I'm impressed," she exhaled into the collar of his shirt, and inhaled his scent of soap and clean wool.

"I thought a cheap thrill would wake you up," he said into her ear. "You've never seen me outwith my jeans, have you?"

"Sure I have, buck naked."

Michael laughed. Something flashed in the corner of Rebecca's eye, and she looked up. A middle-aged couple from her flight had taken a picture of them. Of Michael, rather—their first bit of local color.

Michael smiled graciously, dropped the tourists a curtsy, and drew Rebecca back against the window of the shop. "Dr. Reid, I presume?"

"I don't know yet. They're going to write me."

"But you did hand in your dissertation, Mary, Queen of Scots, and all?"

"Mary, Queen of Scots, and all. It was a strange few months—I haven't studied full time since I was a freshman. But if I'd gotten yet another teaching job, it would've taken me forever to finish." She didn't have to add, "And that would've meant all the more time we'd have been hugging telephone receivers instead of each other."

He gave her a discreet peck on the cheek and said over her shoulder, "How do you do? I'm Michael Campbell."

"Adele Garrity, Dr. Campbell," returned the woman's voice.

Rebecca remembered her duties and peeled herself off Michael's chest. Dennis was standing at her elbow. "And this is Dennis Tucker," she said.

His appraising glance fell to Michael's lower half and stalled there, hung up somewhere between surprise and indignation. Then he noticed Michael's extended right hand. "Oh, hello." He was somewhat shorter than Michael, and almost twice as broad.

Adele hoisted her massive overnight bag with surprising ease, considering that she was as slender as Rebecca—probably from years of jogging and eating tofu rather than years turning over academic compost heaps. "I understand there's a bus to Glasgow," she said. "And I can get a train from there to Newton Stewart, can't I? Would there be a bus or something, do you think, to take me on to Whithorn and St. Ninian's Kirk?"

"Oh, aye," Michael replied. "That's a well-traveled route. There're some fine stone circles in that area, if you've a taste for such."

"I'm going to visit the shrine. King Robert the Bruce went there just before he died. I'm going to pray for Christopher, he was always fond of Robert—such a dashing figure."

"I'm partial to him mysel'," said Michael. "My dissertation was on the Bruce and the Wars of Independence."

"Sorry," Rebecca said, confused. "I thought your husband was Harvey."

Adele's pale eyes didn't blink. "Christopher was my son. He died last year, too."

Rebecca stammered something. Michael's brows tightened. Dennis asked, "Who's Robert the Bruce?"

The boy was woefully unprepared, Rebecca thought. She answered, "He was only Scotland's most famous king. Won the battle of Bannockburn in 1314."

"Turfed oot the English and kept them oot," added Michael. "We could've used a few more like him." He swooped decisively down on Rebecca's and Adele's suitcases and led the way to the front of the terminal. A bus was already loading.

"Well," said Dennis with a sideways glance from the kilt to Rebecca to Adele, "all I'm going to do tonight is check out a few pubs. Thought I'd try some of that warm beer. What would you recommend, Mike?"

Michael flinched at the shortening of his name. "McEwan's Export is quite guid. At room temperature. Our rooms are just a wee bit cooler than yours."

Dennis nodded. Adele smiled brightly.

"There'll be a bus in Galashiels tomorrow afternoon," Rebecca reminded them both. "Sunday. To take you to Rudesburn. See you there!"

Michael took her elbow and steered her across the driveway into the parking area. "Where'd you find that lot?"

"They found me. They've paid for the privilege of mucking about in medieval Scottish mud, remember. Don't criticize. Even if Dennis is only here because he needs a liberal arts course to get his bachelor's in business."

"Business graduates get higher salaries than we poor sods of historians do," Michael conceded. "Just as long as he can use a trowel."

"The other two students might not be as—er—startling. But I've never met them before, either. They'll be here tomorrow."

"We'll let the morn take care of itsel'." Michael stopped by a red Fiat with a "Made in Czechoslovakia" sticker on the windshield and opened the trunk. Boot, it was called here. Wellies, calf-high rubber boots. She had to get a pair for that medieval mud.

Her mind was still a jumble. Rebecca yawned, her jaw creaking. Now *I get sleepy. That figures. But it's all right now. I'm here, Michael's here, everything's okay, I can rest. . . . I have to warn him about the dig,* she reminded herself. *It's American gossip, he won't have heard.*

She stowed her overnight bag, opened the car door, and confronted a steering wheel. *Oh, of course—they drive on the left here.* With a chuckle, Michael escorted her to the passenger side, tucked her in, and climbed behind the wheel. They regarded each other gravely, alone at last.

Tomorrow, Rebecca told herself, swimming a lazy backstroke in the deep blue of his eyes. *We'll talk business tomorrow.*

"I missed you," he said. His forefinger touched her cheek.

She tilted her face against his hand. "I missed you, especially when I was working with copies from the Dun Iain collection."

"There I was, unpackin' the artifacts I'd brought back, and I'd catch mysel' holdin' somethin' and thinkin', ah, Rebecca packed this." He mimed Hamlet considering the skull of Yorick. "I've been makin' a proper gowk oot of mysel' ower you."

"If I had a nickel for every time I caught myself staring at my typewriter and seeing you, I'd have had enough to buy myself a first class ticket." She leaned over the gearshift to kiss him.

A tentative nibble, and then a firm kiss, and then an exploratory expedition that made Rebecca glad she'd brushed her teeth. She came up for air. No doubt about it, a lifetime of burred 'r's and rounded vowels had made his lips and tongue wonderfully flexible.

His face swam, not quite fodused, before her. She'd never known a man who could steam up her contact lenses. As her vision cleared, she saw, several yards beyond Michael's back, the parking lot attendant leaning on his windowsill and taking in the sights with a broad grin.

"Worked yoursel' to a bone," Michael said disapprovingly, and released her rib cage. He started the car and caught the eye of the attendant. His brows saluted cheerfully. The man laughed, and when they pulled alongside his booth, he waved them on without accepting payment.

The Fiat swung out of the parking lot onto the main road just as another car swung in. Rebecca gasped, certain it was going to hit them headlong. But it passed by smoothly to their right. With a long sigh of relief, she settled against the seat. The tendons in her neck and shoulders were slowly unknotting, and her eyelashes were gaining weight. She watched bemusedly as the streets of first Prestwick and then Ayr unfurled themselves, lined with sturdy stone buildings. Only the passing cars, the advertisements, and the dress of the pedestrians—an occasional punk strutting like a peacock among pigeons—assured her that she hadn't dropped into some time warp where the last two centuries co-existed.

To her right she caught a glimpse of the sea, shining blue-gray in the full light of the sun. A pretty day—how fitting. She sighed happily. "And where are you taking me, young Lochinvar?"

"To a hotel in Ayr. A B&B would've been cheaper, but less private."

She turned her head against the headrest and looked appreciatively at his profile. His features were even, unremarkable except for the animation of mouth and brows. Thank goodness he hadn't altered his bravado haircut—short brown strands framing his face, long ones down the back of his neck. He looked like a rock star, an intellectual, and a swashbuckler all in one.

"I booked a room wi' two beds," he went on, "if you dinna want to start quite where we left it last winter."

They'd been colleagues for three months, lovers for only a week. It was almost a matter of starting over. "I intend to start where we left off. But if I don't get some sleep soon, you'll be starting without me."

"Oh, take a snooze, by all means. I dinna have a taste for necrophilia." He shifted gears. The car plunged into a traffic circle, which in the morning rush hour resembled a miniature version of the chariot race from "Ben Hur." Flung by some kind of centrifugal force, the car whizzed out the other side right under the fender of a huge truck.

Rebecca blanched. She'd have to learn to drive all over again.

Unperturbed, Michael shifted again. His wrist caught the hem of his kilt and flipped it up his thigh.

"Just a quick nap," said Rebecca with a slow smile.

He glanced at her expression, down at his leg, and laughed. The car followed a residential street to the driveway of a sprawling red sandstone building that had been new in Victoria's reign. "Here we are."

Rebecca hovered, firmly convinced she'd left something behind. She counted her two suitcases and overnight bag, his suitcase and garment bag, a battered attaché case that looked as if he'd used it as a football, and a long tartan bag with a handle. Golf clubs? He didn't play golf. Then she realized he'd brought his bagpipes. All right! It was Michael's music that had first touched her heart.

At the registration desk Rebecca declined breakfast with a polite mutter. She sleepwalked up the stairs, then into a large bedroom and across it to a dressing table, where she plopped down and took out her contact lenses. That was better, even if she did see the garden below the broad bay window as a smear of green, pink, and yellow.

Michael was looking at her indulgently. "I'll do some shoppin' whilst you evolve yoursel' back into a higher species."

"Something higher than a slime slug, anyway," she said with a laugh.

He ruffled her hair, kissed the tip of her nose, and left.

Rebecca stood basking in the lingering heat of his smile, still mesmerized by the swing and sway of the kilt above his knees, its movement so like the lilt in his voice. Then, with a wry smile at herself, she washed and pulled on a flannel nightgown and a pair of socks—it might be June, but it was also Scotland. She crawled beneath the covers of one of the beds, reached behind her, and pulled one of the thick pillows like a sack of cement from beneath her head. There. She could sleep now. Sleep.

The plaster dadoes surrounding the ceiling light reminded her of the ceilings of Dun Iain, plastered as intricately as wedding cakes. What if she woke up and discovered she was still there, that she'd dreamed the intervening six months, that Michael was leaving for Scotland tomorrow and their ordeal by separation was still ahead of them. . . .

The roar of the jet engines reverberated in her bones. Her body felt weightless, pressed into the bed by the heavy covers. She was in the airplane, ensconced regally in first class, watching the attendant spread a tablecloth over her tray table. No, she was lying across the table. Michael approached. The sgian dubh glittered smooth and hard in his hand. . . .

Rebecca jerked back into wakefulness. *Good grief, Dr. Freud, I'm not that nervous about seeing him again! Thank you, Adele, for talking about ghosts and murders.*

With a snort she turned and burrowed into the covers. She would deal with Adele and Rudesburn and their ghosties and ghoulies tomorrow. Tomorrow would be sufficient unto the evil thereof, or however that phrase went. Rebecca smiled. Today was sufficient unto joy.

Chapter Two

A STRANGE NOISE pulled Rebecca floundering from a dream as deep and dark as water cut by nameless predators. She groped for the eyeglasses she'd left on the bedside table. What she grabbed was her watch. Almost noon.

She was in a sunny room, bed linen crisp and white, the polished oak of dresser and armoire tortured into Victorian opulence. The room would have reminded her of her grandmother's house, if her grandmother hadn't lived in a pink and lime condo in Tampa.

There was the noise again, a kind of trilling gargle. Her eye fell on the telephone on the wall between the beds. That was the culprit. She reached for the receiver. "Hello?"

"Good mornin'. Is this Rebecca, by any chance?"

The warm smile in the man's voice elicited one from her. "Yes, it is."

"Colin MacLeod here, from Fort Augustus. I daresay Michael's mentioned me to you a time or two, if not nearly so much as he's mentioned you to me."

"Oh hello, Colin! Yes, he's mentioned you quite a bit. Even showed me a snapshot of the two of you out hill-climbing. I hear you helped him do the geophysical survey at Rudesburn."

"The North of Scotland Hydroelectric Board doesn't mind my doin' a wee bit of consultin' on the side." He hesitated. "I'm sorry if I woke you, but I need to speak to Michael."

"He's not here. I've still got my days and nights mixed up, so he went out shopping. I'd be glad to take a message." Rebecca perched on the edge of the bed, her sock-clad feet swinging, and smothered a groan. Now what?

Colin emitted a sound that he might have intended to be a laugh, but which didn't quite achieve humor. "Sorry, but it's a right awkward bit of muck, and no mistake. Laurence Baird rang me from Rudesburn, lookin' for Michael. Just to let him know what to expect. Laurence doesn't realize the implications, of course. And it is quite a bargain for them."

"Yes?" prodded Rebecca.

Colin took the plunge. "You already know about the American archeologist, Jeremy Kleinfelter."

Oh, lord. Had that unsavory rumor washed up on British shores already? She replied cautiously, "I've never met him, but I know people who know him. By all accounts, his ego matches his brilliance."

"It's the latter that caused the RDG—the Rudesburn Development Group, the villagers—to hire him. To direct a quick excavation before doin' some preservation work and buildin' a museum—right?"·

"Right. Like what's been done at Jedburgh, just down the road."

"Well, Kleinfelter's made a bargain with a production company to film the dig. For a record for the Historic Buildings and Monuments lot and the museum. The film crew'll work for free—if they can also make a program for the telly about . . ." he cleared his throat and assumed a sonorous announcer's voice ". . . the haunted convent and the lost treasure of the spectral nun."

"Oh, I see," said Rebecca. "The ghostly prioress and the convent treasury looted by Henry VIII. They'll say Henry uncharacteristically left something behind."

"When reality fails," Colin said, "make something up."

"Great." Adele had certainly come to the right place. Rebecca was beginning to wonder if the woman was clairvoyant. As for Kleinfelter—well, publicity was a necessary part of any excavation, but she'd expected the man to be keeping a lower profile after the scandal on his last dig. "I'm sure Michael won't be thrilled at their sensationalizing the dig. But a film for free— you can't beat that."

"You maybe could, Rebecca, when I tell you that Kleinfelter hired Plantagenet Productions, chief producer Sheila Fitzgerald."

Rebecca's brain lurched. The line hummed in her ear. In the garden, a bird sang lustily. Someone banged down the hall outside the door. "You mean," she said between her teeth, "the same Sheila Fitzgerald Michael knew in London two years ago, or else you wouldn't be calling to warn him. Me. Us."

"So he owned up to that one." Rebecca couldn't tell whether Colin was amused or relieved. "Aye, the very same. She left her job as publicity director at the British Museum to form the film company."

"Sheila-bloody-Fitzgerald is what Michael called her."

"I'm not surprised. It's you he . . ." Colin managed a genuine laugh this time. "Well, you know your own business."

Rebecca took a deep breath. "I certainly hope so. I'll break the news to him. That's not the only thing I have to warn him about." Rebecca collapsed back onto the bed, still holding the receiver, and changed the subject. "You're not quite what I expected, Colin."

"Eh?"

"Your accent isn't as thick as Michael's. I mean, he speaks perfect BBC Oxbridge when he wants to, but he does tend toward broad Scots, especially when he's tired, or upset, or tipsy."

"I'm a Highlander," Colin replied. "A teuchter, Michael calls me—just takin' the mickey out of me, mind you. A country bumpkin, you'd say in the States. My ancestors gave up Gaelic for English only two hundred years ago, during the English occupation. Michael's ancestors come from all over—Moray, Argyll, Galloway; the Lowlanders among them spoke Scots, not English."

"So he's a good generic Scot, if you'll pardon the expression?" Rebecca asked.

"More self-conscious, I'd say. Some of his vocabulary is deliberately old-fashioned. He never spoke so broadly until he came back from London. His mates there kept slaggin' him off for bein' a yokel."

"So while some people work hard to lose their accents, he broadened his." Rebecca grinned indulgently. "I always said he had a wee tartan chip on his shoulder."

"Tenacity is one of Michael's more endearing traits," Colin said with a laugh.

"I'd call it stubborn, myself." She yawned. "Thank you for taking the time to call, Colin. I think."

"You're welcome. Do get our Dr. Campbell to bring you up to Fort Augustus. Anjali—my wife—makes a wonderful curry."

"I can't wait to meet you both. Goodbye." With Colin's laugh still warming her ear, she hung up the receiver and pulled up the bedclothes.

Jeremy Kleinfelter. Sheila Fitzgerald. Adele, the missionary to the Other Side. At least Dennis was normal. A normal nerd. The Haunted Convent. Whatever had happened to good old-fashioned scientific research?

Nothing. The concept of dispassionate science was a modern one. Historically, legend preceded science, alchemy preceded chemistry, and magic preceded philosophy. Every science had skeletons in its closet. So did everyone. She herself had just broken an engagement when she'd met Michael. Then she'd almost let herself be swept off her feet by a smooth-talking law-yer, instead of homing immediately in on her thistle-covered colleague.

Rebecca sank into the pillow, drifting into a dream. She wan-dered through a ruined church, lost and alone, calling for Mi-chael. He wasn't there. No one was there. It was raining and cold, and she was frightened.

Someone touched her. She jerked awake. Michael sat on the edge of the bed. "Here, sleepyhead, it's past two, time to be up and aboot. Did you have a good snooze?"

Her mind was fuzzed by the lint of her dream. She catapulted into his arms, almost knocking him off the bed. "No. I had nightmares."

He rocked her, making soothing noises into her ear, and slowly her mind cleared. Her nightgown matched his kilt, she saw, both in blue-green Campbell tartan. He'd given her the gown for Christmas, a reminder that a spouse's tartan counted as one's own. She smiled, straightened, and stretched. "My biorhythms must be scrambled. Sorry."

"For needin' a hug? You're entitled, lass." Michael offered her a quick kiss and then indicated a plastic sack lying on the foot of the bed. "I stopped by Safeway's and got some things for a picnic. It's a bonny day, seventy degrees. A real scorcher. The sunlight'll clear away your cobwebs."

"When I lived in Houston, seventy was cool." Rebecca crawled out of the bed and staggered around the room collecting her clothes. "A Safeway? Here?"

"You've no fallen off the edge of the world."

"I'd rather thought I'd come to its center."

Grinning, he hoisted a bottle of mineral water in one hand and a bottle of whiskey in the other. "I own Safeway's brand of

Scotch is no temptation, but I lost my head and bought a bottle of Cragganmore. Single-malt. There're two things a Scot likes naked . . ."

"His knees?" Rebecca asked from the bathroom door.

"Dinna step on my punch line. There're two things a Scot likes naked, and one of them is whiskey."

Rebecca laughed. She was tempted to rush across the room and push him down onto the bed, but the anticipation was part of the pleasure. And she didn't want to repay his attentions with a growling stomach. "Just a minute," she called, and whisked into a skirt, blouse, and tapestry vest. She inspected herself in the mirror. Her color was better, but her hair was beyond redemption. She hoped she wouldn't detract from Michael's sartorial splendor.

She said to the mirror, "Colin called." That came out just fine. It was the rest she had trouble with. Rebecca stuck out her tongue at her image in the glass. Damn Sheila.

Michael was standing by the door jangling his car keys. This time Rebecca went to the correct side of the car. "Where to?"

"Culzean Castle, a few miles doon the coast. The gardens are open 'til sunset. Past ten in these airts."

He guided the car out of town, following the coast highway. Rebecca looked around so intently she felt like a dog hanging out the window of the car, the clean air ruffling her hair, the colors and textures—green grass, gray stone, blue water—washing over and through her. Michael pointed out more than one ruined castle, crumbling untended into oblivion like abandoned gas stations in the United States. Rebecca shook her head. "At home—I use the term loosely—any one of those would be tarted up with hot dog stands and park rangers. But you have so many you can't save them all."

"Bluidy waste," Michael agreed. "At least the Rudesburn folk realize what a treasure they have. I'm convinced the priory was done by Jean Moreau. John Morrow, whatever his name was."

Treasure? Rebecca rolled her eyes. "Rudesburn was a daughter house of Melrose, not surprising they'd have the same master mason."

"You did your homework." Michael prodded her ribs with his left hand.

"I'm a poor sod of a historian, too." She snaked her right hand across the emergency brake and rested it on his leg. Mi-

chael was an unusual man in not displaying professional jealousy. Of course, he already had his Ph.D., and he probably
considered a degree from Edinburgh more prestigious than one
from Missouri.

Culzean was a massive mansion perched on a cliff above the
sea. Its eighteenth-century graciousness concealed its origins as
a medieval keep, like a socially conscious family hiding its uncouth cousin in the basement. Michael and Rebecca walked for
over an hour among the avenues of pines and beeches. The sunlight was warm, but the dense fluid shadow of the trees was
cool, reminding Rebecca of her dream. In spite of herself she
shivered.

"I'm lettin' you go hungry!" Michael exclaimed. They
wended their way between clumps of picnickers and found a
vacant table overlooking a border of rose bushes. He laid out
the food—rolls, ham, Ayrshire cheese, tomatoes, fruit, and
shortbread—and produced napkins and plastic glasses.

Rebecca sang, "All the roses in the garden would bow and
ask his pardon."

"*Her* pardon," Michael corrected, and finished the verse,
"For not one could match the beauty of the Queen of Argyll."
He pushed his sweater sleeves up to his elbows, pulled out his
sgian dubh and cut thin slices of the tomato.

"I dreamed you were coming after me with that," Rebecca
told him. "I've been reading too much about the Border Wars."

"I ken what a sgian dubh was used for in the past," Michael
returned, carefully wiping the blade. "But this one's never given
the coup de grace to more than the odd vegetable." The knife
slipped gleaming into its sheath and the sheath went back into
his sock.

Rebecca couldn't remember food tasting quite so delicious before. Michael placed morsels between her lips and kept her glass
of whiskey and water full. A couple stretched out under a magnificent copper beech turned on a radio, and the evocative music
of Debussy wafted down the wind. Rebecca unashamedly stuffed
herself before she spoke more than pleasant banalities. "Michael, I have something I have to get off my chest."

"Here?" His brows rose playfully.

"Not my blouse. Business."

"Oh." He sighed, crestfallen. "Well, if you must."

"I must." She leaned her elbows on the table. "You know
about Dr. Nelson, my dissertation director. He had a student a

couple of years ago named Laurel Matheny. She got her degree
and landed a plum of a job at an excavation in Virginia last
summer.''

"No the same one Jeremy Kleinfelter directed?"

"I'm afraid so. Matheny was the research assistant fired for
fudging the results. Her career was ruined before it started."

Michael frowned. "We heard aboot the cock-up in the results.
The dig went ower time and ower budget. Matheny was scram-
blin' to save next year's fundin' by comin' up wi' results that
didna exist—something aboot a Harington farthin' in the wrong
stratum, was it?"

"It was." Rebecca rotated her glass, watching the pale amber
fluid ebb and flow on the sides. Back in Archeology 101, her
teacher had explained the concept of strata by stacking books on
his desk. The book on the bottom had been there the longest
time, the one on top the shortest. The strata of an archeological
deposit were much more complicated, of course; scientists often
had to analyze different kinds of soil. Finding a Harington farthing, a tiny copper coin used only for a few months in the
seventeenth century, was like finding an artifact with a museum
label on it. The stratum where the coin was found could be dated
very closely.

Rebecca sipped at her whiskey. It stung her throat. "Matheny
swore to Dr. Nelson that she recorded that farthing accurately.
It was Kleinfelter who changed the records to make it look as if
the farthing dated a structure. And he let her take the rap."

"His word against hers, eh?"

"The distinguished professional against the neophyte. The man
against the woman." Michael snorted. Rebecca ignored his
comment. "But who would've had the most motive for cheating? The person who was still on probation, or the person with
the reputation to guard and the ego to guard it with?"

Michael asked, "What do you believe, Rebecca?"

Ants trooped across the table, scouting for crumbs. With her
fingertip Rebecca shoved several into their path. "I trust Dr.
Nelson, and he trusts Matheny. She and her husband went back
to Michigan last fall while Nelson tried to clear her reputation.
He has no proof, though. And Kleinfelter's standing pat."

"Where he'll be standin' is Rudesburn. Wi' you and me his
assistants this time."

"Oh, yes. You may have a good reputation at the museum,
but you're responsible to them for the dig. I don't even have my

degree yet. What I have are the volunteers—four loose cannons. We're the perfect patsies.''

Michael tipped up his glass, drained it, and set it back on the table with a solid thunk. An ant barely escaped. "Dinna get the wind up. Even if Kleinfelter's guilty as sin, we canna assume he'll pull the same trick here. We'll make sure the dig goes right and is done by the Festival in August. It's a minor grid and trench excavation, after all, no like that big, corporation-funded expedition in Virginia. Which reminds me.''

"Don't tell me you have a bit of scandal, too?''

"I didna think it was until you told your tale.'' Michael grimaced. "I was talkin' to the archivist at the British Museum . . .''

Rebecca grimaced. British Museum. London. Sheila.

". . . who said that Kleinfelter was researchin' there last spring. He turned doon a job in London itsel' to come to Rudesburn.''

"Why would a publicity hound like Kleinfelter choose such a small dig in what must be to him such an out-of-the-way place?''

"I think I can answer that. I sent you bits of the chronicle written by Mary Pringle, Rudesburn's last prioress, in 1602, did I?''

"Yes. But what . . . ?''

"There're some pages of the manuscript that're no in Edinburgh. I found them in the attic of the old Kerr manor house at Rudesburn last month, when Colin and I went ower the site. Mary implies that the heart of Robert the Bruce may no be at Melrose, after all, but at Rudesburn.''

Rebecca exclaimed, "The first prioress of the Cistercian house was Marjory Douglas, and the Douglases were Bruce's right hand clan! Pringle says that Robert himself had a wheel-cross erected on that hill behind the priory, where there used to be a castle during the years the priory was deserted.''

"Got it in one.'' He poured another splash of whiskey into her glass. "But—and a muckle great but—if I just found that hint aboot the relic heart last month, why did Kleinfelter sign on to the dig in April?''

Rebecca sipped. The smoky-sweet flavor seeped into her sinuses. Trees and lawns, gardens and romping children, were bright as a crazy quilt. The couple beneath the beech were getting down to serious business. She averted her eyes. "I know

why. Publicity. Spectral nuns and hidden treasures. And not necessarily historical treasures like Robert the Bruce's heart."

"What're you on aboot?" Michael asked.

She gritted her teeth and spoke to her glass. "Colin called
while you were out." The inexorable words of explanation fell
like a sudden rain shower from a blue sky.

Michael's hands clenched into fists, his forearms cording with
sinew; his wrists were deceptively slender and his hands delicate, but Rebecca knew how strong they could be. He looked as
if he'd swallowed a goldfish and was trying to keep it down.
"I'm no surprised she'd try to sensationalize the dig. That's her
style, right enough. Flash and cash."

"We all have skeletons in our closets," said Rebecca, more
tartly than she'd intended.

"Oh, aye, like that bastard of a lawyer in yours."

"At least I never slept with him," she retorted.

Michael's chin went up and out, a gesture she recognized only
too well. "Sheila didna come cheap, I assure you. She and her
mates did me ower right and proper. I'll no be makin' excuses
for it the noo."

"You have an excuse. Galloping male hormones."

"Well, I beg your pardon!" he snapped.

They sat stiff and silent, facing away from each other. Several
children rushed by, shouting. Blackbirds wheeled overhead. The
breeze tickled the rich purple leaves of the beech, making them
rustle like distant laughter, and fanned Rebecca's hot cheeks.
The couple turned off their radio, collected their belongings, and
walked away hand in hand.

I haven't been here a day yet, she thought, *and already we're
fighting.* "Sheila's a hell of an insignificant fly to land in our
honey."

"That she is." Michael's hand moved across the table and
clasped hers. "I lied to you once, but never aboot her. If you've
no learned you can trust me by noo, love, when are you?"

"I trust you. That's not what I meant."

He put his arm around her shoulders. She wrapped her arms
around his waist and pressed against him. His sweater was as
soft and warm as a cat. "You're a puzzle, lass. Most women
haver aboot their man's old loves. You're upset because I slept
wi' her wi'oot really carin' for her."

"Confirms my suspicion that men and women come from different planets."

"You may come from the outer rings of Saturn, but I'm no so sure aboot Sheila." He emitted a rueful laugh. "Did I ever tell you what happened? It was the night the museum opened the Jacobite exhibit. I was wearin' my posh claes. A group of us went oot to the pub, and I found mysel' wedged into a booth next to Sheila. She'd been makin' eyes at me—I'm no so dense as to miss that. But there, at the pub, the first thing I kent she had her hand beneath my kilt and halfway home."

"She made a frontal assault, then." Rebecca couldn't help but smile.

"Oh, aye. I was so shocked I almost spilled my beer."

"And what does a Scot wear beneath his kilt, anyway?"

"Traditionally, naething. But that's a wee bit breezy. I canna speak for everyone, but I wear Fruit of the Loom y-fronts, mysel'."

Rebecca laughed helplessly against his shoulder. "With Sheila, then, things went downhill fast."

"At first it was quite stimulatin'," he admitted. "Later I heard her laughin' wi' her friends aboot me. It went ower a cliff then, you might say, wi' a damned hard landin'."

For a time they sat comfortably together. At last Rebecca said quietly, "Rudesburn has its fair share of ghost stories. Let's hope that this time there aren't really any ghosts or treasures. Other than our own. Surely we have enough to worry about."

"Amen," he replied, and suddenly he yawned. "I was up at four-thirty, packin' the car and closin' the flat. Should we be goin' back to the hotel?"

"I should hope so," she told him. Heedless of the ants, the children, the birds, they indulged in another long kiss.

In those far Northern latitudes, the early evening light didn't fail, it thinned, like gold stretched into finer and finer leaf. To Rebecca's eyes the hills, the farms, the sea glowed magically from within, lamps with crystal chimneys. Her friend Jan in Ohio had once opined that distance extinguishes a small flame and fans a large one. Now Scotland itself seemed to be reflecting the conflagration in Rebecca's mind, heart, stomach.

She saw a billboard proclaiming, "Scottish Power." "Are the nationalists making much headway?" she asked.

"Nationalists?" he queried, then laughed. "Ah, that's the electric company, lass."

It was when they were locked away in their room that she noticed the snag in the sleeve of his sweater. She was on him immediately. "Take it off. Careful. Let me see. Either you caught it on something, or a thin place in the yarn separated. . . . Whew, only a couple of stitches undone. Don't wear it again until I fix it for you, okay?"

Michael stood in his shirtsleeves, looking at her with a peculiar expression. "Ah, she'll have my head!" he exclaimed, and opened his garment bag. From its depths he produced a fisherman knit vest in a soft shade of heather green. "My mum made this for you. I forgot to give it to you."

Rebecca stroked the labyrinthine stitches. The color complemented her tawny hair, and it fit perfectly. "It's beautiful! How did she know my size?"

"I told her." Michael's hands outlined a female figure in midair.

"Just how much did you tell her?"

He grinned sheepishly. "My tongue ran away wi' me. I told them all aboot it. Dad looked at me wi' that inscrutable fatherly look, and Mum said she'd just have to make you a sweater. Maddy said you sounded like a fine braw lass who'd be takin' me properly in hand. And she threatened to write and tell you all my bad habits. We may be adults, but she's still my big sister."

"It must be nice to be such good friends with your family. I'm convinced I'm a changeling."

"Left by wee kilted fairies, I doot." Michael patted her cheek reassuringly and handed over a manila envelope. "Here, have a keek at these." Grabbing his shaving kit, he retreated into the bathroom. A few minutes later, his voice rose in song over the splash of water: "Lang hae we parted been, lassie my dearie; now we are met again, lassie lie near me. Say that you'll aye be true, never deceive me . . ."

"Never," Rebecca said to the blank face of the door. She folded the sweater and went through her nightly ritual of makeup removal, contact lens cleaning, nightgown and socks. Then she pulled up a chair and propped her feet on the edge of the bed. Inside the envelope were computer printouts, the results of the geophysical survey superimposed on a map of Rudesburn Priory. That drainage ditch might repay some effort, and there was more extensive vaulting beneath the remains of the lay sister's dormitory than she'd expected from the original description of the site.

Among the printouts was a photograph. Michael stood next

to a nine-foot-tall Celtic wheel cross, his face turned up to it like a saint in a stained-glass window looking up to heaven. Behind him the tracery of the west window of the priory church imitated and multiplied the lines of the cross.

Michael emerged from the bathroom wearing his usual sleeping garb, a pair of soccer shorts. Her interest in the plans evaporated. "I've enjoyed my nightgown," she told him, "even though you once told me you didn't think flannel gowns were very attractive."

He threw his kilt over a chair, tossed the sgian dubh into his suitcase, and leaned over Rebecca's shoulder. "It all depends on how easily the gown comes off." He undid the buttons at the nape of her neck, reached inside the opening and rubbed her shoulders. Gentle sparks of electricity purred down her spine. "Do you still have the metal ring from the wine bottle?" he asked.

"That you put on my finger Christmas Eve? Of course I do."

"Meanin' that we're engaged to have substantive talks."

"That's one very important reason I'm here, love."

His hands met beneath her chin, tilting her head back. She peered at his upside-down face. "Tae you, comin' here is comin' home. Tae me—well, this is home, and I'd no trade it for any place on Earth. But what I want, what I need, is someone tae come home tae. Someone tae be my home. . . ." He stopped, released her throat and turned away.

"I understand," she whispered.

Michael took the envelope and papers and threw them onto the dressing table. He pulled her glasses from her face and folded them away. He removed her socks and tickled her feet. She jumped. Judging by the angle of his brows, her sudden movement gave him an inspiring view up her nightdress.

With the smile of a cat contemplating a pitcher of cream, Michael padded across the floor and flicked off the light. The evening glowed through the curtains, filling the room with translucent shadow. He dropped to one knee and scooped the hem of the gown to her knee. "Welcome home, love."

Rebecca kissed the tousled hair on the top of his head, took his hand and laid it inside her thigh. "And you, too, welcome home."

Chapter Three

To Rebecca, the coffee pot smirked as knowingly at the tea pot as she and Michael did at each other. They clinked cups above the toast rack. The tiny sound was lost in the general clatter of plates and cutlery. "Eat," Michael said. "You've been burnin' a lot of calories recently."

Rebecca's cheeks went as pink and warm as though she'd been basking in the brilliant sunlight outside rather than in his arms. She ducked his amused scrutiny and cut into her link sausage. Usually British sausage resembled a shell casing packed with sawdust, but this one was delicious.

Sometime in the polished gleam of late evening or the fresh glow of early morning, she'd been so overcome by emotion she'd heard herself demanding, "Love me, love me." To which Michael had wheezed, "That's what I'm doin'!" And they'd laughed so hard they'd almost fallen off the bed.

Later she'd embarrassed herself by almost crying. "I'm so happy," she'd explained to Michael's bleary-eyed query, "it's almost frightening."

Gallantly he'd roused himself. "We'll be havin' our ups and doons. We have tae expect that. But there's naething we canna handle." Then, the verbal proprieties observed, he'd fallen comatose.

The birds were caroling as hysterically this morning as they had all night long. Did they sing in shifts, Rebecca wondered, or did they not sleep at all during the short summer nights? She'd slept better in one night than she'd done in months, tucked into the curve of Michael's body, safe at last.

This morning he was back in uniform—running shoes, jeans, and the sweatshirt she'd given him for Christmas emblazoned with a soup can label reading "Campbell's Cream of the Crop."

"When did Colin and Anjali get married?" Rebecca asked. "I thought they were just living together."

"They were. But her mum's from Bombay, you ken, and wisna best pleased at her daughter livin' in sin. So they tied it up formally at the Inverness registry office in March. Just as well."

"Oh?"

"Might as well be hanged for a sheep as for a lamb." He grinned.

Rebecca laughed. She took another piece of toast and smeared it with marmalade. Back in the days of her previous engagement, her mother had found Rebecca's packet of birth control pills. Wringing her hands, Mrs. Reid had wailed, "You'll never get him to marry you now!" Not that her father would come after Michael with a shotgun. She'd long ago reached an understanding with her family—they lived in their world, she lived in hers.

"It's a long way to Rudesburn," Michael was saying. "A hundred miles. We can stop at Neidpath Castle or Abbotsford, if you like, and at Presto's in Galashiels to get groceries for the cottage."

"Let's just hope Dennis isn't too addicted to junk food and Adele doesn't have to have tofu. Heaven only knows what the other students are like. Mark's from Texas—maybe he'll want chili on his corn flakes."

Michael rolled his eyes. "Laurence is rentin' the cottage as usual in August—another reason to finish the dig on time. But it's less expensive for them to have only Kleinfelter and his—well, he was budgeted for a secretary, but I think she's a groupie—livin' in the hotel."

Rebecca lingered another few moments over her coffee while Michael dawdled over his tea. The real world was lurking impatiently outside. All too soon she was folding her clothes and arranging her toiletries in their compartments. She tried not to wince when Michael blithely stuffed his suitcase every which way, hung the kilt in his garment bag, and seemed surprised she wasn't ready yet.

They headed away from the coast, into those rolling hills laced with shining water that Rebecca had seen from the plane. Before long she had a crick in her neck from trying to look every way at once. Michael drove with one hand, using the other to wave at passing sights, to shift gears, and to pat different parts of Rebecca's anatomy, as if assuring himself she wasn't going to vanish like Thomas the Rhymer's fairy queen.

Thomas met his queen on the Eildon Hills, three green mounds rising south of Melrose. By late afternoon Michael's Fiat skirted the Eildons and descended through thickets of beech and alder into Gowandale. He sang, "Seas between us braid hae roared, sin' auld lang syne."

"Should auld acquaintance be forgot," Rebecca chimed in, and finished the song just as they entered the village of Rudesburn. The gardens in front of the houses were breathtaking; profusions of every flower Rebecca had ever seen and a few she hadn't, like some tall, spiky yellow and orange blooms Michael called "red hot pokers."

The narrow highway became Jedburgh Street, the only street in town. Rebecca looked appreciatively at the tidy houses built of rose-gray stone and black slate, many with shops on their ground floors. Some of them provided supplies for the local people while others sold antiques, fishing gear, and toys to tourists. A sign before a glistening new whitewashed structure proclaimed "Craft Centre: Hand-knit sweaters, woollens and needlework." A red phone booth, also freshly painted, stood just in front.

Michael stopped at a much older building across the street. A swinging sign over heavy wood and glass doors read "Priory House Hotel."

"Otherwise known as the old Kerr manor house," he said, climbing out of the car and stretching. "Built of stones from the old castle on Battle Law and from the priory itself. Seventeenth through nineteenth centuries."

"The Kerrs got a little carried away, didn't they? Like crazed children with building blocks." Rebecca peered up at the building. Multiple wings and ells sprawled from a forthright central tower. Windows dotted the facade in eccentric patterns, and chimneys sprouted from the roofs like wagging tails. "Friendly place, though," she added with a smile.

"Aye," returned Michael. "This is where the pub is."

A white police car with blue lettering pulled up beside them. Two navy blue-clad officers clambered out and hurried into the hotel. Michael looked perplexed. "The local bobby was tellin' me last month he never had to deal wi' more than dead car batteries, lost sheep, and the odd drunk."

"I can't see the first two being a problem in a hotel lobby," returned Rebecca. They stepped into the building.

A wide staircase swept upward from the center of the lobby. To the right was a registration desk complete with guest book, flower arrangement, and pigeonholes. Just beyond the desk a glass-paned door opened onto an office. To the left a collection of overstuffed chairs and low tables faced a fireplace filled not with logs but with an electric heater. Beyond the chairs was a passageway Rebecca assumed led toward the pub.

The police constables stood deep in conference with a husky man whose expanse of stomach was encased by a kilt. He had more dark hair on his chin than on his head, as if the follicles were migrating south. His gesture indicated a display case half-concealed in an alcove beneath the stairway. ". . . broke the lock on the case but ignored the cash box below the counter!"

The bobbies nodded and made notes. Another policeman stood just behind them, his hat with its checkered band tucked beneath his arm. When he saw Michael and Rebecca, he came toward them, his long mobile face trying valiantly to suppress a smile. But still the affable creases in his cheeks negated the worried frown that puckered his forehead.

"Hello, Grant," said Michael. They shook hands. "This is Rebecca Reid. Rebecca, Police Constable Grant Johnston."

Grant's huge hand had a firm, dry grasp; just the sort of re-assuring handshake a policeman should have. "Sorry you had tae arrive just as the balloon went up."

"What happened?" Rebecca inquired.

Grant nodded at the kilted man. "Laurence rang me aboot an hoor ago. Sometime the day—he disna ken just when—someone did a bunk wi' one o' the big gold coins and a paper. Theft ower a hundred quid—I had tae knock up the Galashiels force."

"One of the gold nobles of Edward III?" Michael asked.

"Why would a thief take only one?" asked Rebecca.

"That's just it, miss," Grant said. "You'd think a proper thief would take both the coins and leave the paper, bonny as it is wi' a' thae seals."

Michael blanched. "You mean the warrant for Anne Douglas's arrest?" He turned to Rebecca. "The prioress who was tried for witchcraft in 1545; that warrant is all the original documentation we have."

"Anne, the spectral nun?"

Grant glanced furtively at the other officers, and said under his breath, "There're some as say she walks, right enough."

"Just a local legend," called Laurence Baird. He left the Galashiels force examining the display case. "Hello, Michael. Good to see you again. Sorry about all this—I feel quite the idiot, going in and out all day without ever looking into the alcove." He made a dismissive gesture, indicative of spilled milk and locked barn doors, and shook Rebecca's hand. "How do you do, Miss Reid? Did Mr. MacLeod tell you about the film crew?"

"Aye," said Michael. "We'll be needin' a film record."

"We're lucky to get Plantagenet Productions with their museum experience. Have you seen their documentary about Boadicea and her revolt against the Romans?"

"I must've been in America when that was on." The tendons in Michael's jaw twinged.

"I have," offered Grant. "The blond lass doin' the commentary dressed hersel' in a short tunic and went aboot drivin' a chariot. First time I'd ever really appreciated history."

I'll bet, thought Rebecca.

"Miss Fitzgerald has a very creative approach. She hopes to make the excavations more understandable to the general public. It's a shame, after all, to let the priory just fall to ruins when it could be preserved and appreciated by so many." Laurence rocked back on his heels, beaming like a snake-oil salesman with a good audience. "The dig's shaping up beautifully. We were lucky to get Jeremy Kleinfelter. A good omen, wouldn't you say?"

Fortunately one of the other officers called, "Sir?," and Laurence excused himself before anyone answered that question. Michael asked Grant, "The thief didna turn ower those boxes of Francis Kerr's in the attic, did he? Laurence has promised the lot to the museum."

"The attic? I didna think aboot that. But no keys have gone missin'."

"We'll make a recce." Michael leaned over the reception desk, opened a drawer and pulled out a key. He beckoned Rebecca up the staircase.

Once out of sight they shared the same look of mingled caution and exasperation. The Rudesburners were working with the best of motives, keeping their village alive by preserving its past. They'd hired Kleinfelter and approved his choice of Sheila in the best of faith. The troops in the trenches owed it to them to conduct themselves professionally, which still didn't stop Rebecca from muttering under her breath, "A chariot?"

Michael, shaking his head, led the way through a maze of hallways, staircases, and fire doors. At last they emerged in a brightly lit landing at the top of the house. Michael jiggled the knob on the solitary door, then bent to inspect the lock. Threadbare carpet, Rebecca noted, but clean. And the window at her elbow was sparkling. She glanced out.

Jedburgh Street ran down into the furrow of the Gowan Water, crossed the stone arches of the New Bridge—built in 1747—and disappeared to the east, toward Newtown St. Boswells and Jedburgh itself. Beyond the willows on the far side of the stream rose the priory church.

Rebecca gasped in delight. Photographs didn't do it justice. Even half-ruined it was praise sung in stone. The smooth lines of buttress and vault and window tracery guided her eyes toward heaven, as did the bell tower rising above the expanse of remaining roof like a hand lifted in blessing. Its height betrayed the priory's origins as a Benedictine monastery, only converted into a more austere Cistercian convent in 1381. Low walls, the bones of the convent buildings, shouldered aside the rich green turf that swept down to Battle Law. The craggy knoll's harshness was softened by flowering broom, yellow cascading among the tumbled stones of the demolished castle. Beyond the Law the land rolled in green and gold waves toward England.

She leaned so close to the window that her breath fogged the glass and smudged the picture postcard vision. Smiling, she turned away.

The door beside her was open. She stepped into a long room, its low ceiling made even lower by rough-hewn rafters. Three skylights admitted rays of sun, their brilliant shafts filled with waltzing dust motes. Beyond the stripes of sun the room was dim, shapes of furniture and boxes indistinct. But the cleanliness of the hotel extended even here, Rebecca noticed approvingly; the wooden floor was neatly swept.

Except for a matchbook lying to one side of the door. She picked it up. The cover read "Edinburgh Pub." Michael himself might have dropped it last month, except it, like the floor, wasn't at all dusty. She put the matchbook in the pocket of her jacket.

Michael was kneeling beside a stack of cardboard boxes and an ancient trunk. "These should look familiar," he called.

"Just like the haystacks at Dun Iain. Are there any needles in these?"

"I canna say. Kerr's collections were just like this when the Bairds bought the place fifteen years ago. Laurence said he found some schoolboy copybooks datin' from the 1880's and didna look further. He only mentioned them to me last month because I asked aboot the coins and the warrant."

"Did Kerr find the coins?"

"Well, naething's been disturbed, as far as I can tell." Michael dusted his hands and stood. "He found them whilst stravaigin' in the priory grounds, but didna bother to record where. The man meant well, but he was an old-fashioned antiquarian, no a scientist. The best favor he did Rudesburn was to leave the priory to the Historic Buildings and Monuments Commission."

"Who've been prodded by the Rudesburners into finally doing something with it. But the manor house has been a hotel for years, hasn't it?"

"Aye. Laurence never met Francis Kerr. The warrant for Anne's arrest was in Francis's family archives, along wi' the coins and Mary Pringle's history of the priory." Rebecca waited on the landing while Michael locked the door. He went on, "Francis gave the museum the history back in the thirties. Or some of the history, it's turned oot. God himsel' kens when I can go through the rest of yon boxes—typical, naebody thought they were important."

He grimaced and heaved against one of the fire doors, managing to open it far enough for Rebecca to slip through. "The warrant's been a piece of local lore for years, like the ghost. Laurence put it on display because it looked pretty, as Grant said. It was only when Dr. Graham from the museum was makin' a feasibility study last year that he recognized it for what it was. He tried to buy it, but Laurence didna want to sell. And it's well and truly his property, no treasure trove found in a field somewhere."

"You made a copy of the warrant, of course."

"Of course," Michael responded indignantly. "Mary Pringle's account—the part we have—skips very lightly ower the issue of Anne."

"Must've been a heck of a scandal. Whatever happened to her? Was she convicted?"

"Naebody kens. That's why I rang the archives at the British Museum, lookin' for the other side of the story. But all the records were lost. Selfish Sassenach scholars—check something oot and never bring it back.''

"Maybe we'll dig up a first person account," teased Rebecca, "complete with a lurid illuminated cover."

Michael laughed. ''Pull the other one, lass.''

The uneven floors creaked beneath their feet. The building smelled faintly of dust and mold, more strongly of furniture polish, disinfectant, and baking bread. Rebecca inhaled, reminded sharply of Dun Iain. Yet this building wasn't a replica of an old structure; it really was old, and not nearly as hallowed with age as the priory.

As they started down the main staircase, a plump red-haired woman didn't so much walk as propel herself into the lobby. "Laurence? I saw the panda car—what is it?"

"Nora Baird," Michael stage-whispered.

While Laurence explained to his wife what had happened, Grant rejoined Michael and Rebecca. "We'll talk tae the guests who stayed here the night—only three people, an American couple and an old woman frae Nottingham.''

The Galashiels officers folded and pocketed their notebooks and, with various reassuring if noncommittal mutters, left. Rebecca strolled over to the glass-topped display case. Its lock was a mere formality; it could have been broken with a twist of a letter opener or a knife.

The remaining gold coin, artfully spotlighted, shone up at her like a miniature sun. It overshadowed the other archeological odds and ends in the case; a rusted arrowhead or two, a few shards of pottery. The crushed nap of the velvet backing, a round shape and a rectangular one, made it only too obvious what was missing. "What a waste," she said.

Nora peered over her shoulder. "It certainly is. Some yobbo thinks he can get beer and cigarette money with those. I'd like to see him trying to fence the warrant. And the coin—he'll only get the weight of the gold, not its worth as an antiquity. We should've let the museum have them.''

"Maybe the police will find them soon," said Rebecca, with more courtesy than hope.

"They'll alert the antiquities dealers." The two women turned away from the case and introduced themselves. Nora continued, "At least the excavation is finally getting under way. We've been waiting for years. Winnie Johnston—Grant's wife—and I aired the cottage and put clean linen on the beds. Here you go.''

She took a key ring from a pigeonhole above the registration desk and handed it to Rebecca.

"Thank you." Rebecca put the keys in her purse.

"Winnie runs the shop and post office; she's already set up an account for you and the students. We'll be having a supper in the bar for everyone tonight, rather an opening ceremony. Except for the film crew—they won't be here until tomorrow."

Rebecca pretended not to hear that last statement. "You certainly have everything well organized. We do appreciate it. Michael tells me you also run the Craft Centre across the road."

"That I do, with my niece Bridget. Are you interested in crafts?"

Rebecca visualized Michael's wounded sweater. "I sew and knit when I get the chance."

"Come across then, and we'll see you get what you need."

"Thank you," Rebecca said again.

Laurence waved Grant out the door. Michael gestured at Rebecca. "We need to unpack the car."

On the way out Rebecca thought she heard Michael mutter, "Just the one coin, bugger it anyway," but the Bairds' affirmations of welcome were still ringing in her ears. She sighed—historical thieves were the last thing they needed—and essayed, "No wonder the Rudesburners have gotten their act together with Laurence and Nora at the helm."

"Aye. Hard to believe they're English."

Rebecca recoiled in exaggerated horror. "No!"

"I was born there mysel', remember? But Nora's family is from Glasgow, I think, and Laurence has ancestors here. So they're no really incomers, just comin' home, like you."

"At least incomers have the good taste to move here."

"No like the absentee landords who're denyin' us our own land. If no for the incomers, there'd be precious few people left in Scotland. You mind what Samuel Johnson said: 'The most inspirin' sight to a Scot is the high road to England.' Where the jobs are. Which is why Maddy and Geoff are raisin' my nephews in Sheffield."

Laughing, Rebecca turned to the Fiat. Two cats lay in elegant poses on the hood, basking in the sun. "Well," she said. "Hello there." She held out her hand, and each velvety nose gravely saluted her fingertips.

"May I introduce more of the Johnston family?" Michael lifted the completely black cat so that Rebecca could shake his paw. "This is Lancelot, and that is Guinevere. She's the wee nun in black and white."

"Pleased to meet you," Rebecca told them both. And to Guinevere, "Retired to the convent after an exciting life breaking all the commandments? But not to Rudesburn; Cistercian nuns wore all white."

The cat's whiskers went on the alert. A flood of children, one on a skateboard and two whooping behind, swept down the sidewalk. Lancelot did an Olympic backward somersault and hit the ground running. Guinevere's white paws scrabbled for purchase on the hood of the car, then shot off after him.

Michael's hands still held a cat shape. "And there's the rest of the Johnstons. . . . Aaah, she scratched my bonnet!" He bent solicitously over the car's gleaming hood, his fingertip rubbing out Guinevere's tracks.

Rebecca turned away, smothering her laugh—men! Just past the bulk of the Craft Centre was the entrance to a driveway. At its end was the cottage, nesting on the banks of the stream. Two hundred years old, Michael had said. But it, too, gleamed with whitewash, even as the lichen-stained slates of the roof added character.

"I'll walk," Rebecca called. She crossed the street and traipsed down the driveway. Behind the Craft Centre was a fenced-in area. Black-faced sheep peered incuriously at her as she walked by.

The first key she tried opened the door facing toward the village. She entered a vestibule lined with coat pegs, then went through a glass door into a hallway. To her right was a sitting room complete with fireplace, television set, and comfortable chairs. The next door opened onto a bedroom.

Opposite the sitting room was a dining room, and beyond that a kitchen glistening with Scandinavian-style cabinets and counter tops. She looked askance at the propane-fired Aga cooker, a massive piece of iron with lids that raised to expose bare, searing hot metal. It stayed on all day, Michael had assured her, heating the water as well as providing warmth. The window over the sink looked straight across the stream to the priory.

Upstairs were two more bedrooms, huge closets, and a large bathroom. Back downstairs Rebecca found another bathroom just off the rear entry, along with a miniature washer and dryer. She visualized quarrels over laundry rights and vowed to start sign-up sheets immediately.

The front door crashed open, and Michael appeared carrying several plastic bags of groceries. "Which room do you want, hen?" he asked jovially, plunking his burden down on the counter.

"The downstairs one would be more private. But don't you people believe in double beds?"

"No in holiday hire houses, I suppose." He steered her back through the dining room to the bedroom and inspected the two-foot gap between the beds. "Dinna worry, love. That's no so far across as the Atlantic."

She hugged him. "Promise I won't get cold at night?"

"I promise." She'd always been impressed how Michael could kiss her and laugh at the same time.

Over his shoulder the window opened onto the same view as the one from the kitchen. A man was walking across the lawn beside the church, stopping every now and then to poke at bits of broken masonry with his toe.

Michael turned to see what she was looking at. "Guid. A victim for Laurence. Let's go tell him aboot Nora's scones."

"Are you questioning Laurence's motives?"

"Economic power makes the world go around. If naebody paid us for muckin' aboot in dust and mud, we'd be packin' herring or—what do you say—slingin' hash?"

"I've done enough of that, thank you." She squeezed him again, and something squashed between them. The matchbook in her pocket. She pulled it out, didn't see a wastebasket, and tossed it on the dressing table.

"What's that?"

"Just a stray matchbook. Picked it up off the attic floor."

"Always tidyin'," Michael chided. "If you can possibly tear yoursel' away, how aboot a wee dander through the priory?"

"A stroll?" she translated. "Wonderful."

Michael bowed and offered her his arm. Together they walked out of the house and toward the footbridge over the Gowan Water.

Chapter Four

THE GOWAN WATER sparkled and burbled over its rocky bed. Willow branches waded in the stream, and leaves rustled in the breeze. The solitary tourist was nowhere in sight.

Michael and Rebecca paused on the footbridge and looked upstream to where the bridge that carried the modern road arched over the mossy piers of its fourteenth-century predecessor. "There," Michael said, "by the old ford, Marjory Douglas, the first prioress, found her lover's body."

Rebecca leaned on the railing, the sun warm on her back. The murmur of wind and water muffled the voices and slamming doors of the village, sealing the priory in its own secret bubble of time and space. "The rest of his body, you mean? That was downright sadistic, her brothers killing William Salkeld simply because he was English—and then presenting poor Marjory with his heart on a spear!"

"Marjory's family wanted her to marry some neighborin' landowner to extend their own holdin's. That was why they killed William—greed, no ideology. But Marjory took her dowry to the church. Poetic justice."

"No wonder she thought God sent her to Rudesburn, with William dying right on its doorstep. People have always tried to find some higher purpose in human bloody-mindedness." She shook her head with a rueful smile. "The day I got that copy of Pringle's history I dreamed my brothers were after you. Except they were dressed as cowboys, not knights."

"No so keen, are they, at your takin' up wi' a foreigner?"

"I don't think they care one way or the other. You're just

another one of my delusions, like getting a Ph.D." Again she took Michael's arm.

"Thank you," he said, and patted her hand warily.

On the far side of the church, the man they'd seen from the cottage strode toward the parking area, presenting them with a generic jeans-and-jacket-clad back. He disappeared behind the remaining stretch of the perimeter wall, and a moment later the sudden revving of an engine sent pigeons spinning away from the eaves of the church. Gravel spattered, and the sound of the car dwindled. Rebecca sighed. "Shoot. The customer that got away."

"We'll have the place to oursel's then," Michael said. They walked across the bridge and stepped onto the springy grass.

"Is that where the name comes from?" Rebecca asked. "That skirmish between the Douglases and the Salkelds couldn't have been the first one here. Why else call that hill 'Battle Law'? Maybe 'Rudesburn' came from the Gaelic word *ruadh*, red. Poets say the stream flowed red with blood."

"Good theory, except they spoke Brittonic in these airts." He nodded at the tall wheel-headed cross standing before the west door of the church. "See, the rood is as much Northumbrian scrollwork as Celtic interlace. It's your own name that comes from *ruadh*."

"Well, yes, my great-grandfather the immigrant had flaming red hair. I'm sorry it disappeared from the family."

"Recessive gene. All you need is a fresh infusion." Michael tossed his head. In the sunlight, his brown hair had a distinct gleam of red. "Maddy has chestnut hair," he added, as if he were applying for a genetics test. Rebecca acknowledged his inference with a grin.

Despite its age, the cross sprang straight and proud from the turf. Its carved straps, knots, and mythological animals had been smoothed by centuries of weather into organic shapes like muscles flexing just beneath stone skin. Rebecca laid her palm flat against the rock. It was warm. She could almost have convinced herself it was humming, vibrantly alert, noticing but not commenting on the pageant of war and peace played out before it. "Then 'Rudesburn' is from 'rood' and 'burn.' "

"The cross beside the stream." Michael, too laid his hand on the stone. He smiled, as though it tickled his fingertips. "Probably Irish monks carved it when they set up cells on the Law. See the boss in the cross-head, and the decoration on the shaft face runnin' on up onto the head wi'oot a separation. Ninth century, at the least. Temptin' to think it was once a standin' stone markin' a prehistoric sacred site.''

"Very tempting," Rebecca agreed. "I suppose that nick out of the top was made by some gun-happy henchman of Cromwell's in the 1600's.''

"The Puritans were scairt of bonny things, said they distracted you from worship. I'd take the opposite view, mysel'.''

"Definitely.''

Through the wide doorway in the western wall of the church the grass was just as lush, even though it was now barred by the shadows of the remaining vaults and window tracery. "Mind your step," said Michael.

"I see them." Rebecca skirted three stone sarcophagi sunk into the ground, their interiors carved in human shapes and thoughtfully provided with drains. Their occupants had once been laid beneath the flagstoned floor of the nave. Hopefully they'd been long gone when religiously reformed Rudesburners had turned the priory into a handy-dandy local quarry. She visualized zealots breaking the windows and standing with smug self-righteousness as the multi-colored glass rained down. She saw them slaughtering those who disagreed with their revealed truth of how many angels danced on the head of a pin. . . . Not only the reformers did that. People had been murdering each other over religion for thousands of years.

"It's not that I can't understand why people die for their faith," she mused aloud, "I can't understand why other people kill for theirs.''

"Is there ever any excuse to kill?" Michael asked softly.

She looked at his solemn face. That was one question she couldn't answer. She took his hand. *"Benedicite,"* she said, although she wasn't sure just for whom she was asking the blessing.

He squeezed her hand in return. *"Deo gratias."*

A lark swooped beneath the vaulting, its song mitigating the sudden silence, and landed on the shattered sill of the rood screen. "You're a good Presbyterian boy," Rebecca teased, "quoting ecclesiastical Latin at me.''

"I've mucked aboot in the Middle Ages long enough to appreciate the liturgy. A Catholic mother dinna make you one, hen.''

"Most of the time my mother was too tired and disillusioned

to practice any religion—like the Puritans, maybe. We're children of a profane society."

"Who respect the sacred," Michael concluded. "If we ken what's good for us."

The south side of the nave was closed by a row of narrow, carved pillars. Behind them was an aisle centered on a tomb. Michael and Rebecca paused beside the weathered effigy of William Salkeld. His face was a textured lump, his hands holding his sword a suggestion of human form. For being considerably younger then the standing cross, the tomb carvings were in much worse shape. The cross, Rebecca thought, must be made of much harder stone. Why, even the top of the tomb was skewed to one side. . . .

"Look there!" She dropped to her knees and inspected the overhanging rim of the lid. Freshly gouged grooves stood out white and stark against the soft gray of the stone. "Vandals?"

"Grave robbers, more likely. Bluidy idiots. Pringle's history says in so many words the tomb was looted and emptied in the sixteenth century. And Kerr affirmed that it was empty only fifty years ago."

"How many people have access to those references?" Rebecca asked. "That man who was walking around here. . . . Not that it would've been easy for him to hide a crowbar in his pocket."

"Could've been done any time this week. I'll mention it to Grant and Laurence. All this publicity for the dig's no attractin' the kind of business they wanted, is it?" He shoved at the effigy, but the lid wouldn't move. "We'll get some tools and set you to rights," he told the out-of-focus face.

William Salkeld didn't respond. Perhaps the sole purpose of his short, tragic life had been to bring Marjory Douglas to God and to Rudesburn. Unlike Adele's obsessed ghosts, he had no reason to linger.

The remains of a pitch pine roof, dating from the nineteenth century when the church had been the local parish of the Church of Scotland, extended from the tower to cover the chancel and the choir. Here the grass stopped. Rebecca's sneakers crunched over tiles and flags jumbled in a gray, brown, and rose mosaic. Beneath the tower she peered through a grille into a spiral staircase, the steps hollowed from centuries of ascending and descending feet. "Keep Out," read a neatly lettered sign. "Danger. Unstable masonry."

"Time for some preservation work." Michael scraped at the stone beside the door. "Colin says the older parts of the priory are built of agglomerate, the newer parts of sandstone, probably from the same quarries on the Eildons that Morrow used for Melrose."

"Wouldn't it've been easier to use stone from Battle Law? Both the castle and the first priory went up about the same time, didn't they?"

"Aye, eleventh century. The castle was built of Law stone. But Colin says it's some kind of igneous stuff, harder than the priory masons wanted." He pointed to the fine fluted molding edging the chancel arch.

The transepts were lined with empty alcoves, like staring eye sockets, that had once been chapels to the many saints Marjory venerated. Another doorway was blocked with rubble that slumped wearily against several restraining boards. "That was a stairway down to the crypt," Michael explained. "Ceilin' collapsed back in the thirties. A shame—Kerr left a nice map. Something else for us to set to rights."

"I wonder if Marjory's relics were destroyed like so many were at the time of the Reformation."

"Good question. She had a top-hole collection of relics, no doot aboot it. Why else was the place one of the richest in the Borders, all the poor sick folk comin' to ask the relics for miracle cures?"

"Why else," asked Rebecca, "did Henry the Eighth loot the convent during Anne Douglas's time?"

"Vanity and greed," Michael answered.

Rebecca scuffed at the fine dust, the texture of ashes, that mottled the floor. The building was tangible memory, not quite real. The moldings on windows and chancel arch were weathered and chipped, only hinting their original delicacy. The shattered remains of the rood screen, the hacked block of stone that had once held the altar, the scraped and graffiti-fouled piers supporting the roof vaulting—all was suggestion, not statement. The building lacked the animation of a living presence, of song and praise.

The sun sank, and the shadow of the west front crept over the floor, leaving Rebecca in dim coolness. The air was filled with that odor of ancient sanctity she usually found so comforting, dust and must and an elusive sweetness that could have been either incense or decay. But at Rudesburn that air made her uneasy. The chill wind that tickled the back of her neck was not a sigh of peace but a groan of sorrow and pain.

She scurried out the closest doorway behind Michael and found herself back in the sunlight. She would have chided herself for an overactive imagination, but she'd learned the hard way to trust her intuition. "No wonder people think the place is haunted," she commented.

"Peace only an illusion?" Michael's mouth tightened, and his brows signaled a silent message—*here we go again.*

Rebecca took a few steps toward the thick, dark branches of a yew tree, its fronds drooping over rows of headstones. Just beside her was a flat stone, its edges concealed by encroaching turf, an incised skull and the date 1697 barely visible. Beyond that a polished granite St. Andrews cross bore the legend, "Francis Pringle Kerr, 1882-1968." The cemetery with its recent graves was outside the boundaries of the dig.

Michael turned away from the graves and looked toward the shops and houses on the other side of the burn. A car came through the village, picked up speed when it reached the bridge, and zoomed away behind the convent wall. The twentieth century thrust itself into the fourteenth, and the secret bubble of space and time surrounding Rudesburn popped and dissipated.

Rebecca and Michael looked at each other and laughed. Hand in hand, they walked behind the church and around the remains of the convent. The walls of the chapter house still stood, supported by metal braces, and the cloister garth remained a pristine lawn. Most of the other buildings were defined only by collapsed walls almost covered with hogweed, nettles, wild roses, and the daisies that gave Gowandale its name. In the shade the stones were painted with a fluorescent green moss that animation studios would have a hard time replicating. South of the ruins was a well, now closed by an iron lattice and a padlock considerably larger than the one on the display case.

Michael glanced up at Battle Law. "Dinna look the noo, but we're bein' followed."

Rebecca looked. Lancelot and Guinevere were oozing from bush to stone to carved block, their golden eyes winking, their ears pricked and alert. She crossed the footbridge, sensing those curious and yet indifferent feline eyes on the back of her neck.

She and Michael had barely stowed the groceries and started unloading their suitcases when voices echoed through the open windows. Rebecca set her new wellies in the vestibule and looked out the door past the gleaming hood of the Fiat. A blue and white bus had just pulled away from the hotel. Four people were walking down the driveway. "They're here!" she called.

Rebecca recognized Adele's gray hair and glasses and Dennis's rotund figure. By process of elimination, then, the woman in the exquisitely tailored tweed jacket was Hilary Chase, and the man with the silver belt buckle and a guitar case was Mark Owen. Did he intend his short dark hair to stand spikily on end like that, Rebecca wondered, or was it that the wind was picking up? A look upward confirmed that clouds were scudding in from the west. Oh, good. They'd be starting the dig in the rain.

Introductions took only a moment, and a quick tour of the house another few. When Michael finished demonstrating the Aga cooker, everyone continued to stand awkwardly in the kitchen. It was Dennis who broke the silence. "We've got three men, three women, and three bedrooms. Should we draw straws?" He glanced from Rebecca to Hilary with a leer that on his guileless face looked more like, "What, me worry?"

Michael said firmly, "Rebecca and I'll be sharin' the room on the ground floor. I suggest that Adele and Hilary take one of the first floor rooms and Dennis and Mark the other. There's plenty of cupboard space."

Adele considered first Michael and then Rebecca; so much for her assumption of polite courtship in the front parlor. With a pained smile she picked up her suitcase and started up the stairs. Michael rushed to help her. Dennis shrugged resignation and followed.

"The last dig I was on, " Mark essayed, "the volunteers had to live in tents. A roof and indoor plumbing—I'm impressed."

"That's right," replied Rebecca, "you're the only one of us who's a bona fide archeologist. Where were you digging?"

"Pueblo Bonito. Anasazi snakes and dust. But I'm only a larva—just barely have my Master's."

Hilary asked, "Do you play the guitar?"

"I play at it. It's my pacifier."

"Michael plays the bagpipes," said Rebecca. "We'll have to find something you can play together."

" 'Amazing Grace'?" Mark suggested, and turned toward the stairs.

Rebecca, too, was impressed; his grin was almost as appealing as Michael's. And his eyes were very attractive—clear gray and tip-tilted like those of a Tolkien elf. Behind Mark's back, Rebecca and Hilary exchanged a nod, feminine quality control approving the goods.

Hilary had a fresh, open face even if her purse was real leather; her brown hair was tied with a silk scarf, and her luggage was matched Samsonite. *Daddy's money*, Rebecca thought. *Lucky girl.* "I have trouble just boiling water," Hilary confided, with a dubious glance around the kitchen, "but I'll be glad to wash dishes."

Rebecca smiled. "Thank you. We'll sit down later on tonight and work out some kind of duty roster."

Michael bounded down the stairs. "Do you need help wi' your cases?" Hilary declined and wrestled them up herself, throwing Rebecca a quick smirk indicating Michael also deserved a quality control stamp. "Lucky girl," she, too, seemed to say.

In their bedroom, Rebecca found Michael mouthing "how now brown cow" to the mirror. "I asked Adele aboot her trip to Whithorn," he explained, "and she didna—didn't—understand me."

"Just when you thought you were safe at home, you're invaded by American accents." She slid her empty suitcases, a mismatched and much-battered set initialed with her mother's maiden name, under the bed.

Michael tossed several pairs of socks and his sgian dubh into a dresser drawer and looked at his watch. "Past nineteen hundred hours."

"I'm ready." Rebecca combed her hair, applied lipstick, and put on the sweater-vest Caroline Campbell had made for her. It was as cozily warm as Michael's own, and the cable pattern across the shoulders perfectly fit the shape of the arm he draped around her on their way up the driveway.

Hilary cooed to the sheep, Mark inspected a minuscule chip of flint, and Adele stood mesmerized by the vision of the priory across the burn. Only Dennis, following the scent of food, kept pace with his keepers.

A silver Jaguar with a rental sticker on its bumper was parked half across the curb in front of the hotel. "Our fearless leader?" Michael asked.

"Sssh," Rebecca hissed, "don't sow dissension among the ranks."

The car did belong to Jeremy Kleinfelter. They could hear his professorial voice all the way down the hall that led from the lobby to the bar, the faded prints of grouse-hunters and Highland regiments shivering as the words gusted by. ". . . Nimrud and Wroxeter. Thought I should try a little place for a change. Quality instead of quantity."

He was leaning on the bar in a John Wayne pose. In fact, Rebecca thought, he looked like John Wayne, most of his weight carried in the top half of his considerable height. His sandy hair was combed tidily to one side, and his flaring walrus moustache was parted in the middle. He laid down his glass of Scotch and turned to the door with the deliberate confidence of a gunfighter greeting a group of shipping clerks. "There you are!"

A somewhat glazed Laurence made introductions. With an effusive "Call me Jerry," Dr. Kleinfelter lingered a moment longer than necessary over Rebecca's and Hilary's hands, winced perceptibly at Dennis, and bowed to Adele as if offering to help her across the street. He straightened to his full height, demonstrating that of all the men he was the tallest.

"How do you do," said Michael. "I'm your liaison—"

"—from the museum," Jerry finished. "Have to keep on good terms with the local authorities, right?" Before Michael could reply, he turned to Mark. "You're the one studying archeology. Any tips I can give you on getting that Ph.D., don't hesitate to ask—nothing like expert knowledge."

Michael, brows arched up his forehead, ordered a beer.

"Thank you," Mark said. "I'm sure y'all will be very helpful."

Thank you for that second-person plural, Rebecca told him silently.

A woman sat demurely at a nearby table. She was dark-haired and doe-eyed, and her coral lipstick emphasized pouting lips which smoothed into a smile when Jerry laid a proprietary hand on her shoulder. "This is Elaine Vavra. She'll be—er—personing the computer."

Rebecca smothered a groan.

"I can help with that," offered Dennis. "I'm in the hacker club back in Ann Arbor."

Jerry eyed him like a biologist inspecting a microbe. "Everyone will have to wear several hats, since this is such a small excavation."

Laurence started distributing beer and lemonade. Nora bustled through a swinging door and laid bowls and platters on a sideboard. "Food first," she called. "Business later."

Rebecca piled a plate high with salmon, potatoes, whiskey-glazed venison, and Yorkshire pudding. Sitting next to Michael, she decided, was worth Jeremy Kleinfelter's scrutiny pricking between her shoulder blades. For a moment Hilary and Mark watched fascinated as Michael used his knife to plaster his food onto the back of his fork, eating with tidy two-handed efficiency. Then Mark managed to ascertain with various conversational subtleties that Hilary didn't have a boyfriend waiting back in Indiana.

While Nora went from table to table pouring coffee and bringing Adele more lemonade, Laurence delivered himself of a welcoming speech. Rebecca, intent on chasing the last green sprig of cress across her plate, managed to not quite pay attention when he mentioned the film crew. Dennis crept with elephantine grace to the sideboard and took another strawberry tart.

Then Jerry stood up. Every eye followed the ritual polishing of his glasses and the lighting of a thin cigar. Finally, expelling a cloud of smoke that tempted Rebecca to dive behind her napkin, he spoke. "All right, class. Rudesburn Priory. Founded as a Benedictine monastery in the eleventh century. Deserted during the Black Death. Re-founded as a Cistercian convent in 1381 by Marjory Douglas. Worked over by Henry the Eighth's troops in 1545. Worked over again by Cromwell's troops in the 1650's. What we're doing here is salvage. If we find some of the old medieval relics—body parts and personal belongings of saints—we sing the Hallelujah Chorus and hand them over to Mr.—er—Dr. Campbell, here."

He turned to Michael with a smile. Michael smiled back. "Do you have those geophysical surveys?" Jerry asked.

"They're in the cottage. We can go over them the morn."

Rebecca chuckled under her breath. No matter how hard Michael tried to talk "proper," those burred r's clung to his words like thistles to a sheepdog.

"I was hoping to look at them this evening," replied Jerry. With a dismissive gesture, he added, "No matter. I'll check them over tomorrow."

Michael's smile was starting to look like the Cheshire cat's, stiff and disembodied. Beneath the table Rebecca nudged her leg reassuringly against his. She would never understand masculine games of dominance.

Elaine watched Jerry with the dewy-eyed admiration of a candidate's wife watching a campaign speech. Neither, Rebecca thought, would she understand women's games of submission.

Adele spoke, leaving Jerry with his mouth open. "Marjory Douglas collected relics of Saint Margaret, who founded the first priory, and Saints Aidan, Wilfred, Kentigern, Ninian, Columba, and Bridget. Most of the major northern saints except for Cuthbert, who was such a misogynist he'd probably have cursed any convent that tried to appropriate his mortal remains." Her thin face grew luminous. "The medieval belief in relics shows a belief in the survival of the spirit; the saints' spirits were believed to remain in the vicinity of their bodies and possessions. Life after death has always been a vital issue. World literature is filled with examples of psychic energies from beyond the grave."

Jerry cleared his throat. "Thank you, Adele. You aren't from California, by any chance?"

"No. Pennsylvania."

"I see." Jerry turned to an attaché case resting on top of the bar beside the beer spigots. "I have here a cheat sheet of personnel that the University Network sent me. Hilary, you're studying art history. Could you do the sketching for us?"

"I'd be glad to," Hilary returned.

"Mark. You helped survey Pueblo Bonito. If you wouldn't mind . . ."

"Not at all."

"Adele, Rebecca can show you some conservation techniques. And Dennis. You said you'd help Elaine with the computer files." Adele smiled agreement. Dennis shoved his plate away and nodded. Elaine glanced doubtfully at Dennis. "Of course, we'll all be working with shovels and trowels; you have to get your hands dirty in archeology."

Under his breath, Michael muttered, "Do tell."

Laurence offered another round of food and drink. Hilary grimaced and moaned, "No, thank you, I've already blown my diet." Mark's eye traveled contemplatively down her well-filled but hardly overstuffed corduroy jeans.

Jerry, catching Elaine's eye, said, "Let's make it an early night, so we can hit the ground digging tomorrow. Good night, all."

With attaché in one hand and Elaine in the other—her head barely reached his shoulder—Jerry left. The students thanked Laurence and Nora for their hospitality, and went out in an amiable gaggle. Michael lingered to ask, "Did you get a chance to tell Kleinfelter aboot—about—ah, bugger it . . . The coin and the warrant?"

"And this afternoon," Rebecca added, "we saw where someone had taken a crowbar to William Salkeld's tomb."

Laurence's beard bristled. "Blast, that's all we need. I'll mention it to Grant."

"Yes," Nora replied, "we did tell Jerry about the theft. He tut-tutted and shook his head. Damned if you do, damned if you don't publicize."

With a weary nod of agreement and many thanks, Michael and Rebecca strolled out through the lobby. On an easel by the door was a poster, a bright tartan set of bagpipes overlaid by the words, "Borders Festival, Rudesburn, Roxburghshire, 3 August."

"That's your birthday," Rebecca said.

Michael grumbled, "Dinna remind me."

"You make it sound as if thirty is over the hill or something."

"Or something." They walked out into the pellucid shadows of evening. "You were right aboot Jerry. He's fair taken on wi' himsel', and no mistake."

"Probably a sign of deep-seated insecurities."

"That may be his problem, but he disna have to make it ours." Rebecca glanced up at him warningly as they crossed the road. Once again he wrapped his arm around her shoulders. "I'll be behavin' mysel'. I just hope he does."

"Amen," she replied.

They walked around the house and stood on the flagstone terrace outside the back entry. The sun flirted with the horizon, squeezing rich beams beneath the gathering clouds. The priory glowed, polished by the light. *Sleeping Beauty's castle,* thought Rebecca, *awaiting the kiss of the trowel.*

A gray-headed figure knelt at the base of the cross, hands folded, eyes downcast. "Adele?" asked Michael. "The woman's a wee bit bonkers, I doot."

"Well, we all are, to some extent."

A sudden thud rolled across the lawns and the stream, the sound of a massive wooden door shutting. The broad west doors of the priory church must once have sounded like that. Adele looked up and gazed fixedly into the shadowed nave. Something moved, a pinprick of light like a distant candle, an implication of a shape. Slowly Adele raised her hand and beckoned.

"Optical illusion," Michael murmured. "One of the moggies. You know how cats' eyes reflect. . . ."

Adele didn't move. From inside the house came the cheerful if off-key plunks of a guitar being tuned. A pleasant baritone—Dennis's, Rebecca realized—started singing, "Beautiful dreamer, waken to me . . ." The shape and the tiny light vanished. Adele drooped.

"Let's go inside, love," Rebecca said. "I think we'd better fortify ourselves for this."

"Oh aye, I'm afraid so." Michael planted a warm beer-flavored kiss on her mouth. They walked into the brightly lit interior of the house and left the evening and its ambiguities behind.

Chapter Five

IF MICHAEL ROLLED to the right, he'd fall off the bed; to the left, he'd crash into the wall. He managed a wriggle and heave to one side and lay emitting the contented grumbles of a cooling tea kettle.

Rebecca liked being his tea cozy. She snuggled into the crook of his arm, catching her breath and stroking the damp satin and sinew of his back. *Let time stop here,* she thought, *while I can't believe I'm actually with you, while we're drunk with infatuation, while dawn is polished with possibility, not yet tarnished by truth.*

But it had been dawn for several hours. What Rebecca's drowsy myopia had first interpreted as light delicate as melted silver, she now decided must be overcast and rain. When that hopeful voice from the other bed had asked, "Are you awake then, love?" she'd been dozing uneasily, worrying about something. . . . That was it. Today was the first day of the dig. She and Michael would have to answer to Jerry. They'd have to deal with Sheila.

No wonder Michael had been so intent on expressing his devotion the last two days. He'd expressed it so energetically she'd be spending the next two days bowlegged. *Men!* Rebecca thought, and smoothed his hair back from his forehead. He had a nice forehead, high and intelligent, at the moment unlined by anger or worry. "I love you," she whispered.

His reply was a blurred, "Love you—very much—promise."

From the depths of the house a door shut and water ran. Rebecca glanced at the travel clock beside the bed. "Time to get up."

"Right," he said, and didn't budge.

Smiling, she kissed him, extricated herself from his embrace, found her nightgown crumpled on the floor, and slipped it on. She picked up her bag of toiletries. "Time to get up," she repeated, but there was no response.

The overhead light was blazing in the kitchen. Adele stood in the nimbus of glare like a haloed saint in an illuminated manuscript, offering the toaster slices of bread. The tea kettle on the Aga was already bubbling, and a percolator was steaming gently. Rebecca inhaled the blessed aroma of coffee. Thank goodness Adele wasn't trying to convert them to her abstemious habits.

Adele rolled her eyes toward Rebecca and then back to the toaster. "Good morning."

"Good morning." Rebecca padded on across the cool linoleum.

The door to the back entry opened and Mark emerged, a towel draped around his naked shoulders, shaving kit in hand. He stopped as he swung onto the staircase and gave Rebecca what even without her glasses she saw was a broad grin. "Hi," he said, and disappeared up the stairs.

She must look like she'd crawled out from under a rock. Then she saw the rosy-cheeked, dewy-eyed, tangle-haired apparition in the bathroom mirror, and realized how obvious it was that what she'd crawled out from under was Michael.

She grimaced with wry embarrassment and made what restoration she could with cold water and a hairbrush. When she returned through the kitchen, Adele was beating eggs, Hilary was opening a carton of orange juice, and Mark was contemplating a list posted on a cabinet door. "Is this what you two were doing up so late last night?" he asked Hilary and Rebecca both. "Laundry, sweeping, dishes; what if I get dishpan hands?"

"If you'd prefer cooking . . ." Hilary replied.

"Sure, if y'all don't mind grilled cheese sandwiches and salsa."

Adele poured the eggs into a skillet, standing well away from the cooker as if afraid its raised lid would fall on her. "Ten minutes," she said. Hilary took a handful of silverware and turned on the dining room light.

Rebecca found Michael sitting blearily on the edge of the bed. "You were after lettin' me oversleep, were you?"

She threw her towel at him. The kitchen had been warm, but now that her friction-induced glow had dissipated, the rest of the house was cold. Quickly she pulled on jeans, sweater, and socks. By the time she sat down at the dressing table, Michael, no doubt scenting tea, had dressed and disappeared.

Rebecca inserted her contact lenses. A little mascara would be enough makeup. There was the matchbook she'd picked up in the attic of the hotel. Edinburgh Pub. This weekend Michael would show her Edinburgh. When she'd spent her twentieth summer studying in Stirling, she'd made more than one weekend visit there. But only her most wishful thoughts had ever checked the place out as a prospective home. She put the matchbook in her cosmetic tray and went in search of coffee.

Adele made a superior omelette. Even Dennis was persuaded to desert his bed and join the round table, although he didn't remember how to speak English until he'd consumed two cups of sugary coffee. Michael, already wise to the bizarre feeding habits of Americans, didn't balk at the warm, moist toast or at the omelette served for breakfast instead of for tea.

It was Hilary's turn to clean up. Rebecca lingered at the table, indulging in more coffee and frowning at a piece of paper. A salutation of "Dear Mrs. Campbell" was stilted, "Dear Caroline" too familiar, "Dear Mother . . ." No, that wouldn't work. And "Hello there" was right out.

She lifted the paper so Hilary could sweep away the crumbs. "Where are you from?" the young woman asked.

"Nowhere. My family lived all over the United States, my father always looking for a better job. Not that he ever found one. You're an Indianapolis native?"

"Lived there all my life. My family owns half the city. Servants, country club, exclusive girl's school, the works."

Hilary bent over the sink, her expression hidden. She didn't seem to be bragging. Did she think everyone lived like that? "How'd you get interested in art history?" Rebecca asked.

"I always liked museums—so peaceful. Drawing and reading were things I could do alone." Hilary unconcernedly piled the dishes in the drainer.

Poor little rich girl? wondered Rebecca. She wrote "Dear Mrs. Campbell, thank you for the lovely sweater." She couldn't think of any way to thank Michael's mum for the man himself.

Michael slammed the front door, and with Mark and Dennis in tow, walked past the dining room windows. Adele came down the steps and went out the back door. Hilary draped the dish towel over the bar on the front of the cooker. Rebecca sealed her letter, put on her wellies and jacket, and headed up the driveway to the village.

The low clouds were like silver wool. The outline of the Eildon Hills was blotted by mist, ground diffusing into sky. A fine rain kissed Rebecca's face, and she parted her lips to catch the cool, elusive taste of earth and stone. She really had it bad, she thought. A week ago she'd trudged to the University clutching her umbrella, cursing the gloomy day and the puddles spewed onto her feet by passing cars.

Winnie Johnston was just opening the front door of the shop with its red and gold "Post Office" sign. "You must be Rebecca. Come in." She removed Lancelot and Guinevere from the counter and straightened a rack of candy. "A letter for Inverness? Here you go." She pulled a 20p stamp out of the drawer and waited patiently while Rebecca read the denomination of each coin in her pocket, finally producing a tenpence and two fivepences.

Winnie had the rosy-cheeked complexion Rebecca had long admired in Michael's masculine version, fair skin nurtured by the damp dimness of Britain. It was enough to make Rebecca resolve never to get a suntan again. Of course, if she stayed here, she might never again have that opportunity.

She petted the cats, thanked Winnie for tidying up the cottage, and went back out onto the street. The rain had stopped. Elaine Vavra was coming out of the hotel, a drawing board under one arm and a satchel in her hand. "May I help?" Rebecca asked, and took the plastic-covered board.

"We'll be starting in the rain, won't we?" said Elaine. "Sodding climate. Had to leave the computer in the room."

"You're from London, you said? I guess you've had your fill of rain."

"I can't wait to get far away. Jerry says Virginia is nice and sunny."

Rebecca's ears pricked. "I heard Jerry directed a dig in Virginia. Was it successful?"

"There was some god-awful sloppy assistant who caused trouble. He says you have to watch out for assistants." Elaine was blissfully unaware she'd just rammed her foot down her throat. Rebecca smothered a snort.

Across the Gowan the lawn before the priory shimmered the

same green that must surround the pearly gates. The dusty rose buildings stood still and silent, almost leaning forward for a better view. Jerry paced across the cloister, gesticulating with a roll of papers, Dennis trotting behind. ". . . datum point," his voice boomed into the damp quiet. "Mike—over there!"

Michael's slender form stood storklike over a surveyor's theodolite set up by the well. He waved, indicating movement to the right. Mark, holding a staff painted with lines, dutifully took two paces to the right and ended up at the base of the cross. Michael entered the measurements in a notebook.

Adele and Hilary were perfectly explicable shapes inside the church, laying out supplies under the overhang of the roof. "Pretty church," Rebecca commented as she and Elaine stepped onto the bridge.

"It's all right. The new cathedral at Coventry is much more posh. But Jerry says we might find important relics here, enough to be going on with."

To be going where with? Rebecca wanted to ask.

"Nice of you to join us, ladies," Jeremy called, tucking the papers inside his coat. "Rebecca, give Hilary that board. Elaine, get my trowels."

Rebecca quelled an impulse to shout, "Aye, aye, sir," and squished on across the grass. Elaine did an about face and went back across the bridge. Surely it was premature to be calling for trowels, Rebecca thought. It would be pick and shovel work today, at least, cutting down the weeds, peeling back the turf, evaluating the unoccupied layers.

Between them Michael and Mark pulled a string taut and jammed pegs into the turf to hold it, defining the western boundary of the excavation. So Jerry was using some of the theoretically undisturbed land outside the precincts of the convent as a control. He knew his business. But then, his business wasn't what Rebecca doubted about him.

Inside the church, Adele was sorting an array of boxes and plastic bags onto a plywood table. A cold draft blew through the nave, and the bags fluttered. She bent, picked up a rock to weigh them down, then stared. It was a carved bit of an angel's wing. "Label it," Rebecca told her.

She helped Hilary stretch a length of permatrace film down the board and clip it over a sheet of graph paper. "Got your pencils sharp?"

"Shouldn't the records be drawn in ink?" asked Hilary.

"Ink will run in the rain. You can trace the pencil lines to-night, inside. Besides . . ." She stopped.

Hilary laughed. "You're right. I'm not good enough to do it in ink."

They walked out the south transept door into the hollowed shell of the convent's chapter house. The stone piers supporting the walls looked like battered tree trunks, the branching tracery at their tops amputated and their roots overgrown by grass and nettles.

Jerry was in the cloister just outside the chapter house, stabbing the greensward with Mark's staff while Mark himself whittled busily at a peg with a Swiss Army knife. Michael swung the theodolite around. Dennis picked up a shovel and leaned on it. "Here," said Jerry to Hilary. He pulled a tape measure from his pocket and handed it to her. "Plot the four fixed points and the aboveground structures." He waved toward the well, the cross, the chapter house and a tumbled patch of ground to the east, indicating an imaginary rectangle over the site. "When you get done with that, I'll plot out the trenches for you. Get Adele to help you measure."

Hilary nodded and walked back into the church, almost tripping over Dennis. The mist thickened into rain, then thinned again.

Michael stood beside the theodolite whittling his own peg with his sgian dubh. *Scots Army knife,* Rebecca thought. Maybe not as versatile as Mark's, but prettier, with its carved ebony hilt and a serrated edge like the window molding of the church.

"Anyone home?" The voice was a woman's, carried on the damp breeze.

Jerry dropped the staff and strode toward the road. "Over here!"

A shock ran from Rebecca's crown to the bottom of her feet. She looked across the cloister at Michael. For a moment he stood braced, peg in one hand, sgian dubh in the other, chin up and out so that his profile took on an edge as keen as the knife's. Then, in one smooth movement, he thrust the peg into the ground, the dagger into its sheath, and the sheath into the top of his boot. He picked up the theodolite and set it up in the cloister.

Rebecca picked up the fallen staff and stepped into Michael's line of sight. He waved. She edged to the left and collided with Dennis's back. He and Mark were both pointed, as intent as labradors sighting a duck, at the vision wafting around the west front of the church.

For someone who'd bulked so large in Rebecca's imagination, Sheila turned out to be small and slim. She wore a red jumpsuit, storm trooper boots with high heels, and a coat of some fuzzy material that looked like sheep's fleece and mink. Her hair was tormented into bits of fluff that stood out from her head in an aggressive blond corona. Rebecca became acutely aware of what a grotty group they all were, hair either frizzing or hanging lankly in the rain, vinyl boots muddy, jackets and sweaters—except for Hilary's mohair—looking like Salvation Army rejects.

Adele and Hilary stopped in the passage between church and chapter house. One of them emitted a sniff audible to Rebecca's ears several paces away, either from sinus trouble or disapproval. She couldn't tell.

Sheila's heels kept sinking into the turf, giving her walk a provocative wiggle. Gallantly, Jerry extended a hand to help her. Rebecca wondered why he didn't whisk off his coat and lay it down for her to step on. "Sheila Fitzgerald," he announced. "Plantagenet Productions. May I present my staff and the volunteers?"

The lush red mouth smiled. The dark eyes, artistically enhanced by mauve liner and shadow, didn't. "My, you are brave souls to be out in such foul weather. Would you be so kind as to help unload the van?"

Jerry, Mark, and Dennis stampeded toward the road. Hilary and Adele trudged away behind the ruined walls. A raindrop ran down the back of Rebecca's neck, and she shivered.

Sheila shook back her hair. "Hello, Michael. Dr. Kleinfelter told me you were the museum wallah here. How're you keeping?"

Michael straightened. The expression on his face was that of a child contemplating the spinach on his dinner plate. "Quite well, thank you kindly."

"I heard you spent some time in the States last winter. New York? Florida? Those are the only places there worth the effort."

"Ohio. A couthy wee town called Putnam. I quite liked it."

Thank you, Rebecca said silently.

Sheila licked her lips. Her voice was a coo channeled through a sharp beak. "What a gormless place this is. Not like London, is it?"

"No. Thank goodness." Michael's mouth tightened to a fissure. He gestured to Rebecca, who stepped closer to the chapter house wall, and bent again over the theodolite.

Sheila's eyes narrowed. She glanced over at Rebecca. One of her brows arched upward, and the corner of her mouth tucked itself into a supercilious expression. Had she hoped he'd go all hot and bothered at her arrival? Rebecca wondered. And she told herself, *Sheila doesn't know who I am—yet.* By the edge of the staff, where Michael would see it through the scope, Rebecca's hand formed a thumbs-up encouragement signal. His hand directed at Sheila's back the old peasant gesture warding off the evil eye.

Around the corner of the church came the men carrying various bags and boxes. They were followed by another man—a thin, dark-haired individual dressed in the same poor-but-honest uniform of jeans and coat everyone else was wearing. "Tony Wright," he said in introduction. Since he was festooned with camera equipment, Jerry's "The cameraman" was a typically unnecessary comment.

Muttered greetings mingled with Sheila's orders. Her long lacquered fingernails were evidence that she didn't do her own manual labor. Tony laid his bags along the stunted remains of the cloister wall and started pulling out sleek, shiny instruments apparently time-warped in from 2001.

Elaine appeared, carrying a leather case. "There!" Jerry said, snapping his fingers, and Elaine carried the case into the church, but not before shooting a glance of pure venom in Sheila's direction.

Rebecca caught herself digging the end of the staff into the soft ground. She tried smoothing out the divot with the toe of her boot. Was that why Jerry had sent Elaine away, to make sure she wasn't here when Sheila arrived? Despite Sheila's careful "Dr. Kleinfelter," Rebecca was willing to bet she and Jerry had met before—and Elaine knew it.

Obviously, she told herself; Jerry had to hire Sheila for the dig, didn't he? And that archivist at the British Museum had already told Michael Jerry had been there in the spring. . . .

'Rebecca!" Jerry yelled. "Mike!" Michael glanced up from the peg he was whittling and laid down the staff. Tony threw the end of a cord to Mark, who plugged it into a battery pack. Dennis rearranged the bags on the lichen-covered stones. Sheila drifted toward the east side of the excavation rectangle, where Adele was calling out measurements to Hilary.

Jerry asked Michael, "Have you ever taught before, Mike?"

"I've taken tour groups round the museum."

"Working with student volunteers is an entirely different matter. Their enthusiasm is offset by their unreliability."

As if to punctuate his remarks, Dennis knocked over a box of film. "No problem," Tony said tolerantly, and picked it up.

Jerry groaned. "You see? I expect you two to keep a close eye on them, check their work. I had a student once who thought pottery meant Grecian vases and spent an entire afternoon tossing some very nice beaker ware into the rubbish tip. I wasn't in charge on that dig, unfortunately."

"We've both been on digs before," Rebecca offered, "although mine were Indian mounds and nineteenth-century log cabins."

"The Orkneys," said Michael. "Bamburgh Castle. Fishbourne."

But Jerry's eyes were following Sheila's undulating progress across the lawn. Michael slipped his dagger into his boot. Rebecca wiped the damp hair off her forehead. She didn't look at Michael—she knew his expression mirrored hers, disbelief lit by a slow fuse of anger. But too much was riding on this dig to let that fuse burn any faster.

Sheila stopped where Mark knelt, laying out a row of film canisters. She propped a boot on a stone so that the length of her leg was presented for his enjoyment. His hands stopped moving, and his eyes crossed slightly. "Where are you from?" she asked.

"Fort Worth, Texas, ma'am," he said to her thigh.

"Then where're your horse and your gun?"

With a flash of white teeth he laughed. His gaze traveled up her leg to her face. "Don't have either, sorry. I'm just a city kid."

Sheila really was lovely, Rebecca thought with a sigh. Like a glossy advertisement, airbrushed into artificial perfection. No wonder she so insistently asserted her existence.

"All right!" called Jerry. "Everyone! Over here!" As his disciples gathered, Jerry wiped off his glasses and lit a cigar. He pulled the sheaf of papers, Colin's geophysical printouts, out of his coat. "All these monasteries were built more or less to the same plan. Church north, cloister south. The dormitory for the nuns south of the chapter house, the refectory at right angles to it, and the lay sister's dormitory on the west. If there was an infirmary, it would be out of the main range, on the east. Rudesburn did have an infirmary, right? Relics and miracles and all that good stuff.''

Like ducklings following their mother, the students, Sheila, and Tony trailed behind as Jerry paced out the as yet imaginary grid of the dig. Michael and Rebecca brought up the rear.

"If the soil has only a little resistivity, that indicates a drain or ditch,'' Jerry lectured. ''Over there, between the stream and the buildings, is a conduit, and a drain runs back to the water further south. Foundations have high resistivity. So the vaults of the undercroft, the cellars beneath the kitchens, are beyond that corner of the cloister. Third trench.''

He led them past the cross, dismissing it as out of context, but Adele stopped and gazed up at it. ''I went to see the Ruthwell Cross Saturday. 'The Dream of the Rood' is written in runes on its sides. A synthesis of pagan and Christian cultures, transmitting its cosmic energies through the ages.''

Mark muttered to Hilary, ''She's very intelligent, it's just that not all her brain cells are in the same space-time continuum.'' Hilary grinned at him and glanced with—envy? Rebecca wondered—at Adele's serene expression, worthy of a woodcut in a book of martyrs.

In the church, Elaine was arranging a series of well-worn trowels next to the sculptured wing. *Aha,* Rebecca thought. *The ceremonial laying out of the trowels, like a soldier showing off his campaign medals.* Jerry didn't need to actually use them— they just needed to know he had them.

Jerry explained about shovels and heavy work, trowels, brushes, and dental picks and delicate work. He picked up the chemical kit and described some simple conservation techniques. ''Boggy soil like this is murder on bones,'' he said. ''Let's hope any we find are above the water table.''

''Can I get up into the tower for an aerial shot?'' asked Tony.

''The tower's none too—'' Michael began.

''I'm sure we can get you up there,'' Jerry said quickly. He walked out the transept door, delivering them all back into the cloister where they'd started. ''Trial trenches here, here, and here. Then we'll see what we can do about the crypt and the ruins of the infirmary.''

''You haven't turned any dirt yet,'' Sheila said accusingly.

"Start them on that, and then do your orientation again, for the camera, so the viewers will feel like they're participating in the dig."

"Maybe you could arrange for their tellies to get damp-rot," suggested Elaine.

Sheila ignored her. She was putting Jerry through his paces, while Michael and Mark went on about their surveying, when Nora Baird and a young, red-haired and freckled version of herself—Bridget, Rebecca assumed—appeared with steaming pots of tea and trays of hot scones. Tony and his camera would have been trampled in the ensuing rush except he was at the head of the line.

Even Adele accepted a cuppa. Rebecca was grateful for the scalding tea; it took off the chill so effectively that her cheeks flushed. She and Michael found a patch of tile beside the chancel arch, quite dry except for the occasional drip from the roof, and sat down a little way apart from the others. "Now I see," she said under her breath, "just why you once called Sheila a proper little bitch."

"Wi' a capital 'B.' " Michael looked balefully at Sheila, who was sipping at her tea and hanging on Jerry's every word. Mark, Dennis, and Tony were ranged around them like planets around a binary star, while Hilary and Adele joined Elaine—insignificant bits of debris to one side. Nora and Bridget handed out refills and listened to Jerry's war stories.

"I was digging at Colchester," he was saying. "Just a rank kid, wet behind the ears. But I knew we'd found Boadicea destruction level. I kept telling Hargrave, the dig director. Obvious to anyone with half an eye. He insisted it was charcoal from a Danish raid. Went round and round. Then I uncovered a Roman sestertius from the exact year. Old Hargrave had to eat his hat. The next dig I was director—no more mistakes like that one."

"Elaine," Rebecca told Michael, "said something about that Virginia dig. Jerry's still blaming Laurel Matheny. There's no crime worse than excavating and therefore destroying a site without publishing accurate results."

"You're tellin' me? Historians are the first victims!"

"Are you going to tell him about the Bruce's heart?"

"He might already know. Maybe I'll wait until he tells me. That'd be most instructive."

Rebecca knew Michael's look of deliberate insolence, and didn't comment. "You'd like to find it yourself, wouldn't you?"

"Robert the Bruce is as important to the Scottish psyche as a football team that beats an English one," Michael told her.

Adele and Hilary were talking quietly. Elaine sulked. Tony stood, brushed off the seat of his jeans, disappeared into the rain, and returned with a Nikon that had so many attachments Rebecca wondered if it could also gauge barometric pressure. He started by shooting Michael and Rebecca where they sat a discreet foot apart. Obligingly, they smiled. Tony assured them, "We'll have a proper rogues' gallery."

"Anne Douglas was tried for witchcraft in 1545," Jerry said. "Supposedly she still haunts the place. That's the kind of story that catches the public imagination." Adele turned abruptly away from Hilary and focused on Jerry. Michael and Rebecca exchanged a meaningful glance.

"Probably Anne was simply stubborn about handing over the priory treasury," said Sheila.

"But there's no evidence the priory treasury had anything to do with the accusations of witchcraft," said Michael.

Every face turned toward him. Sheila registered Rebecca's proximity. Her mouth straightened in a thin, malicious smile.

She doesn't really exist, Rebecca told herself. *She's just an evil genie and will vanish in a puff of smoke.* She said, "Anne's trial could have been either political expediency or simple greed. Henry the Eighth was trying to force the Scottish government to give him the infant Mary, Queen of Scots, for his son Edward. The Rough Wooing, they called the ensuing English invasion. This was the area that took the brunt of it. Rudesburn, Melrose, Abbey St. Bathans—they were all looted."

"But, Mike," Jerry returned as if Rebecca hadn't spoken, "wouldn't it be fun to prove that there was a treasure involved? Talk about a good story!"

"Not Mike," purred Sheila. "He prefers Michael. Trust me."

"Oh?" Jerry seemed to think that fact was the most interesting thing he'd heard all day. Mark looked around. Dennis remained focused on Jerry.

Rebecca couldn't tell if Michael flushed or whether the damp chill of the day had simply made his cheeks rosier than usual. He heaved himself to his feet and walked out of the church, his steps elaborately unconcerned. Rebecca told herself that pulling out several handfuls of blond perm wouldn't help. She thanked Nora and Bridget, and followed Michael.

He stood in the mist, his hands in his pockets, looking across the stream toward the village. "Did Colin say something about a treasure?" he asked Rebecca.

"Yeah, that Sheila's film is going to be about buried treasure as well as ghosts. Of course, the two go together in the popular imagination, as Jerry would be the first to point out."

"Kleinfelter's a pro. He'd no be confusin' treasure in the form of historical relics with real monetary treasure. Would he?"

"Good question." Rebecca cocked her head to the side. His face was tight and closed, and she couldn't read it. Then the others trooped out of the church and picked up shovels, and she didn't have time to think about it.

Every now and then during the morning, the mist thickened into rain, but after lunch and a welcome hour in the warm kitchen, the mist lifted, and by late afternoon the clouds had become huge fluffy galleons in a deep blue sky.

By six o'clock Michael and Rebecca remained in sole possession of the field. The dark brown stripes of shallow trenches scarred the cloister garth and the lawn. Where they passed over the ruined walls, the sharp edges of cut stone shouldered aside the earth.

In the village, a dog barked. The Plantagenet Productions van pulled into the Craft Centre parking lot, and stopped beside the silver Jaguar. Tony got out, locked up, and saw Michael and Rebecca standing by the church. He waved cheerily and went into the hotel.

Rebecca asked, "Do you suppose he's fallen into Sheila's web, too?"

"I imagine she keeps him on like you'd keep a spare tire in the boot," Michael replied. "The woman'd tease a broomstick if it were wearin' trousers."

"If she delivers on her promises, she's no tease. Just to fit in with the medieval mythology of the place, I'd call her a succubus."

Michael reached out his arm and pulled her close. His coat was wet and cold, but she could sense the warmth of his body beneath. She thought he was actually going to say he was sorry about Sheila. But no, he'd already told her he wouldn't apologize. *He gives no quarter,* she told herself, *and expects none.* She'd liked that integrity from the beginning.

"I'm sorry you had to see her," was what he said, "particularly when we're courtin' wi' intent to commit matrimony. She's no a patch on you."

"I'm glad you noticed." Rebecca smiled against his shoulder. How considerate, to reassure her. Then, like an arrow through her breast, she thought, *He's taking for granted we're going to marry.*

"Hey, Rebecca!" called Dennis from the back step of the cottage. "You're cooking tonight!"

"Coming!" Rebecca shouted, and let her momentary qualm dissipate into the cool evening air and the steady clasp of Michael's arm.

It was when they were halfway across the footbridge that they heard the music. Not specific words, just the murmur echoing in the empty church, the slow rise and fall of Gregorian plainsong chanted by women's voices.

"Is the RDG providing special effects?" Rebecca asked.

"No," replied Michael, his voice thin. "I heard the singin' when I was here before. It's no special effects."

The hair rose slightly on the back of Rebecca's neck. "Oh, I see." Together they sped across the bridge.

Chapter Six

DESPITE THE FIRE crackling in the sitting room and the telly emitting the cultured drone of a BBC documentary, the students gravitated to the kitchen. No wonder, when the aroma of coffee mingled with that of the chocolate chunk cookies Dennis had just pulled out of the oven.

"My sister taught me how to cook," he said as he scooped the warm, sweet morsels into various clutching hands. "She'd stand there making sure I leveled off every measuring cup and sifted the flour and soda together."

"Aye, sisters are tidy creatures." Michael took his cookies and his mug of coffee into the dining room, where he proceeded to pile the table with papers and cardboard boxes.

"Did you get the sheep properly domesticated?" Rebecca asked Adele, and offered her a cookie.

" 'The Taming of the Ewe'?" Adele returned, taking only one. "Very interesting documentary. Pointed up the innate relationship between animals and man. Like in the book *The Way of the Animal Powers*. . . ."

After ten days on the dig they'd learned to indulge Adele's eccentricities. She was even-tempered about them, without the annoying zeal of an evangelist, and had turned out some superb meals besides.

"Here's looking at ewe, kid," said Mark. He handed a cookie to Hilary and took one for himself.

Rebecca and Hilary groaned appreciatively. Adele didn't react. Dennis's mouth was too full to speak.

The students carried plates and mugs into the sitting room

while Rebecca took the cookie sheets to join the dinner dishes. She enjoyed washing up; it was a pleasantly mindless activity leading to a minor but still satisfying accomplishment.

The dining room window overlooked the hotel, the Craft Centre, the shop and the bridge, a stage set across which moved cars, farm trucks, and the Johnston children on their skateboard. From the kitchen Rebecca could see the priory standing aloof from the trenches cut across its lawns. A ray of sun glinted suddenly from the west, and the shadow of the cottage stretched across the Gowan. As if a light had been switched on within its stones, the priory was illuminated against its backdrop of cloud. Too much depth to be a stage set, Rebecca mused. It was more like an oil painting, something by Burne-Jones, a scene of murder and pillage made romantic by gilded sentiment.

Evening was falling early tonight. The showers of the last few days had come and gone, moistening the ground just enough to make it workable. But the thick greenish-gray clouds now building up in the east presaged heavy rain. Rain would flood the trenches and break down the vertical planes of their sides that Jerry, with plumb bob and trowel, had been at such pains to cut. He'd taken the precaution of leaving the working surfaces covered with polythene sheets, and the blue plastic fluttered in the gusty wind.

The yew tree in the cemetery stirred. Something glinted white behind its dark branches. Rebecca leaned across the sink, squinting.

"The ghost of Anne Douglas," said Adele at her shoulder, and Rebecca jumped out of her skin. She turned, saw Mark and Michael looking curiously in from the dining room, and said, "Just a trick of the light, Adele."

"There are no such things as ghosts," added Mark.

"As much as I hate to admit it," Michael said, "some places do have what, for lack of a better word, we call ghosts."

Adele smiled at him, welcoming the prodigal son. Mark still looked skeptical. The ray of sun winked out, and the image of the priory in the window became an old photograph faded into indifference.

Rebecca wiped off the sink and dried her hands. Anne Douglas. Who was she, what was she, what had happened to her? Enough questions clung to her name to make a legion of dead sleep uneasily. Odd, how the saintly Marjory seemed less genuine, less vital, than the ambiguous Anne. Rebecca didn't even know if the two women were related.

Adele said to Mark, "We've all smelled candle wax in the church when no candles were there. We've heard the voices singing. We've seen the cats bristling at nothing."

"Well, yeah, I keep looking for the tape decks and the speakers, and there aren't any," Mark admitted. "But it's not what you sense, it's what your imagination makes out of the sensory input. Like looking at an optical illusion. People see ghosts, or the Loch Ness monster, or whatever, because they believe in them, not the other way around."

"I grew up in Inverness," said Michael. "I never saw anything in the loch, but I've met those who swear they have. It's faith."

"And income from tourists."

"Don't be so cynical." Rebecca sat down, glancing up at Mark where he leaned against the door. "Even if you don't have much faith, you have to admit faith is an important force. The ghost of Anne Douglas is the Rudesburners' Nessie—a mascot, enough to tickle you up but not enough to threaten."

Mark nodded. "You've got a point here."

"The faithful have always prayed to relics," said Adele, "drawn by their power. And those who scoffed at relics were cursed by them. Look at King Sweyn in England, killed for doubting St. Edmund."

"Wonder if that has anything to do with the supposed curse of Rudesburn," Rebecca said. "Some critical mass of relics and reformation?"

No one ventured an opinion. From the sitting room came the canned chuckles of a sitcom. "Oh, no!" wailed Dennis, and Hilary laughed. It was a shame she laughed so infrequently; her laughter was unforced, as natural as the Gowan giggling over its rocks and willow branches.

Mark moved backward toward the sitting room, the male particle attracted by the female nucleus. "Adele," he said over his shoulder, "you and Jerry are a lot alike. You both enjoy a good story." And, from the sitting room, "Hey, Hilary, what's so funny?"

Adele, looking quizzical, followed. Michael and Rebecca eyed each other across the printouts and artifacts. "Hello, stranger," she said.

"The morn is Friday," he returned. "Speakin' of Inverness, my mother invited us to spend the weekend wi' them."

Rebecca's gaze plummeted to the table. Several shards of pottery lay in one box, a lead pilgrim's badge with a crude representation of a woman's face in another. In a bed of cotton batting lay a splendid gold ring brooch, formed of six finely worked dragons in relief, still encrusted with bits of dirt. She asked Michael, "Wouldn't it be rather crowded?"

"My parents run a hotel, love. They have plenty of room."

"The same room?" She looked up from under her brows.

He smiled patiently. "When Geoff and Maddy were engaged, they gave them the same room. They're no goin' to be hypocritical."

Her eyes fell again. Their relationship had become distressingly public. More than once she'd had to traipse through the kitchen with Michael's fingerprints as obvious as a measles rash on her skin. His parents, made of gentler stuff than hers, might well smile fondly at the sound of bedsprings creaking, envisioning rings of both the wedding and the teething variety. "Maybe we should stay here, especially since we came back last Sunday to find someone had been poking around in the dig."

"Grant said he'd keep an eye on the place, although noo that we're findin' gold . . ." Michael looked at the brooch. "Do you no want to meet my mum and dad just yet, then?"

"Not just yet, if you don't mind. Not that I don't want to meet them," she added hastily, "there's just so much going on, so many pressures. . . ."

"I understand. Dinna worry yoursel'." His eyes met hers, faintly puzzled but not hurt. He looked at her with such indulgent affection that what she felt was less guilt than irritation.

Flustered, Rebecca picked up the brooch. The metal was cold and heavy in her hand, but the artifact said nothing to her. She closed her eyes, smoothed her mind, cautiously bent her thoughts toward it. Maybe she sensed a faint resonance, like a tingle in the metal. Maybe not. She looked up. "Are these artifacts less charged than the ones at Dun Iain were, or have we simply developed immunities?"

"I've wondered that mysel'. It could have something to do wi' the objects at Dun Iain bein' so far from their home."

"Or that we've become cautious, less sensitive, in our old age. Not surprising." Michael snorted, whether in agreement or protest she couldn't tell. She turned the brooch, watching the light shimmy along the intricate curves of the dragons' bodies. "Fifteenth century?"

"Probably fourteenth. No tellin' when it was lost, though. Those brooches were family heirlooms."

The label on the back of the brooch was half peeled away; the damp earth had dried and turned grainy. Rebecca tried to stick it down and succeeded only in pulling it off. The glint of gold was scratched. She held it to the light. "Michael, look. There's an inscription."

He took the brooch from her hand, picked up a cloth, and rubbed. *"Ave Maria Gracia Plena.* A.D.''

"Anno Domini? Does it give a year?"

"No year."

"What if the initials stand for Anne Douglas? What if it was hers?'' For a moment Rebecca was rapt by the idea. Then her face fell. "Would she have had something this—well, secular?"

"Secularity was her problem. But there's no way of provin' it was hers or anyone's." Michael laid the artifact in its box, sorted through the printouts until he found its record sheet, and filled in the inscription. Adele strolled by, murmured something about reading, and went upstairs.

"Ave Maria Gracia Plena,'' repeated Rebecca, half to herself. " 'Hail Mary, full of grace.' The angel's greeting at the Annunciation, telling Mary she would be the mother of the Messiah. The priory church was dedicated to Mary, 'Our Lady,' and nuns consider themselves brides of Christ."

"Aye?"

"Oh, nothing really. Just one of those philosophical dichotomies, worshipping pregnancy but scorning the act that causes pregnancy. I guess because it doesn't always cause pregnancy, because there's room for so much pleasure and pain as well."

"Do you mind Robert Graves's poem aboot the Christian nuns? They watch fish circlin' in their chaste and chilly pool and remember that pagan nuns were often temple prostitutes. Though prostitution's no the correct concept. That's just it, sex is sacred and profane both. . . .''

Hilary stood in the doorway, eyes wide. She hurried through the room. Her dishes clinked into the sink, and her footsteps tapped briskly up the stairs. Michael leaned across the table. "Was it something I said?"

"Maybe she gets her mouth soaped for speaking that honestly.

My mother never admitted sex existed. I had to pump my brothers for information.''

Michael grinned, as if to say, *So that's what skewed your perceptions.* ''Immaculately conceived, all of you?''

''Nothing divine about my family.'' She put the cover on the box containing the brooch and turned her attention to the mundane but more useful pottery. Rim of a storage jar. She marked it down. Base of a cruet.

It was Mark's turn to stroll through the room. ''Y'all fixing to head up to the pub, or would you like some help with that pottery?''

''We'll be takin' the brooch to the hotel, anyway,'' Michael replied. ''Might as well have another ceilidh.''

''A what?''

''A party wi' music and drinking, like last week.''

''Oh, I've been going to those for years. Didn't know they had a name.'' Mark picked up and laid down several of the shards. ''The police never found those things that were stolen, did they?''

''Not yet,'' answered Rebecca. ''More's the pity.''

''Get on wi' you,'' Michael told him. ''We'll catch you up.''

''Okay.'' Mark picked his guitar case out of the corner. Dennis turned off the television. The front door slammed.

Michael leaned back and stretched. ''I'm no makin' much of these records the night.''

''Elaine really ought to be doing them. That's her job, isn't it?''

''Even wi' the artifact sheets filled in properly she's made more than one mistake enterin' the data. Even wi' Dennis helpin'. Or maybe because of Dennis helpin'—I dinna ken. She's a nervy one. Did you see her shy that thermos the other day?''

''Yeah. Ten minutes later she was crying like a baby behind the chapter house. I can't remember now what she was mad about—Jerry putting her down, probably. I was rooting for her to throw the thermos at him. Sheila almost hit him when he yelled at her for stepping on the edge of the trench.''

''Sheila has a temper, right enough.'' Michael grimaced. ''And she'll no be wastin' her time throwing dishes or cryin' aboot it. She took the back of her hand to me once—just once, mind you.''

''Did you hit her back?'' Rebecca asked in morbid fascination.

"It was temptin'. But pointless." He started stacking the printouts into their box, declaring the subject closed.

Rebecca packed the pottery. "I think Elaine is reliable—if we double-check her entries. She's just accustomed to crunching numbers at that insurance company. Can't really blame her for running off with Jerry."

"I canna fault her for runnin' off wi' someone, but why Jerry?"

"He probably seems masterful and exotic."

"Eh?" said Michael sarcastically.

Rebecca went into the bathroom. So she wasn't ready to meet Andrew and Caroline Campbell. There was time for that when the dust—or the mud, to be accurate—settled. No need to be irritated at poor Michael.

Last weekend Jerry and Elaine had headed northwest for Glasgow, and Dennis had taken a bus in the same direction. Tony and Sheila had taken off south, Tony saying something about a film processing plant in Newcastle. Mark went exploring along Hadrian's Wall, Adele joined the contemplative community on Iona, and Rebecca and Michael had given Hilary a ride into Edinburgh.

Michael's tiny apartment had been what Rebecca had expected; clean but untidy, books piled on every surface, dishes stacked in the drainer, the double bed unmade. She'd been sharply reminded of her own meager belongings—her grandmother's china, cartons of books, some early Salvation Army furniture—in a storage cubicle in Missouri, financially out of reach.

They'd played house in the blessed privacy of his flat, eaten in his favorite Indian restaurant, walked hand in hand through the Princes Street gardens below the stern face of the castle. It was a dream come true, the place and the man together at last.

He'd taken her through the back rooms of the museum, and she'd seen the Dun Iain artifacts, achingly out of context. "The Forbes Collection," the posters and brochures read; the exhibition would open in October. Michael had proudly shown her her own name listed as visiting lecturer. "You should be the one tellin' aboot Mary Stuart's things, lass, that's your field."

Her return ticket to the United States was for September. Rebecca leaned over the bathroom sink, splashed cold water onto her cheeks and said, "Thanks, I needed that."

She collected the brooch and went into the vestibule to get her jacket. Michael came out of the bedroom with the tartan case of his bagpipes. Hilary stood by the door waiting for them. Despite whatever had ruffled her earlier, her face was now smoothed into its usual quiet if wary expression. Like a fawn, Rebecca thought. Behind Hilary's back, she and Michael exchanged a shrug.

The honeyed light of the evening was turgid beneath lowering cloud. The houses of Rudesburn seemed to lean toward each other, eyeing the gathering storm. "Speakin' of profanity," Michael said to Rebecca from the corner of his mouth, "look who's snoggin' doon by the burn."

Rebecca looked. Two people stood on the footbridge, a guitar case and a canvas bag beside them. Sheila's blond hair looked appropriately brassy in the oddly filtered light. Mark's attitude was more defensive than eager, his back braced against the railing. Rebecca could've sworn that the woman had more than one pair of arms around him, like an octopus engulfing its prey. But he wasn't struggling.

Hilary sped on into the hotel, her expression that of a child opening a Christmas present and finding nothing inside but a pair of socks.

"Bluidy cheek," said Michael, "corruptin' a braw American lad."

"He was hardly fighting her off," Rebecca returned.

From the hotel lobby they could hear Jerry's voice, apparently lecturing Grant about forensics techniques. Rebecca took the gold brooch into Laurence's office and locked it away in the safe. Michael opened his case and removed his pipes. Tenderly he polished the chanter and the drones, then with little puffs began to inflate the bag. The instrument squealed, rather like the obligatory protest of a camel being loaded.

Mark came into the lobby, his guitar case in one hand, wiping his mouth with the other. Sheila's lipstick was a distinctive scarlet; Rebecca had started calling it "Two to Tango." On Mark's face it looked like blood.

He cast a sharp shamefaced glance toward her. She looked away. He went on down the hall. The door of the men's toilet swung shut. Rebecca walked toward the bar, shaking her head. She liked Mark because he reminded her of Michael. It would be no more worthwhile to be angry with her compatriot than with Michael. At least Michael had been vaccinated against Sheila's charms.

With its beamed ceiling, wainscoting, and shine of brass and glass, the pub was a tourist's dream. It was also authentic, Laurence had said; some of the prints of caber-tossing and salmon-fishing had hung on the sprigged wallpaper for fifty years. Rebecca particularly liked the vast stone fireplace, its mantel lined with amiable junk ranging from a model trolley car to some fishing lures to a ceramic Paddington Bear. Tonight the cats were doing their bit to provide atmosphere, stretched out like miniature heraldic panthers on the hearth. The scent of pine from the fire helped to dispel the faint odor of wet sheep that clung even to polyester in this climate. Several local people were scattered around the room, their own muddy wellies and lint-balled sweaters no different from the archeological squad's.

Elaine sat at her usual table, at Jerry's knee as he leaned on the bar pontificating on fingerprints and bloodstains. Grant was dressed in civilian garb—flannels and an Aran sweater. He reached his empty mug across the bar for Laurence to replace with a full one, never taking his slightly stunned eyes off Jerry. Perhaps he was too well lubricated to blink.

Dennis contemplated his own mug across the table from Elaine. Every now and then she'd drop her adoring look at Jerry and shoot a glare at Dennis, shuffling expressions as quickly as a deck of cards. For a business major, Dennis was certainly intent on gathering every gem of wisdom Jerry let fall. He was like a friendly St. Bernard, constantly at the man's heels.

Nora sat with Tony discussing a pile of photographs. Tony had a large nose and protuberant front teeth; when it occurred to his placid nature to smile, he looked like a puppet gone AWOL from a Punch and Judy show. Yes, he and Sheila were sharing a room, but judging from Sheila's indecent assault on Mark, it was more an affair of convenience than of lust.

Bridget and Hilary, bent over a book of knitting patterns, caught Rebecca's eye and beckoned. Rebecca took off her coat—the room was actually warm—ordered a Glenfiddich, and sat down. Bridget pushed a skein of off-white yarn across the table. "Is this what you're needin', then?"

"Oh, thank you. This should work nicely. Michael's really missing his sweater, but I'm afraid if he unravels any more of it, I'll never be able to repeat the pattern." Rebecca stowed the yarn in her pocket.

Hilary's eyes darted to the door, registering Mark's entrance with dull resignation.

Mark ordered a beer. "You brought your guitar!" Laurence

exclaimed. "I thought I heard Michael tuning up out in the lobby."

The locals looked up. Laurence and Nora rushed to pull up a stool for Mark. Little had they realized what a bargain they were getting, not only a scientific expedition, but entertainment as well. Grant evaded Jerry's attempt to sketch something on a napkin and said, "I'll go fetch Winnie and the weans, it's seldom they get tae hear the pipes."

Michael passed Grant in the doorway, the bag of his pipes fat and sassy under his arm. "You've heard," said Jerry, ostensibly to Elaine, "Noel Coward's definition of a gentleman: a man who knows how to play the bagpipes but doesn't." He grinned, virtually twirling his moustache. Elaine and Dennis laughed. Everyone else regarded him with polite but blank stares.

Mark sipped from his drink and strummed his guitar. He segued through "Dixie," "The Yellow Rose of Texas," and "Greensleeves," and ended up on "The Streets of Laredo."

Michael accepted an ale from Laurence, swigged, and left the mug on the bar. The pipes squawked, and he reprimanded them with a firm prod. He put the mouthpiece between his lips and began to play "The Flowers o' the Forest."

The high clear notes of the lament filled the room, the low moan of the drones enriching the melody like gold threads stitched on silk. Mark complemented the tune with soft chords. The Johnstons tiptoed into a corner booth, even the smallest child listening enthralled.

"I've heard the liltin' at our yowe-milkin'," sang Bridget, "Lassies a liltin' before the dawn o' day. But now they are moanin' in ilka green loanin', the flowers o' the forest are a' wede away."

Michael's fingers caressed the chanter, his eyes closed, making love to the music. Rebecca's heart twinged with an oddly pleasant pang of love and sorrow—for him, for the song, for the history, she wasn't sure. When Hilary whispered, "What's it about?" she jumped.

"A lament for the battle of Flodden Field," she murmured. "1513. James the Fourth and half the noblemen of Scotland died, not to mention a good chunk of the peasantry. The country was filled with widows."

Winnie sang, "Dule and wae for the order sent our lads to the border! The English, for ance, but guile wan the day; the flowers o' the forest, that focht aye the foremaist, the prime o' our land, are cauld in the clay.''

"That's why Anne Douglas came to Rudesburn," Rebecca went on. "Her father was killed at Flodden, and she and her dowry were sent to the convent—there was no one else to take care of her. She was five years old.''

"And bided here a' her life," said Bridget.

"The flowers o' the forest are a' wede away," cried the pipes. The melody faded and died into a resonant silence. A log popped in the fire, but no one spoke.

Jerry lit a cigar, the smoke billowing demonically across his face. "Actually," he said, "the English didn't win Flodden by guile. As usual, the Scots were stupid enough to charge. No wonder they were annihilated.''

Frost formed on the silence. At last Michael said with exaggerated courtesy, "Thank you, Dr. Kleinfelter.''

Jerry's expression asked, "What did I say?" Rebecca thought wistfully of the scene in "Monty Python and the Holy Grail" where the pompous lecturer was cut down by a charging knight.

"One, two, three, four," counted Mark, and he and Michael launched into a rafter-rattling rendition of "Johnnie Cope.''

Jerry would enjoy the derision in that song. He was the type who thought derision was wit. Rebecca explained to Hilary, "Prestonpans. The Scots won that one. Cope, the English general, outran his retreating army." She sang, "When Johnnie Cope to Dunbar came, they said to him, where are your men? Why, confound me, I dinna ken, I left them there in the mornin'?''

Sheila appeared in the door of the bar, carrying her canvas bag. She said, as she'd said every night, "How quaint." She strolled over to the table where Tony now sat alone, opened the bag, and pulled out what at first Rebecca thought was a sheet.

Good grief. She hurriedly took a drink of her whiskey. What Sheila had was a nun's habit. "I finished sewin' that the day," said Bridget, suppressing a giggle. "Special order. She'll be wearin' it aboot the ruins for the telly program. Did you see her this evenin', posin' by the yew tree for Tony tae—what did he say, test the light? Ah, that'll come a trick for the tourist trade!'' Bridget's eyes danced. The giggle escaped, infecting Hilary, and her delightful laugh blended with the music.

Rebecca admitted that the best response to Sheila's excesses was laughter. Even so she felt cheated that the ghost she'd seen had been her. Fortunately Adele wasn't here for that revelation.

Mark, frowning in concentration, began to play "Foggy Mountain Breakdown." Michael retired to the bar and refilled his ale.

Rebecca joined him. She must be more stressed out than she'd thought; the tangy Glenfiddich had gone straight to her head. The room wasn't fuzzy but supernaturally clear, each object a source of enchantment. One of the cats yawned, its pink tongue curled. The bubbles in Michael's ale were prisms suspended in dark amber. His eyes over the rim of the glass were as deep and blue as the Scottish sky—when it wasn't raining.

Sheila's voice said sharply, "You pillock, whatever possessed you to use that setting? Now you'll have to take them again."

"Why am I surrounded by such fools?" said Michael under his breath, satirizing Sheila's tone.

Tony murmured equably, "Get stuffed, Sheila," and stacked the photographs into their envelope.

As though considering his directive, Sheila leaned back, her elbows hooked around the chair so that her breasts strained against her khaki blouse. Impressive, Rebecca meowed to herself, and wondered how much was nature, how much chemical artifice.

On Rebecca's other side, Jerry rose to the bait. Rebecca knew that look of Jerry's; it was palpable as a probing hand. He applied it without discrimination to all the women except Adele. Sheila's red mouth turned up, and her tongue licked between her lips just like a cat.

Michael joined in the applause for Mark, who was flushed and smiling, working off his frustration, no doubt. He waved Michael back to join him. They began tossing songs back and forth, "Seventeen Come Sunday," "Silver Darlin's," "Bonnie Blue Flag," and "St. Kilda Wedding."

Rebecca tapped her foot, her thoughts bouncing merrily to the music. Sheila got up and patted Dennis on the head, throwing the young man into confusion. She leaned against the bar. The rich scent of her perfume mingled uneasily with the miasma of Jerry's cigar. "Scots and Americans are all barbarians," her voice cooed in Rebecca's ear. "No wonder Michael fancies you."

"Jealous?" Rebecca inquired sweetly. She turned her back,

not at all contrite, and felt rather than heard Sheila flounce closer to Jerry.

"What?" he asked.

"Nothing," she answered. "How're you keeping?"

Elaine spun toward Dennis and plunged into an animated conversation. Dennis, now doubly bewildered, responded in monosyllables. Laurence left Nora behind the bar and joined Tony. "Do you remember," he said, "when you were here signing the contracts, we saw that owl's nest in the church tower? Well, now it has three eggs."

Tony nodded. "What did I hear about ospreys returning to the highlands?" He glanced toward Jerry and Sheila and smiled in wry amusement. Rebecca blinked. She felt as if she were watching an animated gossip column—with a superior soundtrack.

Tony went on, with a dubious glance at the cats, "I saw in the papers that domestic cats account for half the songbird deaths in the United Kingdom."

"You don't say?" asked Laurence politely.

Michael played "The Cowal Gathering." The Johnstons began clapping their hands. Bridget tapped the tabletop with a spoon.

Mark challenged Michael with "When the Saints Come Marching In." Dennis forgot his confusion and sang. By now everyone in the room was stamping or clapping or pounding on a table. The cats roused themselves and sat sharing glances that required only the shaking of heads and pointing of paws to be outright mockery.

". . . Douglas," said a voice somewhere near Rebecca. *Oh, when the saints,* she hummed, *oh, when the saints.* The voice went on. "The heart of Robert the Bruce—we'd have to call a press conference to announce that."

How I want to be in their number . . . What? Rebecca forced herself not to turn around. She and Michael had never told Jerry about the Bruce's heart, deciding that if they found it, great, if they didn't why inflate his expectations? But—her mind raced—but if he already knew, and found out that they'd known and hadn't told him, he could justifiably call them troublemakers like Laurel Matheny. . . . Ah, hell, the country was teeming with medieval records. He found out about it in London just as they'd suspected.

Rebecca shook her head. Her glass was empty. She'd probably hallucinated those words.

Michael pulled Mark smoothly into "Highland Laddie." The walls of the hotel rattled, the windows bowed outward in the blast.

Then, suddenly, it was over. The pipes exhaled a long sigh of satiation, and a guitar string twanged. The fire died down to embers, Nora collected the dirty glasses, the local people put on their coats, pronounced the ceilidh a roaring success, and went home.

The air outside was a cold, wet slap against Rebecca's warm face. Away from the lights of Jedburgh Street, she felt as if she were squinting through a piece of smoky quartz. The evening was very dark. The priory and Battle Law were dim shapes across the burn. A full moon was a dim orange glow behind the clouds.

"Did you have a wee drop too much, then?" asked Michael. An arm, she assumed his, buoyed her toward the cottage.

"I must have. I thought I heard Jerry talking to Sheila about Robert the Bruce's heart."

The arm stiffened. "Your guilty conscience, lass?"

"*My* guilty conscience?" she retorted. "You haven't told him either."

"And he's no told us, has he? So he is after it."

"Don't jump to conclusions."

"I'm no jumpin'. He's pushin' me."

The footsteps of the students on the gravel driveway sounded like an avalanche. The cottage was dark except for a light in Adele's upstairs bedroom. "It's really sad," said Hilary's voice through the gloom.

"Yeah?" Mark said encouragingly.

"Adele sleeps in an old UCLA sweatshirt of Chris's—her son's. She says it makes her dream about him, as if he's not really gone. He was only twenty-two when he died. A Rhodes scholar, studied at Oxford."

"That's sad," said Dennis.

Michael's heavy sigh lifted Rebecca's hair. *Sympathy?* she asked silently. *Or aggravation? And at what, if not every-thing. . . .*

The glow of the whiskey evaporated into chill darkness.

Chapter Seven

MICHAEL LOOKED AS if he'd been mud-wrestling. Rebecca could barely read the words on his T-shirt, "Monty Python: The Unexploded Scotsman Skit." "You've always said," she told him, "you wanted a bit of the Auld Sod."

"I want to buy land, no wallow in it. But I got the alembic oot in one piece. Jerry's lookin' at it the noo. First real evidence of the hospital—a piece of distillin' equipment."

"They used to think whiskey was medicine, didn't they?"

"What? Do you mean it isna?" With an innocent smile, Michael plopped down next to her and leaned against the sun-warmed stone of William Salkeld's tomb.

The on-again, off-again storms of the last ten days had gathered their clouds and departed to the east. It was now so warm Mark had shocked Nora by inquiring plaintively for iced tea. Her attitude implied that he'd spat on the Union Jack. Chastened, he now sat beside Hilary, staring into his mug and waiting for its contents to cool.

On Hilary's other side, Adele sat looking at the door into the tower. Tony had climbed cautiously up for some panoramic shots, but today the grille was shut. Even so Adele watched so intently, a half-smile on her face, that Rebecca turned to see what—or whom—the woman was watching. But the stairway was empty. Despite the warmth, the back of her neck prickled.

Grant Johnston sat down beside Michael, took off his hat, wiped his face with a handkerchief, and demonstrated Scottish grit by gulping his tea. "Sorry tae ring you in Edinburgh Saturday. I feel a right gowk, askin' you tae come back early and the brooch lyin' on the table at the cottage a' the time.''

''Someone's muckin' aboot wi' the artifacts,'' Michael returned. ''You were right to ring us.''

Nora sat down with them. ''Laurence locked everything away on Friday. But then, the keys to the office were there with all the other keys.''

Rebecca shifted uncomfortably. Anyone could have taken the golden brooch with its ring of dragons and left it in the cottage. Anyone who knew where it was, and which keys went to which locks, and how the cottage would be vacant on a Saturday. The question was why.

''And someone,'' added Michael aloud, ''nicked only one of the nobles from the lobby. There's no sense to it.''

Nora swore. Grant closed his eyes. Rebecca looked at Michael. The three weeks of the dig had accentuated the creases in his cheeks. She knew what the effort of not speaking, of not making one of those suicidal Scottish charges, had cost him. She was paying for the constant gritting of her own teeth with an aching jaw and tendons so tightly corded in her neck that Michael's attentions could ease them only temporarily. Every day one or the other of them slammed the bedroom door and stood glowering over a condescending remark of Jerry's or Sheila's, over some discrepancy in the data, over some mistake on the part of Tony or the students or even the townspeople that caused the puzzle pieces of the excavation to fly apart rather than come together.

Rebecca swallowed her tea and felt the sweat bead on her forehead. So much, she thought, for her visions of gamboling about Gowandale picking daisies and planning the future. They were halfway through the dig, halfway to the time she and Michael had to make a decision, and the decision was as elusive as ever.

Grant drained his cup, settled his hat on his head, and stood. His huge hand patted William Salkeld's stone ankle. ''Thank you kindly for settin' the old boy tae rights.''

''Gave us a chance for a keek inside,'' Michael replied. ''Naething there but dust. Dr. Kleinfelter took a scunner to that, right enough. He's fair droolin' to uncover something glamorous for the film.''

''I'll bet,'' said Nora. Her plump cheeks quivered with indignation. Everyone in the pub last night had overheard Jerry berating Grant and Laurence.

"So the brooch just decided to get up and go for a stroll? And why call Campbell—did you appoint me dig director or not?" Jerry had bristled.

"We had Michael's number," Laurence had replied reasonably. "We didn't know where you were."

Jerry had said, "Don't let it happen again," leaving unspecified whether he meant letting an artifact go stray or taking Michael seriously. No wonder Nora was still seething this Monday morning, and Grant set his jaw so firmly as he paced toward the village.

Halfway across the lawn, he was ambushed by Sheila. She led him to the gatehouse ruins, straightened his tunic, and raised her camera. "Resistance is useless," Rebecca whined in her best alien invader voice, and Michael's strained face relaxed. Encouraged, she went on, "My, you're such a big strong specimen of a bobby to be patrolling a dump like this."

Michael laughed. Ruefully, but it was a laugh. Nora's indignation became disgust. She gathered the cups.

A red Vauxhall crossed the bridge and disappeared behind the perimeter wall. A door slammed. Grant made good his escape—perhaps with visions of his wife emerging from the shop wielding a rolling pin—but did pause long enough to enjoy Sheila's shimmy across the grass toward the dig.

Mark, Hilary, and Adele stretched and walked outside. Michael said to Rebecca, "This is the first time Jerry's worked through his elevenses. He must like my alembic."

"Peaceful, isn't it?" she replied.

A man came across the lawn from the car park. Nora greeted him and gestured toward the church. Michael went to attention. "All right!"

Of course. Rebecca had seen that face in a photograph—horn-rimmed glasses and long dark hair waving around a disarming smile. It was Colin MacLeod. He and Michael shook hands, clapped shoulders, and stood beaming at each other. "Here she is," said Michael.

"So I see," Colin returned. "And a bonny lass, too, just as you said." He took Rebecca's hand in both of his.

She noted the gold band on his ring finger. "Nice to meet you at last, Colin. Where did you come from?"

"It's where I'm goin', to a rock chat in Durham. Thought I'd look in on you. And get another Coldstream Guard from yon toy shop."

"He's doin' a miniature Troopin' of the Colour along his mantelpiece," Michael explained to Rebecca.

She nodded. "Those are beautifully detailed lead soldiers. The Queen Elizabeth on her horse has a side-saddle, a feather in her hat, and even little medals on her jacket."

"Ah," Colin said with a sigh, "that's the piece I really want. But it's awful dear. Anjali wouldn't be best pleased if I brought it home instead of the new electric kettle we need."

"Everyone needs toys," Michael remonstrated with a grin. "If you get her another wee bear wi' the wellies, she'll no complain aboot your soldiers."

Rebecca laughed, approving of Michael's theory of wife management.

"Have you time for the tuppence tour?" Colin asked.

"Certainly." Michael took the current crop of printouts from the box and led the way outside. Going from the cool shade into the blaze of sunlight was like walking into the circle of light beneath a microscope. The radiance defined the landscape so precisely that the images etched themselves on Rebecca's retina—each gray stone of the priory the separate stroke of a brush, Gowandale bright shades of green and gold, the sky an aching fathomless blue. The odors of dirt and mold hung on the still air.

Mark was troweling an occupation surface at the bottom of the first trench. Sheila perched on a nearby stone changing her lens and chatting cozily as much at him as with him. His expression was the wary deliberation of a soldier defusing a live grenade. There was lust in his heart, Rebecca estimated, but what the rest of him was feeling she couldn't say.

Adele scooped Mark's discarded dirt into a bucket and carried it away. A shame she didn't take the opportunity to dump it on Sheila's head. But Adele didn't quite acknowledge Sheila. Rebecca thought of her grandmother tactfully pretending she didn't hear her brothers' four-letter words. Adele might be a flake, but her dignity was impressive.

Hilary sat at her drawing board, sketching several lead pilgrim's badges each with the tiny cross and woman's face—either Margaret, queen of Scotland, or Mary, queen of heaven—that symbolized Rudesburn. Every few seconds she glanced up at Mark and Sheila, her delicate brows drawn together in—in what? Rebecca wondered. Resentful bafflement? Hilary was hard to read, no doubt about it; at times she seemed less shy than carefully guarded. Maybe her wealthy parents had never before let her out without a chaperone.

By the south cloister wall Jerry stood reaming the spout of the alembic Michael had extracted from the cellar of the lay sisters' dormitory. It looked as if he was doing dental work on an earthenware tortoise, Elaine the nurse handing him his picks. Tony circled them, his video camera on his shoulder. Circling him was Dennis. Dennis had never missed his morning tea before, either, Rebecca thought. But he was unlikely to know an alembic from a chamber pot.

Jerry looked up, saw Dennis, and scowled. He threw down a pick for Elaine to retrieve and started toward Rebecca. "I want to talk to you!"

She froze. With raised eyebrows Michael and Colin walked on, Colin inquiring, "The infamous Kleinfelter?"

"Oh, aye," Michael replied. "And that's the glamorous Sheila."

Colin's eyes appealed to heaven. "I see what you mean."

Jerry said to Rebecca, in the voice of a drill sergeant addressing a recruit, "In the future you will keep that geek on a shorter leash."

"Dennis?" Rebecca asked. "He's doing his work."

"He's bugging the hell out of me. Elaine actually saw him in our hotel in York this weekend. She threw a holy fit. It's bad enough I can't turn around at the dig without falling over him. I can't even get a weekend away."

"Don't you want him to help her with the computer?"

"She's having enough trouble entering the data without him breathing down her neck. Tell him to lay off."

"I'll talk to him." Again Rebecca's clenched jaw twinged with pain. Jerry skulked away like a grizzly returning to its den. Damn the man, expecting her to do his dirty work for him. "Dennis!" she called.

The young man ambled toward her, his chubby, child-like face glistening with sweat, his Star Trek T-shirt stained with dirt. "Yeah?"

He was a social klutz, but harmless. As Rebecca groped for words, she saw Tony looking for a place to lay his camera bag. Inspiration struck. "Tony? Could you come here, please?"

Tony's heron-like legs lifted him over a trench. "Yes?"

"We're trying to shift Dennis around to different jobs so he'll have a variety of experiences. We thought it was time to take him off the computer and see if you could show him how to make a photographic record.''

Tony looked at Dennis. ''Do you know anything about videotape?''

''Sure,'' Dennis said brightly, but not without a sideways, reluctant glance toward Jerry and Elaine.

Rebecca smiled. ''Today's sunlight is just the ticket, isn't it?''

''That it is. Come along, then.'' Tony handed Dennis his bag and led him toward the slopes of Battle Law, stopping only to point out a kestrel silently floating overhead.

Rebecca's smile curdled. She caught up with Michael. ''Here's the undercroft beneath the lay dormitory, just where your gadgets said it was,'' he was telling Colin. ''I'm uncoverin' a lovely tile floor, and the cut stone of the piers supportin' the vaultin' is still there.''

After Colin had properly appreciated the surface appearing three feet down in the trench, Michael and Rebecca led him around the refectory and the nun's dormitory, past the site of the infirmary, and behind the east end of the church. Inside Colin eyed the blocked door of the crypt. ''I thought you'd be on to this by now. Kleinfelter's takin' his time, is he?''

''He's a proper professional,'' Michael conceded, ''but he no seems to realize he has a deadline.'' He thrust the printouts into their box. ''And what was that aboot Dennis, hen?''

She explained, concluding, ''Probably he just has a crush on Elaine.''

''Maybe,'' Michael replied. ''Temptin', though, to think Jerry's usin' Dennis and Elaine to cover his fiddlin' the data, just as he did do that lass in the States.''

''But we have no evidence he's cheated here, there, or anywhere; every mistake we've caught he's been perfectly happy to set right. I hate to attribute to malice what can be explained as inefficiency— and not Jerry's. Whatever he is, inefficient he is not.''

''Half a minute,'' said Colin. ''Fiddlin' the data?''

Michael looked at Rebecca. She looked back. If they couldn't trust Colin, who could they trust? Together, interrupting each other, repeating each other, they told him all about it.

''Jesus Christ Almighty!'' he exclaimed when they'd finished. ''The dig from hell, eh?''

''From purgatory,'' said Michael. ''You hope if you work hard enough, you'll be goin' on to heaven.''

''There are compensations,'' Rebecca admitted. ''The music,

the pub, the local people, the students—even Dennis and Adele."
Michael cleared his throat. "And you," she told him, with a pat
on his dirt-caked back pocket.

"But it was only the once you heard Jerry say something about
the Bruce's heart?" asked Colin. "Do you suppose that's the
treasure Sheila meant for her film—the lost treasure of the spectral nun and all?"

"But the spectral nun is supposedly Anne," said Rebecca.
"The heart is associated with Marjory."

Michael tried a shrug, but his shoulders were coiled too tautly.
"Jerry and Sheila want something spectacular for the film. Everyone does. That's why it surprises me he's movin' so slowly.
Unless he realizes we're watchin' him. The uncertainty principle—our observin' him changes him."

"He's outwaitin' you," Colin suggested helpfully. "You lot
are not only witnesses, but also competitors."

Again Michael and Rebecca exchanged a careful look. "The
dig in Virginia went overtime," she pointed out.

"But," Colin went blithely on, "if Jerry—or Sheila, for that
matter—is simply bidin' his time, why are the artifacts goin'
walkabout?"

"If only something would break," moaned Rebecca. "If only
one of the local border collies would be caught with his paw in
the till, or if we found microfilm in Jerry's cigar, or if Sheila
would salt the dig with the Holy Grail."

"Or," Michael said, "if Anne Douglas would jump oot of
the cemetery and tell us all to sod off."

Even as he laughed, Colin glanced over his shoulder. "You
mean the place really is haunted?"

"Something's here, even though it's keeping a mighty low
profile." Rebecca crossed her arms over her chest. "Adele
swears she's seen Anne. Tony even promised Adele he'd try and
photograph her. It. Whatever."

"Mind you," said Michael, "the only ghost photos he's done
so far are underexposed shots of Sheila poncin' aboot in her
nun's habit. She and Tony are oot here at dusk almost every
day, filmin' atmosphere, they say."

Rebecca snorted. "That's a new word for it. Did you notice
the grass stain on the seat of her robe?"

"Havin' it off in a convent'd be to Sheila's taste, right
enough."

Rebecca didn't want to know what memory produced that

comment. Colin looked down at his feet, concealing a grin, then up again, so that his eye met Rebecca's. Sympathy overcame amusement, and he steered the conversation into less controversial topics.

All too soon Colin had to leave. "Gather the evidence, lads and lasses, and save it for Sherlock MacLeod. I'll stop by on my way back from the geology conference—maybe by then I'll decide to buy the wee Queen. Maybe by then you'll have had your break."

Rebecca leaned against Michael's shoulder, watching Colin walk toward the car park. That had been a pleasant interlude. What a shame they had to go back to work. Even though work was half the point of being here.

Michael bent his head to hers, not quite kissing her, but quickly caressing her lips with the tip of his tongue. That particular playful and yet tender sensuality of his always made her go weak in the knees, and for a moment she clung to him, mud and all.

"Now, now," said a voice like velvet draped over acid, "that's not on. You mustn't scare the students."

Rebecca spun around. Sheila picked up a light meter from the supply table and offered them a conspiratorial smile in which her own pink tongue was prominently displayed.

"Christ," Michael hissed between his teeth, "I thought I got shut o' her two years ago."

Two years ago, Rebecca asked herself, *had he kissed Sheila like that?* In the back of her mind, she heard her mother admonishing a grandchild, "Don't put that in your mouth, you don't know where else it's been."

She almost gagged. Wordlessly they walked into the cloister, Michael once again glowering, furrows cut deep into his cheeks.

They'd been with Colin so long that Rebecca expected Jerry to deliver one of his variations on, "How nice of you to come do your work." But all he said was, "Help me put this back." He was lifting the alembic into the trench.

"Here," Michael protested, "that was a right bugger to get oot. Tony already took the still—"

"A good scene in the film," Jeremy interrupted. "Excavation techniques—a professional at work."

Sheila waited, lipstick in one hand and microphone in the other. Tony loped back toward the dig, Dennis at his heels, video camera ready. "Right," Michael said, his tone equal parts fire and ice. He leaped into the pit, nestled the alembic into its muddy hole, climbed out and stalked away.

Oh no, Rebecca said to herself. They wouldn't take credit for. . . . Oh yes, they would. Hell. She looked around for the spade she'd laid down before elevenses, considering whacking Jerry with it.

Jerry accepted a trowel from Elaine, sprinkled dirt artistically over the artifact and posed. "Like this?"

"Posh," said Sheila. She buffed her nails, the scarlet claws of a lioness disemboweling her prey. She tucked her lipstick into a pocket and tied up the bottom of her blouse, an expensive Banana Republic drugstore safari number. "Tony! Move your bum! The light's too good to waste!"

Tony's eyes narrowed. "Yes, your majesty." He brushed by Rebecca, muttering something under his breath that sounded like, ". . . your effing dogsbody, thank you very much."

Rebecca wondered if Tony was prone to headaches at bedtime—not tonight, honey. Unless, like some men, he thought bedtime was a chance to do some domineering of his own.

Dennis sat down, the bag on his lap, and dispensed bits of equipment. Mark leaned on the edge of his trench to watch. Michael bent over Hilary's shoulder and made some comment which must have been inappropriate to what she was drawing, judging by her puzzled look upward. Adele walked by with her bucket of dirt and collided with Tony as he stepped backward, eye fixed to the camera. "Oh," he said, looking around. "Sorry, luv."

Rebecca found her spade. She scooped some mud clods from the edge of the trench. Sheila summoned Jerry, took his glasses from his face and wiped them with a tissue. "We must look presentable, mustn't we?"

"Anything you say," Jerry returned. His oddly naked eyes fixed on her butterfly-wing lashes. Half his mouth curved beneath his moustache in a smug, self-satisfied leer. Sheila simpered and replaced his glasses.

Behind Rebecca, Elaine spat a four-letter word. She stabbed her remaining trowels into the earth at the edge of the trench and stamped into the church. Tony's eye followed her with casual bemusement.

Enjoying the soap opera? Rebecca asked him silently, and gathered her harvest of dirt clods into a bucket. Maybe the knees of Jerry's jeans had, beneath the dirt, grass stains corresponding to those on the seat of Sheila's habit. Rebecca felt sure Mark's knees hadn't bent to Sheila's blandishments, but she'd bet her next paycheck that Jerry's had. Well, it wasn't as if they weren't already using one another.

She hoisted spade and bucket. How about that—Tony really did think it was all a soap opera; now he was aiming his camera and scanning Jerry's and Sheila's little tête-à-tête with no expression on his face except amused calculation. *Men!* Rebecca thought. It must be nice to be so detached.

She took her bucket of dirt to the dump site behind the chapter house and emptied it through the fine mesh screen. A tiny pottery shard. Big deal.

Just as she returned, Sheila called, "Quiet, everyone." And to the camera she purred, "When an important feature is uncovered, the amateur diggers must stand aside for the expert." With exaggerated concentration worthy of the best silent screen comedians, Jerry bent and scraped a layer of dirt from the alembic. "It's very difficult," Sheila went on, gazing sincerely into the lens, "to safely remove a ceramic piece such as this bit of distilling equipment. Notice how carefully the archeologist must work." Jerry blew away a few grains of dust, waggled the alembic, and sucked in his gut.

Muttering Scots and Gaelic curses indiscriminately, Michael picked up a trowel, bounded down into Mark's trench and with short, angry strokes started scraping at the surface. Mark shied, then looked doubtfully up at Rebecca. She shook her head. *Leave him alone. It'll blow over.*

"Dirty trick," whispered Hilary. "Poor Michael."

"Thanks. But for God's sake don't act as if you're sorry for him." Rebecca wiped dirt and sweat off her forehead, climbed into the second trench, and with her spade poked at what promised to be a row of paving stones.

Sheila's voice droned on. Adele carried off another bucket of dirt. Rebecca's spade scraped something lodged in a gutter between the stones. Was that a rust stain? She raised her head to shout and bit her tongue as Jerry's left hand made a frantic shushing gesture out of camera range. His broad grin never wavered as his right hand held the alembic up for the camera.

Rebecca caught Mark's eye. "Bring me your trowel," she mouthed. He brought the trowel.

"Well look at that," she said a few moments later, and Mark's face on the edge of the trench was joined first by Hilary's, then Dennis's. "It's a rondel, a sixteenth-century dagger. See, the iron blade has almost rusted away, but there's the grip—ivory, probably. Soldier's dagger, maybe left here when Henry the Eighth's soldiers sacked the place.''

Now Tony was looking into the trench; good, that bit of film had been executed and could be given proper burial. The shade of the row of bodies emphasized the cool dampness of the ground. Rebecca broke out in gooseflesh.

"What is it?'' Michael asked, clambering down beside her. He took her trowel, scraped at the lump between the stones, then tested it with his forefinger. "Ah, lass, that's no dagger. Can you no see, it's a thirteenth-century wooden spoon and a sort of iron fork called a flesh hook.'' He stood, futilely trying to wipe his hands on his jeans.

His mouth was a narrow fissure; he was still quivering with rage. She swallowed her disappointment at not only her mistake but at his slightly cavalier tone. "Sorry, I guess I blew it.''

"Well,'' Michael said comfortingly, "you have to expect that. I mean, you've studied the place, but I grew up here—naething like personal experience. And the thirteenth century's no your field. Just ask me the next time—no need to mislead the students.''

The air went out of Rebecca's stomach as though he'd punched her. She had only enough breath to articulate, "I see, Dr. Campbell. Thank you.''

That pierced his hide. His brows went lopsided with bewilderment. His eyes blazed indignation. He leaped out of the trench and strode away.

Mark's and Hilary's carefully blank faces disappeared. Dennis's open mouth vanished so suddenly one of the others must have yanked him away. Tony inspected his camera as if suspecting it of imminent collapse. Rebecca sat down hard on the dirty stones, bringing her stunned expression below ground level and out of public scrutiny.

It was only fair, she thought, that she and Michael should contribute to the soap opera. He'd been wounded and had lashed out blindly. She understood and could easily sympathize. What she really wanted to say was, "You jerk, who the hell do you think you are to talk to me like that, especially in front of my students!''

Rebecca picked up the trowel, inched further along the trench, and started scraping another paving stone. Her eyes burned—too much sunlight and shadow and dust, no doubt. *I said I wanted something to break, Michael, but I didn't intend for it to be us.*

Chapter Eight

BY LUNCH TIME, Rebecca felt as if her trowel were imbedded in her skull. The cottage was stifling, and the open windows admitted nothing but flies. The sunshine was too bright, the conscientiously neutral voices of the students set her teeth on edge, and her soup burned her tongue. Every time Michael spoke some cool, correct phrase and avoided her eye, her head throbbed. She choked down a few bites of food and started clearing the table the second the others were done.

Through the window of the dining room she saw Tony enviously inspecting Jerry's Jaguar. Sheila sat on the back step of the Plantagenet van, feeding bits of something out of a greasy newspaper—a fish and chips lunch, probably—to the two cats. Honestly, cats had no dignity at all when it came to food. They'd accept it from anyone.

In the kitchen Rebecca discovered her designated scullery person, Hilary, throwing away the half-pot of leftover soup. "Don't do that!" Rebecca gasped. "That's perfectly good food!"

Hilary's eyes widened. "But it's only—I mean, I didn't think . . ."

Rebecca put the soup in the refrigerator. She could tell Hilary never had to live on a budget. "Sorry for yelling."

"No problem," returned Hilary, who didn't speak again.

Dennis walked out the back door singing, and collided with Michael on the step. "Do you mind?" Michael snarled. Dennis, with the same surprised expression as Hilary's, said he didn't and shut up.

It wasn't so much that it was hot, Mark assured them when

they gathered back at the dig. "It's the humidity. Out in West
Texas you can stroll around in hundred-degree heat and not feel
a thing."

Hilary wadded her hair into a bun. Michael's face registered
horror at the very idea of a hundred degrees and disappeared into
the third trench. Rebecca went into the second trench, Adele
ready to hand her the bottles and brushes of the conservation kit.
Not that Rebecca really wanted to conserve the sneaky spoon
and flesh hook. The sisters had no business cooking in the cloister anyway.

"No!" said Sheila's voice. She and Tony came around the
corner. "You're not going to waste your time and my film chasing that woman's stupid fantasies!"

Beside Rebecca, Adele stiffened.

"Just a few shots," Tony responded. "Adele says she's seen
the ghost in the . . ."

"I don't care if she thinks she's seen it at Brighton Beach.
The woman's bonkers, Tony—all that codswallop about messages from the dead and revenge from the grave and little green
men from Mars."

"We need ghost pictures, Sheila."

"That we do. And I'll arrange them. Right?"

"Right," Tony snapped. Rebecca peeked over the edge of the
trench to see Tony, his expression more exasperated than angry,
raise his camera and target Michael's back as he cleaned the tile
floor.

Adele said, as tightly as Rebecca had ever heard her, "It's
always the disbelievers who are caught out, isn't it?"

"Yeah," Rebecca replied, as noncommittal as possible, and
turned back to the spoon. Not that Sheila hadn't just said what
they all believed. But only she would've said it so loudly and
carelessly. Sheila was enough of a hypocrite to do a film about
a haunted priory and stage the haunting herself.

Jerry and Sheila would drive a saint to distraction, Rebecca
told herself, let alone Michael. Tonight at quitting time she'd
have it out with him. He'd apologize, she'd apologize, and it
would all be over.

Rebecca stabilized the wood and iron with a thin coating of
latex. Then she and Adele dug out the entire block of dirt and
slipped it onto a board. They maneuvered it out of the trench
and into the church where Jerry inspected their find and gave it
his seal of approval. "Okay, fine."

Adele walked away as if she hadn't heard him. Still pondering Sheila's heresy, Rebecca thought. She, too, turned. No point in waiting for Jerry to say something equally heretical like, "Good job, thanks."

Elaine sat hunched over her lap-top computer, typing in the information from the artifact sheets. Her face was as dispassionate as a robot's.

Rebecca paused in the doorway. The countryside drowsed in the heat, the sunlight hazy as the sky inhaled moisture from the earth. Normally the peaceful beauty would have soothed her, but not now. With Michael turned against her, it seemed entirely possible that the hedgerows bristled with knights ready to chase her down and cut out her heart.

Dennis walked backward through the slype, the passage between chapter house and nun's dormitory, focusing the Nikon. Sheila was posing for him, first leaning against the wall, then propping a knee suggestively on a stone. The boy's face was as red as the tomato Rebecca had cut up for lunch. *God, Sheila,* she thought, *have you no pride?*

Something brushed by Rebecca, and she staggered. Jerry walked toward Sheila and Dennis, his moustache at full alert. "Hey you, Tucker, go do your work. Stop bothering her."

"He's not bothering me," Sheila trilled. Laughing, she planted a tiny fluttering kiss on Dennis's cheek. Rebecca thought the boy would melt on the spot, but he pulled himself together, handed over the camera, and with a resentful look at Jerry went to where Tony was now shooting Hilary and her drawing board.

"Sheila," Jerry said, "don't you have any taste?"

Sheila shrugged prettily, tickled Jerry's chest, and strolled away.

Rebecca, slightly nauseous, went back to work. It was a century later that Jerry looked at his watch and bellowed, "Quitting time! Clear up your loose! Clean and stow your tools!"

Dennis went into the cottage, Hilary behind him. Michael collected Mark's and Adele's trowels. Rebecca considered throwing herself fully clothed into the burn. Her head hurt so badly that her eyes bulged from their sockets. She could scream, or pound her head against a stone wall, or against Michael's skull, to the same effect.

What she did was shower. Oddly, the water didn't sizzle on her body like on a hot skillet. In the bedroom she found Michael rooting in his sock drawer. He asked, "Have you seen my sgian dubh?"

"Not recently," she replied, caring not at all about his knife. She closed the door and set down her bag of toiletries. His T-shirt lay in a heap on the floor. She'd already put her dirty clothes in the laundry basket. Normally she'd pick up his things, too. Normally she'd admire his lean body, all sinew and synapses, clad only in jeans. Not now.

"Must've left it somewhere," he said. And with the first direct look he'd given her since the morning he added, "Rebecca, I never thought you capable of professional jealousy."

She heard skirling pipes and voices shouting clan slogans. So he was charging at last, and at her. "I'd say professional jealousy was your problem, making such a big deal out of a misidentification."

"You're the one went all sarkey—'Thank you, Dr. Campbell.' "

"You put me down in front of my students."

"I corrected your mistake. It's my job." He slammed the drawer and picked up some clean clothes.

She put her back to the door, arms crossed. "Rubbing my nose in it isn't your job. I'm painfully aware I didn't grow up here."

"Granted. So what the hell is all this in aid of?" Michael leaned against the wall, leaving a damp handprint on the wallpaper. His eyes were the same blistering blue as the sky.

"I told you, the way you spoke to me, with that bemused contempt husbands always use with their wives."

"We're no married yet, lass."

"Colin gets married so you have to play follow the leader? You expect me to fall dutifully into line?" Her voice arched higher, words rolling off her tongue like lemmings throwing themselves over a cliff. This wasn't going right; the apologies were being trampled in the berserk rush of feet. "Thank God I found out now you're just like all the rest. A man takes a perfectly intelligent, capable woman and whittles away at her until she's a pathetic wreck who says 'yes, master' every time he snaps his fingers!"

"Come off it, woman. Are you daft?"

"I must have been daft to even consider marrying you."

His mouth crimped with annoyance. His brows drew down

like thunderclouds. "Will you move aside? I have tae bathe sae I can cook the dinner."

"I'm standing here with my guts strung out on the floor, and all you care about is dinner!" Rebecca threw open the door. Its edge barely missed Michael's face. She shot into the hall. "Damn, damn, damn!"

Her teeth were clenched so tightly that her jaw writhed. The pain in her head was so intense she couldn't focus her eyes. The dining room was skewed, the table hovering off the floor. The overstuffed chairs in the sitting room were malevolent chintz toadstools. The door to the vestibule bowed toward her. Behind it Mark burrowed frantically through the wellies, his face averted as though from a gruesome accident.

Rebecca leaped toward the boots. Mark dodged. She pulled on the first pair she came to, slammed through the front door, and ran. Gravel spattered, grass squashed, and the boards of the footbridge rang beneath her feet. She didn't stop until she was at the west door of the church, where she leaned her forehead against the cold grit of stone and gasped for air. Any prowling knights were welcome to the numb weight in her chest that was her heart.

Tears condensed from her pain and anger and trickled down her cheeks. She pressed a sob back into her mouth. A hand appeared in her peripheral vision, offering a tissue. She took it, mopped, and sniffed.

Through the moisture in her eyes she saw the late afternoon lying as softly across Gowandale as though photographed through a gauzed lens. A tour bus was parked in front of the hotel, and a dozen or so blurred shapes walked up and down the street.

Mark sat solemnly cleaning his fingernails with his Swiss Army knife. His short, damp hair was as appealing as the fuzz on a hedgehog. He'd changed into a blue T-shirt emblazoned with a mallard in a tuxedo and the words, "Tall, duck, and handsome." Not that he was as tall as Jerry, as dark as Tony, or as handsome as Michael. . . . Different types, Rebecca thought. Mark was solid, Michael spare and elegant. Like Chippendale and Danish Modern, they were both attractive. In spite of herself, she smiled.

"I'm sorry," Mark said, "I didn't mean to eavesdrop."

"You could hardly avoid it. We've all been in each other's pockets the last three weeks."

"Yeah, exactly. Ah—can I barge in even farther?"

"Go ahead."

Mark folded his knife. "It's no surprise Michael's more interested in marriage than you are. The way he talks about his parents and his sister and her family, he has good examples in front of him."

"Yes," Rebecca said, and hiccuped. "He does."

"But you've said you feel like a changeling."

His soft drawl was sympathetic, almost as soothing as Michael's fingertips on her neck. It was nice to talk American. With a sigh Rebecca sat down. "Yeah, my mother married my father right out of high school. All she's ever done is serve him and my brothers. The oldest, Kevin, he's all right. But the other two saw baby sister as a punching bag. A girl, you know. Inferior creature. You ought to hear the way they talk to their wives."

"The way your father talks to your mother?"

"You got it."

"Come on, can you really see yourself in that kind of relationship?"

"That's just it, isn't it? I can't."

"But you're assuming Michael can? You and he are talking different languages—in more ways than one, dinna ye ken." Rebecca laughed. "It's a matter of faith," Mark went on, "like we were talking about the other night. Do you have enough faith in him to trust him to do right by you? And vice versa—can he trust you not to dump on him?"

"Something to be said for biting your tongue," Rebecca admitted. "Although I've been doing that an awful lot already."

Mark nodded abstractedly. "Haven't we all?"

The tour bus gathered its passengers. Bridget ran out of the Craft Centre carrying a package, which she handed in through a window. The bus belched exhaust, rumbled up the street, and turned toward Melrose.

She would talk to Michael after supper, Rebecca resolved. They couldn't let this fester. They'd settle it tonight. "Mark, you're a gentleman and a scholar."

"I can dish it out. I can't necessarily take it."

She looked askance at that. "Do you have siblings?"

"Half-siblings, a couple of little people in grade school. My dad's second marriage."

"Divorce?"

"One of the messiest. They might as well have torn me apart

on a rack. Ten years ago—I was fifteen.'' His face hardened. ''I cut up pretty rough for a while. Acting out, the counselors said. Then—well, something happened that snapped me out of it.''

Rebecca looked discreetly away. Yes, everyone had a skeleton in his closet. So Mark had been in counseling. No wonder he could dish it out.

Footsteps scrambled over the floor of the church. Mark and Rebecca leaped up. Sheila burst out of the door and for a moment clung to the wall, her bosom heaving photogenically. Her wild-eyed glance to right and left didn't register the people staring at her. With an inarticulate cry she looked back over her shoulder and fled across the lawn to the bridge, ran across it and achieved the hotel in mere seconds.

Mark and Rebecca looked at each other. No Tony, no Dennis, no camera. Her terror might actually have been genuine. They looked through the door, Rebecca expecting at least a squad of zombies. Bars of sunlight lay across the floor. William Salkeld's effigy slept peacefully. The grille in the tower door was closed. A couple of jackdaws hopped over the supply table.

''She never struck me as one who'd spook easy,'' said Mark.

''I hope she saw the ghost,'' Rebecca replied. ''Poetic justice.''

Mark cocked his head to the side. ''Like the poetic justice of her seeing Michael in love with you?''

''Is it that obvious they had a—well, they knew each other?''

''I'm the cynic, you know. I expect the worst.''

Rebecca nodded. ''An object lesson, then; don't let her wriggle her way into your past.''

''Oh, a Twinkie can be pretty tempting,'' Mark grinned. ''A nibble even tastes good. But you know if you eat the whole thing, you're going to make yourself sick. Sheila makes you appreciate a nice modest girl like Hilary.''

A cool breeze stirred the willows and fanned Rebecca's face. The sun drifted westward in a sky swept clean of haze. The multicolored flowers in the village gardens glistened like seed catalog advertisements. The green of the lawns and the trees were a new definition of the color, more intense than any Rebecca had ever seen, reflecting hazel in Mark's gray eyes.

They were on the bridge when they heard the singing. Women's voices rose and fell, at one moment lifted on the breeze, at the next evaporating into the sunlight. *''Pater noster qui es in caelis sanctificetur nomen tuum adveniat regnum tuum . . .''*

". . . thy will be done," Rebecca continued, "on earth as it is in heaven." She quickened her pace, Mark on her heels. "Did Sheila see the nuns going into the choir for vespers?"

"I'm not sure I really want to know," he answered. "So far I've done real good with denial."

Back in the cottage, Rebecca discovered she was wearing Hilary's boots. She took them off and set them neatly down. In the bedroom, Michael's dirty jeans lay on top of his dirty shirt. Gathering them up, she took them toward the back entry and the laundry basket. She could hear Adele's voice before she reached the kitchen. ". . . hard to believe anyone could be that unsympathetic to such an aura. All you have to do is walk into the church and you feel it. The relics demand respect, they sense disbelief. They avenge disbelief."

Adele stood chopping vegetables, the long knife snicking up and down like a guillotine. Chunks of carrot and potato lay like heads piled below the scaffold. Maybe she envisioned Sheila's head among them.

Michael stood over the stove browning stew meat, his face as glazed as though it were pressed against a window, but whether from Adele's relentless certainty or from the same light-headedness Rebecca felt, she couldn't tell. At least the explosion had cleared her headache. She threw his clothes into the basket and asked, "Can I help?"

"We've got it, thank you," he returned. His eyes never left the pot. His voice had an edge to it. Probably he'd unbent his stiff spine long enough to follow her outside, and had seen her confiding in someone else. Great. Tiptoeing through the embers of their argument, Rebecca went back to the bedroom and ransacked it for the sgian dubh. It wasn't there. She checked the sitting and dining rooms. Still nothing. He must have left it at the dig. Odd, though, he took such good care of it, always wiping it off and replacing it in its sheath.

The meat was tough, the vegetables underdone, but no one complained. The few bites of stew Rebecca managed to get down lay like a bowling ball in the pit of her stomach. *Look at me,* she ordered Michael silently. *Just look at me, so we can start making up.*

He played with his food, his downcast face obscured by his hair and by thought. He took his plate to the kitchen, muttered to no one in particular, "It's a grand evenin'," and walked out of the house.

Rebecca followed. She got as far as the front step and stopped dead. Michael and Sheila stood next to the Plantagenet van. If Sheila had been frightened a little while ago, she was back to her old self now.

Michael was half-turned away from her, as though she'd grabbed his arm as he strode by. Even as Rebecca shrank back against the door, her heart congealing, Michael shook away Sheila's hand. She leaned toward him, smiled, and spoke. One enameled fingertip traced a line down his shoulder.

He flung her hand away. His scowl would have intimidated a battalion of redcoats.

But Sheila was made of stern stuff. Unfazed, she went on talking. Her scarlet lips moved as if they were independent of her face, caterpillars voraciously consuming everything within reach.

Michael grasped her upper arms. Her hair flew around her face. His voice rose, and his words sliced the evening peace. "You filthy bitch, let me be! Let us be!"

"Or else?" Sheila's lips might have said. Despite his scowl, she still smiled at him as though she sat across from him in a cocktail lounge and sipped delicately from some fruity drink.

He threw her away from him with such force that she smacked against the side of the van. He strode across the car park and disappeared around the side of the Craft Centre, fists clenched at his sides, shoulders braced as though under the weight of armor.

Sheila leaned against the van. Rebecca hoped she was hurt. She was afraid she was hurt, because if she was, Michael had been the one to hurt her.

Sheila straightened, fluffed her hair, and smoothed her blouse. She saw Rebecca on the step. For one crazy, careening moment the glossy photograph of her beauty ripped in half. Her face went as emptily, sharply hungry as that of a child in a famine relief poster. Her eyes raked Rebecca with a look compounded of anger and envy and desperation. Then, before Rebecca quite realized what she was seeing, Sheila began laughing. She squared her shoulders and marched off like a soldier to the cadences of a brass band.

Rebecca staggered into the bedroom. "Can't you leave him alone, Sheila?" she demanded of the blank faces of the beds. "Haven't you done enough? I wanted to hate you, and you won't even let me do that!"

Haven't I done enough? she asked herself. Sheila's face was etched on her mind like the image of a photographic negative. Had Michael ever seen her disemboweled like that? Had he ever heard the peculiar ghastly jollity of that laugh?

Steady on, she told herself. She sat down and forced herself to breathe deeply, counting each exhalation. The bowling ball in her stomach deflated. When her hands stopped trembling, she got out a darning needle and the skein of yarn. She'd mend Michael's sweater while she waited for him to calm down, while she waited for the world to settle back into its ruts.

Adele's voice, saying something about the Egyptian book of the dead, came from the hall. Dennis responded politely. The front door shut. Splashes, clinks, and chatter echoed from the kitchen as Mark washed the dishes under Hilary's supervision.

Rebecca stared at the sleeve of the sweater, half the stitches unraveled in her hand. Well, damn! She couldn't do anything right today! Caroline could fix it, but Rebecca would not let Michael take it home to her and whine, "Look what Rebecca did, Mum." Maybe Hilary could help.

Rebecca arrived in the kitchen door to see Mark offering Hilary a taste of his precious salsa. He'd brought the bottle of tomato, pepper, and onion sauce with him, rightly assuming that British food would be too bland for his Texan palate. Rebecca envisioned the male bird bringing the female a toothsome bit of worm. Courtship had its moments.

Hilary sniffed at the spoonful of lumpy red stuff. "Kinda spicy."

"You can take it." He held the spoon to her mouth.

She nibbled, swallowed, and exhaled through pursed lips. "Oh, my."

Mark considered those lips, bent his head, and kissed them.

Hilary's entire body jerked with shock. "No, don't!" She pushed him away and ran up the stairs. The spoon clattered onto the floor. Mark looked after her, stunned.

Rebecca ducked around the corner before he could see her. Hilary's expression hadn't been coy, playing hard to get. It hadn't been insulted. Her face had been filled with despair, leavened by a hint of the same panic that had contorted Sheila's features at the church door.

Oh God. What had happened to Hilary to make her react like that? Rebecca went back into the bedroom. What a comedy of errors. What a Shakespearean tragedy. The front door slammed. Then the back door.

The evening outside the window was indeed grand. She might as well walk up to the Craft Centre and ask Bridget for help with the sweater. Better than sitting here brooding over Michael and Sheila, Mark and Hilary, motive and opportunity and skeletons in closets. Rebecca secured the loose stitches, put the garment and the yarn into a plastic bag, and walked outside.

Across the stage set of the village, the Johnston children were chasing a soccer ball. Winnie shook a rug out of an upper window. Laurence walked across the street from the Craft Centre to the hotel. Elaine came hurrying out, brushed by Laurence, climbed into the Jaguar, and went roaring off toward Jedburgh. Compared to the clean shine of the sun, the lamps in the van were only counterfeit light. Two shapes moved in their gaudy glow. Dennis chirped breathlessly; Tony replied in monosyllables. Rebecca wondered why Tony stayed with Sheila, whether film jobs were that hard to find.

She trudged up the driveway. The toy shop was next to the hotel. From the step of the Craft Centre, across the street, all she could see in its window was the face of an antique clock. But she'd looked in that window often enough to visualize its contents. She wouldn't mind having a teddy bear wearing tiny wellie boots herself, especially the one in the tweed deerstalker. And the Coldstream Guards, with their scarlet uniforms and bearskin hats like rows of red ants ordered behind their Queen, were enough to tempt anyone.

The clock read eight o'clock. Maybe by nine Michael's rage and frustration would've burned themselves out, and they could start shoveling away the cinders of their argument.

Rebecca went inside and approached Bridget. "Why, of course," the woman said. "Sit you doon, we'll sort it oot."

By the time Bridget announced nine o'clock, closing time, Rebecca felt much better. The sweater was fixed, and under Bridget's tutelage she'd done most of it herself. Everything was going to be all right. She emerged into the street clutching her bag and saw Hilary standing in front of the hotel. "Hi!" Rebecca called. "Is everyone in the pub?"

"Only Jerry," the girl replied, her brow furrowed with irritation. She gazed down at her fancy designer shoes. "I was looking for Mark."

Rebecca glanced curiously at her. Maybe Hilary wanted to

apologize for her abrupt rebuff in the kitchen. Good—Mark hadn't deserved that reaction to his kiss, even if he had accidentally reopened an unhealed wound.

Michael hadn't deserved what he'd gotten, either. He was probably there in the cottage looking over the day's printouts. Blast. She'd never picked them up. Shaking her head—sometimes it was hard to remember that archeology was the reason they were all there—Rebecca asked Hilary, "Would you like to walk over to the church with me? I left the printouts."

The west front of the church reflected the twilight, inscrutable. The wheel cross shouldered its way from the turf. The walls of the priory lay in rocky knots, tensely, across the lawn. In the rising wind, the leaves of the beeches behind the hotel whispered secrets to each other.

Hilary said, "It's pretty spooky over there in the evening."

"That white shape we keep seeing is the resident owl," Rebecca told her, forcing a light tone.

"Really?" They walked toward the bridge that carried Jedburgh Street across the Gowan Water. Grant Johnston, clad in civilian shirt and flannels, was standing in his garden admiring a magnificent display of pink and blue delphiniums. He exchanged waves with the women.

"And what was Jerry up to?" Rebecca asked.

Hilary snorted. "He bought me a glass of wine, in exchange for which I had to listen to him imply that if a man doesn't— er—use a woman regularly, then his metabolism and his intellectual processes suffer. I sat there smiling and playing dumb. Do you think he was making a pass at me?"

Rebecca laughed. The laugh felt good. "Sure he was. Good show, to pretend you didn't understand him. I thought that line had died a justifiable death years ago. Trust Jerry to still be back in Neanderthal times."

The stream gurgled past the bridge, willow branches teasing its burnished surface. The silver Jaguar purred past the priory wall and onto the bridge, Elaine gesturing acknowledgement as she passed.

"Maybe she told Jerry off," suggested Rebecca. "That was why he was window-shopping tonight."

"I almost told him to go find Sheila," Hilary said, "but I thought that would be tacky. You almost have to feel sorry for her."

"The poor little girl looking for love in all the wrong places?"

Rebecca didn't say that as caustically as she would have a few hours ago.

"I just don't understand how she can make such a K-Mart special out of herself. I bet she's been with—well, several men. How can she stand it?"

Perhaps it was the ambiguous evening light that made Hilary look so green around the gills. Not that Rebecca herself had been terribly sophisticated at Hilary's age of twenty-two, but she was beginning to fear that the girl was less an example of arrested development than the victim of a disastrous relationship. That didn't give Rebecca the rights to pry into Hilary's past, however. "Depends on what Sheila's been getting out of it," she said carefully, and Hilary replied with a shrug.

Across the stream the village was muted by dusk and by the fragrant smoke curling from various chimneys. Bright squares of windows defined the hotel from skylights to front door. Next to the lighted van the headlights of the Jaguar went off, and the ceiling light came on as Elaine opened the door. The cottage windows blazed. Dennis was probably propped on his bed reading one of the science fiction novels Michael had lent him. The tenuous chords of a guitar drifted from the open window of the sitting room.

The lawn beyond the gatehouse was so noiselessly soft that Rebecca felt as if she were floating. On the porch of the church, the cats sat still as stone gargoyles. Hilary bent to pet Guinevere. Guinevere hissed and scratched at her, and she jumped back. Lancelot arched, his tail standing up like a bottle brush. As one they turned, fled out of the light, and were swallowed by darkness.

Rebecca looked at Hilary, who bit her lip. They peered in the door. A tenuous light flirted with grasping shadow. The grass in the nave was a deep malachite green. The rims of the granite sarcophagi sparkled with bits of mica. Their depths were filled with darkness as tangible as water. Taking a deep breath, Rebecca plunged into the building, rushed to the chancel, seized the printouts from their box and hurried back, her steps reverberating from the roof.

Hilary was looking down into one of the tombs, so stiff and still that Rebecca's neck contracted. "What is it?"

"There's something in there," Hilary said. Her voice, stretched thin and fine, broke with an upward quaver.

Rebecca stepped up beside her. A white shape lay in the stony embrace, a woman wearing a white habit. Her eyes glowed.

Anne Douglas. The sack and the rolls of paper fell from Rebecca's nerveless fingers and thudded softly on the grass. Her heart did a backflip into her windpipe. "No," she gasped. Her knees gave way and dropped her on the cold stone rim. "No." The woman's eyes were covered by two round, faintly shining objects. Two gold nobles. Below them red lips parted in a grimace of pain. The breath of the sarcophagus carried not only the odor of musty stone, but also that of a rich perfume and of something warm and sickly.

The sunlight faded. The shape, the woman, remained utterly silent, horribly still. Her hands were crossed on her breast. The fabric beneath the clutching, red-taloned fingers wasn't white but dark. *Red,* Rebecca thought. *Like the lips, like the nails. Red as blood. Red with blood.* "It's Sheila," she said, her own voice harshly loud. "I think she's dead."

If Hilary's first scream lacked conviction, her second, third and fourth made the walls bulge. With panicked flappings pigeons erupted from the tower. Footsteps raced across the grass.

Rebecca knelt. The shape in the sarcophagus had its own gravity. It was pulling her downward. Gold and white and red, musky sweet, drowned in shadow. . . . Hands grasped her shoulders and pulled her back. She looked up.

"Here noo," said Grant, "what's all this, then?"

All Rebecca could do was point numbly, dumbly, into the tomb.

Chapter Nine

THE KITCHEN WAS dark, illuminated only by the light from the dining room. Rebecca stood in the shadows rinsing out her cup. She'd had so much coffee in the last couple of hours that acid bubbled into the back of her throat.

The Galashiels force had responded with commendable briskness. So had police and reporters and television crews from so many places Rebecca wouldn't have been surprised to find a New York cop directing the traffic gridlock on the bridge. Rudesburn had its publicity, all right.

The thrum of a generator vibrated in the window. Across the stream the inside of the priory church was lit by arc lights. The broken tracery of the west window was silhouetted like a row of teeth against the glare, and the occasional dark figure moving in or out of the door was a cartoonist's caricature of a human being. Among the remains of the convent buildings pale shapes gathered and parted as though exchanging the shocking news. Traces of mist rising off the Gowan, no doubt. . . . Why bother to rationalize ghosts? Sheila was dead.

Again, Rebecca saw the body laid out in the sarcophagus. The stone had been cold to the touch. Sheila, too, would have been cold—beauty forfeit and tongue stilled forever. Despite the warmth of her sweater-vest, Rebecca shivered.

The back door opened. "Here he is," said Grant, and ushered Michael into the kitchen.

Rebecca held herself back, gauging the magnetic field of his mood. His face was drawn, his eyes oddly pale, as if he'd been kicked in the stomach. "Rebecca," he said, and opened his arms.

She threw herself against him. His cheek was cold, and his T-shirt smelled musty. In the ferocity of his grasp, her ribcage felt like a slinky toy. "Where've you been?" she asked into his shoulder.

"In the attic of the hotel, lookin' through Kerr's old pokes and thinkin'. Thinkin', mostly."

About me? she didn't ask out loud. "You didn't hear the commotion?"

"Oh aye, I heard the sirens, but Nora stopped me in the lobby and Laurence on the pavement and then Grant on the driveway."

Grant had changed into his uniform, making the subtle but important distinction between friend and official. His genial face was creased with lines. "The Chief Inspector'll be lookin' in straightaway."

Rebecca asked, "Would you like some coffee?"

"No, thank you kindly," Grant replied.

Michael was staring out the window at the priory. "What? Oh—I'd like something to clear the dust oot of my throat."

She gave him a glass of water. He eyed her and it. Taking the glass, he found the bottle of Cragganmore in the cupboard and poured a healthy dram into the water. He drank. A faint flush crept up his cheeks.

"Better now?" Rebecca asked.

"I'll do for the moment."

They walked, Grant trailing behind them, into the dining room. The blue lights of police cars throbbed against the drawn curtains. Adele sat at the table wearing her son's UCLA sweatshirt. Her glasses were folded in front of her, her eyes were closed and her hands clasped, but her tranquil, almost translucent, expression was marred by a tightness at the corners of her mouth. Mark leaned on the door, stirring a cup of coffee, his face wiped clean of any expression at all. He'd been stirring when Rebecca walked through the room ten minutes ago. The clink of the spoon was loud in the silence.

Tony sat against the wall of the vestibule, his forehead against his arms crossed on his knees. His clenched fists quivered, his knuckles starkly white, but the rest of his body was stock still. As if the shock of Sheila's death wasn't enough, Tony now had the status of his job to worry about.

Dennis eyed the other occupants of the sitting room couch

with quick, nervous glances that became convulsive shivers in his body, reminding Rebecca of nothing so much as St. Nicholas' bowl full of jelly.

Beside him Elaine sniffled into a tissue, her reddened, mascara-smeared eyes focused on Jerry. She kept trying to press herself into his side, but he responded less to her than he would to a mosquito. His stony profile was sculpted of confusion and resentment, his moustache drooped over pale lips clasped around an unlit cigar.

Hilary huddled, knees drawn up, in the depths of a chair. Her eyes were so like a little lost waif's that Rebecca was surprised she wasn't sucking her thumb. But her spate of hysterics had lasted only moments; since then she'd walked around like a marionette, loose-jointed and clumsy, bringing coffee and sandwiches to the others.

"Where were you?" Jerry demanded of Michael.

"In the attic of the hotel, tryin' to do a wee bit of work." Michael started throwing kindling into the fireplace.

Mark set his cup on the table with a clunk so abrupt Adele started. He hoisted a log from the basket. Tony raised his head from his arms and gazed dully into the sitting room. Grant clasped his hands behind his back and rocked on his heels. Dennis said beneath his breath, "I bet Adele did it. I bet she's into human sacrifice." Elaine rolled her eyes from him to the quiet figure in the dining room and pulled a pack of cigarettes from her purse.

"Suicide," stated Jerry. "Obviously. The woman was way the hell out in left field."

"I don't think so," Hilary said, her voice faint and far away. "I don't think it was suicide at all."

Mark gave her shoulder a quick pat, then groped along the mantelpiece for the box of matches. "Empty. Anyone have any matches? Jerry?"

Jerry pulled the cigar from between his lips, contemplated it, and threw it toward the wastebasket. "No."

"No," Elaine repeated. She put the cigarettes back into her purse.

"I've got some," said Rebecca. She went into the bedroom, scrabbled through the dresser drawer, and found the matchbook. "Here," she said to Mark when she returned.

"Thanks. Nice fresh pack, not a one missing." Mark lit the fire and laid the matches on the mantel. A frill of yellow gnawed at the kindling. With snaps and pops, flame licked the logs and shredded up the chimney.

"Are those the matches you found in the attic?" Michael asked Rebecca.

"Yes. I thought maybe they were yours. Edinburgh Pub."

"The Edinburgh Pub's no in Edinburgh. It's in London, no so far from Temple Tube Station, on Fleet Street." His forefinger sketched street corners in midair. "I used to go there wi' my mates from the Museum."

"There's a phone number written inside the cover," Mark said.

Michael picked up the flimsy piece of cardboard. "071-323-7111."

The front door opened. Tony, in one ungainly lurch, clambered to his feet. Grant pulled himself to attention. Adele put on her glasses. Her eyes looked like museum displays protected under glass.

Three men carrying satchels fanned out into the house. Two men dressed in the dark suits and conservative ties of stockbrokers loomed in the sitting room door. The shorter one said to Adele and Tony, "Would you mind sittin' down in there?" Tony and Adele went into the sitting room and sat down.

The other man was so tall his head just missed the top of the door. He reached into his pocket, pulled out a handful of dark blue booklets, and eyed them as though they were a particularly disappointing poker hand. American passports. Grant had collected them an hour ago. Then Rebecca had caught only glimpses of Detective Chief Inspector Simon Mackenzie and Detective Sergeant Harry Devlin, Edinburgh C.I.D. Now she stared.

With a pipe and deerstalker, Mackenzie's gaunt features would resemble those of Sherlock Holmes. In a robe, his sleek black hair tonsured, he could have passed for St. Bernard of Clairvaux. His dark eyes darted swift uncompromising looks upward, then retreated behind lashes opaque as window shutters. "Rebecca Reid?" he asked in a voice softer than she'd expected from such height. "You're in charge of the students?"

"Yes." *No need to be nervous,* she told herself. *I haven't done anything.* But still a chill of apprehension fluttered down her spine.

"Hilary Chase, Dennis Tucker, Mark Owen."

Devlin's gaze skewered Mark. "Mr. Owen, I see you're from Texas. You are aware that we have strict gun laws here?"

Mark looked as though he'd like to guffaw, but all he emitted was a pained smile. "Never touch the stuff."

"Adele Garrity," continued Mackenzie. "Jeremy Kleinfelter."

"Look here, officer," Jerry said, "it's the middle of the night, and we have work to do tomorrow. Just because the bitch did away with herself . . ."

My, my, Rebecca thought waspishly, *how quickly we forget all those meaningful glances and cozy smirks.*

Mackenzie looked at Jerry much as his forensics team must even now be inspecting Sheila's body. Jerry sputtered into silence.

Devlin opened a notebook and said, "Michael Campbell, Tony Wright, Elaine Vavra. British citizens." With the addition of a grin, Devlin's dark curly hair, blue eyes, and pink cheeks would have made him look like a leprechaun, Rebecca thought. But if he guarded any pots of gold or the ends of any rainbows, his hard, almost belligerent stare didn't invite inquiries.

"Sit down, please." Mackenzie handed Devlin the passports. Devlin handed them to Grant. Grant laid them all on the dining room table.

Michael dropped into the sole unoccupied chair. This was no time to stand on ceremony; Rebecca wedged herself in beside him. Mark settled on the arm of Hilary's chair, his own arm resting behind her head. Dennis gave Adele his seat on the couch and joined Tony on the hearth. A log whined in the crackle of the flames. Heavy footsteps and the snick of closet doors opening and shutting echoed from the bedrooms next door and upstairs. Rebecca tried not to resent the hands prying through her possessions. The detectives were only doing their jobs.

The Chief Inspector hiked back his suit jacket, thrust his hands into his pockets, and addressed the mantel. "Miss Bridget Hamilton has very kindly given the investigative team a room in the back of the Craft Centre, and the Procurator Fiscal has made his report. The deceased is Sheila Fitzgerald, age thirty-five. Film producer."

Michael twitched. So, Rebecca thought woodenly, Sheila had lied about her age.

"Suicide," stated Jerry.

"Hardly," Devlin returned. "She was stabbed in the heart with a small knife which we haven't as yet found. Death was instantaneous. Murder."

"Murder," Jerry repeated queasily. Elaine swallowed a squeak of dismay.

"*Requiem aeternum,*" Adele whispered. Hilary hid her face in her hands. Again Mark patted her shoulder, and this time his hand lingered. Dennis looked ill. Tony closed his eyes and rubbed them as if he could rearrange the reality they saw.

Rebecca had never thought the death was anything but murder. And yet hearing the word out loud was like a blow to the back of the knees. They were all suspects, she thought. They were the strangers, the outlanders. They were the ones Sheila swatted around as though she were a cat playing with an assortment of mice. Death had been instantaneous? No, she'd had time to be frightened, to feel pain. Her expression had been far from composed.

"She wasn't killed in the tomb where Misses Reid and Chase discovered her, but behind the chapter house. We found signs of a struggle there, and a trail. . . ." Not a person couldn't fill in the words "of blood." Mackenzie cleared his throat. "The murderer dragged her body into the church and arranged it in the tomb. She died between 7:15 and 9:15 pip emma. Unless one of you saw her after 7:15?"

Glances caromed from person to person, but no one answered.

"I need to know where each of you were between the hours of 7:15 and 9:15." Even though Mackenzie's mild Edinburgh accent grew no louder, a threat glinted beneath the words.

Everyone began gabbling at once. With a few sharp questions, Devlin sorted out each account and wrote it down. Mackenzie's eyes moved from face to face with the cool deliberation he'd accorded each passport photo.

Jerry had walked in the ruins and then gone to the pub. Before going there herself, Hilary had walked into the fields and woodlands south of the town, playing with a dog. Mark had hiked toward Melrose. Tony had taken some pictures from Battle Law and then worked in the van. Adele had meditated in the cemetery, then walked through the village. Dennis had bought a candy bar from Bridget and also worked in the van. Elaine had driven into Newton St. Boswells. Michael had been in the attic. Rebecca had been in the house and in the Craft Centre with Bridget.

No one, Rebecca told herself, had an—alibi, that was the word—for the entire evening. And Michael had been alone the whole time. She held his hand, trying to warm his cold, inert fingers, without noticeable success.

The voices died away. "So then," said Mackenzie into the thick silence, "until we have a chance to talk to each of you individually, we'll assume the last person to see Miss Fitzgerald alive was P.C. Johnston."

"Aye." Grant surreptitiously polished the scuffed toes of his boots against his trouser legs. "She was in the call box afore the Craft Centre. It was right after dinner, and the weans couldna find their football, so I was moochin' aboot the pavement lookin' for it."

Devlin wrote something in his notebook—"Find out who Sheila was talking to," no doubt. Mackenzie said, "The murder weapon."

More glances. The log expired. Traffic muttered outside, and footsteps tapped inside. Mackenzie played his pregnant pauses beautifully, Rebecca thought.

"P.C. Johnston tells me that Mr. Owen has a Swiss Army knife and Dr. Campbell a sgian dubh. Could we see them, please?"

Mark reamed out his pocket and produced the knife. Devlin crossed the carpet, took it from his hand, and put it in his own pocket. Michael leaned forward as if to rise, then stopped. His hand clenched convulsively. So did Rebecca's heart. *Oh, my God—no, it couldn't be.*

"You're not implying," said Jerry, "that one of us murdered the woman? There are people all over the place—shopkeepers, villagers, busloads of tourists. And some friend of Campbell's was here today. Why couldn't it have been him?"

"We'll talk to him," said Mackenzie. "Is something wrong, Dr. Campbell?"

Michael's body was a dead weight against Rebecca's. He said, very slowly and precisely, "I don't know where my sgian dubh is. I was looking for it earlier, and I couldn't find it."

"Neither could I," said Rebecca. "It's been lost."

"Not stolen?"

Michael said, "It never occurred to me someone might've pinched it, no."

"Why didn't you report it missing?"

"Man, I had a few other things on my mind!"

From the corner of her eye Rebecca intercepted Jerry's sudden look of enlightenment. "Campbell had quite an argument with Sheila this evening. It must've been about seven. He hit her."

"He did not!" exclaimed Rebecca. Michael's hand pulled her

back down into the chair. "Where were you eavesdropping from?"

"I was looking at last week's photos in the camera van," Jerry replied. "I wasn't eavesdropping—they rubbed my nose in it!"

"Aye?" said Devlin. Mackenzie focused on Jerry. Elaine and Adele shrank away to either end of the couch.

"I gather Michael and Sheila had a quick and dirty affair a couple of years ago," explained Jerry. "He was insisting he'd given her the elbow—jilted her—and she was insisting it was the other way around. Then she made some catty remarks about his current girlfriend, Ms. Reid. I gather she'd overheard them having a free-for-all themselves."

Rebecca bit her tongue. It was too late to hate Sheila, much too late. Michael's face was blank with exhaustion. Earlier he might have honorably corrected "girlfriend" to "fiancée," but not now. She'd made it very clear they weren't engaged.

"Aye?" Devlin said again. A furtive sparkle stirred the depths of his eyes. "Must've been quite the day for arguments."

Tony looked up from his grasshopper-like pose on the hearth. Dennis stared at his shoes. Hilary's hand snaked up to clasp Mark's where it lay on her shoulder. His eyes were silver mirrors, reflecting the scene before them but revealing nothing of the thoughts moving behind them.

Mackenzie asked Michael, "You were no friend of the victim's, then?"

"I couldna thole the woman," Michael replied, sliding back into his broader accent. "Oh, aye, I put up wi' her well enough once. But that was a long time ago, in London. Then she wisna . . ." Mackenzie waited patiently while he frowned, groping for a word, "She wisna jinkin' aboot like a frantic hare then."

Jink, Rebecca translated. The word not only meant to swerve or dodge but connoted evasiveness, even dishonesty. Judging by Mackenzie's slow nod, his Scots was good enough to catch that.

"I have to admit," said Adele from the end of the couch, "the woman could be exceedingly obnoxious. Her chakras were misaligned. She needed transcendental therapy."

Mackenzie tilted his head to the side and looked at her blankly.

"A bleedin' tart's wot she was," Elaine spat. "She 'ad it off wiv 'arf the men on this dig." Under stress Elaine's accent tended to migrate from the BBC studios to London's East End.

Devlin's mouth crooked in dry amusement. "Where were you at the time of the murder, Miss Vavra?"

Elaine gulped audibly. "I told you. I drove to Newtown St. Boswells to buy cigarettes."

"We have several brands in the shop," Grant offered.

"I needed to get out, didn't I? The shop assistant saw me."

With the barest of shrugs Devlin abandoned Elaine's red, indignant face. Mackenzie strolled to the fireplace and leaned on the mantel. Tony and Dennis shied away. "This is ridiculous," Jerry muttered.

"Dr. Kleinfelter," said Michael, without bothering to look at the man, "just for once can you no pull your head oot o' your own ego?"

"Who the hell do you think you are, Campbell?"

Michael didn't answer; his tired but dignified expression conveyed that he knew very well who he was.

Mackenzie dismissed Jerry with a thin, undeceived smile and asked Michael, "Tell me again where you were at the time of the murder."

"In the hotel attic, searchin' for items of historical interest."

"I don't suppose anyone saw you there."

"I dinna suppose anyone did, no."

"Where did the coins that were on Miss Fitzgerald's eyes come from?"

Michael shook his head. "Nora, Mrs. Baird, said one of them was the one nicked from the hotel three weeks ago. It was scratched wi' a wee 'F.K.,' for Francis Kerr, who found it. Nora said the other was a spit of the first, but even better preserved— collector's quality, right enough."

"It's not their second coin," said Devlin. "That's still in the display case."

Sheila and her documentary, Rebecca thought. *The lost treasure of the spectral nun. Were the coins on her eyes poetic justice or a macabre joke?*

The pulse of a siren wavered down the air and then stopped abruptly. Devlin glanced at his watch. "They'll be takin' her away now."

"Our work is just beginning," Mackenzie added. It was the first unnecessary thing he'd said all night. "Dr. Campbell, we'll have to ask you to come with us to Galashiels, to help us with our inquiries."

Rebecca looked up, stricken, into that imperturbable face. No, he wasn't gloating. He wasn't conveying any emotion at all except a tired intellectual curiosity. Tired, she estimated, not jaded. His long, thin, mouth was stretched taut as a finely tuned harp string.

Asking Michael to help with their inquiries didn't mean the police regarded him as a helpful citizen. It meant he was their prime suspect. *But, but,* Rebecca's aching mind stammered, *he didn't do it.* But she reminded herself that the more cooperative he was, the faster they'd find that out.

Michael reacted only with a sigh. Rebecca laid her head against his shoulder, then snapped it upright again. She didn't want to embarrass him.

"It's all right, lass," he whispered, brushed her cheek with his cold lips, and released her hand. "Very well, Inspector. Just let me get my coat."

Dennis clambered to his feet, protesting, "But the most obvious person is never the one who really did it!"

"Well, lad," returned Mackenzie, "this is real life now, isn't it?"

Dennis blushed. Tony stood up, wincing as though his muscles were cramping. "May I go back to the hotel?"

"And us?" Jerry stood, hauling Elaine up beside him. *Oh good,* Rebecca thought. Puff himself up as he might, Jerry wasn't as tall as Mackenzie.

"Watch your step," said Devlin. "The press is at the top of the lane."

"Here," Grant exclaimed, "they'll no be badgerin' my wife, will they?"

"I've assigned several more constables to share your beat," Mackenzie told him. "Indefinitely."

Only partly mollified, Grant escorted Jerry, Elaine and Tony out the door. For once Jerry had run out of parting shots.

The officers who'd been searching the house trooped through the hall, exchanging shrugs with Devlin. No sgian dubh, then. Hilary seemed only now to realize she was holding Mark's hand. With a crumpled smile she extracted herself, dodged around Devlin and Mackenzie, and disappeared into the back of the house. Dennis muttered some apology and followed. A moment later his footsteps trudged dispiritedly across the ceiling. Adele remained on the couch, hands folded, gazing into the middle distance.

Rebecca picked up the matchbook from the mantelpiece and

held it out. "I don't know whether it's important, but I found this in the hotel attic the day the coin was stolen."

Mackenzie looked not at the match book but at Rebecca while she explained what Michael had said about the pub. His gaze was steely, and again she reminded herself she had nothing to fear from him. "Fleet Street," he repeated. "There aren't as many newspapers there as there once were. Do you know whose number this is?"

"Aye," said Michael from the door. "It's the number of the library at the British Museum."

I see, said Rebecca to herself. *That's interesting.*

If the flicker of Mackenzie's eye was any clue, he found that to be as significant as she did. He handed the matchbook to Devlin. "Carry on with the excavation, Miss Reid. Except for the inquest—day after tomorrow, probably, and we're rushing that—we'll try not to get in your way."

But you're taking Michael, she wanted to wail. Over Mackenzie's shoulder, Michael's ice blue eyes met hers and melted. He winked, but couldn't manage a smile.

The front door opened and shut, leaving her alone with Mark and Adele. Alone with Mark—Adele was obviously engaging in some kind of astral projection. Rebecca hoped she didn't want to hold a seance and ask Sheila who killed her. She shivered violently.

Mark laid a firm, reassuring hand in the small of her back. They went out to the front porch of the house.

Two constables stood sentry on the driveway. The lights in the church had been turned off, and the building was only a dim shape hunkered down in the darkness. Any will-o'-the-wisps were lost in the thin mist that hung over the burn. Michael's Fiat sat forlornly beside the Plantagenet van.

From a centipede-like mass of people at the end of the driveway came shouts of "Have you made an arrest, Chief Inspector? Have you any comment?" Doors slammed. Blue lights winked out as the car disappeared toward Galashiels. Dim shapes started down the driveway only to be intercepted and shooed away by the constables.

The hotel doors opened and shut repeatedly, swallowing the voices of the reporters. All of the windows in the building were alight. The Bairds would have no vacancy, at least until the press got tired of waiting for the police to produce the culprit.

They wouldn't have a chance to get tired, Rebecca assured

herself. Mackenzie and Devlin would realize Michael wasn't their man; he couldn't prove he'd been in the attic but they couldn't prove he hadn't. By this time tomorrow, the real culprit would be jailed, and the dig would be back to normal.

Normal? Sheila was dead. Rebecca might know a murderer. What she didn't know was why. She pressed her temples between her hands. "Damn, we never resolved that argument."

"It won't fester too badly," said Mark. "Not with everything else going on."

Across the stream, in the dark hulk of the church, two points of light suddenly flared. The eyes of the cats. . . . Something moved along her leg and she jumped. Lancelot looked up, hoping for a handout. A shape whisking off the hood of the Fiat was Guinevere. Mark swore, reverently, under his breath.

More tiny flames appeared in the church. Down the wind came the voices that had grown so familiar, words perfectly intelligible. *"Kyrie eleison, Domine pater, miserere. Christe eleison, miserere, qui nos redemisti sanguine tuo et iterum. Kyrie eleison, Domine, Spiritus Sancte, miserere."*

"I'm sorry, too," whispered Rebecca. "Sheila's blood didn't redeem anything."

Mark said with that world-weary, world-wary air that did not gel with his youth, "Rebecca, is there any possibility Michael did kill her?"

So much for that reassuring hand. "No!" She pushed at him, her blow landing square on his chest. "No! No!"

"Miserere," sang the voices. *"Spiritus Sancte, miserere."*

She turned and blundered into the house, but the voices, both Mark's and the uncanny chanting, followed her.

Chapter Ten

THE HARSH BUZZ of the alarm jerked Rebecca into consciousness, her heart pounding. The first thing she saw was the smooth spread on the second bed. She'd lain awake for hours, knotted and shivering, that bed's emptiness like a chasm at her side. When darkness faded into dawn, she'd at last dozed off, only to grope through a scarlet-tinted nightmare. Now a metallic taste clogged her throat, like that of blood.

She rose, groaning, every muscle as sore as her mind. Quickly she dressed and grabbed some toast and coffee from the kitchen, avoiding the uncomprehending eyes of the students. Yes, the murder really did happen, she thought. Last night they'd all been stunned. Now the shock was wearing off, and everyone was feeling pain.

Rebecca hurried outside and up the driveway. A curtain of mist hid the face of the priory. Shutting doors and curt voices sounded unnaturally loud, as if armies moved invisibly through the haze. Several bobbies were gathered on Jedburgh Street, sharing sips from a thermos, waiting to be sent into battle. The hotel lobby smelled of coffee and bacon. Laurence stood talking to Jerry and Tony, his beard bristling like a porcupine. ". . . impossible to carry on as if nothing's happened, but I think we should . . ."

Tony spoke to the toes of his shoes, as lugubriously as an undertaker. Jerry grimaced like Teddy Roosevelt contemplating San Juan Hill. Laurence nodded encouragement and hurried off. Rebecca shut the door to the office, muffling the sounds of dishes and cutlery and speculation.

All Laurence had wanted, she thought, was to restore and present Rudesburn and make himself a living. All she had wanted was work and Michael. She did want Michael. . . . Sighing, Rebecca sat down and dialed Directory Enquiries.

At the third hotel she tried in Durham she found Colin. The desk clerk dispatched someone into the dining room to look for him; when he answered, he was still chewing. "Eh, hello, MacLeod here."

"Colin, this is Rebecca. In Rudesburn."

"Well, good mornin'! This is a surprise."

"Oh, Colin, surprise is an understatement." She steadied her voice. "You remember Sheila Fitzgerald, don't you?"

"The bitch-goddess of the European Community?"

Rebecca winced. "She's been murdered, and the police suspect Michael."

There was silence—broken after a moment by a distinct gulp.

"Colin? I'm sorry, that was rather abrupt."

"Just draggin' my toes out of my tonsils. Murder? Michael?"

Rebecca told him the tale. She concluded, more lamely than she'd have liked, "Don't you think Michael's family ought to know? The police haven't actually arrested him, and I assume they can only hold him so long without charging him, but he probably could use a lawyer . . ."

"Don't you worry. He's innocent, and he'll be back before you know it."

"Thank you, Colin. I'm so glad to hear you make that assumption."

"I've known Michael since he was eighteen. He has a temper, right enough, but bein' capable of violence is another matter. What happened at Dun Iain last winter bein' the exception that proves the rule."

Memory traced cold fingers down Rebecca's back. The most important memory was of Michael's thistle-covered integrity. "Yes," she said.

"What about the dig?" Colin went on. "Is everyone goin' to stick it?"

"I just saw Laurence talking to Tony and Jerry, telling them to carry on, I gather. The volunteers are upset, no doubt about it, but dammit, Sheila's death would be an even greater waste if we abandoned the work we've already done and ran away whimpering. Not that running away isn't tempting." The pulse in her throat beat a litany: *Who killed Sheila? Why?*

"Steady on," said Colin soothingly. "I suppose the police would like to talk to me, since I was there yesterday?"

"Yes, they would."

"I'll come round this afternoon. If they haven't released Michael by then, we'll get on to a solicitor. As for the family— well, they're all level-headed people. I'll ring Andrew, let him know what's goin' on."

"Thank you, Colin. I really appreciate it. See you later." Rebecca hung up. All she'd done was spread the worries out like a farmer spreading fertilizer. And she'd thought she had worries on the interminable plane ride across the Atlantic.

She slumped in the chair while she called the British liaison of the University Archeological Network. Yes, the students were all right. None of them seemed to be involved. She'd keep the Network posted.

A glossy photograph lay on Laurence's desk. In this country, all someone had to do to get a good picture was take off the lens cap and trip the shutter. But Tony got great pictures. This was one of his best, taken from the Law late in the afternoon, the ruins and the village as meticulously defined as a drawing in a textbook. A human body walked up the driveway, and another stood by the wheel-cross. The cats chased a mouse or something beside one of the grave stones, and the black-faced sheep ruminated behind the Craft Centre. Maybe with Tony in charge the film would be an honest one. Not as flashy, but honest.

Yes, the show must go on. Michael wouldn't want her to be distracted from the gathering of knowledge, from the vital career step, from the . . . "Right bluidy cock-up," she said aloud, in a fair imitation of his accent. At least she could be sure Mackenzie and Devlin hadn't strung him up and tortured him all night. He'd probably get a better cup of tea from them than he could at the American-infested cottage.

Rebecca forced her way, head down, through the group of reporters leaving the hotel and the police entering. Harry Devlin stood outside deploying the rest of the bobbies. "Have you let Michael—Dr. Campbell—go yet?" she asked him.

"He's still helpin' us with our enquiries, miss," Devlin returned. His basilisk stare wasn't any milder; he probably hadn't gotten any sleep last night, either.

Two constables stood in the doorway of the Plantagenet van, speaking quietly to a suited figure inside, ". . . copies of those photos of all the expedition members." Rebecca walked across the footbridge toward the priory, Devlin's steps behind her like the ominous hoofbeats of the Apocalypse.

The morning was clearing. It wasn't as warm as yesterday; the air held a tentative breath of chill. The stones of the priory were damp. Whatever ghostly shapes and voices had thronged there last night, only humans were there this morning, if she counted Simon Mackenzie, who was speaking with Grant by the porch of the church. Beyond them the lenses of reporters glinted like crocodile eyes just above the perimeter wall. Various officers, some in blue uniforms, some in suits, prowled the ruins, the grounds, and the village itself.

Tony wandered disconsolately from trench to trench, every now and then peering through his camera. Jerry leaned against a buttress of the church, nursing a cigar, eyes unfocused. Elaine's back was against the cloister wall as she entered information from data sheets into the computer. Beside her Adele scrubbed bits of carved masonry with a toothbrush. Mark troweled the pavement in the third trench, his shoulder against one of the stone piers of the undercroft. Hilary and her drawing board perched nearby, her pencil poised but unmoving. They were like actors waiting for the director to shout "Action!," only playing at their tasks, in reality watching each other, waiting, listening for cues.

Rebecca ducked into the church. A critical glance showed her the boxes of excavated artifacts—unglamorous but vital bits of pottery, metal and stone—were still stacked beneath the table in the chancel. Rearranged but not disemboweled. That would have been the last straw, if in their zeal to find clues to the present the police had ruined any clues to the past.

Through the doorway Rebecca saw Grant pace off across the lawn, hands folded behind his back. Dennis, hunched like a schoolboy summoned to the headmaster's office, responded to Mackenzie's gesture and sat down on the porch step. Devlin joined them, taking out his notebook and a fingerprint kit. Mackenzie thrust his hands into his pockets, tilted his head to the side, and spoke. Dennis started, shaking his head emphatically.

Rebecca went outside. Hilary glanced up, saying under her breath, "So far he's asked everyone what they were wearing last night, and whether Michael was wearing the same T-shirt at dinner that he was in the sitting room later. He was, wasn't he—the red one with the Dr. Who logo?"

"Yeah," said Rebecca. "Not a bloodstain on it." She selected a trowel and slipped into the trench beside Mark.

"I'm sorry," he said. "That was pretty tactless of me, asking you if Michael could've killed her."

"Tactless, yes, but understandable. You don't know Michael," Rebecca reassured him.

Mark's trowel clinked against the stone. Rebecca started scraping. She caught herself listening and realized it was the beautifully moderated if gracelessly didactic tones of Sheila's voice she was missing.

Concentrate, she ordered herself. The familiar chalk and loam odor of the earth filled her nostrils. The pattern of the paving stones beneath her trowel changed from regular horizontal layering to a less precise diagonal. An experimental poke with the tip of the trowel, and she found rows of thicker stones abutting the pier. Beyond that was the edge of the wall.

"Back corner of the cellar," Mark said. "Probably where they swept all the dust."

"And straw and fruit pits and dead rats and God only knows what, it being the Middle Ages," returned Rebecca. "Look how the pattern of the stones changes here, as if someone had pried them up and re-laid them."

Mark's forefinger dug a furrow in the dirt between the stones. "Maybe they were building a sewer. Although I'd expect the drains to be over there, close to the infirmary. And I'd expect them to get the stonemasons in to do the job more tidily than this."

"Let's give Jerry a chance to earn his keep," said Rebecca.

"Yes, ma'am." Mark pulled himself out of the trench and summoned Jerry. Rebecca scooted out of the way. Dennis was still sitting on the steps, writhing under Mackenzie's scrutiny. Anyone would have thought poor Dennis had a guilty conscience, his face was so pale and sweaty. Clever, to start with if not the weakest then the youngest link in the chain of suspects.

Grant was accosted by a reporter. Another constable walked over the footbridge carrying a brown cardboard portfolio. A third waved a car into the driveway, from which emerged two bobbies and Michael. They walked into the cottage; he waited on the step, his tired, unshaven face attempting a smile and failing utterly. "Good mornin' to you, lassie," he called across the water.

Rebecca pushed Jerry aside and sprinted toward the cottage.

In the vestibule, she and Michael embraced warily. "Are you all right?"

"Of course. What do you think they were doin' to me?" He waved his hand. "I only shed one wee drop of blood, see?"

She focused on his bandaid-shrouded finger. "A blood test? Why?"

"To put it bluntly, someone'd been shaggin' Sheila right afore she died. Someone wi' A-positive blood. Like mine."

Rebecca's stomach lurched, and she swallowed. "A-positive is common enough. So was Sheila. It could've been anyone."

"Oh, I dout they'll be takin' donations from all the men."

His voice thinned and broke, and he turned abruptly into the bedroom. He'd probably been dwelling on what the pathologists had done to Sheila to get that particular piece of evidence. Had done to Sheila's body, that is. The body in which he'd once found comfort.

Rebecca followed Michael into the bedroom and shut the door. He stood staring into the closet. In spite of herself, Rebecca visualized Sheila knotted with him in an act of love. Not that it had been love, Michael had admitted. But they must have laughed together; they must have shared that secret smile of lovers. Making love, like making anything, left debris behind, be it affection or hatred or regret caught like cockleburrs in the throat.

Decisively Michael seized a pair of jeans and a plain white T-shirt. Rebecca sat down on the bed and told him about her conversation with Colin.

"I'd rather Mum and Dad and Maddy hear it from him than from the evening news. And it'll well and truly be on the news." He sat heavily down beside her. "I'll ring them the afternoon, tell them I've no been shipped off to Dartmoor."

Rebecca wouldn't even consider her family hearing the news. Hopefully distance would absorb the shock waves. "Do you know if the police have found the murder weapon yet?"

"Apparently no, judgin' by the way they're still turnin' the place ower." He nodded toward the footsteps echoing from the rest of the cottage. "Sergeant Devlin did share another result of the post mortem wi' me, though; the murder weapon was aboot seven inches long and had a serrated edge. It was probably my sgian dubh."

Rebecca moaned, "I was afraid of that."

"I didna do it, lass." His eyes, slate blue with exhaustion, glanced off her face rather than touching it.

"I know you didn't." She avoided his eyes, too. It hurt to see his defenses breached like this. It hurt to not know whether he wanted her to acknowledge the damage. "I know," she ended lamely.

With slow deliberation he pulled on clean socks. "They may have let me go for noo, but they told me no to leave the dig, even for Edinburgh. If you want to go to the flat this weekend, you'll have to drive yoursel'."

"I don't think I'm ready to drive myself, not yet. I mean, I made it all the way across the Forth Bridge that time, but then forgot I was driving a standard and stalled out at the toll booth. And that was better than I did the weekend before, on those one-lane roads in the Lake District. I swear, just when you think no one's been over those roads since the Romans built them, you round a bend, and there's a herd of sheep . . ." Her voice trailed off.

He was still looking at his socks. "If you're stayin' here in the UK, you'll have to learn to clutch and shift and stay on the left, sheep or no."

"And not expect you to take care of me," she concluded. "That was just my point yesterday, wasn't it?"

He glanced up. Their eyes met like flint striking flint.

A policewoman opened the door. "Oh, sorry," she said, and backed away.

The spark went out. *Hell of a time for an intimate discussion,* Rebecca wailed silently, and clenched her fists in her lap. No wonder their emotional drawbridges were slamming shut. The murder had violated not only the victim, but everyone.

She bounded to her feet and picked up Michael's discarded clothing. He collapsed on the bed, eyes closed, hands folded like William Salkeld's effigy. Like Sheila's body laid ritually in the tomb. But he hadn't seen that. "Rebecca," he murmured, "when this is ower, love. When it's ower . . ."

What? she asked mutely, but he said nothing more. He probably didn't have any more to say.

"Take a nap. I'll be at the dig." She kissed his forehead and went through the kitchen, where a constable was narrowly inspecting each carving knife, out the back door, across the stream, and back up the lawn.

Dennis was setting up a camera on a tripod. His color was

better now, less sickly. In fact, when he glanced up and saw Rebecca. he flushed. "Er," he called, "may I speak to you a moment?"

Mackenzie and Devlin were just inside the church, in close consultation with Grant, the reporter he'd been talking to, and two other constables. What did that reporter have to offer that the others didn't? And what was in the brown portfolio Mackenzie was peering at so intently?

Hilary, Adele. and Elaine bent to their tasks. Tony jockeyed along the trench, sighting his camera between Jerry's and Mark's backs. directed by Jerry's hand which waved above the earth like a shark's fin above the water.

"I'm sorry," Dennis mumbled to Rebecca. "I—well—I thought I really ought to tell them, you know."

Rebecca thought he was going to confess to taking an extra cookie at dinner last night. "What, Dennis?"

"I took Michael's dagger and gave it to Sheila."

Rebecca felt her jaw unhinge and fall almost to her chest. "What?"

"She asked me to get it for her, said she was going to play a trick on Michael. I didn't realize—I thought she was chapped because he liked you better, I didn't know about . . ." The boy's face was contorted with honesty. "I didn't know what was going to happen. She said it was a joke."

Rebecca managed to close her mouth. She wanted to demand, "How could you do such a thing?" The croak that emerged from her throat was, "Nobody can tell the future, Dennis. And Sheila could be pretty persuasive, I'll admit." *Especially for an unsophisticated kid like you,* she added to herself. Chances were the joke would have been on Dennis, not Michael. "You told Mackenzie?"

"Yes. He just nodded, you know. Didn't really react."

Rebecca knew. "Honesty is the best policy," she said, her attempt to smile failing as miserably as Michael's had.

"Er—ah—will you tell Michael? I don't think I can."

"I think it's up to you, Dennis." From the corner of her eye Rebecca saw Michael's tall, slender shape emerge from the house and walk toward the footbridge. Stubborn, she thought. He'd rather be tortured by the C.I.D. than reveal how badly he was shaken. Even to her, it seemed . . . But then, she'd asked for that.

"Okay," Dennis mumbled. He turned back to the camera and

adjusted a dial. His expression was that of a child expecting a blow, a mockery of his usual good-natured innocence.

Grant, the reporter, and the two constables headed toward the village. Mackenzie stepped out onto the porch and called, "Mrs. Garrity, may we speak to you, please?" He seated Adele on the stone step as gallantly as if he held a chair for her in a restaurant. Graciously, she submitted to fingerprinting.

Elaine's face was so near to the screen of the computer that Rebecca wondered if she were rearranging the pixels with her nose. Michael peered into the trench and said with ghastly levity, "What're you on aboot wi' my pavement?"

Jerry glanced up. "So you're back. Couldn't pin anything on you, could they?"

"Could be because there's naething to pin," Michael replied, barely concealing the edge of resentment in his voice.

"We're going to raise these paving stones," said Mark, "and see just why they're laid differently from the rest."

Tony's camera clicked. Michael chose a trowel. Rebecca picked up a toothbrush and started scrubbing the masonry. She would have liked to scrub the dirt from the crevices of her mind. The murderer was from somewhere else, not even a villager, someone from Sheila's past who'd met her here last night. Not one of her own colleagues.

Adele spoke calmly and quietly to Mackenzie, and at last he let her return to work. Rebecca gave her a quick lesson on cleaning masonry: "Don't be afraid to scrub hard. There are layers and layers of grundge to get off." Probably Mackenzie lectured Devlin with those same precepts.

Tony's puppet face curved down like a mask of tragedy. He spent most of his interview shrugging in bewilderment, not least when one of the attending constables showed him the contents of the portfolio. Rebecca craned her neck, but could see only a sheaf of papers.

Jerry's interview coincided with lunch. Michael declined food, saying the fried bread from the police canteen in Galashiels was unfortunately still with him. Rebecca herded her flock to the cottage, pressed soup and crackers upon them, then herded them back. They found Jerry still pacing truculently up and down before impassive Mackenzie, while Devlin held the portfolio under one arm and wrote busily. All three faces turned toward Rebecca as she walked across the lawn, making her feel like a beauty contestant trying to slink down the runway without stumbling. *What about me?* she wondered, and answered herself, *I'll probably be next.*

Elaine was next. She sat, arms crossed, her denim-clad knees pressed tightly together, shaking her head. Once she fumbled in her pocket for a cigarette. No one offered to light it for her, and she held it foolishly for a few moments before shredding it to bits and grinding the flakes into the grass with the heel of her shoe.

A medical officer appeared to take blood samples from all the men. Tony stood stoically silent, Dennis looked sick and had to sit down on the wall. Jerry complied, muttering about American consulates and the Bill of Rights. Mark barely paid attention, holding out his dirty hand from the depths of the trench. Mackenzie looked on abstractedly. *He knows,* Rebecca told herself, *that the man who made it with Sheila last night wasn't necessarily the person who killed her.* The blood tests were just a formality, just official harassment, part of the process of peeling and exposing everyone concerned, innocent or not, to the harsh eye of—of what? Justice?

A constable appeared with several computer printouts. Mackenzie looked over them, then cast a long speculative look at the faces around him. Devlin's brows arched expressively, and he nodded.

Rebecca quelled her growing irritation; she was beginning to feel like the victim of an elaborate practical joke. Despite the slightly hazy sunlight, the afternoon shadows were dark with suspicion. The human figures scattered across the lawns moved in slow motion, their voices distorted. *God,* Rebecca thought. *I'm already sick and tired of this.* She told Dennis to scoop the rich dark dirt the men had piled on the edge of the third trench into a bucket, take it to the rubbish tip, and sift it.

Hilary slumped onto the stone step of the porch, head bowed, and spoke so quietly that Devlin's and Mackenzie's foreheads collided above her scarf-adorned ponytail. When Mark's turn came, he spoke solemnly and sat stiffly. Mackenzie nodded, Devlin capped his pen, and Mark walked away with several frowning glances over his shoulder.

By now a dozen rounded cobbles were ranged on the side of the trench, and Tony lay on his stomach the better to focus inside. "Backfill, right enough," said Michael to Mark when he returned.

"Hilary!" Jerry shouted, and the girl hurried over to accept either a button or a coin from his hand.

Amazing, Rebecca thought. Jerry and Michael were actually working as a team. Nothing like getting rid of Sheila's baleful influence. . . . "Miss Reid!" Mackenzie called. "May we speak to you now?" Her hands jerked on the handle of the spade. How, she asked herself, could a man so perfectly non-judgmental make her feel so guilty?

Nora came across the grass carrying a tray of tea and sandwiches. Devlin gulped thirstily and then bit into a sandwich like a lion bringing down an antelope. Mackenzie peered into his cup, then pulled a sprig of cress from the sandwich and chewed it with his front teeth.

"Dr. Campbell has a phone call," Nora announced. "Dr. Graham from the Museum in Edinburgh, on behalf of the Historic Buildings and Monuments lot. Laurence talked to him, and now he wants to talk to Michael."

"In other words," said Michael, "what the hell is the expedition doin' on the front pages of the papers?"

He and Nora walked off toward the hotel. Mackenzie watched them go, his dark eyes flat. Rebecca wondered if he was any better at reading body language than she'd been today. She could guess at Michael's internal turmoil because she knew him, but even so, his face was closed and locked. As for the others—what they were thinking was anybody's guess.

"Miss Reid," Mackenzie called again.

Rebecca sat on the stone step. Its chill seeped through the denim of her jeans. The wheel-cross rose before her, its weathered face as uncompromising as a Bible held out to swear in a witness. Mackenzie sat down beside her and gazed off across the stream, presumably collecting his thoughts about motive, opportunity, and means.

The wind was picking up. Its damp breath moaned through the empty door of the church, making the grass bend and the willows dance. The back of Rebecca's neck itched. Odd, how of all the emotions she'd felt in the last twenty-four hours she hadn't felt fear. Until now.

Chapter Eleven

REBECCA WONDERED IN an odd dispassionate weariness whether she was afraid of Mackenzie and Devlin or whether she was simply frightened of circumstances beyond her control. She'd done nothing—the police officers were no threat to her or to Michael or to anyone who played fair with them.

Supposedly. Circumstantial evidence was like putty. It could be stretched, bounced, and imprinted with images. No. What frightened her was not the police, but not knowing whether the murderer's secret agenda had been satisfied by Sheila's death.

A good night's sleep would help, she told herself. Time and distance would help. But only finding the murderer would solve anything. And deciding whether that time and distance would come between her and Michael.

Devlin rolled her fingertips across his ink pad and pressed them onto the paper without making eye contact. *Just a job, eh?* she asked him silently. Mackenzie rested his elbows on his knees and cradled his cup between his hands, gazing out over the vista of lawn, bridge, and village. "Well, now," he said at last, "we're trying to make up a timetable of last evening."

"I stayed in the cottage until I went to the Craft Centre at eight," Rebecca reported obediently. "I stayed there about an hour, then met Hilary outside the hotel. We walked over here to get the day's printouts. That's when we found Sheila's—found Sheila."

Behind her back Devlin's pen stopped scratching. Notebook pages flipped. "Bridget thought you came in somewhat after eight."

Rebecca frowned. It wasn't fair, she hadn't known she'd need to account for her movements. "I stood on the step looking around for a few minutes before I went in."

Still Mackenzie scanned the picture postcard scene rather than looking at her, as though, like a blind man, he was hypersensitive to nuances of sound.

"I passed Elaine in the parking lot," Rebecca went on, "and Laurence on the street. Dennis and Tony were in the van, but they probably didn't see me."

"Who saw you in the cottage earlier?"

"Mark and Hilary were in the kitchen, but they didn't know I was there." *I hope,* she added to herself. She stole a quick dubious glance toward Hilary's bowed head, her face concealed by the fluttering end of her scarf.

"Did you see Dr. Campbell at any time?" Mackenzie asked.

"No, but I saw the lights on in the attic of the hotel, through the skylights, when Hilary and I were walking over to the church."

"You're engaged to be married to him?"

She hesitated. Mackenzie turned, striking her with the full force of his eyes. Almost involuntarily, as if he'd jerked the words out of her mind like a fisherman jerking a salmon out of a river, she answered, "I don't know."

"You are lovers, then."

"Yes."

"And he was Miss Fitzgerald's lover two years ago?"

"Yes."

"Was the parting amicable?"

"No."

"How did he feel about her being here?"

"Very annoyed."

"Were you jealous of her?"

Blame the murderer, she told herself, not the police, for this inexorable invasion of privacy like the drop, drop, drop of water torture. "Not jealous, no. Indignant that she'd treat him cruelly; bewildered that he saw anything in her to begin with. But that all happened before we met. It wasn't any of my business until she showed up here and started making snide remarks."

Devlin repeated quietly, "Not jealous?"

"I would've said I despised her, until last night," Rebecca said, responding to Mackenzie's imperturbable expression rather than Devlin's innuendo. "After she argued with Michael, I caught a glimpse of her face. She was desperate for attention. I was actually sorry for her."

"Dr. Campbell says he didn't hit her."

"He didn't. She was hanging onto him, and he shook her away."

"But Dr. Kleinfelter is correct in that Miss Fitzgerald was reminding Dr. Campbell of an argument you had with him yesterday?"

"I couldn't hear what they were saying, except when Michael told her, 'Leave us alone.' She could've been lurking outside the window when we were arguing—we weren't exactly whispering."

"What did you argue about?" asked Devlin.

Rebecca's jaw twinged. "Over personal and professional matters. Not over Sheila. We agreed about her." *If I'd only kept my mouth shut,* she thought. *But no. If that argument killed anything, it wasn't Sheila.*

Mackenzie drained his tea and set the cup down on the tray. Rebecca had to wonder about a man who kept his tie knotted all day long. No wonder Devlin's eyes bulged belligerently above the knot at his own throat. There was competition in those ties.

"Miss Fitzgerald was small and slim," said Mackenzie, half to himself. "Anyone, man or woman, who was moderately fit could have dragged her body across the gravel and the grass. And could have been seen through the church door." He asked Rebecca, "You didn't see anything odd in the church when you were walking toward the Craft Centre?"

"There're usually odd things in the church in the evening. The local people could tell you that."

"Right," Devlin said.

Mackenzie glanced up at him, not at all humorlessly.

"Even Sheila came rushing out of the church yesterday as if she'd seen a ghost," Rebecca went on. "I hoped she had. She'd been sneering at the very idea of anything supernatural, and yet she was making up a ghost story scenario for the film using the nun's habit . . ." She stopped, seeing the white cloth stained with blood. What if Adele was right about unbelievers being punished? What if Sheila had been murdered by the spirits she had teased? Rebecca told herself, *Yeah, and the moon is made of green cheese.*

"Mr. Owen told us about Miss Fitzgerald's running out of the church," Mackenzie said. "That seems to have been the last time anyone saw her near these airts—alive, that is. My lads have had a go at everyone in the village, from P.C. Johnston's children to the old man in the toy shop. Everyone was inside eating, or watching the telly, or in Galashiels shopping. And several people went to a wedding. No one saw anything.''

"Or they're not admitting it if they did. But you realize that.''

"I realize that.''

Rebecca continued, "You think she was killed with Michael's sgian dubh, don't you? But you haven't found it, or any clothing stained with blood.''

"Aye, we think it was the sgian dubh. But it's easy enough to speculate. Now, if you don't mind, I'm asking the questions here.''

Mackenzie reached over his shoulder. Devlin handed him a computer printout. "We're checking everyone's antecedents—standard procedure, mind you. So far the only record we've obtained from the States is yours. I see that you and Dr. Campbell had some trouble in Ohio last winter.''

She'd been expecting this. She looked down at her hands clasped between her scuffed and dirty knees. "Yes, we've seen violent death before.''

"The inquest ruled self-defense during the prevention of a crime.''

"We prevented the crime, not the death. Sometimes I think we caused the death.'' She could feel Mackenzie's look cutting through her sweatshirt and jeans, flesh and bone, as if he were reading her mind. Maybe he wished he could read minds; it would make his job much easier. But his careful use of last names was either an effort to bring some kind of dignity to the undignified crime or an effort to save his sanity by keeping his distance. Mindreading would be insanity.

He flipped to another page of the printout. "Your instructor at the University of Missouri was Dr. Nelson.''

"You didn't leave any stones unturned, did you?'' Rebecca replied, more admiringly than flippantly.

"Your archeologist friends have nothing on us, Miss Reid. Dr. Nelson gave you a glowing reference and then mentioned something about Dr. Kleinfelter. Would you explain that?''

Great. Like a virus, that rumor kept coming back. She explained about the excavation in Virginia, Laurel Matheny, the wronged research assistant, Kleinfelter's ego, the possible job in London, and the heart of Robert the Bruce.

She concluded by darting a glance over her shoulder to Jerry's and Mark's intense, dirt-smeared faces. They must think they were onto something. Tony had the video camera out now; Dennis was wielding a light. Hilary was sketching busily, holding that button or coin or whatever in the palm of her hand. Adele was clearing away the dirt. Rebecca grimaced, feeling left out. But then, Michael wasn't there either, and Elaine sat on the periphery, smoking a cigarette.

"Did Dr. Kleinfelter know you'd heard that rumor?" asked Mackenzie.

"I don't see how. We thought it would be unprofessional to mention it, especially to the Bairds. Of course, you can also accuse us of being unprofessional because we never told him about the relic heart. Whether he knew about that anyway—well, I thought I heard him mention it once." Rebecca sighed. "If his ego is as advertised, so is his competence. We haven't caught him in one underhanded thing. Besides that charade of the alembic."

"How do you spell that?" Devlin asked.

Rebecca told him, and explained about the filmed dishonesty.

"So," said Mackenzie. "Miss Fitzgerald, at the least, wasn't above a wee bit of fiddling with the evidence."

"Did Sheila know about Jerry's alleged malfeasance?" Devlin asked.

"I have no idea," Rebecca replied. "She might have, but I doubt if it would've bothered her any."

"Could she have been holdin' it over him?"

"Blackmail?" Rebecca paused. "No, it looked to me as if they were working together to get publicity for the film."

Mackenzie said, as indifferently as if reading a news report, "Dr. Kleinfelter admitted he'd been Miss Fitzgerald's lover in London this spring. He said, 'Well, it was just lying there for the taking.' "

"He would say something like that, wouldn't he?" Rebecca snapped. "And he'd take everything he could get."

"Mr. Wright," Mackenzie added, "seems to accept that his sexual favors were part of his job."

Devlin muttered something. Rebecca shifted on the cold stone. Sheila had been pathetic. "I can't see Jerry having a motive to kill Sheila any more than the Bairds would kill her in order to sell beer to the reporters. Unless he was desperate to slow down the dig, to get some time alone after the volunteers have to leave, but that hardly seems credible."

"Even if he had inside knowledge about what's hidden here?"

"Yeah, well . . ."

Mackenzie gestured. Devlin picked up the cardboard portfolio and handed it to Rebecca. She opened it and drew out its contents.

Her fingertips identified parchment. The tiny, spidery writing, faded to sepia, was probably sixteenth century. Three pages, one complete document, maybe, with a pinkish stain that meant it had once been sealed with wax. At the bottom was a crabbed signature Rebecca knew well: "Henricus Rex."

"My God," she said. She went back to the beginning, tilting the parchment to the sunlight. "Anno 1545. Anne Douglas, Prioress. Thomas Elliot, Commendator. . . . have most grievously, heinously, and wantonly offended in the unnatural, most odious and detestable offenses . . ."

Someone, four hundred years and a few feet away, cleared his throat. Rebecca looked up, blinking, surprised the church behind her was in ruins and that huge rumbling metallic beasts crossed the Gowan Water. "These are the records of Anne Douglas's trial," she said. "Where on earth . . . ?"

"In Miss Fitzgerald's room in the hotel." A distant flicker in Mackenzie's eye, like heat lightning in the midst of gray cloud, betrayed that he'd been testing her knowledge. "We'll have to take them away for lab work. But you can have them back in a week or so. We'd like a translation as much as you would Dr. Kleinfelter says the sixteenth century is your field."

So that's why they'd been looking at her. "Did Sheila steal this from the British Museum? Did Tony know she had it? Did Jerry?"

"We suppose so, no and, very grudgingly, yes."

"So Jerry and Sheila were trying to make an end run around the rest of us!" Rebecca exclaimed, banging her clenched fists on her knees. "I knew it!"

"Excuse me?" asked Devlin. "An end run?"

"American football analogy. Trying to get to the important finds first and take credit for them. I bet one of them dropped that matchbook in the attic. But I can't see them stealing the coin and the warrant . . ." Her moment's elation evaporated. "But Jerry didn't actually break any rules, did he? If anyone stole anything, or cheated, it was Sheila. Damn."

Rebecca shot a rueful gaze toward Jerry's khaki-clad back as he stood, one hand on his hip, the other slashing the air like a general giving orders to his troops. Mark, Tony, and Dennis nodded in time, their faces reflecting varying degrees of understanding and agreement. Adele carried a bucket of dirt through the cloister and out the slype. The willow branches danced in the breeze, their tips etching the rush of the stream. The shadow of the cross extended toward the church like an accusing finger.

Mackenzie held out his hand. Rebecca gave back the papers. Her fingers tingled from the touch of ancient hands. Much good those fingerprints would do Mackenzie and his minions. "You won't damage them, will you? Those are priceless documents. Like the warrant."

The Chief Inspector tucked the papers into the portfolio and tied the string. "We haven't found that yet, have we? But you'll get these and the gold coins back, I assure you."

"Yeah. That extra coin. Where did it come from, anyway?"

"Do you remember P.C. Johnston saying he saw Miss Fitzgerald in the call box?"

"Yes. Who was she calling, her gynecologist?" Behind her back Devlin chuckled. She bit her tongue, chiding herself. *I'm not jealous, huh?*

Mackenzie, with laudable aplomb, said only, "No. She was calling Bob Jenkins, a reporter with the *Sunburn*. He was good enough to step forward earlier that day and tell us."

"In the hopes of gettin' a better story in exchange," said Devlin.

"I imagine so," she returned. "And what did she want from him?"

"She told him that the expedition had found gold and suggested that he come write up a story."

"Gold? Did she mean the dragon brooch? Or did she mean the extra coin? In which case she found it herself, but where?" Rebecca grimaced. Her brain hurt, just as surely as if she'd been juggling notes and references and sources for a final exam. The brooch had been taken from the safe and yet had turned up in the cottage. The stolen coin had returned with a mysterious mate. The book of matches was from a pub right around the corner from Fleet Street, newspaper alley. . . . No one had the answers to this exam. "Let me guess. She didn't tell him any more than just gold, did she?"

"No," said Mackenzie. "She promised him an interview with Dr. Kleinfelter, but he says he knows nothing about it."

"She was just trying to get some attention after Michael

shoved her aside,'' Rebecca muttered, ''either from Kleinfelter or from Jenkins or both.''

Mackenzie smoothed his printouts. ''Miss Vavra is from Brixton, part of London, and has grandparents in Spain to whom she sends money on a regular basis. She's held a variety of jobs, from exotic dancer to secretary. Mr. Wright grew up in an industrial ghetto in Liverpool, and unlike his family hasn't been on the dole any more than strictly necessary. Twelve years ago he spent some time in a London youth custody center, for vandalism, but since then his record has been clean.''

Tony, Rebecca mused dully, did a better job of hiding his non-university accent than Elaine. Both wanted to rise above their origins. So did she. Who was Mackenzie to say what was necessary and what wasn't with that goal in sight? And was he inviting her to comment on those tidbits of information? Maybe they all had skeletons in their closets, but she didn't want to rummage through them.

Her jaw ached from keeping her upper lip stiff. She rubbed her temples, squinting in pain. Through her lashes she saw Michael come out of the hotel and start across Jedburgh Street. He stopped dead when a car pulled up beside him. Colin got out. The two men stood close together, speaking quietly and intently.

''Who is that?'' Mackenzie asked.

''Colin MacLeod,'' answered Rebecca. ''A friend of Michael's. He was here yesterday morning. You'd probably like to talk to him, too.''

''The more the merrier,'' said Devlin. Maybe he, rather than Mackenzie, was enjoying a murder investigation. Maybe he'd never been in on one before, Scotland being the civilized country it was. Maybe Mackenzie had.

''Did everyone dislike Sheila?'' The Chief Inspector's eyes followed Michael and Colin as they turned and walked slowly down the driveway.

Rebecca saw Sheila's face, first the artistic, glossily presented one, then the one twisted in pain. ''In varying degrees, yes,'' she replied.

''Who killed her?''

Taken aback, Rebecca shrugged wordlessly.

Mackenzie's silence pressed her for an answer.

Rebecca thought they'd been making a lot of assumptions about who was where when. Just because she heard someone playing a guitar didn't mean it was Mark. Just because a light was on in the upstairs bedroom didn't mean Dennis was there. She'd never seen Adele past 7:30 or so. . . .

She said, "Adele's a nut, but I can't see her hurting anyone. The other students, Mark, Hilary, Dennis, are just as incapable of violence as Michael. Elaine was jealous of Jerry, yes. Tony was more irritated by Sheila's high-handedness than by her—her flirtatiousness. Jerry might have fought with her over the account of the trial, but I don't see why."

Devlin's pen scratched. Colin and Michael crossed the footbridge.

"If you're looking for motives," Rebecca went on, in a kind of weary insolence, "I suppose I have one as much as anyone. Sheila had no right throwing that ridiculous argument in Michael's face. But that's what she was, the mouth that roared. And I can't see how our argument had anything to do with her death."

Mackenzie made no move to leap up and arrest her. Michael and Colin arrived at the trench just as Jerry rose up and shouted, "Quitting time!" As every face, expedition member or police, for a hundred yards around turned to him, he added more quietly, "We'll triangulate, plot, and section the feature tomorrow. Elaine, get a piece of plastic to cover it."

"Well, well," said Michael. He climbed into the trench and knelt, his head disappearing below the rim of earth.

Rebecca couldn't stand it any more. "What is it?" she called.

"Human bones," Mark returned with a cheerful grin.

Mackenzie and Devlin both went to point. "Old ones, I take it," called the Sergeant.

"Oh yes," Jerry replied. "There was a silver penny of Henry the Eighth lying right on top, giving us a *terminus post quem* of when, Rebecca?"

King Henry again. "He reigned from 1509 to 1547. Of course, the coin could've been deposited years later." Jerry acknowledged that fact with a throwaway gesture. "Is it a soldier killed in one of the skirmishes during the Rough Wooing?" Rebecca went on.

"Could be, if you can think of some reason they'd bury him in the back corner of the cellar and not in the cemetery."

"Not some nun's illegitimate baby?" Devlin asked.

"Oh no, no. All we've got is the right femur and kneecap so far, but it's an adult's, and I'm pretty sure a man's."

"They had to fold him up to stuff him into the hole," said Dennis, eyes wide. "I bet it's another murder."

"Somewhat out of Chief Inspector Mackenzie's jurisdiction, though," Jerry amended, with a slight touch of acid in his voice.

"Apparently," Mackenzie agreed equably.

Rebecca envisioned the vaulted cellar, a guttering torch, shadows like deep water just outside the light. She saw the nuns, their white habits stained by dirt and sweat, struggling with the unwieldy weight of a body. . . . The image popped and sprayed her mind with droplets of common sense. Any good historian, she reminded herself, knows better than to create theories without facts. But how nice to make an interesting discovery!

Elaine went into the church. Dennis sidled over to the computer and peered down at its screen. Under the eye of Tony's camera, Adele and Hilary started packing up trowels, buckets, pencils, and brushes. The small round whatever, apparently the penny, went into a jeweler's box. Michael emerged from the pit and spoke to Jerry, Rebecca catching only his first few words: "Dr. Graham said to carry on . . ."

Mackenzie stood and buttoned his jacket. "That's all?" Rebecca wanted to ask him. She wondered whether he knew more than he was telling her, even without knowing the identity of the murderer, or whether he simply wanted her to think he was omniscient. It seemed like a nice psychological game, but it was hardly recreation.

Sheila was dead. Someone she knew was capable of murder.

Mackenzie said quietly, "The inquest is in Galashiels the morn, Miss Reid. I'll be sending an escort for the lot of you at nine ack emma. You'll need to make formal statements before the inquest. Other than that sortie, you and the others will stay in Rudesburn until further notice. And I needn't caution you not to talk to the press—let us handle that."

"All right." She must be numb not to resent his imperious tone.

Elaine brought Jerry's plastic tarpaulin. He and Mark tucked it carefully into the trench. Michael led Colin across the lawn and introduced him to Devlin and Mackenzie. Grant ran the gauntlet of the reporters by the gatehouse and strode purposefully across the lawn.

"Would you mind staying here tonight and attending the inquest tomorrow?" asked the Chief Inspector.

"Not at all," Colin replied. "I can doss down in the sittin' room at the cottage."

One end of Michael's mouth quirked at Rebecca. She quirked back. He extended a hand and pulled her to her feet. In the late afternoon sunlight, the stubble on his unshaven jaw glinted red. *You don't marry someone,* she told herself, *just because you like red hair.* "Did you call your parents?" she whispered. "What did they say?"

"The usual exhortations," he answered, his haggard face softening with a faint smile. "Wear clean underwear, stand up straight, and keep in touch."

Colin glanced meditatively from Rebecca to Michael and back. Well, she had spilled her guts to Mark; why shouldn't Michael spill his to Colin? She offered the bespectacled young man a slight shrug. Their argument had started out as a simple spat. It really shouldn't have concerned anyone but themselves. It might have been resolved by now—with or without a happy ending.

Grant Johnston arrived at the step and handed Devlin an ordinary piece of lined notebook paper that looked as though it had been used to polish a shoe. "I found this in the fireplace in the bar. It'd fallen ahint the grate and was only singed."

Devlin read the paper. He read it again and made a triumphant gesture. "Well done, Constable. This should put us in the picture right enough."

Mackenzie plucked the paper from his grasp. Instead of echoing Devlin's grin, his face creased into a frown. "Dr. Campbell?"

By the sudden twitch in his jaw Rebecca knew Michael had gritted his teeth. "Aye?"

She stood her ground, Colin beside her. Mackenzie, Devlin and Grant stood in a row like See No Evil, Hear No Evil, and Speak No Evil. The paper rustled loudly in a sudden gust of wind. Mark, bent over to brush off his knees, glanced up. His eyes went ice-gray in his dusty, slightly tanned face. He spat a four-letter word.

Mackenzie's ascetic face revealed nothing. He handed Michael the paper. "Can you explain this to us, please?"

"I can't. I've never seen it before."

"Then why are your initials at the bottom?"

Rebecca stepped quietly to Michael's elbow and peered around his arm. Black ink. A strong, swooping masculine script, followed by the initials "M.C." But he didn't write his initials that way, the two ends of the "C" reaching toward each other to almost close a circle. None of it was Michael's writing. His was smaller, slanted to the right, the T's crossed with precision, not with a slashing stroke like a sword cut.

The note was undated, the only heading the one damning word, "Sheila." Then, "All right, I'll bite. I'll meet you at the footbridge at 8 to see the artifact."

"I didn't write this," Michael said. He handed the paper back to Mackenzie and rubbed his hands on his shirt as if to cleanse them. "It's no my handwritin'. And I'd no misspell 'artefact.' "

"It's not misspelled," said Rebecca. "In American English, 'artifact' with an 'i' is correct." And she realized where she'd seen that script before, in a letter confirming a place on the expedition, on the chore lists at the cottage, on various site recording sheets. "That's not a 'C,' " she went on, her words choked to a moan. "It's an 'O.' "

"Written quickly, and unclosed," confirmed Mackenzie. "Mr. Owen?" he called.

"I'm coming," Mark said. Devlin, abashed, studied his notebook.

Rebecca bit her tongue and looked at the dirty toes of her wellies. She heard Mark's steps march across the grass. His boots appeared in her peripheral vision, just beside Michael's. "Sorry," she said.

"I don't want you or anyone to lie for me," Mark returned. And, to Mackenzie, his voice edged not with defiance but with the same tired caution Rebecca had heard in Michael's, he said, "Yeah, I wrote that. Not yesterday, but about ten days ago. A Thursday, I think. I'd forgotten about it."

"Was that the night we saw you and Sheila on the bridge?" asked Michael. "Afore the ceilidh?"

"Yes."

Devlin checked his notebook. "That would've been July the sixth. You saw him with Sheila, Dr. Campbell?"

"Several of us did do. He was only wi' her a few minutes."

"Why, Mr. Owen?" Mackenzie demanded.

Mark's eyes flashed. Mackenzie may have been asking him why he killed Sheila, but he wasn't going to recognize that inference. "She left me a note saying she had an artifact to show me. I was curious."

"Did she show you an artifact?" asked Mackenzie.

"She wanted me to go into the ruins with her. She said she'd

show me there. I decided all she really wanted was my body."
He grimaced, acknowledging his appeal to the opposite sex without dwelling on it. "I told her some other time, I wanted to go to the ceilidh."

"And did she approach you again?"

"She flirted like the rest of us breathe, but she never propositioned me again, no."

Rebecca realized everyone had drifted forward, with the same morbid inquisitiveness that used to impel people to make a picnic out of a public execution. Only Hilary was hanging back, her face turned away.

"Mr. Owen," said Devlin, shutting his notebook with a snap, "I think you'll have to come to Galashiels—"

"To help you with your enquiries," Mark finished. "Sure. Why not?"

"Have a care for the fried bread," offered Michael with a ghost of a smile.

"I wouldn't recommend it myself," Mackenzie said, with a sardonic smile. His teeth were white and even, the eyeteeth extending below the rest. He not only could play Sherlock Holmes or Bernard of Clairvaux, he could play Dracula.

"You haven't been cleared of anything yet," Devlin reminded Michael.

"Thank you. Much obliged." Michael turned and headed briskly toward the bridge and the cottage.

Like a group of pigeons disturbed by a passing step, everyone scattered. Rebecca looked after Michael's stiff retreating back. She looked at Colin's grave face turned toward the cross but not really seeing it. She looked at Hilary, packing her pencils with movements so swift and abrupt that Rebecca could imagine the pencils were daggers and their bags Sheila's corrupt and yet pitiable breast.

Mark, blank-faced, walked between Devlin and Grant toward the road. The reporters swirled around the gatehouse like sharks scenting blood. With a shout a police sergeant recalled the constables who'd been searching the grounds, to no avail, all day long.

Rebecca seized a handful of Mackenzie's suit jacket before he, too, could get away. The fabric was smooth and cool, the arm beneath it as rigid as Michael's spine. "Sheila did have an artifact," Rebecca said. "She had the trial records. Maybe she had the gold coins. If I were you, I'd be keeping an eye on Jerry, not hassling Michael and Mark."

"I'll bear that in mind, Miss Reid."

"Was Sheila killed to settle some private score, or did her death have another reason—something to do with the dig?" she went on.

Mackenzie's voice was so crisp and sharp it almost could have drawn blood. "When we know why she died, then we'll know who killed her. Whether it has anything to do with the dig or not. Now, if you'll excuse me." He pulled away and strode off across the grass, long legs stretching and yet not hurrying to catch up with Devlin, Grant, and Mark.

"When we know why," Rebecca repeated.

She only realized she'd spoken aloud when Colin said sarcastically, "Chance would be a fine thing."

"Oh, no," she told him, with the same vehemence she'd pushed at Mark the night before. "No. Chance has nothing to do with this."

Chapter Twelve

REBECCA PUMMELED THE bread dough. If nothing else, she'd end up with bread as tender as her nerves. *I hate feeling helpless.* Punch. *I hate being manipulated.* Punch. *I hate being indecisive.* Punch.

In the dining room, Colin, Adele, Hilary, and Tony were supposedly playing bridge, but no one was paying much attention to the game. More than once Tony had to be reminded that it was his turn, which the others did with the lead-footed consideration afforded the recently bereaved.

In the sitting room, Elaine's long wheedling sentences were met by monosyllables from Jerry. He must find it supremely frustrating, Rebecca thought, to be barred from the reporters who'd practically taken up residence in the hotel bar. He was the type who insisted on being the bride at every wedding and the corpse at every funeral. But it had been Mackenzie who had conducted the news conference, telling the microphones and cameras what he thought they should know and not one sentence more.

With floury hands Rebecca scooped her hair off her forehead. She was taking the first deep breaths she'd taken in twenty-four hours. Her lungs had been whistling and moaning like Michael's bagpipes when he inflated them. Not surprising she should think of that when Michael was playing them just outside the kitchen window.

Dennis opened the back door, admitted Lancelot and Guinevere, and stepped out. The two cats watched Rebecca as though expecting her to magically transmogrify dough to meat. Taking pity on them, she went to the refrigerator and found them each a morsel of last night's stew. With sharp white teeth the cats snapped the pieces of meat from her fingertips and carried them beneath the staircase, there to go through the ritual of stalking, killing, and eating.

Adele made some comment about life after death. Hurriedly Hilary bid three clubs. Colin countered with another bid and a dissertation on lead miniatures. ". . . Troopin' of the Colours. He let me have the wee Queen at a discount, because I'd helped wi' the dig, and it was his daughter's weddin' day to boot. I was lucky to catch him before he left."

Rebecca whacked the dough a couple more times and rolled it into a ball. She wondered how Mark's slow Texas twang was competing with the rounded vowels and glottal stops of the Scottish constabulary. If Michael had survived, so would Mark. He'd be returned like a cow shooed back into the herd, branded with a scarlet "S" for Suspect. As if they weren't all suspects.

Maybe Mackenzie could tie the gold brooch to a fishing line and leave it out as bait. . . . Rebecca laughed at herself, greased a bowl, and plunked the dough into it. She covered it with a clean dishtowel and placed it on the always-warm Aga. The cats finished their snack and sat washing their faces, black and white paws oddly disembodied in the shadow of the staircase.

But the brooch would only be tempting if Sheila died because of greed. Or else—well, if they all had skeletons in their closets, then she probably had mammoth bones. The murder could have been coldly premeditated before the expedition had started. It could have been committed in a moment's heat, her obnoxious mouth uttering some last straw. It might have been personal or just a business adjustment. "When we know why," Mackenzie had said, "we'll know who."

She knew Michael, Rebecca thought. Through him she knew Colin. And she knew herself. But what about the others? Who might have a motive for murder?

Jerry. His reputation was inconsistent, to say the least. Rebecca snorted indignantly at his letting the trial records sit there untranslated and unused. Even if Jerry was an archeologist, not a historian, he would have known the value of written records. What was he planning to do, produce them with a flourish as soon as he had someth.ng to report to a new conference?

Sheila, with her museum background, would have known the importance of those records. But how they fit in with Devlin's theory of blackmail, Rebecca couldn't tell. Sheila seemed too smart to resort to blackmail when she had so many other methods of getting what she wanted.

Rebecca dumped her measuring cups and bowls into the sink, turned on the hot water, and gave the bottle of washing-up liquid a vicious squeeze. She needed to make sure Mackenzie understood the importance of those records.

Adele. She was searching for reassurance. Hilary. She was licking her wounds after . . . Rebecca hoped it was a failed relationship and not something worse. Mark. He admitted to a difficult past, but smoothly evaded any specifics. What a shame Mark and Hilary couldn't get together; they'd each have something worthwhile to offer.

People who lived in emotional glass houses, Rebecca told herself, shouldn't throw spitballs. She piled the soapy dishes in the drainer and poured hot water over them, wishing for a good old American sink with one spigot for both hot and cold water.

Dennis. He'd dutifully told Michael about taking the sgian dubh. Michael's clashing brows and exasperated, "For God's sake, man, why?" hadn't been unreasonable, considering. But all evening poor Dennis had walked around, head hanging, like a child told he couldn't go out at recess. Apparently confession wasn't as good for the soul as it was cracked up to be.

Tony. Elaine. They had similarly poor, even shady, backgrounds. Mackenzie had named one of Elaine's earlier professions "exotic dancer"; Rebecca wondered if she'd worked in a fancy nightclub or a sleazy strip joint. Tony had been in a juvenile delinquent program for vandalism, a sure sign of youthful frustration. Sheila might have been blackmailing either of them, but whom could she threaten to tell when those wretched little clods of dirt were already in the public record?

In the twilight, the priory lay across its lawns in expectant, almost nervous silence, like a veiled bride waiting for her groom. Nuns were brides of Christ. Such a spiritual consummation was all very noble, but Rebecca was willing to bet it left a frustrated itch in the pit of the stomach.

Cautiously, she remembered the first time she and Michael had made love. He'd joked afterward that he now knew how it felt to throw oneself on an exploding grenade. But in time familiarity damped explosiveness into comfort; sex was only part of marriage, after all. If the familiarity of marriage bred only indifference, the couple was lucky; so often it did breed contempt. Rebecca heard Mark saying, "Come on now, can you really see yourself acting that way?" Again she answered, *No, that's something else that has nothing to do with chance.*

Holding his pipes like a child would hold a stuffed animal, Michael coaxed music from bag and chanter. The weft of the melody and the warp of the drones wove themselves into a fabric of emotion colored with wind and water. Rebecca half expected an antiphonal response from the priory. But no music other than the high, clear, silver voice of the pipes touched the dusk.

Michael paced solemnly up and down the terrace. "Fingal's Weeping" segued into "Heather Island" into "If I Was a Blackbird." Of course he'd be playing the slow airs. . . . Rebecca clutched the dishtowel, the next song hitting her like a slap. "Ferry me over, ferry me there; to leave the hills of Caledonia is more than my heart can bear." It had been when he was piping that ballad at Dun Iain that she'd begun to realize how she felt about him.

His fingers moved on the chanter—magician's hands, producing doves from midair. He played "Mo Nighean Donn, Gradh Mo Cridhe," "My brown-haired lass, love of my heart."

It didn't matter whether Rebecca was actually hearing or just imagining the plea in that music. She had more control over the relationship than over anything else at the moment. She vowed over the rack of clean dishes to keep their misunderstanding from getting infected.

The music stopped. Rebecca was startled to realize she was still inside the house. The card players were sitting with abstracted expressions, Tony smoothing his cards, Colin inspecting the ceiling, Hilary leaning on her elbow. Even the cats lay quietly on the stair, ears pricked, eyes gleaming gold slits.

Adele came into the kitchen and ran herself a glass of water. "You have to get in touch with your feelings," she said.

"That's just the problem. I'm not only in touch with my feelings, I'm grappling with them. Can't you see their fingerprints on my throat?"

Adele contemplated that for a moment and realized Rebecca was joking. She smiled politely. "That's the trouble with men. They've been condemned for so long for expressing their feelings, they don't know how even if they want to. You couldn't read my husband with a reading lamp, but then, he was a man of his generation. No wonder he died of a heart attack. As for

Chris . . .'' She paused, her pale eyes focused beyond the window, beyond the dusk itself.

Rebecca waited.

"He was a lot better at expressing what troubled him," the older woman continued. "Until there at the end. He never told anyone then. If you'll excuse me." She turned and walked with steady steps up the stairs, avoiding the cats as they lay like fur wraps on the treads.

Rebecca frowned. She didn't like the implications of that. How many people around here had those rattling, grinning skeletons, anyway?

Dennis's baritone filtered in from the back porch. "Oh, Shenandoah, I'm bound to roam, across the wide Missouri."

Thanks, Rebecca said silently to him. She checked the bread dough, found it acceptably puffy, and divided it into loaves. Elaine took Adele's place at the card table. A subtle hint of cigar smoke drifted from Jerry's lair in the sitting room. Michael taught Dennis the words to "Flowers o' the Forest." Maybe if he convinced the boy that all was forgiven Dennis would stop looking so uncomfortably guilty.

Had Sheila really wanted the dagger to play a trick on Michael? She had, however inadvertently; the manner not only of her death, but also her life made him a prime suspect. Or had she intended to get Dennis into trouble? She'd certainly achieved that, too.

Bugger it anyway. Rebecca sat down at the counter with last week's grocery receipts, filling out a report for the Archeological Network. The volunteers may have found themselves involved in violent crime, but at least she was feeding them properly. . . . Her head fell forward in a doze, and she jerked herself awake.

Elaine had to be jogged into action at the bridge table every bit as frequently as Tony. Dennis came inside and sat down with a magazine. Then Michael, too, walked in. As he passed behind Rebecca's back, he rested his hand on her shoulder. By the time she looked up, he'd vanished toward the bedroom, and the kiss she blew after him missed by a mile.

Rebecca put the loaves of bread into the oven and went out onto the back porch, the cats at her heels. Dusk had thickened into night. The lights of the village reflected in fitful gleams from the priory walls but illuminated nothing within—profane light turned back at the gate of the sacred. What stars Rebecca could see in the cloud-mottled sky were as smeared and uncertain as her mood.

Eyes narrowed, she peered toward the trench and its unexpected grave, imagining a blurred white apparition wafting upward like the ghosts in "Fantasia." But she saw nothing. Whoever the man was—if it *was* a man, and she was willing to take Jerry's word for that—if he rested uneasily, he was not sharing his unease with her. She couldn't blame him for disdaining the orgy of public disclosure everyone else was caught up in.

The cats disappeared into the darkness. Rebecca inhaled the scent of baking bread and went back inside. Before long all the others had drifted casually into the kitchen, just happening to pick up knives and napkins. Rebecca took the brown loaves from the oven and started slicing them while they were still hot, producing not neat slices but uncouth haggles. No one complained.

Dennis and Hilary asked for milk, Adele for juice. Michael proffered the remains of the bottle of Cragganmore to the others, and its sweet smoky flavor perfectly complemented the warm wheat of the bread. Solemnly Michael and Rebecca touched glasses, although whether they were toasting a beginning or an end, he was probably no surer than she was.

Jerry drank his whiskey and water in a gulp. Elaine hung back, waiting for him to pass a glass to her, until Tony finally reached over and gave her one. Colin's dark eyes, like Michael's with their depths of intelligence, peered around the group. Between sips and munches he said, "Do you think Mark was havin' it off with Sheila?"

Jerry snorted. "Sheila would tease anything male, from the Pope to Don Juan."

"Maybe she had a vitamin deficiency," offered Adele.

Tony pensively licked crumbs from his lips. Rebecca passed around the butter. Michael said, "No, Mark's just payin' dearly for a bit of snoggin'."

"Snogging?" Dennis asked.

Hilary answered expressionlessly, "Necking."

Dennis colored and refused a third piece of bread.

Rebecca said, "Yeah, Mark was just telling me yesterday about his Twinkie principle. How a nibble is all very well, but the whole thing will make you sick."

The Americans emitted various kinds of laughter, from Jerry's acid guffaw to Adele's thin chuckle. Michael groaned in agreement, but the other Britishers looked blank. By the time Rebecca had explained what a Twinkie was, the joke had died a well-deserved death.

She saved the last two pieces of bread and wrapped them up for Mark.

"Thank you," Tony told her. "That was a treat."

"You worked for hours, and now it's all gone," said Elaine sadly, and smeared butter on her last morsel of crust.

"That's usually the case, isn't it?" Rebecca replied. "Anticipation, and then crumbs . . ." Michael, upending the bottle of whiskey so that the last drop would fall onto his tongue, didn't seem to hear.

"Would you like to have Mark's bed tonight?" Dennis asked Colin.

"No, thank you, I'll take a blanket into the sittin' room."

Dennis nodded earnestly. "I guess you don't want to walk on his grave or anything."

That did it. With various polite mutters the gathering unraveled—Jerry, Elaine and Tony out the front door, Adele, Hilary and Dennis up the stairs, Colin into the bathroom. Rebecca left the pans to drain, smoothed the washcloth over the faucet, and went into the bedroom. She didn't bother to turn on the light but sat down on her bed and slipped off her shoes. Michael stood in the doorway, a silhouette against the light glowing into the hall from the dining room. "Are you fair clapped oot, then, lass?"

"Yes, lad, I do believe I am."

"No surprisin', is it? I'm well and truly knackered mysel'."

He stood and she sat, in silence. Water ran and footsteps echoed from upstairs. They both started speaking at once. "I'm sorry . . ." They stopped, eyeing each other through the darkness that bandaged their wounded expressions.

"I'm sorry," Rebecca said. "About a lot of things, but mostly about our argument. I didn't have to hit you with all that."

"I started it," Michael returned. "I was thoughtless, inconsiderate, rude. . . . Choose one of the above."

"Or all of the above," said Rebecca dryly. "Jerry and Sheila would drive a saint to distraction. I should've backed off."

"I should've understood what you were on aboot. I should've tried to understand."

Again silence fell. Colin tiptoed through the hallway into the sitting room and shut the door. Faint music emanated from the wall as he turned on the television just loud enough to muffle whatever they were saying. Normally he was considerate, Rebecca thought; why had he blurted that question about Sheila in the kitchen? Did he have some idea of drawing hints from the assembled suspects? Too many detectives spoil the broth, or something to that effect.

Michael collected his soccer shorts and shaving kit, kissed her forehead and went off toward the bathroom. "That's it?" she wanted to call after him. "You think that solves everything?" And she answered herself, *Yes, he probably does*. He'd never found sackcloth and ashes becoming.

Groaning, she put on her tartan nightgown and wool socks. During the dark nights of winter and spring, she'd made a ritual out of putting on that gown, of propping herself up in bed, of dialing the long string of digits that would make the phone ring in Michael's flat just as he was getting up in the morning. They'd talk, her in her bed alone, he clattering about his kitchen fixing his toast and tea.

She took out her contact lenses. When she came right down to it, Michael had opened himself to her a lot more than she'd opened to him. His map of himself was finely scaled, the elevation lines of anger, joy, boredom, precisely marked, the crosshatched city labeled "Dun Iain," with all its palaces and slums, duly recorded.

His map was marked with green braes and sparkling burns, snow-topped bens towering over ancient castles, deep lochs from which smirking monsters waved their fins at tourists. Her map had dry arroyos, cypress-haunted bayous, vast grassy plains, and skyscrapers strangled by jostling steel freeways.

On her map, Dun Iain was a bomb crater softened by a lush growth of loosestrife and rambler roses. The swampy coastline of her childhood was edged with fortresses of education and experience. Beyond those was a blank area labeled "Here be Dragons."

Rebecca picked up her brush and dragged it painfully through her hair. Poor Michael, to stumble into that blank area. They'd shared a difficult journey last winter, and they were sharing another this summer. Perhaps there was a limit to how far they could travel together when their maps depicted such different landscapes.

Michael walked into the room, threw down his clothes, and said, "It's all yours." Rebecca took her bag of toiletries and headed for the bathroom.

When she came back, Michael was a long lump in his bed. She climbed between her ice cold sheets and curled into a ball, willing to herself warmth, sleep, and amnesia. Instead she shivered. Her tired mind mocked her with dart-like images: Sheila's body, the wheel-cross, Michael smiling in the airport as though he'd never known unhappiness or doubt in his life.

A quick sob of frustration and cold escaped her throat. She clapped her hand over her mouth. Too late. Behind her back, Michael stirred and made a soft query under his breath. Blankets slid aside.

He climbed into her bed and wrapped her body with his own. How could he be warm in nothing but shorts? But he was, his skin radiating heat through the flannel of her gown as though she stood before a fireplace on a cold, raw afternoon. Surely he didn't think—not now. . . . She stiffened.

His breath stirred the hair on the back of her neck. "Hush. I promised you I'd keep you warm, that's all."

"Yes," she said, with a short laugh. And in mingled gratitude, affection, and exasperation, she went limp in his arms.

Chapter Thirteen

THE RAIN DIDN'T conceal the countryside but illuminated it, each drop a miniature lamp dispersing a tender, silvery light. Pink and maroon foxgloves edged the gray stone fences, yellow broom splashed across the green fields, and the equally green hills were shaded by dark brown heather. Streams burbled merrily beneath the patent-leather ribbon of road that bound Galashiels to Melrose to Rudesburn.

Laurence and Nora's mini-van led the way, followed by Jerry's Jaguar and then the Fiat. Grant Johnston's car was at the end of the procession, dutifully keeping them all under surveillance. Mackenzie had told them they'd have an official escort. That Grant was also a witness was an exemplary bit of Scottish thriftiness.

Rebecca eyed her reflection in the car window. Her own face looked funny, as if she'd caught it unaware before it had time to assume a suitable public expression.

The verdict of the inquest had been murder. No one was astonished at that. It wasn't that Rebecca had expected any dramatic revelations, but neither had she expected the inquest to be quite so anticlimactic. The Procurator Fiscal had required only bald facts—who had or hadn't seen what. Any inferential details such as Jerry's collusion with Sheila were in the formal statements that Mackenzie was holding like a poker hand close to his chest. His omniscient attitude, she told herself, had to be a bluff.

Michael said, "The do was gey perjink, right enough, but that'll no winkle oot the daft slaisterin' gowk."

Rebecca smiled; Michael was being deliberately obscure.

Mark, slumped in the back seat beside Colin, pried open his eyelids. "Would you mind translating that?"

"The inquest," said Michael obligingly, "was all very fine and proper, but it dinna find the stupid dirty fool who killed her."

"Not so very stupid," Colin put in. "Whoever dragged the body into the church was damned lucky no one saw him. Her. It."

Rebecca asked, "Beginner's luck? No one's suggested we have a serial killer in our midst. Thank goodness."

"Just serial suspects," Mark said dryly. He smothered a burp. "Michael, thanks for the warning about the bread. Let me warn you about the coffee. Pure battery acid."

"Very good of you, but I've no intention of goin' back there, let alone drinkin' their coffee."

"Yesterday you looked as if you'd been rode hard and put up wet."

Michael said, "You'll have a go at translatin' that, will you?"

"Worked half to death without adequate care," explained Mark.

"Right." Michael nodded emphatically.

A black and white collie bounded suddenly into the road ahead of Laurence's van. Brake lights flared. The dog turned to look back the way it had come, head erect, tail flattened. Rebecca leaned forward. "That's a professional dog if I ever saw one."

The brownish-white blobs of sheep spilled down the hillside and clustered at the side of the road, the dog's stance letting none cross. Black faces looked incuriously at the waiting cars. Rebecca saw Hilary's face, a pale, taut oval, watching the dog and his charges from the Baird's back window.

Hilary had avowed that around the time of the murder she'd been playing with just such a border collie in the fields south of Rudesburn, while Tony encountered Dennis in the camera van. While Jerry lurked in the bar. While Adele meditated beneath the yew tree in the cemetery, seeing and hearing nothing of Sheila's death. Of course, Adele meditating was the next best thing to a stone statue; the murderer would have had to blow a trumpet fanfare to get her attention. Unless Adele had done it herself. . . .

Rebecca grimaced. She could flog that damnable list of suspects all she wanted, but no one, not even Simon Mackenzie, could formulate a hypothesis without facts, or get facts without reliable testimony. But even her own testimony was suspect. How did she know she went into the Craft Centre at eight? she asked herself. By the clock in the toy shop window. How did they know it wasn't eight? By Bridget's watch, which she didn't look at until—when, almost nine? Either clock or watch could have been off.

A piercing whistle cut through the murmurs of car engine and rain. The shepherd, a young man in slicker, wellies, and shapeless hat, waved at the waiting cars. The dog shooed the sheep across the road.

Michael shifted gears and accelerated. His wrist didn't flick the hem of his kilt up his thigh. Rebecca hadn't known he owned a coat and tie, but in honor of the occasion, he'd produced both. He'd also smoothed back his hair. Now it once again flopped casually over his forehead. Except for the dark circles of exhaustion beneath his eyes and his knotted brows, he wore his usual expression of alert, almost startled, intelligence. He didn't kill Sheila. Someone else did it. That brought her right back to the list.

Colin pulled a notepad from his sporran. "The pathologist testified that Sheila died of a stab wound to the heart, made by a dagger with a serrated edge like Michael's sgian dubh, between seven-fifteen and nine-fifteen. Rather earlier, he thought, but admitted that's too broad a time to be helpful."

Everyone nodded gloomily.

"The reporter, Bob Jenkins," Colin went on, "said he had a bargain with Sheila, exclusive rights to report on any interestin' finds. Dr. Kleinfelter says he didn't know that. Although he had, of course, every intention of makin' the finds available to the press."

"Flannelin' like a proper politician," scoffed Michael.

Colin said, "All the men tested, bar Dennis, have A-positive blood."

"No point to DNA tests," said Michael. "No proof whoever was shaggin' her killed her. No proof a man did it at all. Mackenzie's a canny one, he'll no be missin' that."

Colin had easily proved he was at the conference in Durham that night. Not that Rebecca had ever suspected him anyway. Mark—well, he'd been out walking, alone, unnoticed. *Not Mark,* part of her mind said, and another part said, *Why not? Just because you like him?*

This morning Devlin had not seemed at all chastened by his

second suspect slipping through his fingers. As the group greeted Mark at the police station and handed over a set of clean clothes, Devlin's bellicose leprechaun face still seemed convinced that with patient excavation his pot of gold would eventually materialize.

Not to mention the murder weapon. The sgian dubh was conspicuous by its absence from Michael's sock. "Did Sergeant Devlin give you back your Swiss Army knife?" Rebecca asked Mark.

"Sure did. Reminded me of a toreador turning his back on the bull."

"Stopped badgerin' you about that note, did they?" Colin asked.

"Finally. If I can't prove I wrote it ten days ago, they can't prove I didn't. Like you and the attic, Michael."

"Just that," Michael muttered.

A night in jail under Mackenzie's chilly version of the third degree, Rebecca thought, hadn't hit Mark as hard as it had Michael. But then, the murder victim hadn't been Mark's lover, just a snack. . . .

The car tires hissed along the wet tarmac. The windshield wipers scraped and thudded softly. Rebecca abandoned her futile efforts at mystery-solving and visualized Melrose Abbey. Today, as they'd passed, she'd seen the rosy gray ruins streaked dark red by the rain, as if blood flowed over the stones.

In 1545 it had. Edward Seymour, Earl of Hertford, had sacked Melrose just as he'd devastated Rudesburn and ravaged Edinburgh. The destruction went against his grain; he'd protested to his master, Henry VIII, that it served no purpose. But the corpulent old spider had only two years left to live and more than one old score to settle.

Hertford's name had been just above Henry's on the records of Anne Douglas's trial. Probably Hertford had presided on behalf of the king, and then, like a dutiful flunkey passing around an office memo, had brought the records to be initialed by the boss. "Odd," Rebecca said, "that Henry himself was concerned about Anne's trial."

"She was a Douglas," said Michael.

"But it was here in Scotland that the Douglases had fallen out of favor. That would explain why the Scots didn't help her—but then, they couldn't, could they? They were at war."

"So there's a reason we found a body in the cellar?" Mark asked.

"Oh, yes," Rebecca replied. "One of the old mossy stones in

the far corner of the cemetery marks a mass grave of soldiers from the battle of Ancrum Moor, just down the road from Rudesburn.''

"Mary Pringle," said Michael, "thought the commendator, Thomas Elliot, is the one who was in London several years later workin' for Edward the Sixth. I'd no have stayed for the Rough Wooin', either.''

"A commendator is some kind of tax collector?" asked Colin.

"More of a lay administrator. By the sixteenth century many of the religious houses owned vast property. Here in Scotland the kings granted abbey revenues as political rewards. Beginnin' of the end of the monasteries.''

"So Elliot would've been checkin' Anne's accounts?"

"Some commendators worked wi' their religious counterparts, some against. How Anne and Elliot got along I canna say.''

"From the glimpse I had of the trial records," said Rebecca, "they were both accused of gross malfeasance—even though if he went on to London later, he must've been acquitted.''

There was Rudesburn, nestled in its green fold of land like a bone china model enfolded by tissue paper. "Naething like a four-hundred-year-old mystery," said Michael, "to take your mind off the new one.''

Rebecca darted him a sharp look. Sure. He turned the car onto Jedburgh Street and sent her a rueful sideways gleam.

The toy shop clock read one-fifteen. A constable opened the door of the van, even though the reporters had migrated to the inquest in Galashiels—much good it had done them. Michael parked the Fiat between the Plantagenet van and the Jaguar. Jerry climbed out into the mist and cursed, probably wishing for windshield wipers for his glasses. He hurried into the hotel, Elaine sulking right behind. Tony trudged after them. Colin and the students went into the cottage debating the merits of coffee or tea for lunch.

Across the Gowan Water the gentle rain dampened the priory into the same ambivalence as its parent Melrose. Rebecca thought of a nun, her wimple and veil hiding her expression so well she could pretend devoutness when actually her thoughts were far from benevolent.

As Anne Douglas might have looked, facing her accusers. "Her foreign English accusers," Rebecca said aloud to Michael, "who'd sacked the only home she'd known, who'd brutalized her people, who were adding insult to injury by bringing her to trial for—well, the charge was witchcraft, but that covered a lot of territory in the sixteenth century.''

Michael was used to picking up on her non sequiturs. "There was guid precedent for disposin' of the unwanted—mostly women—wi' a charge of witchcraft."

"Like the English disposing of Joan of Arc."

"And was Anne a saint, too?"

"If I had any evidence, maybe I could tell you." Rebecca frowned. "If Mackenzie doesn't bring those records back by this weekend, I'll go to Galashiels or Edinburgh or wherever he's lurking and shake them out of him."

Michael laughed. A police car pulled up in front of the hotel, and Mackenzie and Devlin got out. The Sergeant peered dubiously up at the sky. The Chief Inspector hoisted a slim briefcase and looked straight at Rebecca, exactly as if he'd heard her threat. She tried a manic smile in his direction, turned toward the cottage, and skidded on the gravel. Michael grabbed her arm to steady her. "Who decreed high heels as proper dress wear for a woman, anyway?" she demanded.

"The same sod who invented the tie," he answered, jerking his from his throat with his free hand. "Or else a man invented the shoes, and a woman the tie, each meanin' to disable the other."

Rebecca snorted. She couldn't imagine why he'd visualize the sexes in an adversarial relationship.

In the kitchen, the students were ranged around Colin while he confirmed his notes of their testimonies. "I wouldn't be at all surprised," he told Michael and Rebecca, "if someone saw something or heard something he or she doesn't realize was seen or heard." He thrust the pad back into his sporran and looked around expectantly. Adele seemed amused, Mark and Hilary puzzled, Dennis oddly sullen. No sudden revelations, no abrupt confessions.

On the one hand, Rebecca wanted to scurry into the bedroom and slip her exacerbated nerves into jeans and a sweatshirt. On the other hand, it seemed a shame to take off her tweed suit and pantyhose—she hadn't dressed up in months. Adele was resplendent in an ultra-suede pantsuit and a blue and green Hermes scarf. Hilary's wool jacket and Black Watch tartan skirt she'd bought in Edinburgh were similarly spiffy. Dennis's tailored suit lent him an unaccustomed air of gravity, and Mark's navy sports jacket dusted his gray eyes with blue. His silver buckle and tooled leather belt clashed with his conservative tie; Rebecca didn't know whether he'd forgotten to bring a plain belt or whether the gaudy one was native costume. Like Michael's and Colin's kilts, which had drawn more than one admiring glance from the ladies, and subsequently jaundiced glances from Mark and Dennis, Tony and Jerry.

"Everyone looked awful posh today," Rebecca said. "Did us proud. But we'll have to get back to work after lunch."

Silently, avoiding eye contact, everyone plodded away to change. By the time Mark and Rebecca fixed a plate of sandwiches and a vat of tea, Michael and Colin had shed their plumage and were back in international uniform—jeans and T-shirts reading, respectively, "Mitsubishi Glendhu Distillery Pipe Band" and "Keep Scotland Tidy, Throw Your Rubbish in England."

Half an hour later, she was sweeping the kitchen floor while Mark, his shirtsleeves rolled up, washed the dishes. She opened the back door and threw a handful of crumbs onto the porch for the birds. But no birds were there, only cats. "How about some leftover ham?" Rebecca asked Guinevere's upturned face. Lancelot was looking down, pawing at a reddish lump, disappointed it didn't fight back.

Good grief, he'd dragged the remains of a mouse onto the porch. Rebecca stepped forward, wielding the dust pan. No, that wasn't anything organic; what she had taken for a tail was a strip of fabric.

Lancelot delicately picked up the fabric with his teeth and trotted inside, lump dangling, Guinevere and Rebecca on his heels. Quickly Rebecca bribed the cats with pieces of ham and took possession of the object.

Mark looked around. "What's that?"

"Good question." Rebecca took a dirty spoon from the sink and poked.

"Curiosity killed the cat," Mark teased, even as he laid down the dishrag and knelt beside her.

Cautiously she picked up the object. The cloth strip was stained and damp, but wasn't too disgusting. Its end disappeared into the cold, strangely slick lump. The dark red material looked as intricately carved as a Chinese sculpture. Rounded edges, Rebecca deduced, now folded over and perforated by tooth-marks. Probably it had once been flat and deeply incised. She scraped with her fingernail. A thin paring came off. Below the surface the material was lighter red, almost pink.

"Wax?" asked Mark.

"Sure is. I don't suppose it could be the remains of a wax seal?"

Mark took the lump from her hand. His elfin eyes glinted. "Paraffin? Or beeswax?"

"In other words, Mr. Archeologist Larva, how old is it?"

"That would depend," he replied, "on whether it's been lying in a trash heap for six months or in someone's strong box for a century. But if it's been in a strong box, how did the cats get it?" He shoved away an inquisitive feline nose and scratched its owner's ears.

Michael walked into the room. "Havin' a prayer meetin', are we?"

"Look what the cat dragged in," said Rebecca. "Lancelot, to be exact."

Mark stood and offered Michael the lump. The belt buckle gleamed in Rebecca's eyes, a strand of labyrinthine engraving turning itself into words. She blinked. The legend "Mark and Karen Forever" was etched in the metal. The words had once been inlaid with a contrasting copper or gold wire, which someone had gone to a great deal of trouble to pick out. Probably Mark himself, reluctant to part with a fine piece of work but only too eager to forget the woman who'd given it to him. And how short a time forever had apparently turned out to be.

Mark offered Rebecca his hand and helped her to her feet. Once again she thought, *You don't pry into your friends' psyches.*

Michael was peering at the object with his own feline inquisitiveness. He announced, "It's a wax seal."

"Told you," said Rebecca to Mark.

"I wasn't arguing," he replied. And, to Michael, "How old? Where did the cats dig it up? What does it go to?"

A fiendish grin like a carnival mask spread slowly over Michael's face. "The warrant for Anne Douglas's arrest! It was nicked wi' that gold noble last month. It had several seals on it. What if the thief hid them together, somewhere around here?"

"All right!" Mark exclaimed. "A treasure hunt!" He seized his coat and rushed upstairs, calling to the others, "Come one, come all!"

"If that's no a hell of a leap of faith." Michael's grin skewed.

"Hey. It's worth a try." Rebecca rushed to the sink to finish washing the dishes while Michael opened the back door and scanned the priory grounds, evidently hoping that X marked the spot. The cats, licking their whiskers smugly, padded off into the wet grass.

Soon the entire company was standing by the bridge, kitted out in wellies and jackets. Above them, billowing gray and white clouds played tag with pools of blue sky. "Good," said Hilary. "It's clearing up."

"Now," Rebecca said, assuming her best lecture hall voice. "We'll assume the seal is mashed up because the cats dragged it off the parchment and were playing with it. We'll not assume the parchment was dumped into the burn and has disintegrated or anything like that. We'll also waive the question of just why the thief hid the warrant and coins here instead of carrying them away. Has anyone seen the cats poking around?''

Every head moved solemnly back and forth, signifying negative recall. A crunching on the driveway heralded the arrival of Tony, carrying his camera bags, Elaine, carrying the bag of trowels and the drawing board, and Jerry, carrying his moustache and a smile mimicking that of a used-car salesman. "Back in the right gender, I see,'' he said to Michael and Colin.

The two Scots exchanged a look of pity for those afflicted with cultural dyslexia. Once again Rebecca gave her spiel.

Elaine refused to touch the lump of wax. Tony regarded it cautiously, as if it would bite. Jerry took it, considered it, handed it back. "Okay, sure, no problem. Mark, we'll get back to work on the bones. Elaine, I'll need you to gopher, as usual." Elaine didn't blink at his slang—she'd learned the hard way what gophering was. "The rest of you guys go ahead and look for needles in haystacks. If you know what you're talking about, Campbell.''

"I always know what I'm talkin' aboot,'' Michael responded. His smile was saintly and sharp at once, like that of his namesake, the warrior archangel who went around killing dragons.

Rebecca quelled both her lecture hall voice and an impulse to push Jerry into the burn. He was right about needles in haystacks. He was also dig director. She couldn't help but wish he wasn't so casual about what could just as well turn out to be yet another time-waster.

And here came Mackenzie and Devlin, Don Quixote and Sancho Panza tilting at windmills of human deceit. Although at the moment they actually looked calm, almost mellow—the effect of a couple of pints of McEwan's Export and Nora's superlative ploughman's lunch. Time for them to start work, too. Rebecca took the lump of wax from Michael, trudged across the spongy turf and confronted the officers with the latest find.

Mackenzie listened, his head tilted to the side, his eyes narrowed. Devlin's brows registered skepticism, but with a glance at his superior he said nothing. "Sergeant,'' Mackenzie directed, "ask the Bairds and the Johnstons where the moggies usually play, then put some of our lads onto the search.''

"Thank you." Rebecca was surprised Mackenzie would take her seriously.

"You're welcome,'' he returned.

Mark helped Jerry fold up the plastic sheet from the trench. His face was a sketch by Picasso, half-yearning toward the searchers, half-intent upon the bones at his feet. Tony laid out an array of cameras and tried various sight lines both into the trench and toward the church, ready for anything.

Rebecca found a box for the mangled seal and left it with Elaine. Elaine was interested only in Jerry's and Mark's backs showing above the rim of the trench like humps of dolphins above the surface of the sea. It wasn't justice that was blind, Rebecca thought, but love.

The same cool, damp wind that was shoving the rain clouds toward the east fluttered her jacket and set her hair dancing across her forehead. The grass was so wet it squeaked beneath her boots. Michael was standing by the grate-covered well. The police had dredged up assorted coins, styrofoam wrappers, and a truly awesome pile of green muck, but not the sgian dubh. "Let's try the Law," he suggested to Rebecca. "We saw the cats stravaigin' aboot the first day we were here."

"We saw a man that day, too, remember? Not skulking, just walking through the ruins. We wondered if he'd vandalized the tomb; how about him hiding the warrant and the coin?"

"He'd be a cool one, hidin' the goods in sight of the hotel."

"Like whoever was cool enough to drag Sheila's body into the church in full sight of the village? Those coins are a connecting thread, if you'll pardon the mangled metaphor."

"Oh, aye, they are. And you're pardoned."

Colin gathered the students, and under the combined eyes of Tony and the video camera began delivering geologic incantations. "The Eildons are the remains of a stratified laccolith intruded into the Old Red Sandstones characteristic of the area. Wester Hill, closest to us here, is two layers of fine-grained reibeckite-felsite."

"Sounds like a Hebrew tribe from the Bible," said Michael.

Colin turned, gesturing expansively. "Yon hill is a phonolitic intrusion, younger than the Eildons, a much-eroded lava neck like Traprain and Berwick Laws. The wheel-cross here is made of whinstone from Battle Law. . . ." His voice disappeared down the wind.

Michael and Rebecca fell into step, side by side, toward the steep, stony sides of the hill.

Chapter Fourteen

BATTLE LAW LOOKED like a child's sand castle half-washed away by an invading tide. Only lumps of stone now protruded from the thick undergrowth. Rebecca could hardly tell which stones were the original igneous blocks of the Law and which had been shaped by hands that were long since dust. The ground seemed to ring hollow, as if concealing fairy caverns.

For a time she and Michael turned over small rocks and probed at larger ones. They found an intact arch, a rubble-filled cistern, and on the eastern extremity of the hill the stump of another wheel-cross, arms and halo lying shattered amid heather and hogweed. "This is the one Mary Pringle said was set up by Robert the Bruce?" Rebecca asked. "Somewhat older than his time."

"He appropriated it," Michael replied. "Standard procedure. Also standard procedure for Cromwell's troops to break it during the 1650's invasion. I imagine they were billeted up here, in the remains of the castle, and got bored."

"So they found something to smash. Things haven't changed much."

They walked on through the dark green gorse that spread over and between the stones and sprinkled yellow blossoms like confetti over the ruins. Vast ferns sprouted through a pavement similar to that in the newly excavated cellar. "My mother slaved to grow ferns half that size," Rebecca said, "and here they grow wild."

"My mother was always tryin' to grow cactus."

"Yeah, the grass is always greener, isn't it?"

They leaned against a bit of wall. To the east green billows of land faded into gray billows of cloud, and the wind was brisk and chill. A ray of sun illuminated the priory, village, and lawn as precisely as an architect's model. Colin's class strolled through the church. The others clustered around the trench. Two uniforms prowled around the remains of the infirmary, Mackenzie's attenuated figure following as aloof as a wolf. Cars flowed down Jedburgh Street as the reporters returned to Rudesburn like swallows to Capistrano.

"Is that why you want me?" Michael asked. "Because I'm greener?"

"That's part of it. Although I guess I'm just as exotic."

"But I'm no so intent on runnin' away from home as you."

His keen perception could be downright annoying—probably because it was usually correct. Dryly she said, "Thanks."

He shrugged.

"Colin thinks one of us knows something we don't know we know." She sighed. "Something the killer doesn't know anyone knows."

"The only window in the attic is the one on the landin', ootside the door. A guid view ower the priory, true, but I only looked oot the once. Maybe twice. I didna see a thing."

"You weren't trying to see anything that night. Neither was I. Now I keep going over and over the holes in that timetable. Makes my teeth itch."

"Serial suspects," Michael said. "Includin' me and you."

"We were suspects last winter. We ended up being the detectives, too."

"And we almost didna survive."

"Our mistake was in not being frightened enough soon enough. In not trusting each other soon enough. Now I'm frightened, and I do trust you."

Michael shook his head and said softly, "Oh, aye."

Colin strode toward the cottage, glancing at his watch. Hilary scuffed along the dormitory wall as if expecting the warrant to explode into the air like a grouse. Adele and Dennis poked around in the chapter house. Tony and Elaine sat on the edge of the trench where Mark and Jerry were apparently making mud pies. The police scouted the perimeter wall.

"Noo we have real detectives," Michael said, "who'd be narked if we got in their way."

"Would they? Mackenzie seems to expect me at least to poke

and pry into everyone's lives just as he is. What else is there for anyone to do?''

"Wait and see what bluidy well happens next?'' Michael demanded between his teeth.

They looked at each other. Maybe, Rebecca thought, two minds at work could reach some kind of critical inspirational mass. Interesting physics, two substances reaching critical mass without really touching, without really—what had Mark said about Adele?—being quite in the same space-time continuum? "One thing we can do,'' she said, "is look for the warrant.''

"A hint of where to look widna come amiss,'' said Michael.

Colin came out of the cottage carrying his suitcase. Elaine held up a measuring stick. Tony knelt on the wall, focusing one of his cameras. . . .

Rebecca grabbed a handful of Michael's shirt. "There was a photo on Laurence's desk—one of the ones Tony took from up here. The cats were poking around in the far corner of the cemetery where the graves are marked with flat slabs instead of headstones.''

Michael leaped up. "Let's go!''

They went, first scrambling cautiously down the Law, then skimming past the wheel-cross and around the corner of the church. The dark fronds of the yew tree drooped beneath their burden of moisture. Depending on the type of rock and the degree of weathering, the various headstones either sparkled or stood smudged and stolid. Some of the slabs covered vaults; around those the ground had ebbed, leaving dark, muddy gaps between the rims of stone and earth.

Michael and Rebecca walked past Francis Kerr's grave and approached the flat slab marking the soldiers' resting place. The skull and crossbones etched upon it was camouflaged by dirt and moss.

"We ought to try a charcoal rubbing of this one sometime.'' Rebecca indicated a sandstone slab covered with script almost as indecipherable as the feathered angel's wings surrounding it. "I'd like to know who it belonged to. Eighteenth century, I guess.'' She bent, resting one hand on the cold, wet, gritty stone. That wasn't just a gap between the earth and the slab—that was a cavity, the grass flattened at its edge. "Look!''

Michael knelt and rolled up his sleeve. "If something tries to pull me in, will you save me?''

"Yes, dear,'' Rebecca replied. From the corner of her eye she caught a movement. She glanced around. Adele stood in the transept door, her mouth turned down. *We're not robbing any graves*, Rebecca told her silently.

Dennis appeared beside Adele, his face a question mark. Two constables looked through a gap in the perimeter wall. Michael reached into the darkness. His features stiffened in alarm. For a moment Rebecca thought something really had seized him. Then alarm moderated to disgust, and he pulled out the sodden paper wrappings of a takeaway fish and chips meal. A long black slug clung to one piece. "Canna blame the moggies for wantin' this," he said, and threw the garbage down.

"I appreciate someone not littering," said Rebecca, trying not to be too disappointed. "But shoving it under a gravestone . . . ."

Michael was staring at his hand. Red wax particles were mingled with the greasy dirt on his palm. He threw himself down on his stomach so forcefully that water squished around his chest, and he pressed his face to the cavity. "I need a torch," he said.

Rebecca spun toward the constables at the wall, only to discover they were standing right behind her. One was already proffering a flashlight. As Michael shone it into the hole, Dennis came around the corner of the church leading a stampede. Jerry waved his trowel like a cheerleader's pompom. Tony, with a grin not unlike that of the carved skull spreading from ear to ear, loped along with his video camera on his shoulder. Hilary, Mark and Colin jostled each other for the lead, while Elaine brought up the rear with a here-we-go-again expression curling her features.

The hurrying steps must have sounded like a herd of buffalo. Michael looked up, bellowed, "Watch your step!" and reached again into the hole.

The constables started forward with crowd-containment gestures. Mackenzie, Devlin, and Grant Johnston spurted through the gateway and across the grass. The reporters were at their heels.

"Eureka!" Michael exclaimed, and sat up holding a dirty crumple of plastic that had once been white. Rebecca laughed. Mud and grass particles plastered his jeans, his shirt and jacket, even his face. His grin was a ray of sunlight glancing through cloud.

"Let me have it," said Jerry.

"No," Michael returned, "I get first look."

Jerry backed off; apparently there wasn't enough of an encroachment on his territory to make a scene. Tony closed in, looking like a giant insect with the whirring camera held before his face. A pair of creased trousers at Rebecca's shoulder was

Mackenzie; the flipping notebook pages no doubt belonged to Devlin—unless they were from Colin's little notepad.

Michael laid the tangle on the slab of stone and smoothed it out. "Plastic garbage bag secured with a wire strip," he said, in his best museum-guide diction.

"We have ones just like that in the dustbins at the hotel," said Nora's voice. Rebecca glanced up—the crowd now included both Bairds, Winnie Johnston, and Bridget. The reporters were photographing not only the find but also Laurence's kilt fluttering photogenically in the wind.

"One corner torn," Michael went on. "Perhaps when the bag was shoved beneath the stone. Perhaps by the cats. I don't think we'll be able to tell whether the takeaway wrappers were hidden at the same time."

"I wouldn't be so sure of that," said Devlin. He gestured. One of the policewomen pulled a clear plastic bag from her pocket and, using only her fingertips, stowed away and labeled the greasy, crumb-encrusted papers and their attendant slug.

Michael wiped his dirty hands on his dirty jeans and undid the twist-tie. He handed it up to the policewoman, took a deep breath, and peered into the bag. He excavated. The only sounds were of plastic rustling, the whirrs and clicks of assorted cameras, and the sighing branches of the yew tree.

"It's the warrant, right enough!" Michael exclaimed. "Just a bit damp and gnawed at one end." He tenderly drew the heavy parchment from its cocoon of plastic. The ink was faded by time but smeared only in the one corner. The seals clung like stubborn multi-colored jellyfish to the lower edge.

Rebecca heaved a sigh of relief. "Boy, it could have been ruined out here in the rain. At least the thief wrapped it up."

"They knew how to make documents back then," Jerry said. "A piece of today's newsprint would have disintegrated in five minutes."

"I should have donated it to the Museum," moaned Laurence.

"Why," Mackenzie asked, "did the thief leave it here? You'd think he—she—would want to take better care of his investment."

Rebecca looked up and met the dark, sober eyes gazing down. *What do you want to bet,* she replied silently, *it's because whoever stole it and hid it is working here? Because the cottage is too small, or the hotel could be searched, or . . .* Mackenzie nodded in silent agreement.

"Were the coins here, too?" asked Dennis.

"What coins?" demanded several voices from the rank and file. "Those found with the murder victim?"

Devlin shot Dennis an irritated look. Lower lip protruding, Dennis stepped back. Hilary smiled compassionately at him.

Rebecca's knees were wet and cold. She and Michael stood and tried to brush themselves off. The grass particles clung like tiny green leeches. "The coins might have been here," she said under her breath to Mackenzie.

"Then why were they removed the night Sheila was killed?" he returned.

"To compare Kerr's coin with the other one?" she guessed.

Michael stopped, half-stooped, and looked up sharply. "Is that it? Did someone find a new—old—one but wisna sure if it was genuine?"

"Well, now," said Mackenzie. "A wee bit of buried treasure, eh?"

"What?" asked Jerry, leaning forward to hear.

Devlin snapped his notebook shut and smiled blandly. Jerry rolled his eyes, sat down on the grave slab, and picked up the parchment. Michael said to him, "Have you no respect for the dead?" With an aggravated snort Jerry slid off into the grass and continued his inspection.

No one respected the dead like archeologists did, Rebecca told herself. No one committed more indignities on the dead than archeologists, with the possible exception of police pathologists.

At Mackenzie's gesture Devlin set off at a run toward the Craft Centre and the temporary lab in the back room. Two constables began to cordon off the area. With miscellaneous mutters, contented and otherwise, the cast and crew of the Rudesburn follies began to disperse, aided by Grant's and Laurence's diplomatic skills. Dennis helped Tony with his camera and his bag. Adele walked away, head bowed. Mark whispered something to Hilary and received a giggle. Hope springing eternal, he followed her through the transept door.

Jerry helped Elaine slip the parchment into a fresh plastic bag. "I suppose you'll want to take this away, too," he said to Mackenzie.

"Of course."

"Then get it back PDQ. And the trial records. I have to get Rebecca onto a translation. Written records are useful to an excavation, you know."

"I know," Mackenzie said.

Rebecca turned away before either man could see her exasperated expression. She, Michael, and Colin left the cemetery to the formal inquiries of the police and strolled to the front of the church. "You lot attract buried treasures, do you?" Colin asked.

"Dun Iain's treasures weren't exactly buried," Rebecca replied.

Colin went on, "As much as I'm enjoyin' this, I need to be goin'. The Hydroelectric Board and my wife are both waitin' for me. Not necessarily in that order, mind you."

In the cloister, Dennis was gabbling excitedly to Mark, who laughed and replied in kind. Hilary waited, drawing board poised, seeming to consider the back of Mark's head more interesting than any artifact he might produce. Rebecca smiled—not that she considered herself a matchmaker, but it didn't hurt to do some cheering from the sidelines.

Adele was nowhere to be seen. Tony sat on the remains of the dormitory wall, holding several oddments of camera and staring off into space. No, Rebecca realized, he was staring at the roof of the church where several ravens sat, feathers fluffed against the chill, looking appropriately ominous. As she walked by, she said, "A penny for your thoughts."

He dropped a lens cap and laughed. "I was imagining what it'd be like to be a bird, looking down on hills and rivers and cities. To be able to fly, not to have to crawl on the ground."

"To be free?" Rebecca asked. "I think we'd all like that."

Shaking his head, he retrieved the cap and put it on a camera. "Some people have a better go at it than others."

Rebecca murmured something and walked on. *Spoken like a true child of poverty,* she thought. Tony took skilled photographs, but perhaps of the team it had been Sheila who had the drive and the know-how to market them. Maybe he'd really cared for her.

She asked herself when it was she had heard Tony talking to Laurence about bird-watching. Laurence mentioned something about the owl in the belfry, and that Tony had been in Rudesburn earlier setting up the film deal. She sped up, passing Colin and Michael on the driveway. "I'm going to talk to Laurence. Be right back."

She found the cats adorning the lobby furniture like Oriental potentates resting on their laurels. The hotelkeeper was in his office contemplating a stack of receipts. She refused his offer of a chair, of hot tea and scones, of a glass of whiskey—tempting as that prospect was—and leaned against the door.

In answer to her question, he said, "Yes, Tony came round two weeks before the dig started. He could've seen the coin and the warrant. Anyone could—we never hid them. But he wasn't here the day they were stolen. Why?"

"Michael and I saw a man walking around the priory that day. It could have been anyone."

"Even if Tony did steal the coin and the warrant," Laurence pointed out, "that doesn't mean he murdered Sheila."

"Immutable logic," Rebecca admitted. "Sheila herself wasn't here earlier, was she? Or Elaine or Jerry? I thought maybe one of them dropped the matchbook in the attic, but a matchbook isn't much of a witness."

"I didn't see any of them, no. None of the students, either."

"I came in with two of them myself," Rebecca told him. "Laurence, I know there are rumors of ghosts in the priory—I believe the rumors myself now . . ."

The man hunched as though feeling that last straw settling on his back.

". . . but have you ever heard any rumors of treasure? I thought maybe your—Francis Kerr's—coin was stolen to compare it with another one. Maybe one someone found here."

"The priory treasure was looted by the English. We know that."

"How do we know that?"

"From Pringle's chronicles. What're you on about?"

"Mackenzie says that when we find out why Sheila was murdered, we'll know who did it. I think her murder has something to do with the priory and with the dig. And lust for money has always been a great motive."

"For all of us." Laurence peered blearily at a receipt and tossed it aside as though it were written in code. "To tell you the truth, Rebecca, Nora and I regret ever having called in Plantagenet Productions. Sheila wasn't at all what we had in mind. I think someone killed her because he couldn't tolerate her cheek anymore."

A twitch in his expression made Rebecca wonder how many midnight arguments the Bairds had had over Sheila's big game hunting. Poor Laurence. "The dig needed to be filmed. Getting Sheila was just bad luck." She straightened. "I'd better get back. Thanks, anyway."

"Thank you," said Laurence, summoning a smile. Well, he, at least, didn't object to a little bit of freelance sleuthing.

Michael and Colin stood beside Colin's Vauxhall admiring the figurine of Queen Elizabeth on her horse. "May I see?" Rebecca asked.

"It's a fine one," Colin assured her, handing it over. "But I think I'll buy a wellie bear for Anjali, just in case."

"Insurance," stated Michael. Rebecca laughed.

Duly admired, the bright colors of the lead figure disappeared into a box and the box into the car. For a moment Colin looked at Michael and Rebecca as though considering some admonition along the lines of "Don't shoot until you see the whites of their eyes." But he confined himself to, "Well then, keep your peckers up. Come see us, the kettle's always on." He climbed into the car, reached into his pocket, and climbed halfway out again. "Here. Keep my wee notepad. Add your own clues."

"As we make them up?" asked Rebecca. "Goodbye. See you soon."

The Vauxhall moved away. Michael waved. Rebecca's smile tightened. Maybe she would see Colin again. Maybe not. As much as she liked him, he was a feature on Michael's map, not hers. She shoved the notepad into her pocket and walked with Michael back down the driveway.

"Eh, Ms. Marple," he asked, "what did you want wi' Laurence?"

"I was wondering if anyone besides Tony—and you and Colin, of course—had been here before. He didn't see anyone."

"And the priory treasury was looted by the Sassenach, as per Pringle, right?"

"Right."

"Ah, well, that was a guid idea aboot the coin. And right inspiration aboot the warrant."

She glanced at him, wondering if her lover's paranoia had sharpened his voice. "If you'd seen the photo, you'd have noticed the same thing. . . ." His face remained noncommittal. "The cats did it," she concluded.

They walked the rest of the way in meditative silence and found everyone connected with the dig ranged along the edge of the trench like medical students watching a famous surgeon operate. Mark and Jerry were muddy but unbowed. Brown bones glistened in the dark, damp ground before them. Rebecca quelled an instinctive shudder and said, "Making progress, I see."

"Basically we've got a crouched inhumation," said Jerry. "Not horizontal, though. As Dennis put it so bluntly yesterday, whoever buried him crammed him into the hole headfirst."

"Like the Duke of Clarence drowned in a barrel of wine," Mark said brightly over his shoulder.

"Don't get dramatic," retorted Jerry. With a spoon he scraped a thin layer of mud off one of two kneecaps, one slumped slightly away from the other. Two femurs extended downward into the undisturbed soil, two tibiae now lay on the surface. Those black gummy strips adhering to the thin foot bones must be shoe leather.

"See all those rusty spots?" Mark asked, pointing with his own spoon. "Little bitty nails. Whoever this was, he was wearing expensive shoes."

"A robbery victim?" asked Adele.

"Could be," Jerry said. "Could be we'll never know. Campbell, get down here and relieve me for a while."

The men changed places. Dennis held a light while Tony's video camera whirred. Jerry looked unctuously into the lens and intoned, "One of the most interesting finds on any dig . . ."

Rebecca was curious as to what the final film would say about the sudden disappearance of its original narrator, unless they cut Sheila out of the earlier portions, making her the face on the cutting-room floor as well as the face in the tomb.

Her shoulder blades tightened. She turned, bumped into Elaine, excused herself, and headed toward the first trench. Maybe she could uncover a cache of gold nobles while everyone else clustered around the bones. Jerry should have told Adele and Dennis, at least, to work on something else—Elaine could have held the lights now and filled in the records later on.

They'd found the warrant, at least. She rummaged among the array of spades lying on the grass of the cloister and chose one. Finding the warrant was an accomplishment. She and Michael could bask in the glow of discovery for a while. Maybe all they needed was a bit of a glow. . . .

She stood up and came eyeball-to-eyeball with Harry Devlin. "Miss Reid?" he asked, gesturing toward the church steps where Chief Inspector Mackenzie waited. "May we speak to you, please?"

Rats. No one expects the Scottish Inquisition. Her glow fluttered and dissipated into the cold wind.

Chapter Fifteen

REBECCA DROPPED HER spade. The grass was so soft the implement didn't make a satisfying clang but instead produced a frustrating thud. The excavation wasn't supposed to be like this. Nothing was supposed to be like this. She plodded over to the steps thinking, *I could try one of Michael's martyred expressions, but that wouldn't help anything.*

The chill of the stone step through her jeans made her flinch. She forced herself to sit still, hands folded. Once again the late afternoon shadows lay in rivulets of darkness across the lawn. "Yes, Inspector, what can I do for you?"

"Chief Inspector," corrected Devlin from behind her back.

"Sorry. Chief Inspector."

Mackenzie himself said, "That was a bit of luck, finding the warrant."

At least Michael, annoyed or not, had attributed it to her cleverness. "The cats did the hard part."

"The forensics team examined the cavity and found this."

Mackenzie had the incredibly long fingers of an artist. In his palm lay a small curving red object, like a scale shed from a scarlet dragon. "A fake fingernail," Rebecca said. "Sheila's?"

"We found a packet of them in her room."

"Sheila must have hidden the warrant there herself; I did see her eating some fish and chips the other day. Or maybe she got he coin or coins out herself. And someone killed her for them. That's as good a motive as Laurence's jealousy theory."

Mackenzie's fingers closed over the dragon scale. He handed

it to Devlin and sat down on the steps beside Rebecca. "You've been discussing the case with Mr. Baird?"

Mackenzie might need all the help he could get. It depended on his definition of help. "Yes, I have."

Devlin clucked disapprovingly, but Mackenzie tilted his head and smiled as though to say, "The worm turns, eh? Remember there are birds about who eat worms." He said, "Mr. Baird was experiencing a bit of jealousy himself, wouldn't you say?"

"Yes, I would."

"If Miss Fitzgerald was killed for the coins, why didn't the murderer take them away? Wouldn't that indicate the coins are irrelevant?"

"I don't think anything's irrevelant, especially the coins. Remember that call Sheila made to the reporter, Jenkins, about finding gold?" Rebecca saw again that blank stare in the depths of the tomb. Her folded hands tightened. "You've heard the story about the betrayal of Kildrummy Castle? Time of Robert the Bruce—you'd have to ask Michael, that's his period."

Michael himself looked up out of the trench and saw Rebecca sitting with Mackenzie. His brows signaled curiosity and concern. Then Jerry turned away from the camera and blocked his view.

"Anyway," Rebecca continued, "one of the castle minions sold it out to the English besiegers. For a price, of course. They paid him off by melting the gold he asked for and pouring it down his throat."

Devlin's pen stopped scratching, then started again.

"Not that I really want to believe the killing was connected with the dig, the priory, buried treasure or publicity or whatever," Rebecca finished. "That makes it look like one of us did it. But you remember the old saw about the lust for money being the root of evil."

"And not lust itself as the root of evil?"

"Like I said, nothing's irrelevant."

Mackenzie nodded sagaciously. He reached out, palm up. Devlin handed him another sheaf of computer printouts. "We'll be talking to everyone again in the next couple of days," he said, flipping pages.

"Like archeologists," said Rebecca, "scraping away a layer at a time."

Adele carried a bucket of dirt across the cloister. By the set of her shoulders it was evident she was avoiding glancing over at Rebecca and her official chaperones. Tony, with similar forced disinterest, sat down in the shadow of the church wall to change film. Dennis leafed through the artifact records while Elaine packed away the lights. Hilary glanced over her drawing board at Rebecca, offered her a quick smile, and went back to work. Michael and Mark moved aside as Jerry climbed back into the trench, trowel at the ready. The sun sank toward the west, and the breeze stiffened.

Rebecca focused on Mackenzie's barbed profile. He thought the murderer was someone on the dig, or he'd be picking on the townspeople. He wouldn't take the easy way out.

Mackenzie deflected her scrutiny with a half smile. "Why did you and Dr. Campbell argue?"

That was one question she hadn't been expecting. "I told you. Personal and professional differences."

"Be more specific."

"Oh. I see. You're checking my story against his." Rebecca gazed off into the middle distance, seeing the bright afternoon inlaid with Michael's angry face. "I made a mistake at the excavation, and he corrected me much more harshly than necessary in front of my students. I told him how I felt, also more harshly than necessary. The next thing I knew we weren't talking about that anymore, but about the nature of our relationship, whether we wanted to marry after all." She paused. The image of Michael's anger faded into one of his sensitive and sensual introspective moments as he played his pipes. "At least *I* was talking about our relationship. I don't guess you can really understand that kind of thing, can you? Business worries lapsing over into personal ones."

Mackenzie laughed. Rebecca stared at him. But no, he wasn't making fun of her, he was ruefully considering some image of his own. "I don't suppose you've heard of Amanda Fraser."

"No."

"She's a barrister. Quite a good one. Specializes in—shall we say, in making sure the C.I.D. doesn't do anyone over too enthusiastically?" His laugh dwindled and died. "She's my wife. You may be competing with Dr. Campbell for academic laurels, but I doubt if you'll ever oppose each other in court, as Amanda and I have done."

Rebecca glanced at Mackenzie's left hand. No ring. Was that disclosure his and Devlin's version of good cop/bad cop? "I

didn't know you were married. I apologize. You do understand.''

"Most of us marry," said Devlin darkly, "at one time or
another.''

"At any rate," Mackenzie went on, "your argument with Dr.
Campbell wasn't over his relationship with Miss Fitzgerald.''

"Her attitude, to us and to the dig, helped to spark it. But
then, the issues are so important it was bound to happen eventually." Rebecca looked again at the trench. Michael was leaning on the edge expounding on something—another coin?—to
Elaine. She nodded and went toward the church.

Mackenzie rattled his printouts. "Miss Reid, were you aware
of the fact that one of your students has a court record?"

Rebecca eyed that damnably impassive face. She'd only imagined the wry laugh, that personal admission. "No, I wasn't.
Who is it? Mark? He said he'd had a rough time when he was
a kid. Was he busted for pot?"

"You're jumping to conclusions. I said court record, not criminal record. And I'm talking about Miss Chase.''

"What?''

"She was the plaintiff in a rape case three years ago.''

"The—you mean the victim?" Rebecca's heart plummeted,
landing with a surge of nausea somewhere behind her navel. Her
head snapped around. Hilary was drawing, her hand steady, her
face as calm and peaceful as that of William Salkeld's effigy.
"My God. So that's it. Oh, Hilary.''

"What do you mean, so that's it?" asked Devlin.

Rebecca dredged her queasiness for coherence. "Just some of
the things she's said and done. She's very defensive when it
comes to men.''

"You didn't ask her why?" Mackenzie prodded.

"Good Lord, no! I hate to pry into other people's lives. I hate
people prying into mine.''

Devlin said, "We're not doin' it for amusement.''

Rebecca took a deep breath. She hoped the man who had
violated the innocence Hilary was so desperate to affirm would
rot in jail for the next century—hanging, drawing, and quartering
not being an option in Indiana.

"If you please," said Mackenzie, "imagine whether, with
Miss Chase's background, Miss Fitzgerald's—proclivities—
might have disturbed her.''

"Come on. Hilary couldn't have killed Sheila. She found the body."

"So did you."

Rebecca opened her mouth, found no words in it, closed it. Elaine reappeared carrying a box which she gave to Michael. Jerry gestured. She tramped off toward the hotel.

Notebook pages rustled. "Hilary told us yesterday," said Devlin, "quote, 'Women like that make it hard for all of us. They make men think we're all like that.' "

And two nights ago, Rebecca thought unwillingly, Hilary had been green around the gills just thinking about Sheila and her many lovers. She dropped her face into her hands, massaging her temples, trying to forestall another headache. Mackenzie and Devlin ought to come equipped with bottles of aspirin, like Saint Bernards and their kegs of brandy. "All right. The girl has some hangups—and understandably so. We all have hangups to some extent. Most of us don't commit murder because of them."

Mackenzie shrugged. "Mr. Owen says he and Miss Chase left the cottage about seven-forty-five, but went in different directions. Dr. Kleinfelter says she came into the pub at eight-thirty. Between those times Miss Chase herself says she was walking in the fields."

"I've heard all that already. None of it makes me believe Hilary is capable of murder. Period. Got any more skeletons to drag out of their closets?"

Mackenzie didn't refer to the printouts. He'd probably memorized them and was using them only as a prop. A trick he'd learned from his wife, the barrister? "Mrs. Garrity is a widow. Her only child, Christopher, died last year."

"How?" Rebecca asked. From the corner of her eye she saw Adele removing yet another bucket of dirt with antlike persistence.

"An automobile accident. He was driving alone late at night and lost control. The car hit a retaining wall head-on."

What had Adele said rather hopefully on the plane, about spirits lingering because of unfinished business? And that speech last night about men hiding their emotions. . . . Rebecca asked, "You have the police report there? Was there any suggestion of drugs or alcohol? Were there any skid marks?"

"No." Mackenzie frowned slightly. "And no. The death was ruled a suicide after an unhappy love affair. How did you know that?"

"Again, just something Adele said." Rebecca shook her head, trying not to exacerbate her pain.

"Is it Mrs. Garrity's interest in parapsychology?" asked Devlin.

"She's searching awfully hard for evidence of an afterlife. Not surprising. Surely you're not going to tie that into the murder."

Mackenzie sorted his printouts, admitting nothing. Rebecca was beginning to understand why Devlin had such a contentious air; he was a boat constantly off the lee shore of implacable Mackenzie.

Her lips tight, Rebecca looked over to where Jerry, Michael, and Mark were standing on the edge of the trench in close conference. They were trying to decide whether to take the skeleton out piecemeal or try to lift it all at once, no doubt. The way the bones were positioned would make them the devil to dig out, the upper ones collapsing as the excavation extended to the ones below.

Jerry's hands moved in vertical swoops. Ah, they could come in from the side—the ground was damp enough. Elaine returned down the driveway, leading Grant Johnston and a waiter who were carrying several boards. So Jerry had already sent for wood to shore up the side of the trench. He was trying to keep the skeleton complete. Good for him.

Dennis edged away from the computer. Tony gathered up his cameras and stood poised. Mark leaned over, whispered something in Hilary's ear, and tickled the back of her neck. *Watch it,* Rebecca told him silently. Hilary had almost self-destructed on him once before. But all Hilary did now was look up at him and blush.

"Are you going to talk to Hilary about—about the court records?" Rebecca asked.

Mackenzie, too, was watching the activity at the trench. "Aye."

"Then get another woman to sit in. So Hilary won't be as likely to think it's an adversarial situation."

"All right, Miss Reid. When the time comes, we'll call on you."

She should have seen that coming, Rebecca told herself. The headache swelled. She slitted her eyes against the glare of the westering sun, but that blurred her vision. She'd rather tolerate the pain and see clearly.

"As for the other students," said Mackenzie, "Mr. Tucker has two married sisters, and his father works for a computer software firm. His story of stealing Dr. Campbell's sgian dubh is a wee bit thin, but unless he's a superb actor, I doubt if he used the dagger on Miss Fitzgerald."

Devlin muttered, "The lad's a bungalow."

"Nothing up top?" asked Rebecca. "I wouldn't be so sure of that."

Mackenzie glanced back at his sergeant, counseling him to avoid the editorial comments. He said to Rebecca, "And, despite your suspicions, Mr. Owen has nothing in his closet but two young half-siblings and an ex-wife, all of whom he told us about last night."

Rebecca winced. The silver belt. "Karen. Is that her name?"

"They were married at seventeen, divorced at eighteen. He's told you about her, then?"

"No. Just another guess." That was what had happened to shake him out of his "rough time." A shotgun wedding, probably. Mark must have a seven- or eight-year-old child, about the age of the middle Johnston kid. But as a graduate student, he could hardly be contributing to the child's upkeep.

Love and money, Rebecca told herself. This is where she came in, sitting on that plane worrying about Michael and love and money. And she thought she and Michael had skeletons in their closets. Maybe this was a typical assortment of people, but she hoped not. Surely not every random collection of ten or so people had quite so many bones rolling about underfoot.

Boards and plastic sheeting waved above the top of the trench. The scene would have degenerated into a Three Stooges routine if it wasn't for Jerry's gesticulating arms and shouted directions. Damn. He would have to be competent. That made it a lot harder for Rebecca to suspect him of lying and cheating, of scapegoating assistants and conspiring with Sheila.

"Tell me, Miss Reid," said Mackenzie. "Who killed Miss Fitzgerald?"

"How the heck should I know? You're the detective."

Mackenzie's onyx eyes gleamed. "Have a go at it."

"Laurence and Nora," she stated, frowning in aggravation and concentration both. "They were unhappy with the way Sheila was presenting the dig. But for that they would have fired her, not killed her. I wouldn't be surprised if they argued over her flirtatiousness. Maybe that got one of them mad enough to kill her. Motive—lust. I can't see them being after the gold coins, the treasure, whatever, and planning to skip out on the RDG.''

Mackenzie leaned his chin on his hand and his elbow on his knee. "Very good. Do go on.''

"Jerry. He and Sheila could've had a falling out between thieves, exacerbated by the on again, off again affair. Lust and money both. Elaine. She could've been jealous of Jerry and Sheila—Jerry's her ticket to ride.'' Rebecca forestalled Devlin's question by adding, "She told me he was going to take her away with him, rescue her from her background. Lust and money again.''

Mackenzie didn't blink.

"Tony. He could've been resentful of the way Sheila bossed him around. Maybe he, not Jerry, was working some kind of scam with her. Maybe he made the same deduction from the photo that I did, and found the coins. Money, again exacerbated by lust. There's an echo out here.''

"And the warrant?'' asked Devlin.

"Don't confuse me with a wild card,'' Rebecca told him. "Mark. Well, he spurned Sheila's advances, being understandably wary of relationships, and she became angry and attacked him. She had the knife, after all—assuming Dennis is telling the truth about that.'' Her sinuses hurt. "For Mark, self-defense more than lust. Even though he might have needed money to support his family. . . . No, that's just too long a shot.''

"What about Miss Chase?''

"You've already got a motive for her, haven't you? Temporary insanity sparked by her—her emotional mutilation.'' Rebecca plunged on. "Adele. Some weird religious ritual. The belief she was avenging the priory ghosts for Sheila's slighting remarks. Sending her son a companion. I don't know. She's our human wild card.''

"The coins on Sheila's eyes,'' murmured Mackenzie.

They understood each other altogether too well. "Right,'' Rebecca said. "That does rather point to Adele, doesn't it?''

"And Mr. Tucker,'' Mackenzie continued. "The bungalow. Perhaps Miss Fitzgerald spurned his advances.''

"Perhaps there's a lot more going on than we know about, Chief Inspector.''

"Oh, I have no doubt that's very much the case.''

Rebecca dropped her face into her hands, concealing the light, Mackenzie, everything. No, not everything. Here she was calmly, coolly considering motivations. Here she was actually entertaining the idea someone she knew was a murderer. *How far I've come in just a couple of days,* she thought caustically. *The police are infectious.*

"You left out two suspects," Devlin said quietly.

Rebecca looked up. "Not Bridget or Grant—" Mackenzie's half-amused, half-regretful expression stopped her. "Oh. Michael and me. Poor as church mice, the both of us, trying to get our acts together. Sheila barges in and bad-mouths me to him and him to his face. Bludgeon us with love or money, if you have to, but neither of us killed the woman."

The maddening scratch of Devlin's pen went on and on. Mackenzie's eyes rested on Rebecca's, probing like a surgeon after a tumor. She let him look; she had nothing to hide. She had nothing left to hide.

"Quitting time!" shouted Jerry. "Clear your loose! Clean your tools!"

"That's a good idea," Mackenzie said. He pressed his fingertips against his eyelids. Only the fact that his skin wasn't quite as fair as Michael's kept the circles under his eyes from being just as dark. Rebecca wondered suddenly if he'd slept since Monday. "I'll talk to you again tomorrow, Miss Reid."

Devlin snapped shut his notebook and put it in his pocket. He and Mackenzie marched off toward the village.

Rebecca felt as if she'd been dropped from about twenty feet. She stood and stretched, groaning. Her buttocks were numb from the cold stone. Michael appeared at her elbow. "How was the conference wi' Lestrade, Miss Holmes?"

"Don't tease me," she told him. "My nerves are shot."

"I wisna teasin' you," he replied indignantly.

The others shouldered their equipment and walked off toward the cottage and the hotel, Mark whistling "Heigh ho, heigh ho." The trench was beginning to look like the excavation of Tutankhamen's tomb, the crevice between the ancient stones swathed in plastic, the supporting boards protruding like sentries. "How far did you get?" Rebecca asked Michael.

"To the pelvic arch. It is a man, right enough. Gold threads and a few shreds of what appears to be silk aboot his hips. A rich man, I doot, wi' gold points on his doublet."

"What were you showing Elaine?"

"One of his hands is lying by his left femur." Michael crouched slightly, miming the posture. "He's wearin' a ring."

"A signet ring, with a coat of arms? That might help identify him!"

"It certainly might. I told Elaine to put the box in the cottage —we'll get to work cleanin' it the night, then you can take a keek at it. Sixteenth century, that's your field."

Rebecca visualized their respective fields staked out, guarded by mines and lit by arching flares, while they each peered out warily from separate trenches. She rubbed the bridge of her nose, wondering if anything short of a flamethrower would help her headache.

He set his arm around her shoulders. "Tired, lass? Mackenzie'll do you over properly."

"And improperly," she replied. "Come on. I'll tell you about it."

They walked around the church to the cemetery. Rebecca related the substance of the interview, from the intriguing fact of Mackenzie's marriage to the horrible facts about Hilary. Michael spat, "Ah, by all that's holy, it's enough to make you give up sex as a bad job!"

Rebecca shot him a sardonic glance.

"Adele's in shock ower her son's death," he went on. "And I assume Mark's learned by noo where babies come from. What I wonder is why Mackenzie asked you to name the killer? Givin' you permission to play detective?"

"I doubt it. Just testing intuition against logic, I guess."

Michael growled something in his throat, a noise of assent, Rebecca supposed, although it could have been miffed skepticism. What did he want, for Mackenzie to ask his opinion, too? The Chief Inspector would be getting around to it, Rebecca was sure of that.

Grant was in the cemetery shoveling dirt back into the cavity from whence had come the eclectic assortment of clues—fish and chips wrappers, ancient warrant, and fingernail. "Just settin' it to rights," he told them. "Whoever's sleepin' there, it's no their fault, is it?"

"Hardly," Michael told him.

They walked on around the church, behind the east window, and came to the chapter house. It was on this soft blanket of greensward Sheila had died. The grass was resilient; nothing marked the spot except a wilted bouquet of daisies. The Johnstons had probably placed it there, punctilious to a fault.

The sun had sunk far enough to the west that the wall of the chapter house shaded the grass and the derelict flowers. Rebecca leaned into Michael's grasp, remembering the nightmare she had had her first morning in Scotland, of darkness through which moved nameless predators. And yet beyond the shadow, the sunlight glinted green and gold on the nearer hills, making the hills on the horizon ethereal blue. To the south the Law was the weatherbeaten face of a crotchety but well-meaning old man. The dark spoil heap of excavated soil was piled against the perimeter wall, the sieve leaning beside it.

A cold draft spilled through the tracery of the east window, carrying first a distinct odor of onions, ale, and sweat, then the sound of voices. Rebecca broke out in gooseflesh. Michael's arm went rigid.

"Salve Regine," sang the high, clear voices. *"Salve Regine, mater misericordie. Domine Deus, Agnus Dei, Filius Patris."* The words faded, then returned. *"Christus resurgens ex mortuis iam moritur mors illi non dominabit."*

"Maybe Christ rose from the dead," said Michael under his breath, "but Sheila'll no be comin' back."

Wishful thinking, Rebecca reflected, and then bit her lip. The flowers stirred uneasily in the wind. Again the music ebbed, along with the odor not of sanctity but of life. Together she and Michael stepped cautiously along the slype until they could see into the church. Through the transept door oozed the radiant cold of an iceberg. Something moved through the chill, glimmering gauzy pale in the blocks of sunlight, in the stripes of shadow a solid white.

Rebecca felt her face go steam-hot, and her eyes open so far that flecks of dust settled on her contacts. She could hear only the wind, and the trees rustling, and the prosaic scrape of Grant's shovel from the cemetery. The shape glided through the choir of the church and disappeared into the nave. The cold drained away down a cool evening breeze.

There was a sudden movement. Rebecca jumped. Michael's hand convulsed on hers. Adele was standing beside them. "It's Anne Douglas," she stated. "She's still here, waiting for redemption. Her task isn't done."

"What does she want?" asked Michael hoarsely.

Adele shook her head. "I'm not sure. She died a martyr; maybe she wants revenge on her murderers. Maybe she's guarding something important—maybe that's the reason they killed her."

"We don't know they killed her," Rebecca said. The heat was draining from her cheeks, leaving her dizzy.

Adele regarded Rebecca and Michael as calmly as a Sunday school teacher setting out the day's lesson for heathen pupils. "I do. She told me. She died for love, you see. But that love has yet to be redeemed." On that non sequitur Adele walked through the door and into the church, where she knelt before the slab of rock that had once supported the altar and began to pray. The sun glancing through the west door made her gray hair shine.

"I'd advise retreat," said Michael, "dignified or otherwise."

He and Rebecca trotted past the excavation, across the bridge, and to the cottage. Once on the step they exchanged a long, speculative look. "And how much of that is true?" Rebecca asked. "I can believe the English killed Anne, although you'd think if it was anything really spectacular, like Joan of Arc, it would have been recorded."

"A martyr dyin' for love. I take it Adele dinna mean profane and uninspirin' love for a man. For her faith? For her country?"

Rebecca shook her head. "Notice, Michael, how neither one of us doubts that she really has been talking to Anne."

Michael swore softly. He and Rebecca exchanged dazed smiles, turned, and went into the cottage.

Chapter Sixteen

IT WASN'T FAIR. Her brain was numb, but not her nerves. It would be much more helpful if it were the other way around.

Michael sat at the dining room table, using a needle to probe the artifact ring. Right now it was the least glamorous piece of jewelry Rebecca had ever seen, encrusted thickly with God only knew what. "Gold?" she asked.

"That it is," he replied. "Nice and heavy. Get the water, please."

In the kitchen Adele was dismembering the remains of dinner's roasted chicken, looking like a greeting card version of a grandmother. "Nora gave me a recipe for cockie-leekie soup," she said. "I'll try that tomorrow."

"Whatever you want," Rebecca said cautiously.

Hilary was washing dishes. At Rebecca's step she looked around. Her smile was pleasant enough, but it was obvious she'd been hoping for someone else. Rebecca restrained herself from hugging the girl, patting her head, and delivering an unhelpful and much too late "There, there, I understand." She didn't understand. She had had her share of trauma, but not, thank God, that one.

She got the container of distilled water from the pantry and a saucer from the cabinet. From the door Mark called, "Would you like me to dry?"

That's who rated the dewy-eyed smile. Rebecca wanted to tell Mark to leave Hilary alone. And yet, after her first rebuff he was making his new approach as carefully as an airplane circling a foggy airport. Maybe it would work, after all—it wasn't only a matter of Hilary trusting him, but of him being trustworthy.

Michael arranged the dental picks and the soft brushes from the conservation kit. Rebecca poured the water into the saucer and wet a cotton swab. Her first tentative swipe at the ring brought off a layer of brownish green grundge that made her stomach uneasy.

Dennis walked by. "Shouldn't you be using that chemical kit?"

"It's gold," Michael replied. "Water'll turn the trick quite nicely. If it was latten or bronze, we'd be usin' the kit."

Rebecca went on, "Remember how all of Tutankhamen's gold grave goods were in perfect shape? Dry climate, of course. But gold holds up very well."

"Oh. Yeah." Dennis turned on the television.

Another layer of dirt parted company with the ring, revealing a flattened side. "I do believe it is a signet," Rebecca said. "Keep your fingers crossed for a device of some kind."

"Let me." Michael took the ring and applied a brush.

Adele put the chicken in the refrigerator and went upstairs. Mark and Hilary went out the back door. Rebecca felt like a mother watching her daughter leave on a first date.

She pressed her fingertips against her sinuses. Dinner and an aspirin had helped her headache. A Mackenzie headache, a new variety of migraine. A Michael headache. Through her lashes she inspected Michael's solemn, intense face. They'd actually retrieved a bit of affection today. Maybe there was hope yet. *He's trustworthy*, she told herself. *I trust him.*

"Give me a yes or no answer, Michael. Do you want me to stay here?" she said abruptly.

He shot her an upward glance, the typical queasy male. "Aaargh, she wants to talk personal relations." With a sigh that was remarkably ungrudging, considering, he replied, "I'd like for you to make a decision you can live wi'. Whether you live wi' me or no."

"What decision can you live with?"

Michael wriggled like a butterfly skewered to a collection box, the chloroform descending. "I told you. I want a home. I want a wife. Sometime doon the way, I'll be wantin' a family. Proper enough."

"Standard operating procedure," Rebecca agreed. "The question is, do you want a wife who not only has a career but the same one you have? Or do you want one who'll make a career out of being your wife?''

''I want you, Rebecca,'' he said. ''I want you to want me.''

She, too, was a carrier of headache. Now Michael was rubbing his temples, eyes shut, lips thin. She shouldn't have put him on the spot like that. Rebecca took the pick and the ring and levered a chip of damp dirt from it. A gleam of gold winked at her. ''Sorry,'' she said.

Michael attempted a smile, but his eyes showed annoyance. With himself, Rebecca estimated, for not giving her what she wanted, and with her for wanting something he couldn't give.

A chunk of debris fell off the ring. The flat surface gleamed in the overhead light. They exchanged a quick, pleased glance. ''All right! A coat of arms!'' Rebecca turned the ring back and forth, inspecting the finely incised lines, Michael's breath warm on her cheek.

''A diagonal bar,'' he said. ''I'd rather expected the crowned heart of the Douglases.''

''Did you really? He could've been working for the Douglases, I guess.'' They bumped heads and laughed. ''There's the motto. *Fortite et recte.* 'Guts and truth,' more or less.''

''Mean anything to you?'' Michael asked.

''Yeah, it jingles a little bell in there somewhere . . .''

The back door opened. Hilary's giggle receded up the staircase. Mark's solid body loomed behind Rebecca's shoulder. ''Thank you for saving the bread for me. It was delicious.''

She glanced up. If he'd been a cat, he would have been licking feathers off his whiskers. Got yourself a kiss this time, eh?

''Is that the ring from the skeleton?'' Mark asked, dropping into another chair. ''Is it gold?''

''Signet ring,'' Rebecca replied. ''You press it into wax to seal a document. Appropriate enough, considering today's discovery. We knew the man was wealthy from his clothes, and he must've been in a position of some influence to have had a coat of arms.''

Fortite et recte. She saw those words incised in wax. She saw the seals clinging to the bottom of the warrant. A diagonal bar, a simple enough device. She grimaced, eyes screwed shut, trying to see not the warrant itself—her glimpse this afternoon had been too brief—but the photographs of it in Michael's collection of plans and printouts. One seal, in the corner, was askew on its wax blob.

From far away came Mark's voice. "Does she do this often?"

"Oh, aye," said Michael. "A directory scan takes a bit of effort."

Rebecca's eyes flew open. "It's the coat of arms of the Elliots!"

Mark stared. "Elliot? Rudesburn's commendator? Is he in the cellar?"

"This is Elliot country," Michael cautioned, "and Pringle says Thomas, the commendator, was in London several years after Henry the Eighth's death."

Rebecca laid the ring in its box. "We have no proof that the body is Thomas Elliot's. It could be another Elliot, or Joe Blow wearing an Elliot ring. All we know is that Thomas had to have been in political favor to have gotten the post as commendator, and that that didn't matter anymore when the English came through."

Michael snorted aggravation. "We dinna ken if Elliot was acquitted of those charges, or if he simply escaped. Damn Mackenzie, scarperin' wi' the records!"

And Jerry, Rebecca thought. *And Sheila.*

"I can hardly wait to get out there tomorrow," said Mark. "I like this mystery much better than the real-time one."

Michael and Rebecca groaned their concurrence and went back to work on the ring, debating possibilities and lamenting the shortage of facts. At last Mark drifted away. Michael said under his breath, "Do you think someone ought to tell him aboot Hilary?"

"She needs to tell him herself." Rebecca leaned back and stretched. "I do believe everyone's gone to bed."

"I'll tidy up. You go on yoursel'."

Rebecca kissed the top of his head, collected her things, and went into the bathroom. Serial suspects, she thought, as she washed her face and brushed her teeth. Mackenzie had collared Michael and then Mark; who would he focus on next? Michael, Mark, and Mackenzie. Sounded like a law firm.

She found Michael putting the box with the ring into the drawer of the bedside table. "I'll no be takin' chances," he told her, and disappeared toward the bathroom.

He knew what not to leave to chance. Every morning he handed her her packet of birth control pills. And yet someday he wanted a family. She assumed she'd want children, too—it seemed a normal enough part of existence. She'd much rather bear Michael a child than any other man she'd known. He'd be there for her, unlike her brothers, who had followed their father's example and decreed the business of labor and delivery rooms "women's work." Rebecca had finally shamed Kevin into finishing what he'd begun at the birth of his third child. Her sister-in-law had gazed at her in mute gratitude, her parents had, as usual, been baffled that their swan had turned into an ugly duckling. "But, dear," her mother had murmured, "that just isn't done."

She lay down and pulled up the covers. She saw herself like her sisters-in-law, frazzled by two a.m. screams, S-shaped from toting a baby on one hip, smelling of sour milk, the desperation of a trapped animal lurking in her eyes. And she visualized eighteen-year-old Karen Owen, a child herself, staring in despair at a baby who had Mark's gray eyes. How hard had he pressed her to sleep with him? Had she enjoyed it? Had he bothered to hold her, to help her, while she give birth to the consequence of their folly?

Michael came into the bedroom, stood for a moment, leaned over and laid an affectionate if cautious kiss on her forehead. "Good night."

"Good night," she returned.

Rebecca lay in the darkness listening to the slow rise and fall of his breath repeating the wind through the willows outside. Maybe she heard singing from the priory, maybe not. She was too tired to care. Her thoughts slipped in and out of her consciousness like Anne's ghost in and out of shadow—murder mysteries and mysteries of love and sex—nothing was solved, nothing was soluble. She heard the old song about the battle of Sheriffmuir in 1715. *We ran and they ran and we ran. . . .*

And they ran and we ran, echoed her breathless dreams, until at last dream solidified into image.

She was in an oddly distorted version of the cloister. The sky glared a brassy blue. The walls were tinted gold, their shadows dense as smoke. Out of the corner of her eye she saw quick glints of light, sunlight flashing off camera lenses or the sharp beaks of ravens. She was wearing a Cistercian nun's white habit, rucked up around her thighs. The material was thin as cheesecloth, and she felt the grass pricking her shoulders and buttocks.

Mark lay on one elbow beside her, wearing nothing but jeans and a towel draped around his neck. His hand moved teasingly between her legs. "Tibia," he murmured. "Patella. Femur. The soft tissues are all gone now. All that appealing, stimulating, flesh, all gone.''

His hand slipped beneath the material of her habit. She woke with a start, her only too substantial flesh achingly humid. The bedroom and its dawn-silvered light barely registered. Mark. That wasn't right. Michael.

Michael was sleeping on his side, imitating the fetal position of the bones in the cellar. But his flesh was just as tangible as hers. In one movement Rebecca threw back her covers, lunged across the gap between the beds, dragged his covers away. She fumbled with the waistband of his shorts and abraded her lips on his stubbled cheeks.

With a sharp inhalation of surprise he awoke. He exhaled in comprehension and seized her, brushing aside her nightgown. *He must have been a Boy Scout*, she thought incoherently. He was certainly quickly prepared.

It seemed like seconds later she was rubbing the back of her neck—whiplash—and gazing crosseyed and trembling at his sweaty, slightly stunned, face. Well, that was one way to relieve stress. ''Ah, lass,'' he said with a slow smile, ''I didna think you cared.''

Thought condensed from the steam misting her brain. She drooped, unable to meet that acute blue gaze. Wham bam, thank you, sir. That wasn't caring. She'd been dreaming about some-one else; what that had been was cheap.

Michael's hand pulled her face around. ''Eh, love?''

Hell of a posture. She extricated herself from him, yanked down her gown, and plunked onto the edge of the bed. The alarm went off. She batted the small travel clock across the table.

Michael's face crisped into bafflement. ''What have I done the noo?''

''You exist,'' she said. And, realizing that had come out wrong, tried to explain without incriminating herself. ''I was just using you. I'm sorry.''

''If that's the way you want tae use me, go right ahead.''

''God, Michael. That's cheap.'' The heat drained from her body. The room was cold. She was cold. She hugged herself. *Give me the right words*, she pleaded with her own recalcitrant mind. *Just a few right words.*

Michael sat up and wrapped his arms around her. ''Do you remember the first night we were together? I was sae worried aboot doin' right by you. And you told me I couldna do wrong by you, because it was me. Do you want me tae tell you the same noo?''

Even if she told him she'd been dreaming of someone else, it wouldn't bother him. It hadn't bothered him telling her about his affair with Sheila. What did she want, she demanded of herself, for him to throw a possessive fit? "I don't know what the hell I want," she said.

"Oh, aye?'' Bafflement became irritation. His arms fell away. He stood up, remarkably dignified despite his shorts puddled around one ankle. "Tell me. Were you born daft, or did I make you that way?''

"It wasn't you," she replied. "I promise you that."

He shook his head, adjusted his clothing, took his shaving kit and went out the door. Rebecca got up and made not only her bed, but also his, which prompted another puzzled look when he returned. "Why did you do that? I'll only be sleepin' in it again."

"Why wash your clothes? You'll only wear them again. Why eat? You'll only be hungry again."

"Never you mind," he said, like a police chaplain talking to a potential jumper perched on a high ledge.

Rebecca went into the bathroom and splashed cold water on her face. She hated women who kept testing their lovers. And yet what was she doing with Michael? Why was it so hard to do right by each other? It was certainly one of Nature's dirtier tricks to make the opposite sex so damnably attractive and so damnably bewildering at once.

Mark was peering out of the dining room window at the dark clouds gathering in the north. She tried to scurry on by, not sure she could look him in the face, but he said over his shoulder, "Looks like it's comin' another frog-strangler, right enough."

"You're getting your dialects mixed up," she told him.

"Waal, lil lady," he drawled, "it's y'all have them there dialects, not me." He shot her a quick grin and headed into the kitchen.

With an appreciative chuckle she fled into the bedroom, threw herself onto Michael and clung like a vine. "I'm sorry, I'm an idiot."

"Will you stop apologizin'?'' he replied, resting his chin on her head.

"August third. Your birthday, the first day of the Festival, the end of the dig. On that day I—we—will make a decision. No matter whether anything else is settled by then or not.''

"Thank you. Much obliged." He kissed her nose, shook her like a malfunctioning vending machine, and with glazed eyes headed toward the kitchen.

By the time she was dressed—in Caroline Campbell's sweater-vest, as proof of her good intentions—Michael and Mark had breakfast ready. After a few healthy swallows of caffeine she was ready to face the day. Friday. No weekend in Edinburgh or the Lake District this time. Not that it would hurt to work through the weekend, especially with the skeleton half-excavated.

She lingered to wash the dishes. On her way out the front door, she saw the red and gold postal van. She walked up, got the mail, took it back inside and spread it out on the table. Nothing for either Michael or Hilary. A letter for Dennis, return address L.M. in Ann Arbor. For Adele, a smiley face sticker from an ashram in Arizona. An Austin address painfully printed in a child's hand for Mark. One of his siblings or his own child?

For her, a large brown envelope from the University of Missouri. She ripped it open and read the enclosed papers in one predatory gulp: "The University is pleased to inform you you will be awarded the degree of Doctor of Philosophy in History. . . ." She jumped up and down, did a jitterbug around the table, shouted, "All right!" to the house. The house didn't reply.

She threw the envelope onto Michael's bed and ran out the front door. *Everything's all right now*, her mind caroled. *Everything's. . . .* She caught herself and assumed a more sedate pace. Well, no, everything wasn't all right now. That was only one worry eliminated, and she'd actually forgotten it over the more immediate worries of the last few days. The Ph.D. would make a difference with Michael—just what kind of difference she couldn't say—damn, she hadn't been worrying about getting a job, either. What an emotional roller coaster. No wonder she had a crick in her neck.

She was grinning like a squirrel with a mouth full of nuts. She tamped her expression into a crazed smile and headed for the footbridge. On an intercepting path with Harry Devlin, she noted. Reality struck again.

Mark was right. It looked as if it was going to rain; the northern horizon was ominous with dark clouds. The wind was stronger than it had been yesterday, gusty and damp. She should have put on her jacket. But then, she saw the Johnston children as they wandered along the banks of the stream. Their spindly, chill-reddened legs protruded from shorts even though their torsos were covered by sweaters. Well, Scots had tough knees.

A ray of sun glanced from beneath the advancing cloud and illuminated the church. The brassy light reminded Rebecca of her dream. She stood on the bridge rotating her shoulders and head, wincing, wondering if Rudesburn had a chiropractor.

At the excavation Michael was showing Hilary the ring. Elaine was adding to the ring's artifact record, and Tony was taking its picture. Rebecca half expected Dennis and Adele to rush forward to thrust microphones at it, but instead they were removing the plastic wrap from the skeleton under Mark's direction. Whether Jerry knew about the ring and its suggestive coat of arms was hard to say. He was in the hot seat on the porch of the church, puffs of cigar smoke emanating from his mouth like toxic fumes from a diesel truck, while Mackenzie stood on the lawn considering him as his wife would no doubt consider a hostile witness.

Detective Sergeant Devlin passed behind Rebecca, saying from the corner of his mouth, "His nibs is playin' up again, I see." She smiled at his departing back. Anyone who realized what an ass Jerry was couldn't be all bad.

The Johnston children were clustered at the edge of the burn, where the water invaded a willow's tangled roots. The oldest held onto the second while he fished a smudged white blob from behind the tangle. The youngest stood with her thumb jammed securely in her mouth, her eyes huge and frightened. A chill traced a cold fingertip down Rebecca's spine.

The oldest child lifted the blob. All three of them huddled around. The little one shrieked. Ravens shot from the trees. The middle boy spun around and saw Rebecca on the bridge. "Here, miss, here. . . ."

Rebecca ran. Part of her mind thought, *Why are children's accents always exaggerated versions of adults'?* The rest of her mind reeled with dread.

There among the reeds at the edge of the stream lay a white cloth bag. From the opening protruded two black and white paws and a small face. Guinevere, mouth open, eyes closed, whiskers matted.

With an incoherent cry of her own, Rebecca fell to her knees beside the animal and pulled her from the imprisoning cloth. Who? Her thoughts stuttered. Who could do such a thing? Why?

For a moment she stared, the cat's wet body a heavy weight in her hands. Then she detonated with rage. She picked the cat up by her hind legs and swung her up and down. Encouraged to see water trickling from her mouth, she stretched the animal across the grass and pushed at her ribs. Careful, careful, her bones were thin. . . . Water gushed from Guinevere's mouth, and she wriggled.

Someone else was kneeling in the muddy reeds. Long, tapering fingers were pressing on the cat. "Poor little beggar," said a male voice. And a young female voice said with a quaver, "Is she going to be all right?"

Rebecca glanced around. The stream bank was thronged with people. Mackenzie knelt beside her, pressing gently on the cat's ribs. Devlin and Michael knelt in the mud and reeds and pooled water. Adele clasped the sobbing little girl. Tony's mouth hung open, as limp as his hand dangling a camera. Dennis looked ill. Hilary and Mark stood protectively over the two boys. Elaine's eyes bulged as she clutched Jerry's arm. Jerry himself hung back uncomfortably, his cigar plugging his mouth like the little girl's thumb plugged hers.

Rebecca wondered with a trace of hysteria whether Mackenzie's duties had ever before included administering artificial respiration to a cat.

Guinevere hissed and spat. Her claws left bloody grooves in Mackenzie's hand. Rebecca took off her sweater, and she and Michael managed to wrap it around the animal before she inflicted any more damage on her rescuers. Caroline would surely approve—the sweater was being used for a good cause.

Grant rushed up, shouldering his way through the crowd, collecting his children in one giant hug of his long arms. "There, there, they've sorted her oot. Thank the Chief Inspector and the lady."

The children's expressions were instantly transformed into joy. Dutifully they said their thanks. Guinevere, having none of it, yowled and struggled.

Without so much as a grimace Mackenzie wrapped his hand in his handkerchief. *He* would *carry a handkerchief*, Rebecca thought. Went with the tie. She stood up, clasping the spitting bundle, and gave her to Grant. "We'll put her doon afore the fire," he said, and directed his daughter, "Run, lass, tell your mum tae warm some milk."

The girl took off running toward the village. Cautiously, with admonitions of "Have a care" from their father, the two boys took Guinevere and carried her away like Cleopatra in her carpet. Mackenzie examined the sodden, muddy bag and the length of twine that had bound it shut. "A pillowcase. P.C. Johnston, can you identify it?"

Only now, with his children safely away, did Grant's rosy complexion go ashen. He took the pillowcase and flipped out the hem. In small precise letters were inked the initials "G.J." "It's ours, right enough. Winnie left the wash on the line, it was such a grand night."

The silence was so profound that the noise of the stream sounded like a flood. A gust of wind rattled the willow branches overhead. Rebecca stepped back and collided with a lean body. A firm, familiar hand closed on her arm. Michael's voice said, "Bluidy hell, all she did was bring in the wax seal."

If anyone could make a quantum leap of perception, and be unafraid to put it into words, Michael could. Rebecca's horror-struck eyes met Mackenzie's blank stare. It was not comforting to know the man could be taken aback. She said, her voice grating her throat, "It wasn't Guinevere who brought me the seal. It was Lancelot."

"The other cat?" Devlin asked. "Where is he?"

With a universal mutter of concern the group scattered, leaving Rebecca, Michael, and Mackenzie like jetsam on the banks of the burn.

Rebecca's wet legs and feet were icy, but not as icy as her face. What sick, evil spite, to murder the cat in revenge for exposing the warrant. She'd been right. Not only wasn't Sheila killed for personal reasons, but also the murderer hadn't achieved his or her aims with Sheila's death. "Now," Rebecca said under her breath, "I'm really scared."

"That makes two of us," Michael returned.

They stood together on the banks of the stream. Mackenzie paced grimly toward the church. It started to rain.

Chapter Seventeen

AFTER HALF AN hour's frenzied search, Winnie Johnston found Lancelot asleep in her kitchen cabinet, draped gracefully around a deep fat fryer. He considered the dozen people in his audience, yawned, and stretched. Devlin made a note in his notebook, the children carried Lancelot into the sitting room to join Guinevere, and everyone went back to work.

The cloister was swathed in funereal gloom, silent except for the scrape-slap of Mark's, Jerry's, and Michael's trowels. The wet grass muffled Adele's footsteps. The click of Elaine's keyboard was absorbed by the stone walls of the church. Mackenzie and Devlin cornered Dennis by the blocked crypt door, their voices low and studiedly casual. Tony swathed his cameras in little plastic raincoats and carried on.

Rebecca's spade ground against some lumps she identified as pottery. She picked up a trowel and pecked carefully at the assorted lumps. *Who knows which cat dragged in the seal?* she asked herself. She did. And Mark. And Michael because they'd told him. A few surreptitious glances had shown her no scratches on anyone except Mackenzie, who'd earned his honorably. But Guinevere was a trusting soul; chances were she hadn't realized what was happening until it was too late. It always came down to trust.

Not one of the circle of faces watching her and Mackenzie resuscitate the cat had betrayed any guilt. Even Tony, who preferred birds to cats, had looked as sick as the rest.

Guilt? she asked herself. Whoever tried to kill Guinevere, like whoever did kill Sheila, probably considered his or her actions

perfectly logical. And surely the same person was responsible
for both. Having two separate killers on the premises was just
too much.

Nothing happened anymore without that circle of faces closing
in like the drawstrings of a bag. For a moment Rebecca felt cold,
clammy cloth sealing her mouth and nose, and she shuddered
violently. The cat had been caught in the roots of the willow.
Like Moses in the bulrushes, some supernatural power had saved
her from being swept into oblivion. Maybe it was Anne's power.
And yet Anne supposedly cursed lovers who came to Rudesburn
carrying the baggage of other places and other times.

Rebecca rubbed her cold, raw hands on her legs and tried to
ignore the prickle between her shoulder blades. The attack on
the cat was almost more frightening than Sheila's actual murder,
evidence of a terrible malice at work. Guinevere was an innocent
bystander, but Sheila had been involved in something. . . . No
matter what Sheila was up to, she hadn't deserved a knife in the
heart.

Rebecca mopped a piece of pottery on the damp grass. Just as
she'd thought. Typical Cistercian ware made in the north of
England, red fabric with a brown glaze. The shards looked more
like the sweepings of the kitchen rather than a complete implement. Just the same, she should borrow Hilary's drawing board
and make a sketch.

She clambered out of the first trench. Tony was juggling two
different cameras, peering down into the third trench where the
body lay upside down like an astronaut in free-fall. A free-fall
into death, Rebecca thought. It happened to everyone eventually. The object was to not be hurried into it.

"I'll be damned," called out Jerry. "Tony. . . ."

"Dennis!" Tony shouted. "Fetch the lights!"

Dennis and his chaperones appeared in the doorway of the
church. "Now what?" asked Mackenzie.

"Come look at this, Inspector," Jerry returned.

"Chief Inspector," corrected Devlin.

Jerry's hair was matted brown by the rain. He pulled off his
glasses, mopped at them, put them back on and blinked in owl-
ish smugness. Michael's hair hung lank over his forehead and
ears. Mark's stood up spikily. Both blue eyes and gray sparkled.

Rebecca accepted Michael's wet, cold hand and stepped down
into the musty depths of the trench. The skeleton was framed by
its supporting timbers, a macabre bas-relief sculpture on a dark

brown wall. Its head and shoulders were still buried, but its ribs stood out in stark parallel lines against the mud. Between two of them was a ridge of rust extending into a knob that could have been either wood or ivory.

Michael said, "There's your rondel, Rebecca. A dagger through the heart. He was killed."

The walls of the trench seemed to ooze forward. The watching faces registered various expressions, calculated interest from the police and Jerry, nausea from Hilary and Elaine, a firm nod from Adele. Dennis hoisted a light, and the whir of Tony's camera was loud enough to blank out the murmur of the rain. In the sudden luminescence, the brown bones looked doubly ghastly.

"Was he a Scot killed by a Sassenach?" Michael went on, so quickly she deduced he was trying to break the silence. "Or vice versa? Or was it something else entirely, no political at all?"

"Got him from the front," said Devlin. "Someone he knew, perhaps. At least a fair fight."

"If it'd been a fair fight," Michael asked, "would they've bunged him into the cellar?"

"He's not wearing armor," said Jerry. "Not a soldier."

"At least," Mark added, "not soldiering when he was killed. A duel, maybe? Look at the traces of gold thread there and there. And the shreds of cloth—I bet they'll turn out to be linen or even silk. Somebody wealthy and influential. The rondel might have been his own."

"A hurried burial," asserted Jerry, turning up his volume. "The murderer didn't even retrieve his weapon."

Unlike Sheila's killer, Rebecca added silently. *And this body wasn't meant to be found.* She said aloud, "The signet ring has the Elliot coat of arms on it. I suppose there's a chance he, the body, is the commendator."

"Why the hell didn't you tell me that earlier?" Jerry demanded.

"Sorry," she said with a sigh.

"We'll have to call a news conference," the archeologist continued, his face lighting eagerly behind its scum of dirt and damp. "This ties in with the brouhaha about Anne. Wasn't he accused along with her?"

"Aye, that he was," said Michael.

"No news conferences," Mackenzie directed, "until you have a lot better evidence than you have the now."

"Circumstantial evidence," huffed Jerry. "Men have been hanged on less than we have now."

"Not in my jurisdiction, Dr. Kleinfelter. Rudesburn is getting altogether too much publicity already."

"That's the object of the excavation!"

Tony's camera whirred on, recording the discussion and the faces of its spectators moving back and forth as if they were watching tennis at Wimbledon. With a boost from Michael, Rebecca climbed out of the trench, followed by Mark. "My money's on Mackenzie," he whispered, stifling a grin. And, louder, "Let me check the site records on those little nails. I'm under the impression one of his shoes was tossed in after him, not left on his foot."

Elaine said, "I'll find the file for you . . ."

"Elaine!" shouted Jerry. "Gather up the tools, it's lunch time." And to Mackenzie, "Let's see what Baird has to say about this. The reporters are all here. It'd be a waste not to use them." He gestured toward the perimeter wall, but only one or two stubborn faces showed above it, hats dripping. The reporters were no doubt entrenched in the hotel bar.

Devlin followed Jerry as he started purposefully in that direction, like a dog nipping at the heels of a recalcitrant sheep. Mackenzie walked behind them with a determined expression that boded ill for Jerry's delusions of grandeur. Tony gathered his cameras, probably hoping for more fireworks.

"I'll find the file, Mark," Dennis said as he stowed the lights.

"I'm computer-friendly," protested Mark.

Hilary looked hopefully at Adele. "Do you think your soup is ready yet? I could sure use something hot."

"Tea," stated Michael. "Lots of tea."

Adele's soup was delicious. After Rebecca helped clear the table she went into the bedroom and found Michael reading her letter from Missouri.

He glanced up. His brows struggled to find equilibrium among the several expressions fighting for control of his face, finally settling on a wary slant which diluted his pleased grin into a polite smile. "Were you no goin' to tell me?"

"Of course I was. This is the first time we've been alone since I got it." Rebecca embraced him. Still he held the letter extended behind her back. "Should I wait until Mackenzie or Jerry say 'Miss Reid' and then correct them? How about a party?" His body in her arms was as cautious as his brows. Even when he put the letter in the envelope and hugged her back, his arms were stiff. She gabbled on, "I think I detect the fine hand of Dr. Nelson, pushing the committee to move a little faster, to decide while I was still here."

"Congratulations," Michael said. His arms tightened into a fierce embrace that made her ribs protest. His breath caressed her hair in a laugh.

The rue in that laugh made her look sharply into his face. "Michael?"

His eyes were glassy. He kissed her, missing her mouth by an inch. "Congratulations. I knew you could do it, Dr. Reid." He walked not only out of the room, but also out of the house, shutting the door quietly behind him.

Rebecca stood staring after him. Never in her worst nightmares did she think he'd want her to fail. Never did she think she'd have to tiptoe around his ego. Never, that is, until Monday. Her rondel, he had said—he didn't have to remind her of that mistake.

Her jaw hurt as she suppressed something between a scream and a moan. She stamped out into the hall, only to be captured by Dennis. "Look at this, Rebecca."

Mark sat at the table, tapping on the computer keyboard, his eyes fixed on the screen. "Elaine made these entries, didn't she?"

With considerable effort Rebecca squashed down her emotions and peered at the dark tracks of letters on the silver screen. "Yes."

"It says here that the penny we found in the layer above the skeleton was in a pouch hanging from its belt."

Rebecca's heart, already overloaded, lurched. "Implying the dating is more exact than it really is. Associating the body with Henry the Eighth—a name familiar even to the culturally deprived. Archeological evidence is easy to fudge, isn't it, because you destroy it as you go along. Hell."

"You think the record was altered deliberately?" demanded Mark.

"By Jerry," Dennis stated. The stabbing sharpness in his voice made Rebecca spin toward him. He ducked her scrutiny, looked down at the floor and added, "Why would Elaine fudge the records? She handed over the computer without a squawk, not as if she was trying to hide anything."

I didn't think you were a dummy, Rebecca said to herself.

"Why don't we go and ask Dr. Kleinfelter just what's going on here?" She headed out the door, Dennis beside her, Mark and the computer just behind.

It was still raining, even though the sky looked a little lighter, the cloud cover thinner. The face of the priory was as silver as the computer screen, inscribed not with liquid crystal letters but with cracks and shadow. Laurence expostulated to Jerry's glowering face, Mackenzie standing to one side, Elaine to the other, Tony just behind. Devlin and a couple of bobbies strolled diffidently by the gatehouse as several reporters beat up and down outside. Jerry had probably been dropping hints in the hotel gent's room. Hilary and Adele waited in the doorway of the church, while the top of Michael's head showed in the trench.

"No news conference," said Laurence, in a tone that indicated this was his last repetition. "Not until we have something positive to present. The opening of the grounds at the Festival, in two weeks, will be time enough. The publicity we've been getting isn't the kind I bargained for."

"Jesus!" Jerry snapped. "Why'd you hire me if you won't cooperate . . ." He saw the trio with the computer. "What are you doing with that?"

"Our work," said Rebecca. "I'm afraid we've found a discrepancy in the files. The penny was in the dirt above the bones, wasn't it, not actually connected to them?"

Behind the misty lenses of his glasses Jerry's eyes bulged. "Elaine! Where do you get off fouling up the site recording sheets?"

Michael came out of the trench like a jack-in-the-box. Elaine's lipsticked mouth opened and shut. Rebecca's frazzled nerves could almost hear her thinking, "What does he want me to say?" It was to Rebecca she spoke, her dark eyes flaring. "Are you accusing me of not doing my work proper?"

"Somebody made a mistake," Rebecca returned. "I didn't say it was you. Although I'd appreciate it if you'd fix it."

Elaine snatched the computer from Mark's hands. With a piercing glance at Jerry, she marched back into the church. Jerry looked belligerently around the group. "Well," he said to the air between Laurence and Mackenzie, "women, you know. Not very good with machines. I'll keep a better eye on her."

Rebecca fantasized integrated circuit cards plugging Jerry's gaping mouth. She turned, collided with Tony, and picked up her trowel. Michael slipped back into the trench, muttering something about "fair scunnered." Just as long as it was Jerry he was mad at, not her.

The debate over a news conference, deftly moderated by Mackenzie, concluded with an agreement to wait until further evidence was found, but not necessarily until the Festival. Laurence offered Michael a few complimentary words and returned to the village shaking his head. The rain slackened and stopped, leaving the stone and the grass sparkling damp, the air fresh as a lover's kiss. . . . She would have to think of that, Rebecca reprimanded herself.

She looked for Hilary—time to make a drawing of the shard jigsaw puzzle—and saw Devlin escorting her into the church. He beckoned to Rebecca.

No, she wailed silently, *I've had enough for one day, no!* Gnashing her teeth, she climbed out of the trench, laid the spade carefully down on the grass, and trudged into the church. Devlin was just doing his job. They were all just doing their jobs.

Elaine sat by Salkeld's tomb, her back turned, her fingers clicking on the keyboard. Beside her several site recording sheets were weighted by a brick, their edges curling in the chill breeze. Hilary sat on one of the folding chairs liberated from the Craft Centre, her ankles held primly together, her hands folded, her face helpful if somewhat puzzled at Rebecca's entrance. Her pinned-up hair left the nape of her neck exposed in all its fragility.

Devlin sat just behind her, Mackenzie to one side. Rebecca sat down and asked him, "How's your hand?"

Mackenzie seemed surprised at her question. "It will heal." Despite Nora's best efforts, his suit still showed traces of those harried moments on the soggy banks of the burn, but his dignified bearing wasn't at all damaged.

Notebook pages flipped. Devlin said, "No usable fingerprints on either the coins or the warrant, Miss Reid."

Still confiding in me, she thought. "I heard from my university this morning. I've been awarded my Ph.D. It's Dr. Reid now."

"Wow!" exclaimed Hilary. "That's great! Congratulations!" She wasn't in competition with Rebecca; her grin was perfectly genuine.

So was Mackenzie's nod of acknowledgement. "Best wishes, Dr. Reid." Devlin's pen scratched something out.

Mackenzie turned to Hilary. "Miss Chase, I'd like you to tell us about the court case in which you were involved three years ago."

Hilary's eyes grew round. She looked quickly from side to side. There was no escape. Embarrassed, Rebecca focused down the nave. Tony sat on the porch outside the west door cleaning his lenses, every now and then sighting toward the wheel-cross. Elaine's fingers tapped on the keyboard, sounding like the rattle of small arms fire.

"The—court case," murmured Hilary. "Is it important now?"

"Aye, lass, I'm afraid it is," Mackenzie said.

Hilary compressed herself into a defensive bundle. Her voice was staccato with haste. "I got myself—I was raped. By my mother's step-brother. He'd been after me for years, I guess, but I never understood what all his jokes meant, I just knew I never liked the way he touched me. Then he came to the house one night when my parents were out."

The roof creaked gently, and something fluttered in the tower. Rebecca reached over and laid her hand gently on Hilary's knotted fingers.

Hilary didn't look up. Her face drooped, abused by gravity, but she didn't cry. She probably didn't have any more tears to shed. "I fought. I screamed. But the house is big, the servants have their own rooms beyond the kitchen, and they didn't hear. Or maybe they did hear and didn't want to get involved. I didn't tell anyone, not for several days.

"But then I, well, I hurt so bad I had to go to the doctor. And told my parents. At first they didn't believe me. Then they fought, and threw things, and finally called the police. Ben told everyone I'd led him on. Dressing in pretty clothes and smiling at him. Everything a girl's supposed to do. Then they found pornography in his apartment and found out he had a charge account at a brothel in Chicago. He went to prison. I went into therapy, and then away to college. The horrors—they come and go. But you wouldn't understand that."

"No," Mackenzie agreed.

Rebecca felt Devlin's gaze on the back of her neck. Her neck hurt. With her free hand she rubbed it.

"Ben's out on parole," Hilary said, a little louder. Elaine stopped typing and looked up, but not around. "That's why I'm here. I might just live here in Europe for a while, after the dig is over."

"He's out already?" Rebecca asked. "I would've thrown away the key."

"He had a good lawyer," said Hilary. "He could afford one."

Like Amanda Fraser Mackenzie? Above Hilary's bowed head Rebecca met the Chief Inspector's eye. She wanted to ask tartly, "Are you happy now?" But his face was set, mouth tight, eyes narrowed, in acute discomfort. Devlin's pen scratched raggedly on.

Hilary's face was haggard and pale. "Do you think I killed Sheila because of what happened to me? Some kind of *ex post facto* reasoning, that it was her fault? That it was the fault of her kind of woman?"

Mackenzie said, "We're just exploring every possible motive."

"I saw her with Mark once," Hilary continued. "I was really disappointed that a nice guy like him could be taken in by such sleaze. But I guess he realizes that . . ." Her voice trailed off, and she bit her lip.

Rebecca waited for Mackenzie to assure Hilary that her tentative probings toward Mark were none of the police's business. He didn't. With a defiant glance toward him she said, "Hilary, Michael had an affair with Sheila a couple of years ago. I know how you feel, in spades. I'd say I had an even better motive to kill Sheila. But I didn't, just as you didn't."

Hilary looked gratefully at Rebecca, squeezed her hand, and shoved it gently aside. She sat up straight, squaring her shoulders. "The thing is, I was pretty upset the night Sheila died."

"Why?" asked Mackenzie.

"Because I went over to the church to get the computer printouts right after supper and saw Sheila vamping Jerry."

"What?" Rebecca asked. Hilary had withheld evidence? Mackenzie's black eyes glinted.

"Doin' what?" Devlin asked.

"Making up to him. Coming on to him. Flirting suggestively."

"And how did he respond?" Mackenzie asked.

Hilary snorted. "Like any man would. They went through the slype, toward the back of the chapter house, groping each other. I wasn't about to follow them. I forgot the printouts, came back to the house, and helped Mark do the dinner dishes. Then he kissed me, and I panicked. I went for a walk until I felt better. When I ran into Jerry in the bar, I couldn't figure out why, if he'd just been—been with Sheila, he was coming on to me so strong."

"It's an addiction," said Rebecca, and received Mackenzie's warning glance pertaining to editorial opinions.

"Maybe his performance wasn't satisfactory," offered Devlin, "and Sheila slagged him off about it."

There's a thought. Rebecca nodded. Sheila evidently had unorthodox tastes. Jerry's macho posturing could well mean that he didn't.

Elaine bent over the keyboard. She must have caught something of that revelation. Beyond her Tony worked on his cameras, oblivious to the drama behind his back. Rebecca wondered how bothered he would have been if he'd seen Jerry and Sheila intent on a carnal encounter. If anything, he'd always seemed amused by her untiring efforts to serve mankind.

"Why," Mackenzie asked, "didn't you tell us when we spoke with you on Tuesday about Dr. Kleinfelter and Miss Fitzgerald?"

Hilary met his indignant gaze, chin up. "But you already knew they were getting it on, didn't you? I sure didn't want to talk about it."

"Aye, we knew. But to be having it off at that particular moment . . ." He glanced at Elaine. "Did you hear them talking?"

"Only a few words about the dig, about relics. Jerry said something to the effect that all the legends are well and good, but we don't know for sure Marjory brought it here until we find it. I guess he meant Marjory Douglas, who founded the priory."

"Go on," urged Rebecca, on the edge of her seat.

"And Sheila said something to the effect, you're the expert, that's the bargain, you find it and I publicize it. I don't know what 'it' was."

Again Mackenzie and Rebecca shared a glance. The reliquary containing Robert the Bruce's heart? Maybe it was mentioned in the trial records, for them to know about it. . . . "Here we go again," she said with a sigh. "All this time, and we get two flecks of evidence against Jerry in one day, mostly by wild extrapolation, which doesn't make Jerry a killer."

"Did you ever doubt Jerry and Sheila had been planning an end run?" Devlin asked, relishing his new bit of American slang.

"No, I didn't. Not after what Dr. Nelson told me about Jerry's dig in Virginia."

Elaine's shoulders were coiled, radiating anger.

"Miss Chase, you should've told us this earlier," Mackenzie chided.

"I didn't know it was important," said Hilary miserably. "I'm sorry."

Rebecca grimaced. "I should have told you about our suspicions of Jerry and Sheila. You would have realized what you were hearing. And yet I really couldn't." She sighed. "Catch me later, and I'll explain."

"It's our job to decide what's important," said Mackenzie. "Thank you for helping us. If we've caused you any discomfort. . . ." He stopped, cleared his throat, and made a show of looking over Devlin's notebook.

Thus dismissed, Hilary stood and shook herself. She walked out the door, lifting her feet as though they wore cement boots.

"May I go?" Rebecca asked Mackenzie.

"Oh, aye. Ask Dr. Kleinfelter to come round if you would, please." Mackenzie turned his gaze on Elaine, much as Jerry would contemplate an artifact, trowel in hand. "Miss Vavra, may we speak to you a moment?"

Elaine snapped to her feet, tossed her head, and advanced on Mackenzie with the clicking steps and flashing eyes of a flamenco dancer. *The worm turns*, Rebecca thought. *Serves Jerry right*. She went outside and walked toward the trench. Jerry was holding forth on some arcane aspect of bone preservation. Hilary sat down with her drawing board and stared blankly at it. Mark looked at her, his brows knit with puzzled concern.

Rebecca told Jerry the inquisitors were waiting.

Chapter Eighteen

ADELE SAT ON the stump of the wall cleaning Jerry's trowels. She kept eyeing the third trench, her face somber, as if she were the next of kin of the emerging skeleton. Dennis did some desultory spade work in the second trench, glancing over his shoulder at Jerry rebelliously continuing his monologue on bones rather than jumping to attend Mackenzie. Hilary settled her drawing board and poised her pencil.

"I'm sorry you had to go through that." Rebecca's trowel exposed another lump of pottery, this one a curved handle.

"Telling about it isn't the hard part," Hilary returned.

Through the transept door came Elaine's voice, angry enough to scatter its "h's" far and wide. " 'E gave me that paper and said to copy hit hinto the computer. I didn't change sod-all."

"And what were you and Dr. Kleinfelter going to do after the dig?" asked Mackenzie, his voice the bass line to Elaine's treble.

" 'E was going to take me back to the States, wasn't 'e? Even if 'e scarpered then, I'd be away from 'ere."

"You'd like to emigrate?"

"Who wouldn't? Cost of living's over the top, and the dole pays more than anything you can get at the job center."

Jerry strolled into the church, fashionably late. Elaine stopped abruptly. Rebecca uncovered a pottery piece the size of her hand, the curved side of a bowl or beaker.

"Sit down, Dr. Kleinfelter," said Mackenzie. Chairs scraped on the tile floor. "Are you sure the data you gave Miss Vavra to enter into the computer was completely accurate?"

"Anything I did was accurate," Jerry answered, in his favorite "why am I dealing with idiots" tone. "Of course, I'm the only professional here."

Mackenzie went about on another tack. "Miss Vavra, tell us again about the night Miss Fitzgerald was killed."

Elaine's voice was cold enough to reclaim her BBC accent. "I waited in the hotel room for Jerry. He said we'd suss out the pubs in Jedburgh, but he had to do something first. He was chuffed over it, whatever it was."

"I was pleased the dig was going well," said Jerry. The faint odors of cigar and cigarette smoke fouled the breeze.

"I waited," Elaine continued. "When he came back, the knees of his trousers were stained. I asked him if he'd been with Sheila. He laughed at me, said he'd slipped into one of the trenches. Mind you, this is the same toff who'll tick off anyone who comes within a foot of a trench. I'd taken enough aggro. I left, went to Newtown St. Boswells by myself."

"We took statements from the barman at a pub," Devlin said, "and from the cashier at the petrol station where she bought cigarettes. She returned here just after nine o'clock."

"The stains on his trousers were what color?" asked Mackenzie.

"Green and brown, not red." Elaine sighed. *Regret?* Rebecca wondered waspishly. *Or relief?*

"Bloodstains do turn brown," Mackenzie pointed out.

Jerry snorted. "Not that fast."

"Do you know, then, Dr. Kleinfelter, when Miss Fitzgerald was killed?"

Rebecca carefully pulled the curved piece of pottery from its matrix of mud. Beneath it were several dark specks. Some kind of grain, probably. A storage jar. She needed to put some in a plastic bag for analysis, but the conservation supplies were in the church. Obviously Mackenzie didn't realize how well the building's acoustics were broadcasting his interview.

"You were here at the priory with Miss Fitzgerald," Mackenzie insisted. "You were seen."

"All right, all right," Jerry exclaimed. "I was with Sheila in the ruins. She'd asked me to meet her, said she had information about some relics. That's when she told me she'd found those records misfiled at the museum. She knew there was something about the heart of Robert the Bruce, she could read that much. When she looked old Bobby up and saw the Douglas connection, she figured she was on to something."

"And you didn't urge her to return the records she'd stolen?"

"Not stolen, really—I mean, we needed them for the dig. They'll get back to the museum. Assuming you let them go."

"Last Monday night was the first time you'd heard about those records?"

"Yeah, well, I'd heard rumors in London last spring."

Aha, said Rebecca to herself. *Michael, we twigged it.*

"When you were hiring Miss Fitzgerald to make the film?"

Elaine said parenthetically, "That's not all he was doing with her."

Jerry didn't speak. The smoke wafting from the doorway thickened, as though a small angry dragon lurked inside, watching for passing princesses.

Rebecca's trowel clinked against metal. She probed and scraped. A horseshoe. Interesting—kitchen debris shouldn't include a horseshoe. The priory didn't even have a stable. She put a measuring stick across the horseshoe. Hilary drew it onto her plan.

Adele set down the last of the trowels, scooped the pile of dirt beside the trench into her bucket, and carried it out through the slype. Dennis picked up an earthworm from the bottom of the second trench and set it aside. "Jaw ahoy," said Mark. Michael responded, "Well done. Have a care for the teeth." Tony walked around the inside of the cloister, stopping every few paces for a shot of the entire field.

"Why didn't you tell us of your bargain with Miss Fitzgerald," Mackenzie prodded, "you to discover the artifact, she to publicize it?"

Feigned ignorance was hardly Jerry's style. "The same person who was spying on us was eavesdropping, I see."

"Why didn't you—" Mackenzie began to repeat.

"In the process of scientific investigation," Jerry interrupted, "we scientists have to keep our cards close to our chests. Just like detectives. You aren't telling everybody what clues you have, are you? You have to keep the hoi polloi from stepping all over the evidence."

"Why didn't you tell us about the possible existence of the relic?"

"It wasn't any of your business, that's why."

But Mackenzie did share clues, Rebecca thought. His game was more complex than Jerry reckoned. Rebecca visualized Devlin shooting a sharp glance at the back of Jerry's head and

Mackenzie leaning back with the slow smile of a leopard perched on a branch above a waterhole. "You had another reason for meeting Miss Fitzgerald that night."

"Nothing like a woman scorned, right, Elaine?" Jerry's voice was as taut as a tight-walker's rope. "Sheila was insatiable. She liked getting it on in all sorts of strange places."

There was a moment's silence, but he didn't elucidate. Tony stopped outside the transept door, not even pretending not to listen. His placid expression soured, indicating that no one knew Sheila's tastes better than he. God, Rebecca thought, there really were other ways to make friends and influence people. "Jerry thinks Elaine turned him in," she said to Hilary.

The girl replied, "She can deal with him better than I can."

"Was Miss Fitzgerald wearing her nun's robes?" asked Mackenzie.

"Sure," Jerry said. "That's how she got her jollies."

"Did you enjoy . . ." Mackenzie paused, weighing his words ". . . meeting her in unusual places?"

"Inspector, none of this is even remotely relevant to the murder."

"Or was it expected of you, part of your bargain?"

Jerry didn't answer.

"Was she pleased with your efforts that evening?"

"They didn't half have a row," offered Elaine. "His nibs here wasn't best pleased when he came back to the hotel. Not at all that airy-fairy look men usually get afterwards."

Devlin cleared his throat, as if smothering a laugh. "So then you had a row with him yourself?"

"Right."

"And you, Dr. Kleinfelter," Mackenzie stated, "went into the bar and started talking to Miss Chase."

Hilary's pencil slashed at the paper, completing the horseshoe. Tony walked away from the door, his face creased with disgust. Adele returned to the cloister and starting scooping up Rebecca's loose dirt. Rebecca's trowel scraped against another piece of pottery, the rim of a plate, perhaps.

"When did P.C. Johnston see Miss Fitzgerald in the call box, Sergeant?"

"Seven-fifteen," Devlin answered.

"So you met her when, Dr. Kleinfelter?"

"Right after seven-fifteen. She was waiting outside the phone booth. We walked into the ruins."

"When did you return to the hotel?"

"Hell if I know."

"It was seven-forty-five," said Elaine. "I left straightaway."

About eight, Rebecca said to herself. She'd seen Elaine drive off. And Laurence crossing the street, and Winnie looking out her window.

"So," Mackenzie said, neither questioning nor stating, "we know Miss Fitzgerald was alive at seven-forty-five."

"She was alive and kicking when I left her," asserted Jerry.

"And Mrs. Baird," Devlin added, "saw you come into the bar at eight-fifteen."

Silence. Rebecca could work the equation for herself. If Jerry killed Sheila, it had been between seven-fifteen and seven-forty-five. If Jerry was telling the truth, she hadn't died until later. Elaine and Jerry confirmed each other's alibis, unless they were conspiring together. That matchbook with the phone number written on it indicated a smoker. But then, someone could have used it as a notepad; none of the matches was missing.

Rebecca levered up the piece of pottery, telling herself it was entirely likely that plots were lurking beneath. But nothing was there but a thick bone. Ox, maybe. Kitchen remains, jumbled together with a horseshoe. And that malicious spoon and flesh hook in the other trench.

Her fingers stroked the slimy piece of ceramic. The gray-green of the afternoon swam before her eyes. 1545. English troops sacked the priory. They threw away bones and pottery as worthless and rode their horses through the cloister, hooves tossing dirt and grass. Women screamed, robes fluttering, as mail-clad soldiers. . .

Her mind sputtered faintly and she shook herself. Never mind what the soldiers might or might not have been doing. Hertford, their commander, had a decent streak.

The edge in Elaine's voice was blunted. "I'm leaving. I'm going back to London. I'm tired of this argy-bargy. It's not bloody worth it."

"Go on," Jerry retorted. "The nerd can do the hacking. There's plenty of what you have to offer available elsewhere."

A chair clattered. Feet scuffled. Devlin exclaimed, "Here now, that's not on. Stop it."

"Let me go," spat Elaine. The sounds of struggle subsided, but not before every face in the cloister had swiveled toward the church. Michael went so far as to climb out of his trench and amble toward Rebecca's, head cocked to the side like a bird dog spotting a grouse.

Mackenzie said sternly, "Miss Vavra, whether or not you continue to work for the expedition is your decision. But you aren't leaving Rudesburn. Dr. Kleinfelter, you're coming to Galashiels to help us with our enquiries."

"I have a dig to run!" Jerry shouted. "God only knows what those students will do without proper supervision! Archeological evidence is irreplaceable—if anything is damaged, Inspector, I'll hold you personally responsible. The dig is behind time anyway due to all this, this nonsense—"

"I wouldn't call a woman's death nonsense," said Mackenzie. Steps rang down the nave. Jerry, flanked by Devlin and Mackenzie, stalked off across the lawns toward the road. Perfunctorily the reporters raised their cameras.

Michael called, "Do try the police station's coffee, Jerry!" To Rebecca he said, "Has he been caught oot at last?"

"In some minor fiddling with the evidence, both archeological and criminal, yes." She quickly summed up the conspiracy to find the Bruce's heart, concluding, "But I can't see Jerry killing anyone. He's the type that's more bark than bite."

"And what type is it that kills?" Michael asked. "Bluidy hell. I actually wish we'd been wrong aboot the man."

"Yeah." Rebecca scuffed the dirt with her toe.

Adele headed purposefully toward the church, from which issued the sounds of desperate sobbing as Elaine either reached the extremity of her anger or already regretted burning her bridges with such vengeance. She'd made quite an investment in Jerry. But then . . . Rebecca thought with a glance at Michael.

Tony raised his video camera and focused on the skeleton. "Women," he muttered. "Always cutting up rough. Bonkers, the lot of them."

The angle of Michael's brows indicated wry agreement.

Hilary went on drawing, her pencil making abrupt jerks on the paper. "At least they didn't take me away. I guess that's a point in my favor."

"I think it is," Rebecca replied, "although I sure wouldn't make any assumptions. I'm surprised they didn't take Elaine, too."

"She wasn't here when Sheila was killed," Hilary said, and bent over a difficult part of the sketch.

Mark leaned on the edge of the trench and wiped his hand across his forehead, his clear gray eyes contrasting oddly with his dirty skin. Dennis watched Jerry and his keepers drive away. The young man's face reflected the grim determination of Sergeant Preston of the Yukon out to get his man. Not that Jerry hadn't been extremely rude to him, Rebecca thought, but Dennis was overreacting just a bit. The tension was contagious.

Rebecca chose one topic, quelling the rest, and showed Michael the scatter of pottery and the horseshoe. When she sketched out her conclusion, that this was the 1545 destruction level, she earned a smile and a "Well done."

"I need narration," said Tony, camera poised.

"After you, Alphonse." Mark bowed to Michael.

Michael brushed back his hair, straightened his jacket, and assumed his impeccable BBC accent. "The skull of the skeleton is now almost exposed. The mandible is slightly dislodged, perhaps because the mouth was hanging open as dirt was shoveled in upon it. The teeth show remarkably little wear; he was probably a young man of no more than thirty."

So, Michael admitted he was a man, Rebecca thought, not just an artifact. But they all knew academic-speak; like Mackenzie and his incessant use of the honorific, it was a way to distance oneself from emotion. The sleekly gleaming arch of the cranium didn't look that different from the pieces of pottery. She was glad the face of the body was still turned into the mud, a neophyte actor leery of his moment on stage. Dirt filling his mouth as he screamed. . . . Was he dead when he was buried? She did an about-face and saw Nora beckoning from the footbridge.

Rebecca tiptoed away from Tony's microphone. "You're wanted on the telephone," said Nora. "Kevin Reid. Your father?"

"My brother." With a smile that expressed both fondness and annoyance Rebecca hurried toward the hotel. The telephone receiver was lying amid a jumble of bills and letters on Laurence's desk. "Hello? Kevin?"

"Hey, Squirt!" His voice was as warm and unaffected as a ball park hot dog. "What time is it over there? I was afraid if I waited until the rates went down, I'd get you in the middle of the night."

"It's five in the afternoon. I was working. No problem."

"There was a paragraph in the paper about a bizarre ritual murder at a place named Rudesburn. I looked, and sure enough that's where you are. I know better than to ask you to bail out and come home, but, well, it's not any of those Satanists, is it?"

"There was a murder here, yes, but the bizarre aspects are just someone's sick sense of humor. I was hoping Mom and Dad wouldn't hear about it.'' The door of Laurence's safe was slightly ajar. She pushed is shut, but wasn't sure how to lock it.

"Mom and Dad won't unless Johnny Carson or Vanna White mentions it. I won't tell them, just as long as you're all right.''

"I'm tired and more than a little scared. But all right.''

"And your boyfriend—is he okay?''

"Michael's fine, thanks.''

"I'm glad you have someone to take care of you.''

"I can take care of myself.'' How quickly she fell back into the habitual cadences. She concluded lamely, "Don't worry about me.''

"Will you be back for Mom and Dad's fortieth anniversary in September?''

"I don't know. If I'm not, I'll send a present. Some Strathearn glass or something nice.'' *Like I usually do,* she thought, but Kevin didn't offer any rebukes. "I heard from the university. I got my Ph.D. I'm Dr. Reid, now.''

"You really wanted that, didn't you? That's great! Good for you!''

"Better not tell Mom and Dad just yet. They'll want to know why you were spending money calling me. I'll write.''

"You'll have to convince them you're not the kind of doctor who can treat sprains and bunions, but they'll be proud of you. Really, they will.''

Rebecca winced. Sometimes her parents called her a smart-alec college girl. "Thanks for calling. Nice to know you're thinking about me.''

"Take care, Squirt. I'm here if you need anything.''

"Thank you.'' She stood with her hand on the receiver, wondering just how Kevin had survived all these years when he insisted on calling her by such an appalling nickname. Probably because he'd always been so refreshingly banal. Once, when she was four and Kevin fourteen, he'd found her crying over a puddle of melted popsicle. With some of the money he'd earned mowing lawns he'd bought her a new treat and laughed at her sugar-smeared smile. She wished he could fix the murky puddle she was in now as easily. He would if he could. He meant well. They all meant well. She hurried through the lobby, feeling like something an entomologist would find under an overturned rock.

The reporters, having had their amusement for the day, were flocking back into the hotel. The various constables stood cross-eyed with boredom, probably dreaming of tea and scones. With sympathetic clucks Adele escorted a red-eyed Elaine across the street. Tony tagged behind, swathed with cameras, and said, "Cheer up, luv," to Rebecca as he passed.

She forced a smile. "Do you have siblings, Tony?"

He stopped, equipment swinging, startled. "I don't know. My mum was on the game—haven't a clue who my dad was, let alone any siblings."

"Oh." Blushing furiously she hurried away. Tony looked quizzically after her, then shrugged and went into the hotel, less perturbed about his mother having been a prostitute than Rebecca was.

Her cheeks were still flaming by the time she returned to the site and found Hilary collecting the day's site recording sheets and Michael and Mark covering the skeleton with plastic. "I'll ring Dr. Graham the morn," Michael was saying. "He'll be bringin' a team from Edinburgh to take the puir chap oot all of a piece and do a proper analysis in the lab." He saw Rebecca and asked, "Did someone ring us?"

"The call was for me. My brother Kevin."

"Ah." Dennis hurried the computer into the cottage, evading a shower of rain that spilled suddenly from the still cloudy sky. The evening would close in early. Already a damp, muffling silence hung over Rudesburn. "Kevin heard aboot the murder?" Michael continued, escorting Rebecca across the bridge.

"Yes. I managed to calm him down. And I told him my news."

Michael glanced around at Mark and said, in perfectly moderated nonchalance, "Rebecca just heard. She got her Ph.D."

"Great!" exclaimed Mark. "Congratulations! Let's have a ceilidh to celebrate—I can strum a few bars of 'Pomp and Circumstance.' "

Rebecca laughed. "Thanks."

"Will your family be pleased, then?" Michael held open the door.

"Pleased, I guess, if not particularly impressed. I'm the only one of them to even have a bachelor's degree."

"You've come a long way, baby," muttered Mark.

Hilary asked, "What would you have to do to impress them?"

"Get married and have children," Rebecca replied automatically.

Michael went toward the bathroom, Mark and Hilary up the stairs. Rebecca could read Michael's thought: "A fine thrawn lass you are, deliberately refusin' to do what your folks want you to do." She went into the bedroom and flopped down at the dressing table. In her pocket she found Colin's notepad with "Rudesburn Toys and Fancies" embossed on the cover. Meticulous handwriting filled the tiny pages. "5:30. Mark and Rebecca see Sheila running out of church. 7:30.

Adele meditating under yew tree.'' But Jerry hadn't volunteered the information that he and Sheila were holding wrestling matches behind the chapter house at 7:30. She wondered what other facts were missing—no blame to Colin.

Rebecca considered the rows of names and figures. The pathologist had estimated Sheila's time of death as between 7:15 and 9:15. And yet, if Mackenzie's assumption that someone from the dig had killed her was correct, every suspect was in some way accounted for after 8:15—except for Michael, but he hadn't done it. Add that to Jerry's assertion that Sheila had been alive at 7:45. . . . Rebecca frowned. Half an hour. It might have happened in half an hour, as Devlin and Mackenzie had no doubt already noticed.

She put the pad in the drawer. Her packet of birth-control pills lay on the edge of the dressing table where she always left them at night so Michael could bring her one in the morning. . . . Oh no. This morning they'd started fighting before they were even out of bed. Rebecca seized the packet and counted. Sure enough, the one for today was still nested in its plastic bubble. With one convulsive movement she punched it out and swallowed it, but her throat had gone so dry she almost choked. Birth is the flip side of death, after all—damn it all, something else to worry about.

Michael came in the door, his hair shining around his face, his chest and shoulders glistening above clean blue jeans. Odd how he wasn't at all appealing. ''I missed taking my pill this morning,'' she told him.

His expression did a slow doubletake into a sickly grin. ''A few hours'll no be makin' that big a difference.''

''The things aren't a hundred percent reliable as it is, Michael. A fact we've been conveniently ignoring.''

''There're only three days left in the packet. Dinna worry yoursel'.'' His hands squeezed her shoulders. Gravely they regarded each other's images in the mirror. His eyes were faceted so intricately with thought and emotion that she didn't know which surface to consider first. It wasn't that his emotional cannon were loaded and run out; she'd coped with that before, either by direct assault or by subterfuge. This was something more complex than defensiveness.

His hands fell. He finished dressing and went toward the kitchen. Rebecca dropped her face onto her clenched fists.

She sat there a long time, watching the thoughts crash and collide in her mind, but could find no pattern in them.

Chapter Nineteen

REBECCA FELT FOOLISH locking the doors behind her, but to assume the cottage was somehow beyond the territorial boundaries of the murderer would have been even more foolish. In a subdued knot, the students and their not-so-intrepid leaders trooped up the driveway, the cloud hovering above their heads almost visible.

The evening was painted in watercolor shades of green and gray. Rebecca squinted suspiciously at the priory, but it maintained its bland silence—as did the sentries dotted along the street, whose expressions now betrayed internal musings on the virtues of beer.

Michael lingered in the lobby, inflating his pipes, while everyone else homed in on the bar. From the reception desk, Bridget commented to Rebecca, "Michael looks right posh in his sweater."

"Thanks to you," Rebecca returned. "He was very grateful." She'd only remembered to give him back the mended sweater this evening. His punctilious courtesy had almost hurt.

"Your sweater's in my basket," Bridget went on. "Winnie's already cleaned it. I'll get it to you the morn's morn."

"Thank you. No rush. I'm just glad I could help the cat." Rebecca went on into the bar, avoiding the questioning glances of various strangers. Tourists and reporters, she guessed. Fortunately the Bairds didn't have room for more than a few guests; most of the ambulance-chasers were staying in Galashiels or Newton St. Boswells.

Rebecca made her announcement to Laurence more diffidently

than she'd have liked. Banging a spoon on a glass, Laurence transmitted the news. Congratulations poured in, leaving Rebecca blushing and bemused. Getting her degree wasn't what she'd imagined . . . she could no longer use it either as a carrot or a crutch.

Laurence gave her a glass of Laphroaig, then drew a pint of ale for Michael and a lager for Mark. Mark begin tuning his guitar, his fingertips cajoling trills from the strings like water laughing down the burn.

Tony and Elaine sat in a corner booth indulging in English slang and gin. ". . . po-faced berk Mackenzie," said Elaine, her expression indicating that it wasn't a compliment.

"Gormless," Tony agreed.

"And there's Dr. High and Mighty Kleinfelter. He's a proper wally."

"So you shopped him. Well done." They nodded over their glasses.

Dennis slid into their booth, smiling affably despite their blank stares. Adele accepted a glass of apple juice from Nora and sat down alone. Rebecca and Hilary headed toward the corner between the fireplace and the end of the bar. The cats reposed on the hearth in patrician splendor, rising above the indignities of the morning, although not so far they wouldn't accept Hilary's offer of tidbits saved from the dinner table. Rebecca pulled a chair around so that she could feel the warmth of the fire and still see the rest of the room. Making sure her back was to the wall, she thought, as if someone might attack her here in the pub. But still a spot between her shoulder blades itched just beyond her reach.

Guinevere leaped up into her lap. *How gracious I am*, said her smug expression, *to have allowed you to serve me this morning*. Rebecca smiled. She stroked the purring bundle of fur and sipped her whiskey. Mellow was unobtainable, but at least she could relax a little.

A weedy young man sat down next to Adele and greeted her with an ingratiating grin. At one moment Grant Johnston and two of his colleagues were leaning decoratively on the bar, at the next they were escorting the curious man back to his own seat.

That was Bob Jenkins, the reporter for the *Sunburn*, whom Sheila had called just before her death. Called about finding gold, he'd testified at the inquest. That he hadn't yet publicized the presence of gold at Rudesburn, and set off a rush of prospectors, Rebecca attributed less to his common sense than to Mackenzie's judicious blend of promises and threats.

Michael came down the hall playing an emphatic "Scotland the Brave." He followed that with "Tranent Muir" and a verse or two of "Johnnie Cope," making a trio of defiance. Mark enthusiastically strummed accompaniment. Someone else strolled in from the lobby, and Rebecca blinked. No, she wasn't imagining that hatchet face.

Simon Mackenzie joined Adele at her table and ordered lemonade. His raptorial gaze made a slow circuit of the room, considering each face. When he met Rebecca's eyes, he bowed over his glass. She lifted hers in return.

Michael stopped to catch his breath. Mark broke into "Dixie." The smooth amber whiskey slipped down Rebecca's throat, filling her senses with sunlight and smoke. Everyone was in the bar, she mused. This would be a good opportunity to search bedrooms. Except the police had already done that, were maybe doing it again even as she thought about it, would no doubt continue doing it on into the future.

The future. Rebecca fantasized Devlin and Mackenzie apprehending Sheila's killer. But the central role in that scenario had yet to be cast. She hadn't killed the woman. Neither had Michael. Or Hilary. Or Mark—she trusted her instincts enough to make that judgment. And she'd already discounted the townspeople. Unless further evidence presented itself, the list of suspects was down to five names.

Guinevere opened her eyes and glanced up with that peculiarly feline gleam that indicates profound skepticism. Rebecca continued stroking the animal's head until those accusing eyes closed.

"Dixie" ended with a flourish. Mark took a pull at his beer and began something classical. Michael leaned against the bar, cradling his pipes against his chest. Mackenzie made circles of condensation on the table with his glass.

For a moment Rebecca toyed with the classic mystery in which all the suspects were guilty. Some of these people, she thought, had known each other before the dig, but most were segregated geographically, economically, and intellectually. No. Any conspiracies were small ones.

Dennis. Rebecca was beginning to wonder how much of the young man's clumsiness was a front for some kind of secret agenda. She shifted uneasily and received a set of claws in her knee.

Elaine. She'd attacked Jerry this afternoon when he'd insulted her. God only knew Sheila had been proficient at insults. But had Elaine known of Sheila's plan to find the relic heart and the treasure?

Tony. He must have known something of Sheila's plan. And Sheila hadn't hesitated to play men off against each other; perhaps she'd been playing conspiracies as well.

Jerry. His bluster could well have teeth. He'd lied about being with Sheila right before her death, trying to salve his ego. What else had he lied about—the mistake in the computer record? The question was not so much whether Jerry's academic skulduggery fit into Sheila's murder as how far it did. The matchbook with the number of the British Museum on it was a minor point. So was the call to Jenkins. But they added up.

Adele, Rebecca thought. What about Adele?

"There is a ghost in the priory," Adele was insisting. "I've spoken with her. Anne Douglas. She was murdered."

"Oh aye?" Mackenzie said softly.

"An unhappy soul lingers for many reasons. Guilt, or to guard something, or to get revenge. In Anne's case, it could be all three. She's still in the priory because the soul persists in— haunts—the locale in which its strongest emotions were played out."

"Not everyone can sense a lingering soul."

"You have to open yourself to the resonances. Or else the resonances grow so strong even the unbeliever is taken unaware."

"Like Miss Fitzgerald, not long before she was killed?"

"Quite," said Adele. She smiled serenely into her glass. Mackenzie looked at her as if she were sliced, stained, and flattened on a slide beneath a microscope, but she seemed unaware of his scrutiny.

Mark caressed his guitar, annotating Battlefield Band's "Peace and Plenty" with subtle grace notes. The evocative melody filled the room. Rebecca indulged in another fantasy—a wedding, and she and Michael dancing to those delicate notes, wounds healed, commitments made. . . .

The music stopped. Mark acknowledged his applause with a shy grin. Michael advanced to center stage, and together they played "Amazing Grace."

Hilary scooted her chair a little closer to Rebecca's. "It's scary how much sense Adele makes sometimes."

"If she wants to explain the whatever-it-is at the priory as some poor tortured ghost," Rebecca replied, "let her. They don't kill people for witchcraft any more."

Hilary looked puzzled.

"One of the classic accusations of witchcraft was 'summoning spirits,' " Rebecca explained. "Seeing ghosts would have put you into real hot water in Anne's day."

"You said you and Michael saw ghosts last winter."

"Heard them, smelled them, felt them—seeing was only a part of it. Something about Celtic blood, I guess; your receiver is tuned to ghoulies and ghosties and long-leggety beasties and things that go bump in the night."

"My ancestors came from all over, and I hear those bumps coming from the priory just as much as you do." Hilary eyed her glass of wine and found it uninhabited by any ghoulies. She drank. "If anyone haunts the priory, you'd think Sheila would. But maybe she's glad it's all over. Having to keep up so much pretense must have been exhausting."

That itch on Rebecca's back became a slow crawl, like worms beneath her skin. Guinevere stirred in her sleep, her eyes slits of gold. The song finished, and Mark put down his guitar and headed for the bar.

Mackenzie left Adele with a murmured farewell and slid in beside Elaine, facing Tony and Dennis. All three looked at him with varying grades of misgiving. He made some comment about the weather.

Hilary said, so quietly Rebecca hardly heard her, "I bet Sheila was sexually abused as a child. I learned in counseling that the trauma, the loss of self-esteem, drives some people out of control. Kind of like alcoholism. Thank God I didn't get hit that way."

Whatever Rebecca had been thinking was expelled from her mind like air from her lungs at a blow to the stomach. Mark, Hilary, Sheila, Tony, Marjory, and maybe even Anne; all of us, walking wounded in the sexual wars. There was a common strand that knit it all together—without explaining a thing.

A movement beyond Hilary's back was Mark, approaching their table carrying a fresh pint of lager. He stopped so suddenly at Hilary's words the beer slopped over the rim of the mug and ran onto his hand. His brows arched, and his eyes widened, flooded with comprehension and yet hating to comprehend. Rebecca ducked the question in his face. He turned back to the bar and wiped his hand and mug with Laurence's dish towel.

The fire died down, filling Rebecca's and Hilary's corner with shadow. Mark walked more heavily across the creaking wooden floor than necessary and sat down next to them, his expression muffled by gloom. Hilary sipped at her wine, not looking at him.

Michael was playing Runrig's "Pride of the Summer." "She was the pride of the summer that year, she was my sweetheart, my lady." His eyes peered around the thicket of drones, cautious, almost wistful, and yet characteristically stubborn. "Like a heartbeat, lonely and strong."

Lonely and strong? We've tried that. Rebecca looked into her empty glass and thought, *That's something I can remedy.* Gently she removed Guinevere from her lap, went to the bar, and refilled her whiskey.

Behind the bar was a poster advertising the Borders Festival, the old Lammas Fair, beginning on August 3rd—Michael's thirtieth birthday. No matter whether anything else was settled or not, she'd told him, on that day they would decide. . . . Baloney. Everything had to be settled, or no decision was possible. Her ghosts, and his, and all those other ghosts figurative and literal thronging the priory, had to be put to rest.

It was like her and Michael's sweaters. While his mother was knitting them, she had seen only one stitch at a time. But now all the separate strands, the seemingly unrelated knits, purls, cables, skipped stitches, together formed one overall pattern. Rebecca had to find that pattern even if a happy ending for her and Michael wasn't part of it.

The last strains of the song faded and died. Michael went to the lobby to put his pipes away. Now that the show was over, several tourists and reporters left, trailed by the extra constables. Dennis collected the keys and wandered off, muttering something about working on the computer records.

"Be my guest," Elaine told him. Picking up another gin and tonic, she walked out, too, leaving Tony and Mackenzie eyeing each other across the booth.

Mackenzie, Rebecca thought, hadn't questioned either Elaine or Jerry closely enough about the discrepancy of the penny. But then, the dig's academic problems weren't his. Fudging results caused only professional deaths, not human ones. Rebecca could lose everything here. . . . Her swallow of whiskey went down the wrong way, stinging her windpipe, and she coughed. She went back to the table where Mark and Hilary were intent on their respective drinks and dropped into her seat.

Adele said goodnight and left. Tony slipped out behind her. With a resigned shrug, Mackenzie joined the others at the bar. Michael returned and accepted another ale. Rebecca recognized the look in his eye; it was the same one she had. Attack the issues, force them if necessary, but never give up. He, too, seemed prepared to sacrifice their relationship to get to the truth.

Without asking Mackenzie's leave, Michael started telling Grant and the Bairds—the leaders of the Rudesburn Development Group—about Jerry's possible sins. Laurence's face contorted with horror, Nora turned chalk-white, and Grant sputtered his ale.

"Sorry I didna tell you sooner," Michael concluded, "especially when you kept that rumor aboot the Bruce's heart quiet, like I asked. But we didna ken if Jerry's business was just a rumor. You hired the man in good faith, after all."

Laurence pulled nervously on his beard. "You were between a rock and hard place, were you? No harm done. We'll watch him right and proper now."

Grant said, "Assumin' you let him go, Chief Inspector."

"More lemonade, please," Mackenzie replied. Nora refilled his glass.

"I hope no harm done," Mark muttered. "So that's what that bit about the penny was all about. I thought y'all knew more than you were letting on."

"Poor Jerry," said Hilary. "No one's even missed him tonight."

Rebecca finished her second glass of whiskey. No wonder the voices around her were bursting in slow satin bubbles against her senses. Even without the heat of the fire her cheeks were warm. The remaining strangers in the room left, their figures swimming through the shadows like jellyfish in an underwater nature special. Bridget came down the hall from the lobby and joined Nora behind the bar. There was a whispered colloquy, and Bridget's eyes bulged. "The hell he was!" she exclaimed.

Returning the cats' curious glances, Mackenzie pulled out the vacant chair at the corner table. "May I join you? I was hoping, Dr. Reid, that you could tell me something about this relic Dr. Kleinfelter is so keen on finding. All I know about Robert the Bruce is that he skelped the Sassenach at Bannockburn."

"The thirteenth and fourteenth centuries are really Michael's field, but I can tell you enough to be going on with." Rebecca spoke slowly, trying to compensate for the slight thickening of her tongue. "Robert died in 1329 at the age of 55. He'd been excommunicated for killing one of his rivals in a church and had always intended to atone for that, buy some grace, you might say, by making a pilgrimage to Jerusalem. But what with all the war and mayhem, he never got around to it. So on his deathbed he directed that his heart be cut out and his right-hand man take it on the pilgrimage instead."

"Ah," Mackenzie said. "James Douglas has almost as many myths told about him as Bruce."

"He got as far as Spain where he found some convenient infidels, the Moors, to fight. Untypically, he let himself be drawn away from his followers and surrounded by the enemy. No way out. He threw the reliquary into the thick of the fray, shouting, 'Forward, brave heart, as ever thou were wont to do, and Douglas will follow thee or die.' "

"He died, didn't he?" Mark asked.

"One of his men picked up the reliquary and brought it back, supposedly to Melrose Abbey, although it could well be that Marjory Douglas brought it here to Rudesburn, fifty years later, as a safety measure. The English would have loved to have gotten their hands on Robert the Bruce's heart."

"Because it was magic?" Hilary asked.

"The medieval mind feared magic because it believed in it," said Rebecca. "Like we fear and believe in science and technology."

Hilary nodded. Mark looked at her and looked away again. He asked, "What did the reliquary look like?"

Out of the corner of her eye Rebecca caught a movement at the far end of the darkened hallway, in the lobby—a late-roaming reporter heading upstairs, or a constable taking a break, or her own addled senses playing tricks on her. "It was a silver and enamel casket on a chain. It might look somewhat like the Monymusk Reliquary, a bit of religious magic from the eighth century that held either a relic or a communion wafer. It was carried at Bannockburn and is still around."

"And Henry the Eighth was after the Bruce's heart?" Mackenzie said.

"Probably. He had a record as long as your arm for relic-bashing. He called it smashing superstition. Maybe he had some atavistic idea about taking the power of the relics for himself. He certainly wasn't reluctant to take the treasuries for himself, the offerings made by pilgrims over the years."

"He took Rudesburn's treasure," said Hilary thoughtfully, "but he might not have gotten the relic. That particular relic, that is—wasn't there a whole pile of them here?"

"Oh, yes. The religious houses were the Disneylands of their day, vying with each other to get the biggest attractions."

"How does this tie in with Elliot?" Mark asked. "Assuming the skeleton is Elliot, which is a leap of faith. I do wonder how whoever it is came to be buried so haphazardly in the cellar of a convent."

"I'd say it was a quick and dirty job, hiding an inconvenient body." Mackenzie drained his lemonade. "I'll have those records to you next week, Dr. Reid. You should find some evidence in them."

"Thank you," Rebecca told him. She wanted to shake him and demand, "You're the expert! Get this case solved already!" But it wasn't that simple.

The whiskey lingered warmly in the back of her throat, but her tongue was starting to burn. She got up to ask Nora for a glass of water. At the bar Michael was holding forth with his fellow countrymen. "You can have economic and political justice in the modern world wi'oot goin' back to some mythical time that never existed. Rob Roy was a thug and Bonnie Prince Charlie a twit—so much for truth. We folk in the Celtic Fringe have to keep the romance alive, I suppose, but I wish we'd no muck it aboot wi' politics."

"Celtic Fringe," repeated Mark from the table. "Scotland, Ireland, Wales, bits of Cornwall and Brittany, right?"

"Right," Rebecca returned.

"Then I'm qualified. My ancestors were Welsh."

"Can you see ghosts?" Hilary asked him.

"Depends on how you define ghosts."

"Ah," said Grant teasingly to Michael, "but you're a Campbell, a race wi'oot the least bit of romance in their wee graspin' hearts."

Michael feigned indignation. "If I were graspin', I'd no be makin' a livin' siftin' dust and ashes, would I?"

"What about the Campbells of Cawdor? They supported Prince Charlie, romantically if not politically correct." Rebecca negotiated the floor to the bar and clasped Michael's arm. "But then, Castle Cawdor is seven miles from Culloden. Did they rush out and get themselves beaten to a pulp with the rest of Charlie's Highlanders? Heck no, they pulled up the drawbridge and said, 'Battle? What battle?' Sensible to a fault, the Campbells.''

"Oh, aye, it's easier to talk a good romance than live one.''

Rebecca didn't mistake the slight edge in Michael's voice. But his arm beneath her hand was firm, not tense, not trying to throw off her touch. She got her water, and together they returned to the table. He seated her and leaned against the mantelpiece at Mackenzie's shoulder. The cats stirred themselves to make figure eights around his ankles, imprinting him with their personal pheromones. She'd done more than a bit of that herself. Wherever she and Michael went from here, they'd always carry something of each other.

"Do you suppose, Chief Inspector,'' Michael said, "that Sheila was a mistaken victim just like Guinevere here?''

"How do you mean?''

Michael grimaced exasperation. "We've been makin' a lot of assumptions. Did someone try to kill Guinevere because of the seal? Is that someone the same one who killed Sheila? Did the person who killed Sheila also drag her body into the church and arrange it so nicely? Was Sheila really plottin' to scarper wi' the reliquary—or did someone think she was?''

The room was so silent that the sigh of the dying embers sounded like a train whistle. Laurence laid down the mug he was drying and leaned on the bar. "Occam's Razor,'' Rebecca murmured. And louder, "Michael's fond of saying the simplest explanation is the best one.''

"I daresay it is,'' said Mackenzie, and added, not entirely without sarcasm, "You'll have noticed, Dr. Campbell, that of all our suspects only you have no alibi after eight-fifteen. Or before, for that matter.''

So he had noticed that hypothetical 7:45–8:15 window. Michael had, too, since he reacted only with another grimace. But Rebecca found it hard to believe that Mackenzie regarded Michael as more than a hypothetical suspect.

The Chief Inspector continued, "I'll sleep on your comments. Thank you.''

You? Rebecca queried silently. *Sleep?* His hooded eyes didn't look as if they were capable of more than a quick nap. Even then he would doze like the cats did, flinty crescents of perception gleaming between his lids.

The suggestion of sleep swept like a psychic avalanche across the group. One after the other everyone yawned. Bridget and Laurence trudged toward the office. Nora collected dirty glasses. Grant stood before Mackenzie, nodding at a low-voiced series of instructions. Mark took his guitar case in one hand and Hilary's hand in the other. The firm and yet gentle way he pulled her down the corridor made Rebecca hold Michael back. "He overheard her say something about her . . . her problem," she explained.

Michael winced.

Rebecca didn't have time to turn away before Mark stopped in the lobby, tugged Hilary around to face him, and spoke.

Her entire body quivered, a ripple moving from crown to toe and back again. She answered, facing him, chin up, eyes direct.

He stood frozen. Only the guitar case hanging at his side trembled.

Hilary pulled her hand away and walked out the door like Mary, Queen of Scots must have walked to the scaffold, pride and pain in every move.

Mark took a step back, bumped against the banister, and sank onto the bottom tread of the stairs. The guitar case thunked down at his feet. His back bowed and his head swiveled back and forth in negation.

"Bluidy hell," said Michael. "I wish we'd no seen that."

"We're on display," Rebecca returned. "Every one of us—"

"Damn and blast!" Laurence's voice shattered the hush. He galloped into the bar, kilt flying. "Someone's stolen the brooch again!"

Grant and Mackenzie jostled each other down the hall and almost trampled Mark as he leaped to his feet. Michael and Rebecca dashed into the office just after Laurence and the police, Mark behind them, Nora bringing up the rear. Bridget sprawled in the desk chair. "When did you last see it?" Mackenzie demanded.

"This mornin' when Michael brought in the signet ring," she answered. "I was in and oot o' reception a' day, but no in here."

"The ring!" Michael exclaimed. "It's no gone, is it?"

Rebecca's head swam from too many alcoholic breaths concentrated in one small room. Mackenzie pushed Bridget aside and tried the door of the safe. It swung open. "Baird, don't you ever lock up?"

Laurence bent and peered into the safe as warily as though it harbored a nest of cobras. "No, the ring's not there. But nothing else is gone. See, here's the penny. . . ." He sat down on the chair. "Tony Wright wanted to photograph the brooch and the ring. I left the safe unlocked, and told him to lock it when he was done. With all the reporters and the tourists coming back and forth, I never checked. I'm not even sure he did those photos. God, I'm an idiot, certifiable, ought to be locked up myself!"

"The safe was open about five," offered Rebecca. "I came in here for a phone call."

"Bridget or I watched the office all day," Nora said. "I think. Except when everyone were running around looking for Lancelot, and during that argy-bargy about the news conference."

"And just a little while ago," Rebecca said, remembering that subtle movement in the lobby during Mackenzie's history lesson.

"Jenkins," said Bridget. "He's awful keen on a story aboot gold."

"P.C. Johnston," Mackenzie ordered, "alert the other constables that there's been a theft. Two thefts. Knock up Jenkins and Wright. And everyone else, too." He scowled.

His scowl was terrifying, like the Phantom of the Opera when he removed his mask. Rebecca shrank back and bumped into Michael's chest. "Clean oot from under his nose," he said in her ear. "I'm no surprised he's right scunnered."

Michael, Rebecca thought, did not have a future in the diplomatic corps. With a snarl Mackenzie shoved them both aside, strode through the lobby, and burst out the door. With a rush of feet, everyone followed.

The night was dark, the air suddenly chill after the warmth of the bar. The lights of the village glowed feebly, and the priory buildings were shadows across the dark furrow of the burn. Indistinct human forms milled around Jedburgh Street, either asking questions or refusing to answer them.

Grant stood on the sidewalk holding Hilary's arm. "I didn't take anything," she protested. "I was just standing here." In the light spilling from the door, her face was racked with emotion. *Good timing, Grant*, thought Rebecca. But he hadn't realized he was kicking someone already down.

Mark pulled Hilary away. "Leave her alone."

"Sorry!" said Grant, perplexed and indignant both.

Hilary stood in the circle of Mark's arms, her face concealed in his shoulder, her fists clenched on his chest, her back stiff, permitting the embrace but not surrendering to it. Mark raised his face from the top of her head and spit out a mouthful of hair. His steely expression read, "Just let someone try to hurt her. Make my day."

Flashbulbs popped, preserving for posterity an array of startled expressions. Police pounded into the cottage, ejecting Dennis and Adele and once again scouring the premises. Every window in the hotel lit up, flooding the street with light and plunging the priory even further into obscurity.

Elaine, a gaudy Japanese kimono clasped snugly across her breasts, peered out of the lobby door. She looked like an animal caught in the sudden glare of headlights, stunned and frightened. A gaggle of constables swept her aside and escorted Tony, looking oddly lopsided without his camera bags, and the stumbling, half-comatose figure of Jenkins toward a waiting police car.

The wind's chill damp breath stirred Rebecca's hair and tickled the nape of her neck. "Another night's sleep shot all to hell," she muttered.

Michael nodded, mouth tight, cheeks deeply creased, eyes cold.

If they lost only sleep, Rebecca thought, and not their lives, their fortunes, and their honor, they'd be lucky.

Chapter Twenty

A POLICE CAR stopped in front of the hotel, its racing stripe of fluorescent orange a defiant gesture against the rain. Rebecca peered at it through the window of the shop. Jerry's posture as he emerged from the car was similarly insolent. He went into the hotel with an imperious nod, as if the police officers were so many footmen attending his glass coach.

A second car, this one white with blue lettering, pulled up behind the first. Bob Jenkins and Tony climbed out of it and went inside together. If they hadn't been colleagues before being swept away last night, they certainly were now—fellow survivors of Galashiels police station food and Simon Mackenzie's frustration.

Mackenzie himself stood on the pavement in front of the hotel. His expression was granite-edged, his eyes narrowed, as he registered any changes that had occurred since last night—a new bud on one of the Johnston's rose bushes, perhaps, or a paper cup lying in the gutter. Devlin eyed his superior as a soldier on a bomb squad would eye a suspicious package.

And then, Rebecca thought, there was Battlefield Band's version of the battle of Sherriffmuir: "We both did fight, and both were beat, and both did run away." Except she was willing to bet that running away wasn't in Mackenzie's vocabulary any more than it was in hers.

Winnie handed her a sack embellished with a potato wearing a kilt and labeled "MacSpuds." "Here you go. Was that Dr. Kleinfelter?"

"Yes, I'm afraid it was."

The two women exchanged a wary look. "He'll no be foolish enough to try any more fiddlin' wi' the data, will he?"

"He might not see it as foolishness, but as career enhancement." Rebecca hefted the sack of potatoes. Under her arm she tucked a box overflowing with sultana bran and Weetabix, MacVittie's biscuits and milk. With the other she cradled a box filled with tomatoes, cucumbers, and cress, chicken, and stew meat. She thanked Winnie and headed out into the rain. She was getting used to walking in the rain. "Good morning, Chief Inspector."

Mackenzie, with admirable restraint, didn't snap back, "What's good about it?" He instead returned her greeting, helped her carry the sack of potatoes and a box, and walked beside her across the street and down the driveway.

Emboldened, Rebecca asked, "Make any progress last night?"

"Only by process of elimination," replied Mackenzie. "As you see, we had to let the lot of them go. Mr. Jenkins says he never saw the ring and the brooch, and he can prove he was in London when Miss Fitzgerald was murdered. Mr. Wright says he never photographed the artifacts—and judging by his exposed film, he didn't. Neither he nor Dr. Kleinfelter can prove their innocence of the murder, but then, neither can we prove their guilt."

"I know that verse already," said Rebecca.

"I thought Dr. Campbell's comments about our assumptions were very interesting. You and he make a good trouble-shooting team, do you?"

Rebecca laughed ruefully. "As long as the trouble isn't up close and personal." She glanced across the burn toward the priory. Through the west door of the church she could see Adele cleaning pottery shards. Elaine, having nothing else to do, tapped away on the computer. If Dennis's attentive attitude over her shoulder was any indication, nothing else would be filed inaccurately.

In the cloister Hilary stood respectfully by while several raincoated figures arranged a block and tackle above the skeleton. It and its matrix of earth were now encased in boards, the four sides of a packing crate fitted into grooves around it. Michael and Mark emerged from the trench, so smeared with mud Rebecca could tell them apart only by their body shapes. Both were grinning; they must have just embedded the all-important bottom of the box below the skeleton. Jerry would be livid at such a tricky operation performed successfully without him.

Michael assumed his habitual posture, hands in pockets, beside the slender, upright form of Dr. Graham. Rebecca half expected the old gentleman to pull out a swagger stick and poke Michael in the chest with it—"A fine mess you've made of the dig, boy"—but despite Graham's military bearing, his exchange with Michael appeared quite genial.

Rebecca unlocked the door of the cottage and ushered Mackenzie inside. "How much did Tony know about the relic heart?" she asked.

"Very little—or so he says. He pointed out that a mummified heart would bring little on the open market."

"Notwithstanding who the heart belonged to?"

"I'm not sure he fully appreciates that point. Or else I don't. It seems to me the relic would only be valuable for its publicity value, not like, say, gold coins and jewelry, that he or Miss Fitzgerald or even Dr. Kleinfelter could sell to a private collector."

"Museums would bid frantically for the relic, but you couldn't hold that kind of auction in secret. The government—the Crown—would claim it first and then parcel out compensation."

"Exactly." Mackenzie laid the box and bag down on the kitchen counter. "Mr. Wright knew Miss Fitzgerald was after historical artifacts to build her reputation. He stayed with her because he knew his reputation, and therefore the prices he could charge for his work, would be similarly strengthened. Another version of Dr. Kleinfelter's story. Very straightforward."

"Oh, yes, it's all very straightforward." Rebecca put the meat and vegetables in the refrigerator. Mackenzie found a piece of leftover toast and picked it into crumbs, watching through the window while Mark and Michael eased Graham down into the trench. Rebecca visualized Graham asking the skeleton for its name, rank, and serial number. "Why confide in me?" she asked.

Mackenzie looked around at her. "Confide?"

"Discuss the case with me. As much as I hate to agree with Jerry, he did have a point when he said you wouldn't want people trampling your clues any more than an archeologist would."

"Then I'd advise you and Dr. Campbell not to trample any clues."

Even Mackenzie's features were in code, revealing little.

Maybe he was trying to tell her she and Michael were no longer suspects. Maybe he was warning them about playing detective. Yet he actually seemed to be asking them for help. "We won't, assuming we find any clues at all," she said.

Mackenzie considered the pile of crumbs and wiped his hands on the dishtowel. "Thank you," he said.

"Thank you for the help," Rebecca returned, with only a trace of sarcasm, and went with him to the front door.

Tony and Jerry walked past, heading toward the footbridge. Tony carried a camera, Jerry his trowels. Rebecca anticipated a struggle for seniority—as director of the museum, Graham outranked Jerry.

Jerry saw Rebecca standing familiarly with Mackenzie on the step of the cottage. His supercilious glance was the equivalent of a mocking, "Teacher's pet!" Tony trudged stolidly on, eyes averted in distaste.

A scuffle of gravel announced Devlin. He stopped in front of the cottage and offered Rebecca a cardboard portfolio. "Here you go. Forensics have done all they can."

"I'd like a report on the contents when you get a chance," Mackenzie added, and walked toward the excavation, where Jerry was shaking hands with Graham with every appearance of amiability.

Clutching the portfolio to her breast, Rebecca carried it into the dining room. Yes, the trial records and the warrant both lay wrapped in conservator's tissue inside.

The tissue rustled loudly in the silent house. The cooker in the kitchen gurgled. A beam creaked overhead. Rebecca ignored the slow crawl between her shoulder blades—she reminded herself that the cottage wasn't haunted—and laid the thick pieces of parchment on the table.

The seals ranged along the bottom of the warrant were dried and cracked. There was Hertford's, smack in the center. And there was the one she remembered, stuck to the edge like an afterthought. Not the diagonal bar of the Elliots, but the winged heart of the Douglases.

Rebecca frowned. A James Douglas had been commendator of Melrose in 1590, when the last monk died, but was he even alive in 1545, let alone collaborating? She stroked the wax, visualizing a signet ring pressing it. This other Douglas, whoever he was, had barely made an impression, so light was the pressure of the seal on the wax. And the device was off center, a crescent of untouched wax bulging along its edge. Interesting.

She needed to get out to the dig, but her knees folded, and she fell into a chair. She smoothed the sheets of the trial records. detecting a faint resonance like that of a plucked harp string.

Some nameless scribe had labored long over those pages. The spidery handwriting danced just ahead of Rebecca's eye, and she squinted, willing it to be still. "Thomas Elliot, commendator . . . Anne Douglas, prioress . . . Grievous crimes against God." That was medieval legalese for "one size fits all." It could mean anything. Defending the priory. Refusing to hand over its treasure. Much good it had done them, Anne and Thomas, to stand on principle.

Rebecca shook herself. The house was silent, focused around her and the table. An elusive odor of incense and mold tickled her nostrils.

The words "summoning spirits" pirouetted on the paper, drawing her forward. The back of her neck twinged, and absently she rubbed at it. In her mind's eye, she saw the darkened cloister, will o' the wisps thronging the as-yet unbroken archways. Anne's white shape walked alone, head down, hands folded. But she kept glancing up, from the corners of her eyes, at the gibbous forms that danced in the shadowy corners.

Except one shape wasn't pale. It was dark. blending into the night. A man in a doublet laced with gold points, an ivory-handled rondel at his belt. Bearded, probably. Frowning in concern. . . .

Wait a minute. Goose bumps rose on her arms. Thomas had been charged along with Anne—she knew that. There must have been another warrant, although it would be a miracle if it had survived, too. But there, right there, the crabbed letters said that Thomas was being tried in absentia.

Hands soothed the back of Rebecca's neck. She released the document and its images evaporated. She cuddled into the massage. "Why thank you, love," she said.

"You're welcome, but the name's Mark." Rebecca spun around. Mark stepped back, hands raised in surrender. He'd even washed them without her hearing. Anyone could have crept up on her. "Sorry. I saw you rubbing your neck. I thought you knew it was me."

"No problem." Her skin tingled, from the documents or the touch or from fear, she couldn't tell. It had been a long time since Michael had massaged her. It was his fault she had the crick in her neck to begin with. Sort of. Showed how far gone she was, that she hadn't realized those hands weren't his. And it was lunch time already, a whole morning's work gone—no, reading the records *was* her work. . . .

She stood up so abruptly that the chair almost fell over. Mark saved it, set it down, and headed bemusedly for the kitchen. Adele appeared in Rebecca's peripheral vision. "Are those the accounts of Anne Douglas's trial?"

"Yes." Rebecca wrapped them in tissue and slipped them back into the portfolio.

"Poor Anne," said Adele. "Her love for God, for her country, for a man—all betrayed."

"Love for a man? She was a nun."

"She was sent to the convent as a child."

"True. You're not thinking she and Elliot had something going?"

Adele's face was somewhat scrunched, as if she was trying to remember the words to a long-forgotten song. "Could be."

"And how was she betrayed?" continued Rebecca.

All Adele replied was, "I don't think the trial was a fair one."

"Now that wouldn't surprise me." Rebecca tied the string around the portfolio.

"Artifacts can be haunted like places," Adele went on, her expression now one of certainty. "And for the same reason: lingering emotions, vibrations in the life force. Like we inherit genes from our ancestors, some artifacts have a genetic code. . . . Here, Mark, let me slice those potatoes."

Rebecca looked after Adele's retreating figure. She had wondered if she'd grown immune to the power of old objects after living with the haunted artifacts of Dun Iain, but the documents in the portfolio showed every promise of supernatural twinges. How did Adele know? She'd never touched those documents. Unless she'd stolen and hidden the warrant, or Sheila had showed her the trial records. Or unless she'd heard it all already, from Anne. . . . The woman had a good imagination, Rebecca told herself, as well as the ability to tell a compelling tale. And she didn't hesitate to jump to conclusions.

Rebecca patted the portfolio. If the priory was haunted by Anne's ghost today, then which spirit was haunting it when Anne was still alive, one that she could be accused of summoning?

Marjory? Now there was a thought. They were probably even relatives. Very tidy.

Too tidy. Shaking her head—imagination is helpful, but jumping to conclusions wasn't her job any more than it was Mackenzie's—Rebecca stowed the portfolio in her bedroom and went to help with lunch.

Adele's superb french fries and Mark's crusty, peppery hamburgers—he'd found at least one thing he could cook—left Rebecca nicely warm and content. Later Michael walked beside her over the footbridge, gazing truculently up into the overcast sky. As though responding to his silent threat, it stopped raining. "Dr. Graham was askin' aboot you, lass."

"Sorry. I got hung up on the trial records. There's something, well, none too couthy about them."

"Eh?" he returned, with a wary sideways gleam. "Do you mean to say they've those damned mental mine-fields planted aboot them, or that the accounts dinna match what we already know?"

"The former, mostly. I need to go over them much more thoroughly before drawing any conclusions about the latter. But I can tell you one thing. Thomas Elliot's seal is on Anne's warrant. Then he's charged along with her. But he wasn't here for his trial."

"Scarpered, most likely. Unless that's him, there, in the crate."

"Adele seems to think it is. But you know Adele."

Michael's brows commented on Adele by lifting at the outward corners, wing-like, tempted to fly away for the duration.

They arrived at the side of the trench in time to see Graham's crew wrapping cords around the block of mud in which the skeleton was embedded. Jerry made flapping motions with his hands, directing traffic, but seemed otherwise content to let Graham murmur the orders. He was like the class bully busily polishing apples whenever the teacher walked in the door.

Graham stood beside Mackenzie, hands folded behind his back, his white moustache combed tidily. His eyes gleamed from beneath the brim of his tweed hat. "Ah, that's lovely," he muttered under his breath.

"Impressive," agreed Mackenzie.

A murmur swept through the watchers, the Bairds, the Johnston clan, the police, and assorted reporters allowed across the demilitarized zone for the occasion. Even the cats sat gravely on the porch of the church, paws neatly together, heads cocked to the side at the manifest strangeness of humans. They wouldn't be found playing in the mud.

"So he was murdered, too?" asked Jenkins brightly.

"Hard to say," replied Graham. "We'll finish removing the bones from their matrix in Edinburgh—they're so soft, they'll need conservation work."

"Sixteenth century?" Jenkins persevered.

"If the clothes are any indication, yes." Graham glanced around and saw Rebecca standing beside Michael. "Ah, there you are, my dear. I hear you're Dr. Reid the now. Well done!" He took her hand and bowed over it like Bonnie Prince Charlie greeting Flora Macdonald.

So Michael had told him. Rebecca smiled. "Thank you."

Graham said, "Dr. Nelson sent me a copy of your dissertation and told me the good news. Since we have the Forbes exhibition opening soon, your comments on the artifacts belonging to Queen Mary were most interesting."

Somehow Rebecca had imagined a genuine Scottish scholar would laugh at her conclusions about Mary's role in sixteenth-century politics. During their brief meeting in Edinburgh two weeks ago, though, Graham had never been anything but scrupulously polite. She stammered her thanks.

Michael inspected his boots. He hadn't told Graham about her degree. He was feeling guilty. He should.

"Have a care!" shouted one of the workmen. In a wave the audience stepped back, Mark colliding with Hilary, Tony with Dennis. Elaine inched even further away from Jerry, but he paid no attention to her.

Before long the skeleton and its cocoon of mud landed with a thunk in the back of a small truck. One of Graham's minions released the tackle, and another drove carefully across the lawns to the car park. The trench yawned, empty, the huge gouge in its side looking like a bomb crater. Shards of pottery and a row of stones peeked above the coffee-colored water in its bottom. "Thirteenth-century level?" Jerry queried, of no one in particular. He seized a trowel and climbed down, Mark hot on his heels. Hilary picked up her drawing board.

Tony followed the truck, taking pictures. Laurence inspected the ruts left in the lawn. Elaine, without formal dismissal, walked toward the hotel, leaving the computer with Dennis. Adele vanished.

Graham looked at his watch. "If we leave the now, we'll reach Dalkeith at the rush hour. Of course, the rush hour lasts all afternoon on Friday."

"Must be a universal occurrence," said Rebecca. "I bet in Mongolia they have camel jams on Friday."

"Not necessarily," Michael returned. "The concept of Friday night depends on the dominant religion of a given area. . . ."

"Thank you," Rebecca said, and bit her tongue before she followed with "Dr. Campbell," even jokingly.

"I'd recommend waiting until the morn," Graham went on, "to move the artifact to the museum. I'll arrange for a—er, if you'll pardon the expression, skeleton crew to come in on Saturday. Michael?"

"I'll drive the lorry to the museum, if you'll appeal to the Chief Inspector there to let me off my lead."

Mackenzie, on cue, turned from the assortment of constables he was instructing. "Oh, aye, Dr. Campbell, you're free to go."

"Decided I didna do it, then?"

"Sergeant Devlin will go with you. Dr. Reid will have to stay here."

"As hostage?" she asked. Mackenzie gave her his best we-are-not-amused look.

Jerry called, "Dr. Campbell, if you wouldn't mind giving me a hand with these stones—might be a conduit—would you like to look, Dr. Graham?"

Shaking her head at Jerry, Rebecca went into the church, found Adele scrubbing pottery shards, and settled down to help.

Graham and his crew left an hour or so later, after working out a roster of bobbies to guard the truck and its tarpaulin-covered burden. Jerry's conduit seemed all-absorbing; Tony collected his video camera and recorded a disquisition on medieval plumbing. One moment Mackenzie and Devlin were conferring with Bridget outside the Craft Centre, the next they were gone. Even policemen deserved the odd afternoon off, Rebecca supposed.

The clouds clotted into gray and white billows. Between them shone splayed rays of sun. More than once Rebecca caught Adele gazing off into the sky as though seeing angels descending on those beams of light. Adele, she thought, was a sweet lady, but she sure gave her the creeps.

After the heavy lunch, Rebecca fed her flock a light supper of vegetarian lasagna and salad. Dennis made garlic bread of positively lethal potency; Mark lapped it up, but Michael went crosseyed. Later the group strolled up to the pub, still smelling faintly of garlic. Dennis stayed behind, tapping happily on the computer, and Adele sat on the porch of the priory much as the cats had sat there earlier.

In the bar, Jerry was deep in conversation with Laurence. Or *at* Laurence, rather; the hotelkeeper looked like a sterling example of the taxidermist's art, his eyes focused glassily on Jerry's moving mouth. The cats occupied two bar stools, sound asleep.

"You know," Jerry was saying, "kind of like a double agent. Keeping an eye on her. She was up to something—she called that reporter without checking with me first."

From his perch at the end of the bar Jenkins didn't even glance around. If Laurence looked stuffed, Jenkins looked pickled.

Michael held a chair for Rebecca, his expression carefully noncommittal. Mark seated Hilary, equally neutral. Rebecca whispered, "Does Jerry know just how much Sheila knew?"

"No one knows how much she knew. Even him." Hilary nodded toward the corner booth, where Elaine and Tony sat poring over a pile of photos.

"I'd no be so sure of that," said Michael. "Wine, Hilary? Whiskey? Lager?" He headed toward the bar. With a start Laurence awoke and reached for the McEwan's tap.

"Just giving her enough rope to hang herself, right?" asked Jerry of Laurence's back. "Entrapment, like Abscam."

Elaine laughed, and Jerry stiffened. She stood, head cocked to the side coquettishly, while Tony gathered his photographs. His expression was no less taciturn than it usually was, except for something sharp in the glance he sent toward Jerry.

With an elaborate yawn Jerry called across the room, "Elaine, you left a pair of your pantyhose on the back of the bathroom door. But I see you won't be needing them."

An abrupt silence fell on the room. Elaine's look was one Medusa would envy, but Jerry didn't turn to stone. He held out his pint mug to Laurence, smiling affably, unconcerned. Laurence, rolling his eyes heavenward in silent appeal, refilled it. Lancelot stretched and fell off the bar stool. Embarrassed, he glanced belligerently around and sauntered away.

Tony and Elaine left. The conversational buzz sparked by their exit rolled down the passageway behind them. Rebecca accepted her glass of whiskey from Michael and tried not to guffaw. "A creative solution to no room at the inn, I must say."

Mark made a manful effort to hide his grin in his pint of beer.

"Ah, well, that's one up for us Brits," Michael said, and toasted the departing couple.

"Poor Jerry," said Hilary. "You almost have to feel sorry for him, with all his plans unraveling. Assuming they are," she added darkly.

Jerry slumped over the bar, nursing his beer.

Rebecca sipped. The whiskey tickled her mouth, and its aroma wafted up her sinuses. Sheila was still lying, alone, in the Galashiels morgue. Not that her relationship with Tony had been anything but business—or Elaine's relationship with Jerry, for that matter. Both Tony and Elaine were accustomed to paying for services rendered, so why not throw in their lots together?

She caught Michael's jaundiced look. Sure, Tony and Elaine could have been working together all this time. Why not? The more complicated the merrier.

Michael shrugged, lifted his mug to his lips, and choked as running feet thudded down the passageway. Winnie Johnston burst into the room. "Here, come see what's on in the car park. Grant came loupin' into the shop as if the deil were after him."

So now the priory harbored devils. Okay. Rebecca and her cohorts joined the rush out of the hotel, down the street, and across the bridge.

Twilight gilded the landscape, the sky above a thin, ethereal blue-gray. The priory sat innocently on its green lawns. In the car park, the truck waited just where it had been left, the tarpaulin tied around the ominous crate. Supported by a couple of other bobbies, Grant stood shamefacedly at the opening in the wall and traced patterns in the gravel with his toe.

"Are you all right?" Laurence demanded.

Grant attempted a smile. His face cracked. "Oh, aye. Sorry aboot all the haverin'. I—I . . . ."

"You asked me to bring them, and I did," said Winnie sternly. "Noo, what happened tae you?"

"I went checkin' the bindin's o' the tarpaulin—a' shipshape, mind you—and I walked around the corner o' the lorry into a ghost. *The* ghost. The air went awful cold, fair froze my bones."

Grant accepted the existence of the priory ghost much as his children accepted the existence of Mickey Mouse. And there was a lingering chill in the air, as if a refrigerator door had briefly opened. Rebecca crossed her arms. Hilary shrank against Mark and with a delighted double-take he put his arm around her.

"A nun," Grant went on. "In white robes. I could see the fabric floatin' around her, the veil draped ower her head, everything. And yet she wisna really there, not quite solid, like. And when she turned and looked at me, she had nae face. Shadows, that was a', in the circle o' her wimple. That's when my feet took ower and I ran. Sorry." Winnie patted his arm.

"Good story," scoffed a voice from the back row. Jerry. No one paid any attention to him.

"Have you ever seen the ghost before?" Michael asked.

"No so close. A light across the burn a time or two, when I was a lad, or a shape-thing glidin' oot the door o' the priory . . ."

A thud reverberated across the lawns. Every body in the group seemed to jump six inches off the ground. Every eye turned to the priory doorway. *We heard it shut*, Rebecca thought. *We heard the door shut, but it's not there.*

Adele strolled out of the open doorway, down the steps, and paused at the foot of the wheel-cross. Her look toward the multiple eyes staring at her was as blandly self-absorbed as that of the cats. "Is something wrong?" she called.

Her voice drifted away down the soft evening breeze. No one replied.

Chapter Twenty-One

REBECCA CLOSED THE door behind Bridget and took the mended sweater-vest into the bedroom. She put it away and turned her attention to Michael's bed, which, as usual, looked like a fabric strip mine. Not that the issue of whether he made up his bed was an important one.

Mark and Hilary, Dennis and Adele, collided in the vestibule as they put on their wellies. "What Grant saw," said Adele, "was Anne making sure that Thomas's mortal remains are treated respectfully."

The others greeted that statement with noncommittal murmurs.

"However," Adele went on, "I don't think Anne has enough psychic energy to follow Thomas to Edinburgh."

"Museums," said Hilary, "ought to be the most haunted places on earth."

"Not necessarily," Adele said. "Artifacts are out of context in a museum; their vibrations don't reach critical mass. And the sheer quantity of them keeps the sensitive person from tuning in on an individual echo."

Sounds good to me, Rebecca said to herself. She fluffed the pillow.

Mark asked, "Didn't you say your sister worked in a museum, Dennis?"

"She did once," he replied. "Kind of a summer internship, dusting the display cases and stuff."

Hilary glanced in the bedroom door. "Coming, Rebecca?"

"Be right there," Rebecca looked out the bedroom window

as the others traipsed toward the priory. So they had to work on Saturday. They were so far behind that they would have had to work weekends, murder or no murder.

It was a beautiful morning, the sky a clear cerulean blue like a ceramic bowl filled with cotton puffs of cloud. The rosy stone of the priory blushed, and the grass sparkled. Tony was hanging over the railing of the footbridge, camera ready, while Elaine stood behind him juggling his bags with a slightly smug expression.

Jerry strode across the lawns, right through Tony's viewfinder, ignoring them both. He shooed the students along with semaphoric arm-wavings, like a policeman hurrying onlookers past an accident.

Rebecca picked up Michael's soccer shorts and folded them into a drawer. Then she poked out the last birth control pill, swallowed it, and threw the packet away.

Michael and Devlin had started for Edinburgh right after breakfast, Michael driving the lorry, Devlin following in the Fiat. Grant and the other bobbies had stood and watched, frankly relieved, as the entourage disappeared toward Newtown St. Boswells and the A68.

Mackenzie had yet to appear. Devlin said he'd gone straight to Edinburgh last night and would be back in Rudesburn on Monday. Guess he had to say hello to his wife every now and then, Rebecca thought. Maybe he and Amanda Fraser were competitors, but at least they didn't work in each other's pockets. Michael's parents had been working together for years, but hardly in competition.

The portfolio with the trial records sat beside the dresser. She could have sworn she'd left it on the bedside table. She picked it up. The string was untied. Although the papers were crammed untidily inside, they were all there. Michael could have been looking at them. Or Dennis. Or . . .

Swiftly she turned, lifted the covers on her bed, slipped the portfolio between the mattress and the box springs, and smoothed the spread. Maybe she was being paranoid. Maybe not paranoid enough.

In the vestibule, her wellies and Michael's were slightly pigeon-toed, turned away from each other. She straightened his and put hers on. Michael, she thought. His reaction to her Ph.D. She could put "Doctor" in front of her name, but the degree was only a hunting license; it didn't come with a job. Maybe she could find a job if she broadened her horizons and searched back in the United States. "Sorry," she could hear herself saying, "I just couldn't find a job here. Guess the relationship is off."

She started to slam the front door, caught herself, and shut it carefully. Michael wasn't giving her any clues about his feelings—no playing on her emotions, no persuasion one way or the other. Chances were they could break up and remain friends. She saw them as seventy-year-olds meeting at a conference, smiling with wistfulness and relief over what might have been.

Rebecca's boots scuffed across the bridge, slapped on the damp grass, and carried her to the edge of the third trench. Mark and Jerry were down on their knees in the muck. "Looks like a comb," Jerry was saying.

"One of the most important pieces in the Jedburgh museum is a comb," said Rebecca.

Jerry looked up, face puckered against the brilliant sunlight. "Go stake out the infirmary for some test trenches. We've spent too much time on this side of the priory. We've got to get moving. Working with volunteers is like jogging through molasses."

Rebecca stared down at him, her mouth open in surprise. The arguments she'd carefully formulated, how despite his slowness she needed time away from the dig to translate the records, evaporated like cotton candy on her tongue. "May I borrow your knife?" she asked Mark. He fished it out and handed it over with an expressive flick of his brows that would have done Michael proud.

Tony and Elaine were setting up some lights in the doorway of the chapter house. Elaine's jaw moved rhythmically, and a distinct odor of spearmint clung to her. Maybe she was trying to stop smoking. The usual contingent of policemen, some in uniforms, some in civvies, roamed about the dig. A couple of reporters and a gaggle of tourists stood in the gateway to the car park, inspecting the blank stretch of gravel. The ghost of Anne did not perform.

In the church Dennis sorted through a pile of site recording sheets. Rebecca got some pegs and twine from the worktable. "How's it going?"

"No problems yet," he replied. He seemed almost disappointed.

"Was anyone in the cottage last night while you were working?"

"Not that I know of. Of course, I was upstairs with my tape player going most of the time."

"With the doors locked?"

"Well, no—I mean, I was there, I was keeping an eye on things."

Rebecca gritted her teeth. "Get the transit and help me, please."

"Oh. Sure. Be right there."

Rebecca went through the slype and found Adele sieving the excavated dirt. She held up a nondescript lump. "Look. A coin."

Rebecca rubbed at the lump. Its dirt crust was unusually fragile, and flaked away to reveal heraldic creatures enameled on metal. "No, I think it's a decorative disc. See the stud on the back? It was attached to a piece of leather, probably a horse's harness. How on earth did somebody miss that? What bucket did it come from?"

Adele considered the spoil heaps. "First trench."

"Oh." Rebecca grimaced. "Then I missed it. I could've sworn I crumbled up all the lumps. Here, put it in a box, please, and label it."

Adele carried her booty back into the cloister. Shaking her head at her apparent mistake, Rebecca squished on across the grass to the lumpy ground concealing the foundations of the infirmary. She'd obviously been distracted when the disc was found.

Test trenches, my left femur, she told herself. All they could do was peel a few layers of dirt and weeds away from the remaining stones and get a vague idea of the general layout. Taking Mark's knife, she whittled a peg and lodged it between two blocks of masonry. "There," she told Dennis when he arrived with transit and meter stick. "That's the datum point for this grid. When Michael gets back, he and Mark can tie it in with the main one."

"Okay," said Dennis, and they went to work.

By elevenses Rebecca was able to report to Jerry that the grid was laid out. "Very good! We'll backfill the first trenches tomorrow and get the grounds people to re-sod them. Time to get going on the crypt and the tower." He beamed as jovially as an evangelist at the door to a tent show, shaking hands and picking pockets.

Nora passed around the cups of tea. "Kerr did a layout of the crypt back in the thirties, before the doorway collapsed. Stone walls, a brick wall, lots of dust and old bones. Nothing exciting.''

"No scientists have looked at it." Jerry gulped his tea. His face suffused with red.

"It's hot," said Nora blandly, and offered Hilary a scone.

"I'll need you, Mark," Jerry went on, clearing his throat, "and Dennis, and Michael when he decides to come back, to clear out the blockage. And we have to survey the tower, too— it's in bad shape."

"Some of the steps have settled," offered Nora, "and the upper walkway has some loose stones."

Tony added, "Have a care—the owl's nest is in a window slit."

Jerry barely glanced at Tony, and at Elaine nibbling her scone beside him. "This isn't a bird sanctuary. The owl can find another place for its kiddies." He went on, before Tony could articulate a protest, "Tomorrow Hilary and Adele join Rebecca at the infirmary. Light probes, right? Remember that the medieval idea of first aid was bleeding—you bring in a guy with his leg cut off and they say, 'Hey, we'll just drain away the rest of your blood, speed up the process.' '' He grinned. No one laughed. With a shrug Jerry continued, "So don't start investigating any drains without latex gloves and lots of disinfectant. Over at the medieval hospital at Soutra Aisle they found all sorts of biological nasties."

"I thought they were still testing the area to see if any disease-carrying bacteria had survived," Rebecca said.

"Yeah, well, whatever. The possibility is still there."

"Super," said Elaine under her breath, and looked around as though expecting the black plague to come up and lay a skeletal hand on her shoulder. But she didn't have to worry. Jerry hadn't assigned her a task. It appeared that as far as he was concerned, she no longer existed.

"So, troops," Jerry went on, "we're going to have get our behinds in gear. Our funding's only good through the fifth of August. The cottage is booked then, too. No more of this stalling around."

The entire crew and Nora regarded Jerry with varying degrees of incredulity and disgust. Now what was he up to? Rebecca wondered. Maybe he had a conversion experience on the road to Galashiels.

She went back out to the infirmary, spade in hand, worrying

about Jerry, worrying about the trial records, worrying about having missed the heraldic disc. It hadn't been there, she decided. Adele had got her buckets mixed up. Dennis had missed it in his trench.

Lunch time came and went. The afternoon sun was as brilliant as the morning's, with that crystalline clarity peculiar to the British Isles. By the time Jerry shouted "That's all, folks!" a six-foot-long strip of dark earth lay like a velvet ribbon across the infirmary foundations, turf rolled up tidily to the side, foxgloves and loosestrife clumped to the other. A row of stones was almost dry, the moss that had covered it now a green blob outside the taut string. With a trowel Rebecca cut the edge of the nascent trench just a little more neatly—artistically, even—and contemplated her handiwork.

Two constables strolled outside the perimeter wall, nodding cordially. A door slammed. Judging from the absence of smoke fouling the breeze, Jerry must have gone to his lair in the pub. Rebecca cleaned her trowel on the grass, picked up spade and meter stick, and started toward the church. She had been worrying about something. What was it?

She stopped at the edge of the cloister, hearing voices from the chapter house. No, not Tony and Elaine, but Mark and Hilary. She backpedaled, meaning to go back the way she'd come and around the south side of the conventual buildings, but her movement brought her next to a lancet window. *Aw*, she thought sentimentally.

Mark and Hilary were thoroughly engrossed in a kiss. And yet there was something in Hilary's posture. . . . Rebecca visualized herself pressed against Michael. That was it. Hilary was angled stiffly away from Mark's body, only simulating compliance.

Mark's hands moved down to the back pockets of her jeans and tried to press her closer to him. Tactical error—Hilary jerked away. "I—I . . ." she stammered, not panicked, just perturbed. "I'm sorry, Mark, I just can't."

She pulled herself from his arms and walked quickly out of the chapter house, through the cloister, and toward the cottage. Mark stood looking after her, his hands still outstretched, holding nothing. His face went from a frown to resigned expressionlessness.

Rebecca, her cheeks flaming, trotted back around the priory buildings. She reached the church from the west side, strolled nonchalantly down the nave and deposited her tools, knowing she wasn't fooling anyone. Mark was leaning on the frame of the transept door, arms crossed, looking for all the world like an upended effigy. "You saw that," he stated.

"Sorry. Don't mind me, I'll just slink away."

"No, I want you to tell me something."

"Oh. Okay." She leaned on the opposite doorpost, the stone cold at her back.

Even though they were standing in shadow, Mark's eyes shimmered with the blue-tinted sunshine outside. They were searchlights, illuminating every crevice, leaving nothing unexamined. "I know she's hurting. I know why. Am I some kind of sex maniac because I still want to make love with her?"

"I don't think so," Rebecca replied, "but what's important is whether she thinks so. Did she say that?"

"God, no. I wish she would. She keeps apologizing."

"Planning on seducing her, were you?"

"I was planning on letting nature take its course."

"I'm afraid it is." Rebecca sighed. "You're in the unfortunate position of being the man who convinces her most men will take no for an answer. You get to teach her to trust men again."

Mark laughed, short and bitter. "I'm not martyr material."

"Sure you are," retorted Rebecca, "if you care about her."

He muttered something under his breath about "Catch-22, damned if you do, damned if you don't," and added more loudly, "Well, there is something to be said for simple affection."

"A great deal to be said. She'll get more out of your affection than any amount of—well, groping."

Mark shook his head. A bus rumbled up the street outside the church. In the distance children shouted, car doors slammed, and a sheep bleated. The priory itself was silent, the faintest of breezes stirring the dust in the chancel and branches of the yew beyond the opposite door.

"I've always heard," Rebecca went on, "that any time a man meets a woman, any woman, he appraises her as a bed partner. At least you seem to have some control over whatever pernicious instinct that is."

He smiled lopsidedly, brows slanted. "Not just any woman. I mean, I never looked at Adele the way I looked at Hilary and . . ." His eyes fell as abruptly down to his muddy wellies as if he'd just stepped in something.

"And me?" Rebecca finished for him.

"Guilty. Consider yourself flattered."

Remembering her dream, she thought, *We're even.* "From you, I will. But don't tell me Jerry's appraisal is flattering. He'd leer at a stalk of broccoli."

"Looks more like a rutabaga man to me." Mark grinned.

They leaned against their respective doorposts, laughing. Great slapstick, Rebecca thought. Maybe they should take this show on the road.

From the corner of her eye she saw a movement in the opposite transept. It was Michael. She willed herself not to look guilty—she had nothing to look guilty about. "Hey!" she called, and walked briskly toward him. "You're back. Did everything go all right?"

Mark scuffed along behind her. "No deductions about the body yet?"

Michael's face was stamped with the same resigned expressionlessness she had seen on Mark's. She slipped her hand under his arm and drew him toward the cottage.

His arm pressed her hand against his side so firmly that she had to flex the blood into her fingers. "The puir chap's set up right and proper in the lab. Graham says he'll ring us if he finds anything. A little late for a formal post-mortem. No dental records, more's the pity."

"Could it be Elliot?" asked Mark.

"We got on to London to see if there're any records of Elliot workin' for Edward the Sixth."

"Did Graham say anything about Jerry?" Rebecca asked.

"Nelson warned him, and he's on his guard. He told me Jerry wisna exactly complimentary aboot us ower lunch yesterday, but he wisna tryin' to stab us in the back."

"Too much to hope he's given up wasting research assistants," said Rebecca. "I guess even Jerry, though, realizes you already have a good reputation with Graham. And me with Nelson, helpfully enough."

"Jerry even admitted the discrepancy in the records, said mistakes happen and promised to keep a better eye oot."

"For his own interests," Mark said. "Maybe he won't frame you, but what about us larva?"

"We're all in this together," Michael replied.

Rebecca glanced at his profile. His jaw was set, his mouth taut with obduracy and unease. "Have you been looking at the portfolio?'' she asked. ''This morning it had been opened, and the trial records disarranged.''

He spun toward her. ''Good God, no. Did someone do a recce through the cottage?''

''I don't know. None of the papers were gone. Of course, I haven't done a translation yet, either, and they wouldn't be as tempting without that.''

Michael muttered something profane. Mark annotated it. They walked across the footbridge and into the cottage, to be greeted by a delectable spicy smell. Hilary, Dennis, Adele and, strangely enough, Harry Devlin were ranged around the dining room table. Flat boxes of pizza lay open in the center. ''Is it still warm?'' Michael asked.

''Just right,'' said Dennis around a mouthful.

''Those old newspapers turned the trick,'' Devlin explained, and sucked a string of cheese into his mouth.

''What a treat,'' said Hilary. ''Mark, does your knife have a corkscrew? They even brought a bottle of chianti.'' She pulled out the chair beside her and patted it, looking sheepishly up at him. Rebecca handed over his knife and with a flourish Mark opened the bottle and shared it out.

It was Devlin, Michael said when they were mopping up the last crumbs, who'd bought the wine to go with the pizza. Rebecca looked at the policeman over the rim of her glass. ''Why, thank you, Sergeant. Should I accuse you of trying to loosen up a few tongues?''

''Chance would be a fine thing,'' Devlin snorted. ''You lot talk more and say less than any suspects I've ever dealt with.''

Dennis looked up at the ceiling. Adele dismembered a stray piece of pepperoni. Mark's mouth thinned; Hilary looked at her lap. Michael and Rebecca glanced at each other, conveying little more than caution.

Rebecca looked around to see Devlin watching her watching the others. ''Actually,'' he went on with an engaging smile, ''I was thirsty.'' He poured himself another glass and relaxed enough to loosen his tie, but not without a swift glance at the door, as if Mackenzie would leap out of the vestibule lecturing him about neatness and propriety.

''You're single, I take it, Sergeant?'' asked Mark.

''I am the now.'' He pulled out his wallet and produced a photograph of a little girl about five years old. She had his Irish coloring, fair skin, dark hair and blue eyes, but her expression betrayed youthful optimism rather than adult belligerence. Not that Devlin was particularly belligerent at the moment. He explained quite equably about the joint custody arrangement with his former wife. He was trying to draw them out, Rebecca thought. First Mackenzie, then Devlin, both playing good cop.

Adele admired the picture, then gathered the boxes and took them to the garbage can outside. She didn't come back. Dennis slipped away to finish the day's computer entries. Mark held the photo a long time, his expression distant. When Hilary gently took the photo from his hand and returned it to Devlin, Mark shook himself, as though someone had walked over his grave.

Michael shared out the rest of the wine and told Devlin about his nephews. "They intended to have only the two, mind you, but the second one turned oot to be twins. A wee bit ower the top, I told them. But they're fine braw lads. Andrew, after my dad, Patrick and David."

"The patron saints of the Celtic Fringe," said Rebecca. "Good names."

"I'll tell Maddy and Geoff you approve," Michael said into his glass. But he took care to smile, mitigating his sarcasm.

Quelling a groan, Rebecca went to the sideboard and got the boxes with the day's choice artifacts. "Would you like to see what we do when we're not causing problems for the police?" she asked Devlin.

Mark explained the recovery and preservation of the ivory comb. "Not as nice as the one at Jedburgh," he concluded, "but a good piece nonetheless. And, not being gold, not tempting to thieves."

"Let us hope," said Devlin.

Rebecca pulled the tiny heraldic device out of its jeweler's box. "This is in remarkably good condition."

Michael took the disc and rubbed it delicately against his sleeve. "Lion and greyhound supporters—the arms of Henry the Eighth. Might've belonged to some personal envoy of Henry's in Hertford's army."

"What really bothers me," Rebecca admitted, as the disc passed from hand to hand around the table, "is that somebody dug this up and didn't see it. I swear it wasn't in my trench, but I really hate to blame anyone else. It's not a big prize, but not something you'd want to get away."

"It's a good thing Adele spotted it," said Hilary.

Something loomed at Rebecca's back. "Where'd you get that?"

She swung around. "Oh—Dennis. Out of the spoil heap."

"But Sheila had it," he said.

Like a tidal wave of glue, silence fell upon the room. Then Devlin tightened his tie, reached into his jacket draped over the chair behind him, and pulled out his notebook. "Did she show it to you, then?"

Dennis looked hurriedly from face to stunned face. No help there. "Yeah. She told me she'd bought it at some antiquarian's shop in London, that it had come from Hampton Court. Jerry asked her to get it for him. . . ." First comprehension and then outright elation swept his features. He dropped into the chair. The chair squeaked a protest.

The back of Rebecca's neck corded, sending a throb of pain through her head. "Great. Jerry was out salting the dig last night."

"Not necessarily," said Hilary. "It could have been Sheila. It could have been Adele, for that matter."

Devlin wrote in his notebook, saying, "It's worth the askin'."

Michael swore through his teeth. Mark simply looked sick.

"It was Jerry who was planting artifacts that don't belong here," Dennis said. "That's what he did in Virginia with a Harington farthing."

Rebecca's thoughts churned. Not only had Dennis not been in the pub when Michael had told everyone about Jerry's possible wrongdoing, but also no one except she and Michael knew specifically what that wrongdoing had been. With a jolt she remembered seeing a letter for Dennis from Michigan, return address "L.M." Matheny was married. She'd gone home to Michigan. Dennis had two married sisters, one of whom had worked in a museum.

Rebecca turned to Dennis so fiercely, eyes blazing, he shrank back in his chair. "You're her brother, aren't you? You came here to get something on Jerry! That's why you were breathing down Elaine's neck, to get closer to the computer. That's why you volunteered to check the records."

Dennis turned pale, but he didn't flinch. "Yeah. I'm her brother."

"Who?" asked Hilary faintly. Devlin leaned forward, his pencil poised. Rebecca explained.

"Man," Michael exclaimed to Dennis, "you should've put us in the picture straightaway. We're natural allies!"

"It was something I had to do by myself."

"You told Sheila!" retorted Devlin.

"She could be very persuasive," Mark said dryly.

"The more people who knew, the greater the chance of Jerry catching on," Dennis insisted. "I had to catch him in the act. What he did to Laurel—someone should've killed *him*, not Sheila."

Devlin frowned. "Could it be," he said quietly, "that someone thought it would be poetic justice to frame Jerry for something he didn't do?"

One moment ticked by, then two. Dennis's pale face went beet red. "Me? Kill Sheila and make it look like Jerry did it?"

"You stole Michael's sgian dubh and gave it to her. She showed you the . . ." pages flipped ". . . heraldic disc."

"I told you about the dagger. She said it was going to be a joke. She said if I helped her, she'd help me. I don't know why she showed me the disc—maybe to convince me she'd help me." He leaned his elbows on the table and sank his face into his hands.

"Oh, Dennis," said Rebecca, "she was just playing with you."

"Maybe he realized that, that evening behind the chapter house." Devlin stood up. He put on his jacket and stowed the notebook in a pocket. When he put his hand on Dennis's shoulder, he at least had the courtesy to look solemn instead of triumphant. "You'll have to come with me to Galashiels, Mr. Tucker, to help us with our inquiries."

Chapter Twenty-Two

THE SOUND OF bells punctured Rebecca's doze. She groped for pencil and paper—the exam was starting, she hadn't studied. . . . With a gasp she lurched into wakefulness. The ceiling shimmered with the fine, clear light of morning. Sunday morning. Church bells ringing. There was no church in Rudesburn except the priory, and the bells in the tower came down centuries ago.

She clambered over the foot of the bed, opened the curtains, and unlatched the window. The sun was low on the eastern horizon, so bright that it hit her eyes like an exploding flashbulb. The priory was an indistinct outline beyond a translucent mist rising from the burn. Shapes might be moving in the dimness of the church. They might not.

Hands touched her shoulders, and she started so violently her head collided with something hard. "Ow!" Michael exclaimed. "I've no need of a nose job, thank you just the same."

She spun around. "I'm sorry. Are you all right?"

He wiggled his nose. "I'm all right. Can you hear the bells?"

Still they rang, trills spilling into the soft morning air like crystal coins down a well. The breeze through the window was cold and damp, and gooseflesh rose on Rebecca's arms. Then, as sharp and quick as a gunshot, the back door of the cottage shut. "Come on," said Michael.

They rushed into their clothes and dashed outside while Rebecca was still hooking her glasses over her ears. A prosaic human form hurried over the green lawn toward the church. The sun cleared the roof, and a ray of light illuminated Adele's silver hair.

Beneath the bridge the babble of water played counterpoint to the bells. Mist wreathed upward, touching Rebecca's face with chilly kisses. On the far side of the stream, the air was palpably cold.

"Hey! Wait for us!" Mark's shout was subdued into an urgent stage-whisper. He and Hilary ran hand in hand toward the bridge.

Adele rushed into the church like a parishioner late for services. The bells faded away, quieter and quieter, until they were only an echo quivering in the ground and pealing gently through Rebecca's blood. The cold ebbed. Together the four walked across the bridge and swished through the grass.

The ancient stone of the wheel-cross glistened with rivulets of light and damp. Inside the church the sunlight shining through the tracery of the eastern window made an intricate pattern of light and shadow on the floor. Adele knelt at the altar. Beside her knelt someone or something else—a white contour of draperies and light. A curtain of cold air blocked the door.

Michael and Rebecca, Hilary and Mark, edged away. Toward them across the lawns came Laurence and Grant, shoulder to shoulder, like Ghostbusters summoned to an early shift. "What is it?" called the bobby.

"Naething couthy," Michael responded.

They peered into the church. Adele didn't move. Neither did the ghostly form. Faint and distant women's voices sang, *"Angelus domini descendit de caelo et accedeus revolvit lapidem."*

"An Easter verse, " whispered Rebecca. " 'God's angels came down from heaven and rolled back the stone,' or something like that."

"The stone covering Christ's tomb," added Hilary.

"Angelus domini . . . " sang the voices. The broken arches and the shattered tiles glowed, the stone seeming to flow like a viscous liquid, healing itself from centuries of injury.

As one they all turned from the door, blinded by the glowing light. Silence fell, even the wind and the stream muted. After a long moment Grant asked plaintively, "Any chance of a cuppa?"

Nora welcomed them into the hotel kitchen where a massive Aga cooker emanated warmth. Rebecca's glasses steamed up. A cup of blissfully hot and sweet tea and a mound of wholemeal toast chased the shiver from her spine and almost relaxed the back of her neck. The roses returned to Hilary's cheeks. Lancelot and Guinevere lounged in front of the oven door, knowing better than to go chasing ghosts on a chilly morning.

"My grandfather used tae say," offered Grant, "that Anne and her nuns didna realize they were dead; they kept right on doin' their duty."

"Guardin' something?" Michael asked. "Wantin' revenge? What else did Adele say was a motive for hauntin'?"

Mark stirred his tea. "Adele fits right in, doesn't she? No more grasp of reality than a ghost."

"Reality?" Hilary retorted. "We all saw her."

"Serve us right," said Laurence, "if Adele really has been chatting with Anne Douglas."

"But we'll no be able to summon Anne as a witness." Grant scooped marmalade onto his toast. "Speakin' o' witnesses, I dout they'll be bringin' Dennis back straightaway, just like all the others."

Mackenzie's quest for a motive for murder was producing too damn many, Rebecca thought.

Jerry's voice boomed suddenly from the door. "Is this shindig invitation-only? Sorry, don't have my black tie." He pulled a chair from a stack against the wall, forced a space between Michael and Rebecca, and sat. "Damned bells woke me up. Somebody's idea of a joke?"

Rebecca considered Jerry's jowl, gleaming pale and cold beneath a mousy stubble of whiskers. He knew quite well that the bells hadn't been a joke.

Jerry yammered on. "Where's the nerd? I figured free food would pull him in like a moth to a candle."

Over Jerry's shoulder Rebecca saw Michael stifle a wicked grin. Grant gazed innocently at the ceiling. Laurence and Nora buttered toast and handed around marmalade. That had been a good ploy of Devlin's, worthy of Mackenzie himself, to quietly haul Dennis away and no doubt wring him dry before giving Jerry a chance to pile on any wet blankets.

"Oh, you know Dennis," said Mark. "A brass band wouldn't wake him up, let alone a few bells."

Jerry offered anecdotes about Colchester and Nimrud, but no one took the bait. He ventured an opinion on Thatcher's economic policies. The British taxpayers concealed smiles, and the Americans yawned. He pontificated briefly on crime detection, but gave up when there was no response but the desultory clink of spoons in cups. Before he could begin speculating why Tony and Elaine hadn't heard the bells, everyone muttered excuses and sidled away.

By the time everyone had washed, brushed their teeth, and gathered at the dig, the mist had been absorbed into a cloud-laced sky. Adele didn't ask why she'd had to breakfast alone. She set to work at the infirmary trench with the virtuous air of a child who'd earned a good-conduct badge in Sunday School. The church was once again a silent shell of rock.

Laurence, not wanting to waste Jerry's enthusiasm, volunteered some lads from the village to help with the ditch-filling. Elaine trotted behind Tony, juggling the pieces of equipment he tossed to her, while he filmed the closing of the old trenches and the opening of the new. Judging by Michael's suffused expression, he had to squelch more than one sardonic comment about Jerry's metamorphosis from slug to butterfly. He took a miniature pick and a level and started tapping his way up the tower staircase, recording arcane aspects of subsidence and decay. Rebecca sent Adele and Hilary on to the infirmary trench while she lingered in the church; with Dennis gone someone had to get the computer booted and spurred for the day.

She hit "enter," watched yesterday's artifact records unfurl on the glowing screen, and looked up. Simon Mackenzie came striding down the nave toward her with Devlin two paces behind. A pinched look about Mackenzie's mouth, and Devlin's truculent air, made Rebecca suspect Devlin hadn't bothered to call his superior back to Galashiels until this morning. She called, "Good morning."

Mackenzie sat on one of the folding chairs and stared at William Salkeld's effigy. Salkeld was unimpressed. Mackenzie looked up at the tatty wooden roof that had replaced carved stone bosses. The heavens didn't open with inspiration. He pulled a small white box out of his pocket and said, "There is no one more dangerous than a successful murderer."

"Thank you, Chief Inspector, for easing my mind," said Rebecca. "Especially since I think someone was snooping around the cottage, looking at the trial records, the other night. But I haven't done a translation yet."

Devlin whipped out his notebook and wrote that down.

Mackenzie seemed unsurprised. "Once you start translating, don't leave them lying around." His scratched hand opened the box, revealing the damning enamel disc. "Mr. Tucker is either a superb actor or just what he says he is. Which way would you vote?''

"Just what he says he is. A lifelong klutz who finally found a crusade, saving his sister's honor. I should've realized ages ago what he was up to—he's been an elephant tiptoeing through a china shop.''

"You think, then, the subtlety of killing Miss Fitzgerald and making it look like Dr. Kleinfelter did it is beyond him.''

"The only thing that could possibly make me think Dennis killed her is that he failed utterly to make it look like anyone else did.'' Rebecca leaned her chin on her hand. "Besides, we're assuming Sheila's killer also tried to kill the cat—in other words, Sheila's killer is after relics or treasure. How do you dovetail that with Dennis's revenge motive?''

Mackenzie indulged in a sardonic laugh. "I don't. That's why Mr. Tucker is even now outside in the cloister, free to go.''

Devlin retired behind a pillar, presumably to bang his head against it.

Jerry appeared in the doorway. "Dr. Kleinfelter,'' said Mackenzie. "Good of you to come. Please sit down.''

Taking her cue from Mackenzie's labored courtesy, Rebecca gathered up computer and records and went into the cloister. Dennis and Mark were comparing notes on police station cuisine. Michael's hammer tapped away in the tower. The local lads seemed to work harder without Jerry supervising. Word got around quickly, Rebecca thought, and set the computer on a flat column base. "Glad you're back, Dennis. Here it is, all ready to go.''

His bearing was as dignified as one of Colin's toy redcoats. "Thank you, Rebecca. I'll get right on it.''

From the church came Mackenzie's most casual voice. "You saw this yesterday afternoon, I take it?''

"Ah, yes,'' Jerry replied. "A heraldic disc of Henry the Eighth. Establishes that the man took a personal interest in Rudesburn.''

"How does it do that?''

"Because old Henry must've sent one of his personal flunkies up here. Not just any Tom, Dick, or Harry could wear the king's arms.''

Mackenzie went on playing out the rope and tying the noose. "So you'd say this was dated quite solidly, an important find.''

"Well,'' Jerry replied in his favorite speaker-to-peasants

voice, "since it came from the 1545 destruction level in the first trench . . .''

Dennis sat down by the computer, fingers poised. Mark leaned on his spade. A shadow inside the door to the tower was Michael.

"Actually, Dr. Kleinfelter," said Mackenzie, "the disc came from an antiquarian's shop on the Edgware Road in London. We knocked up the shopkeeper this morning and faxed him a copy of the disc. It's in his records."

Silence, except for the thud-slide of dirt filling the trenches, the squeak of a wheelbarrow, and the harsh call of a crow high overhead.

Mackenzie continued, "The shopkeeper sold the disc to Miss Fitzgerald last month—along with the second gold noble. He recognized her at the time, from her telly programs."

Rebecca nodded. So that's where the coin came from. Sheila was checking Kerr's coin, then, not her own. So she could plant hers, maybe?

Jerry sputtered, probably with his patented codfish stare, "Well, that goes to show you, doesn't it? The bitch'd resort to anything to get herself some publicity. Salting the dig. Absolutely beyond the pale."

"That level hadn't been uncovered when Miss Fitzgerald died."

"Okay, so she left it in the spoil heap."

"That particular spoil heap," said Devlin amid a rustling of notebook pages, "wasn't here when Sheila was killed."

Jerry's voice was getting louder and louder. "Then it was that nut who turned it up—Adele. She was in it with Sheila."

Mackenzie said quietly, "We have a deposition from a witness who was told by Miss Fitzgerald that she bought the disc for you."

"This is ridiculous! Why don't you just do your job, Inspector, and let me do mine? Thank God I don't pay taxes in this country. The quality of public servant is pathetic, leaving murders unsolved to harass foreign nationals who are simply going about their business!"

"I am doing my job," said Mackenzie.

"We have a deposition," Devlin said. "Sheila bought the disc for you."

A chair scraped abruptly. "Someone's out to get me, huh?

That figures. People are always jealous of a man at the top of his profession.''

Jerry stormed out of the transept door, pushing Rebecca against Mark. He strode back to the trenches, grabbed a shovel from one of the lads and started scooping dirt as fiercely as though he were stoking a fire.

Mark scowled at Jerry's back. Dennis tapped the space bar on the computer keyboard, watching the cursor bounce across the screen, his mouth tight. Footsteps trudged up the tower. Devlin took a step after Jerry but was recalled by a quiet word from Mackenzie.

Of course Jerry would stonewall. How could Rebecca have thought Michael had an ego when she was confronted daily with Jerry's brass-plated gall? Scowling, she headed toward the infirmary.

Grant was stationed by the spoil heap, supervising every shovelful of dirt that went back into the trenches. Tony and Elaine sat cozily on Battle Law; he was letting her look through his video camera. Adele and Hilary were turning out a very nice vertical baulk that revealed a jumble of broken pottery. Rebecca ran out of profanity and bent to help.

After a time Mackenzie and Devlin came strolling through the slype. With casual greetings they passed the infirmary trench and approached Tony and Elaine. Despite Elaine's quivering outthrust lower lip and Tony's head-lowered stare, like a bull considering a charge, they were both hauled off toward the Plantagenet van.

They were still there at lunch time, Mackenzie evidently insisting on seeing every inch of tape and every frame of film shot since the beginning of the dig. By the time the detectives finally emerged, Elaine's face was as red as her lipstick, and Tony's was ashen.

In the afternoon Mackenzie and Devlin talked again to Dennis. At quitting time they cornered Laurence and Nora. Jerry climbed in his Jaguar and roared off in a cloud of gravel. Michael looked up from helping Rebecca collect the day's printouts. "They're no lettin' him go, are they?"

Devlin and Mackenzie calmly climbed in a police car and followed. "I wonder where Jerry's been hiding that disc," asked Rebecca.

"I'd like to say the same place he's been hidin' my sgian dubh."

"But can you really see Jerry killing Sheila?"

"No. But then, I canna see anyone killin' Sheila." He tucked the printouts under his arm. "Will they be tellin' Jerry who Dennis is?"

Rebecca shook her head. "Would Dennis be safe?"

"Aboot as safe as any of us." The creases beside his mouth deepened. With a sigh Rebecca took the computer and headed for the cottage.

The clear afternoon slipped subtly into a clear evening. After dinner Mark and Dennis compared the original site recording sheets with the computer records, Hilary touched up her drawings, and Adele went over the budget for the Archeological Network. Rebecca, deciding she couldn't watch everyone at once, went into her bedroom and stood with her back against the door.

Michael was sitting on his bed, writing something in Colin's notepad. "New information," he said to her questioning look. "Besides Hilary seein' Jerry and Sheila at seven-thirty. The ring and the brooch have gone missin'—Tony or Bob Jenkins suspected. Dennis is unmasked. The nets are closin' aboot Jerry."

She settled down beside him, took the book and flipped back a few pages. "Monday, July Seventeenth. God, it's only been a week since—"

"Sheila died."

"Eight o'clock. Mark takes a dander along the B6359, Hilary through the fields. Tony takes photographs from the Law, then goes to the camera van. Dennis goes to the camera van. Yeah, that's right, I heard their voices in there when I left the house. Jerry, Elaine, Adele. . . . Michael searches the hotel attic, and Rebecca sulks in the cottage."

"Colin didna say that."

"Just adding color commentary. Eight-fifteen—look, Colin tried to catch Adele out. He has in parentheses, when Adele walked through the village she noticed the toy Queen was gone from the store window. And here, he asked Jerry what time Hilary got to the bar. You're sure Colin doesn't have a secret urge to be a policeman?"

"He's always liked detective novels."

A pattern, Rebecca thought. The pattern she was looking for might be right on that page, but she couldn't see it. She was too close to it. She was too close to Michael. They leaned together cautiously, not speaking. A valedictory pose, like Bogart and Bergman on the runway in Casablanca. Neither of them had broken the dignity of the moment by blurting, "Talk to me, tell me what you feel, spill your guts."

A knock on the door heralded Mark, reporting that Jerry was back, and that the police car had lingered in the street until he'd gone into the hotel, there to be shadowed by Grant, unless it was Grant's duty tonight to shadow the students.

After the ITV Scottish news—nothing about the Rudesburn murder—everyone went silently and separately to bed. Rebecca tossed and turned, not quite dreaming, not quite remembering, and finally lay in a stupor as sunlight leaked into the room. But she heard no bells, no singing, no doors shutting. It was only when Michael turned off the alarm the instant it rang that she realized he, too, had been lying awake.

At least Monday promised to be another clear and sunny day. The herd of reporters diminished, and the number of tourists increased, as did that of police shepherds. Mark and Michael started prying boards and heaving blocks of stone at the crypt door while Jerry wandered from church to infirmary and back, wafting cloying clouds of smoke. He seemed sure that the person who had turned him in yesterday had been the same one who had revealed his assignation with Sheila, and his bellicose remarks to Elaine left no doubt who he thought the culprit was. Elaine responded in kind. Tony looked on, dryly amused. Hilary and Dennis ignored all three.

Rebecca set up shop on a warm stretch of the southern cloister wall, by the broken doorway of the refectory. From here she could keep an eye on the infirmary trench and the door of the transept. No way was she going to sit alone in the cottage, trapped in the sights and sounds of another era. "Come and pull me out in an hour," she told Michael.

"You're a better man than I am, Gunga Din," he said with a salute.

She took a deep breath, like a scuba diver going off the side of the boat, and opened the portfolio.

At first there was only the parchment dry and dusty on her fingertips and the spiky script crawling before her eyes. The seal of Edward Seymour, Earl of Hertford. The seal of somebody Douglas, a half-hearted ghost of an imprint. The seal of a Salkeld, a descendant of the Salkeld done so cruelly to death on this very spot. The seals of Howard and Sadler, English nobles.

The script writhed, words like worms burrowing deep in her senses. A cloud passed over the sun—no, the world darkened into night. Torches burned in the corners of Rebecca's eyes. The odors of sweat and ale filled her nostrils. *Anne, prioress of Rudesburn, come into the court.*

The slender figure was clothed all in white, her face paler than her garment, only the dark eyes alive, frightened but too proud to show fear. Anne Douglas, prioress. Thomas Elliot, commendator, tried in absentia. Unlawful carnal knowledge—aha, Adele was right; if Anne and Thomas didn't have something going, then they were suspected of it. Convenient, that Thomas had disappeared, that he couldn't testify either for or against his lover.

Summoning spirits. Witchcraft. The holy spirit of Marjory, 1 st prioress. Demons, perverted woman—lies, all lies. Committed to close questioning. . . . Rebecca felt her head moving in a gesture of negation. Close questioning. They'd tortured the woman. Pigs.

Relics of superstition and idolatry—St. Margaret's veil, St. Aidan's cross, a finger bone of St. Kentigern. A relic of the traitor de Brus. Church plate and jewels. Where are they? They must be commended to His Majesty. . . .

The traitor de Brus. . . . To the English, Robert the Bruce would have been considered a traitor. It was here. It really was here. The parchments quivered in Rebecca's hands. She knew she was crouched over the papers, pencil and notebook clutched in her hand. She knew she was in the chapter house, roof complete, columns whole, torches burning smokily and smearing the eager faces of the men. Men in the convent, the white-clad figures banished to the kitchens except for the one, Anne—swaying weakly but facing her tormentors, chin up, eyes pools of shadow and pain and pride.

Did any of the men step forward to support her? Even the one named Douglas? . . . There was his name. Alexander Douglas, cousin to the defendant, at first standing among her accusers and then gone, wiped from the record. Rebecca felt her teeth grinding. Coward. But what could he have done?

Her neck hurt. Her whole body hurt. Since Anne withstood questioning, she was possessed of demons. She was proved a witch. She wouldn't give them the relics or the treasure. Inventory attached. Did that mean they found it and took it anyway? Anne—what did they do to Anne? What was the verdict of the court?

"Rebecca!"

"Ah, sweet Jesus, spare me!" Sparks swirled from the torches. The convent burned. Women screamed, and horses stampeded through the cloister.

"Rebecca! Wake up! Graham just rang with news from London."

Michael sat on the wall beside her, hands clenched on her arms. Other faces hung blurred in the sunlight behind him. "Oh," Rebecca croaked, and cleared her throat. "Oh, hi."

"What the hell is her problem?" Jerry demanded.

"Reality displacement," explained Michael.

"Hmph," said Jerry.

Adele nodded understanding. Hilary looked as if she'd just seen Rebecca sprout an extra head. Mark's brows angled up his forehead. Dennis's mouth hung open.

"London?" asked Rebecca. "Thomas Elliot?"

Elaine gazed into the distance, bored to tears. Tony raised his camera. Great, Rebecca thought, she was being immortalized like this. She straightened her hair.

"Aye, Thomas Elliot," replied Michael. "The assistants at the Library couldna find any record of him workin' for Edward the Sixth."

"Then it was him in the cellar!" Jerry chortled.

"No so fast. The story aboot Edward's a flannel for the folk at home. Elliot's in other records—those of Newgate prison. He was hanged in 1548 for highway robbery."

"What?" Rebecca exclaimed. "The same Elliot?"

"He rated a mention because he was a minor Scottish noble reduced to robbin' coaches in Surrey. You ken the story—barbarian Scots, raise the drawbridges. It's our Elliot, right enough."

"So he ran for it, apparently without the treasure," Rebecca mused. "I'd almost wondered if Anne had killed him herself, for collaborating maybe, or for ripping off the goods, or simply for doing her wrong."

Adele frowned, shaking her head, no doubt wondering why her psychic receivers had fuzzed out on her.

"The night afore he died," Michael went on, "Elliot confessed to his jailor that he'd killed a man in a convent."

A ripple of *aha!* went around the group. "He didn't bother to give the man's name, did he?" asked Dennis hopefully.

"No, more's the pity. And he didna bother to explain why he left his ring on the corpse's hand. If he did."

"Restitution for a sudden death? That ring reminds me of the coins on Miss Fitzgerald's eyes." Mackenzie sat down on Rebecca's other side and signaled Tony to put away the camera. "Tell me about the treasure."

"The priory plate, mostly, and probably the odd jeweled reliquary," answered Rebecca. "Although Hertford and crew did put on a show of wanting the relics—to destroy them, I bet. Among them something I assume was the heart of the Bruce. Anne wouldn't give them up even when they tortured her. I don't know whether the English got them in the end or not. There's supposed to be an inventory. . . ."

Warily, with only her fingernails, she flipped through the sheets of parchment.

"Did Anne die under torture?" Adele asked faintly.

"There's a page missing," Rebecca replied. "This one ends in mid-sentence, and this one, with the signatures, is just legal formulas. No inventory. No verdict. I don't know how or when she died."

Now Adele looked worried. Tony held his camera on his hip like a woman holding a child. Michael leaned back, his fingers enlaced around his knee, and exhaled through pursed lips. "A page missin'. Back to the attic, then."

Rebecca folded the trial records into the portfolio, added her embarrassingly messy notes, and asked Mackenzie to put them in Laurence's safe. "No more today?" he asked.

"I got the heart out of them. No pun intended. No more today." She stood. Her knees wobbled in separate directions. "I wonder if the body in the cellar is Alexander Douglas."

"Who?"

She explained, concluding, "Just a hunch. He disappears awfully abruptly. And Elliot confessed to a murder. Maybe Alexander attacked first."

"Understandable, if he caught Elliot scarperin'," said Michael. "Well done, lass. Come on, I'll help you wi' lunch."

"Thank you," she said, and they headed toward the kitchen.

Mackenzie and Devlin sat with Jerry on the porch of the church while the afternoon sky filled with white and gray thunderheads. At last, worn away by the spate of inconsequential braggadocio, they dismissed him and invited Adele to join them. She was released unperturbed at quitting time, and proceeded to fix smothered steak and rice for dinner. Devlin and Mackenzie skulked around the ruins until the first shower of rain drove them away. Michael and Mark spent a fruitless hour in the hotel attic. Rebecca wrote yet another report for the Archeological Network, tempted to conclude, "So far no students have been murdered, but stay tuned."

That night the soothing sound of rain on the roof put Rebecca right to sleep; she didn't even lie awake weighing the significance of Michael's neither perfunctory nor enthusiastic good night kiss.

She dreamed she was standing at the altar of the church. The whole, undamaged altar, swathed in a richly embroidered cloth. The Monymusk reliquary lay amid a dazzling display of silver plate, salver, paten, chalice. . . . She awoke, blinking, in pitch blackness. The inventory might be in the attic. Everyone had heard her say so. The attic should be watched.

The clock read one-fifteen. The rain had stopped. Rebecca padded cautiously through the house. From the kitchen window the priory was invisible. From the dining room window a few lights gleamed in the village. A gusty wind tossed the branches of the trees. Raindrops spattered on the roof like a throw of dice. No, all was quiet. . . .

Wait a minute. Those weren't car lights reflecting in the attic skylights. No cars were passing. Someone was up there with a flashlight. The bastard moved fast. She caromed off the doorway and catapulted into the bedroom. "Michael, wake up! Someone's in the attic!"

His bleary look indicated she had bats in her attic.

"Michael, I can see a flashlight in the skylights. Someone's up there looking for the missing page!"

That roused him. Again they threw on shirts and jeans and rushed outside, this time into darkness. Puddles ambushed them on the driveway, and the gutter beside the call box ran with water. Rebecca was so hot with anger at the unseen culprit that she was surprised the water didn't turn to steam around her boots. "Every time I've turned around this week I've fallen over a cop," she hissed, "and now there's not one in sight."

"You knock up Grant. I'll go on up, catch them afore they leg it."

"No way. We're supposed to be a team, remember?" Michael shot her a skeptical glance, but didn't contradict her. The hotel door was open. "Did some late guest not lock it? Or did our prowler help himself to a key?"

"We'll find oot," replied Michael grimly. "I've had enough of this jiggery-pokery."

They hurried up the staircase and tried to ease through the fire doors, but they were so heavy they creaked and swished. Rebecca and Michael groped up the shadowy staircase to the landing outside the attic. The door was open. The room was dark. Rebecca flicked the switch.

The ceiling lights threw boxes, trunks, and old furniture into sharp relief. Michael stepped inside. Rebecca waited outside, straining her ears, trying to look everywhere at once. She heard another patter of rain on the roof, and the wind in the trees, and Michael's footsteps. He pounced behind a dresser and emerged shrugging from the other side.

"No one's here," he said. "No one's here the noo. Look." He pointed to a large wooden crate. The top was open, nails still protruding from it. The velvets and flounces of century-old clothes spilled from it onto the floor. Several musty leather-bound books lay among them. Michael picked them up and piled them to one side. "Can the gowk no read? It's labeled 'Elizabeth Kerr,' no, 'Mary Pringle.' "

Somewhere in the dim corridors behind Rebecca's back a door clicked. Her heart jumped into her throat. A patch of white slithered along the floor. . . . Oh. She smiled. It was Guinevere's white breast and paws.

Her smile withered. The cat was stalking something. Michael and Rebecca tiptoed down the staircase from the landing and stepped slowly along the hallway below.

The cat crouched in front of a door designated "Ladies" at the head of the main staircase. Her tail twitched. From her throat came a low growling hiss, like a small steam engine on the verge of explosion. Another shape a few feet away was Lancelot, hunched and bristling, puzzled by Guinevere's mood and not liking a bit of it.

Someone's in the bathroom, Rebecca told herself. Michael's jaw twitched. Two steps away from the door, with Michael's hand already extended, Rebecca put her weight on her right foot and beneath the carpet a floorboard squealed like a set of pipes.

The door flew open. Pain exploded in Rebecca's shoulder and her glasses flew off her face. She staggered backward as a pale shape lunged from the black interior of the room. Michael shouted and grabbed. Something glinted. Cats shrieked. Michael fell, saving himself from tumbling down the stairs by a frantic grasp of the banister. Footsteps raced away. Doors slammed. Voices bellowed for silence.

Rebecca recovered her balance and rushed forward. Something crunched under her foot. Her glasses. Never mind them.

Michael was still clutching the banister, his forehead against the wood, exploring the possibilities of profanity in a thorough listing from A to Zed. Rebecca skidded to a stop beside him. The arm of his sweatshirt was stained dark . . . It was stained with blood. "My God!" she gasped.

She seized his arm and pulled it up into the air so vigorously he cried out. "It's nae sae bad as a' that, dinna pull it off, woman!" She ignored him, groped for the pulse point, found it and pressed her hand into it.

Someone was thumping down the hall toward them. Rebecca looked up and saw a blurry Nora, nightgown hitched up, armed with a skillet. The woolly shape behind her was Laurence wielding a cricket bat. "Who's there?" Laurence demanded.

"No the U.S. Cavalry, I'm afraid," Rebecca answered.

"My God," said Nora. The skillet clanged to the floor.

"Right embarrassin'," Michael said with a wan smile, "tae be stabbed wi' your own dagger. And my pipe-pumpin' arm, tae boot."

Laurence galloped down the stairs, calling for Grant, for Mackenzie, for medics. The two cats, whiskers bristling, crawled out from under a chair and proceeded to lick themselves down, as though a bath could get rid of the sickly scent of blood.

Chapter Twenty-Three

THIS WAS AS close to a hallucinatory experience as Rebecca ever wanted to come. Her myopia intensified the sway of the car into the lurch of a carnival ride. Glittering blobs along the road were the eyes of startled sheep. Two passing police cars were blue comets, the wah-wah of their sirens a textbook example of the Doppler effect. Grant's face, illuminated by the dashboard lights, peered worriedly from the rearview mirror.

It had been Grant and Laurence who'd swathed Michael's arm in gauze bandages. "It's no so bad," he'd kept insisting, "there's nae need tae mummify me!" By the volume of his complaints Rebecca estimated not only that he was going to survive, but also how badly he was hurting. She'd bundled him into Grant's car without getting her contact lenses from the cottage or acknowledging any of the vague shapes seething up and down the sidewalk.

Michael's head lay on her shoulder, his right arm wrapped her waist, his hurt arm rested in her lap. Shadow and pain pared his features to a minimum. His long, limber mouth, parted on a ragged breath, was startlingly vulnerable, and his brows were knotted, making him look aged beyond his years. His forehead as she smoothed his hair felt clammy. She tugged the hotel comforter around him.

His eyes opened with a blue spark. "Can you no offer a bit o' artificial respiration?"

"Michael Campbell, you are incorrigible."

"I should hope so—" She cut off his response with a kiss. Grant's face in the mirror softened.

Rebecca's heart was still hammering. That had been too damn close a call. She envisioned a Michael-shaped void in her consciousness, forever haunted by words left unsaid and doubts unresolved.

"I'm all right," he said again.

"You'd better be." She'd often wondered whether she had much of a nurturing instinct. Now she knew. She relaxed her grip before she choked him.

Melrose flashed past. Grant took the Abbotsford roundabout on two wheels. Bright lights spilled onto the pavement—Galashiels at last. Faceless figures pulled Michael from her arms, laid him on a stretcher, and wheeled him away. "I'll find the car park," said Grant. Rebecca blundered into a hallway and stood rotating the shoulder knocked and bruised by the opening door.

Someone thrust a clipboard into her hands. A pen appeared in the blur of her peripheral vision. Name: Campbell, Michael Ian. Date of Birth: August 3, 1959. Sex: She almost wrote, "when appropriate," then looked up.

She thought she recognized that pen. "What's all this in aid of?" asked Detective Sergeant Devlin.

Only now, in the glare, did Rebecca see her gold Missouri sweatshirt mottled with red and brown stains. The floor moved beneath her feet. Devlin grasped her arm, released it at her cry of pain, and whisked a plastic chair behind her as her knees gave way. *Oh, Michael, why is this happening to us?* Tears spilled from her eyes and burned down her cheeks.

Rebecca groped in her pocket and found a tissue, telling herself sternly, she was not going to help the situation by crying. Devlin vanished and returned with a squishy cardboard cup of hot tea. She drank, pushed back her hair, and thanked him. "I guess you'd like to know what happened."

He pulled out another pen and sat down beside her. "All Laurence said when he rang was that you'd surprised someone in the attic."

"Yeah, we did that, all right. We should've backed off when we couldn't find the police. We should've done a bed check to see who was missing. But, dammit, we were mad, we were afraid they'd get away." She was still mad, trembling with fear and anger both—not the least at not even knowing what pronoun to use.

Devlin shook his head over the ineptness of civilians. "You couldn't tell who it was, I take it."

"Everything happened too fast. I just saw a white shape. I have no idea of height or weight. No face, even, just shadow. But it wasn't Grant's transparent ghost—it knocked me back with the door, stabbed Michael, and almost threw him down the stairs." She took a deep breath. Starting from the time she woke up worried about the missing page, she progressed in a more or less orderly fashion to the appearance of the Bairds.

"And no constables on duty? Well, Mackenzie'll be sortin' them out." Devlin's smile was that of a crocodile relishing a victim.

A body loomed behind Devlin, and a masculine voice said, "We'll be needing the completed forms, Miss."

"Oh, sorry." Rebecca produced something almost legible and handed over the clipboard. "Is he all right?"

"Right as rain," replied the blur. "The cut's one of those long gashes that bleeds like hell but isn't really bad. He needed a few stitches at the puncture end, where the knife first went in." With left forearm and right forefinger the figure mimed an upward thrust. Rebecca shuddered.

"Check her out, too," Devlin said. "Her shoulder's hurt."

"Half a minute." The blur faded into the background and reappeared with a wheelchair. "Pop in."

"I walked this far," Rebecca protested, and for her efforts received another clipboard. Name, rank—she could check Miss, Mrs. or Ms., but there was no space for Dr.

By the time she'd been poked, prodded, x-rayed and medicated, her head was filled with moths and her stomach with lead. She emerged from the curtained cubicle with little ambition beyond taking a bath and burning the blood-stained sweatshirt.

Michael was waiting with Devlin and Grant. His face was greenish-pallid beneath the reddish stubble on his cheeks, and his hand emerging from a bandage and sling was shaking. At her glance he clenched his fist to stop the trembling and managed an anemic smile. "How's it goin', hen?"

"I'm turning black and blue, but nothing's broken. And you?"

"They said I could play the pipes at the Festival, if I behave mysel'."

"No more chasin' either ghosts or criminals," warned Devlin.

Grant said, "Let's be gettin' back home."

Michael and Rebecca flopped, groaning, into the back seat of the car while Devlin climbed in beside Grant. Dawn crept up the sky, so clean and pure Rebecca wondered if a loud noise would cause it to shatter, and the delicate roses and lavenders break away to reveal permanent night behind. Back in Rudesburn she and Michael plodded past assorted worried faces and collapsed in the cottage.

Rebecca started awake more than once at Michael's mumbling outcries, and at last struggled from her bed to his. His face was now flushed rather than pale. He stared foggily up at her. "What day is it?"

"Still Tuesday. Nightmares?"

"Time to get up," he replied, admitting nothing.

They tried to embrace. His left arm and her left shoulder were too sore for more than a quick inclination toward each other, like two puzzle pieces that didn't quite fit. She opened her mouth, swallowed what felt like glue, tried again. "Giving you up for a philosophical principle is one thing. Having you—permanently gone—that's something else again."

He stroked her cheek with his fingertip. "No good lettin' that bluidy bastard make our decisions for us, is it? We're fighters, the both of us; no wonder compromise comes so hard."

"I'm not so sure it's as simple as compromise, Michael."

"Naething's simple." He levered her gently aside and went to bathe.

They arrived at the excavation just in time for elevenses. Nora rushed over with tea and shortbread. Everyone else was ranged along the stump of the wall, the sunshine defining a variety of weary expressions. Probably no one had slept much after the one a.m. alarm.

Jerry said, "Hell of a way to get out of a morning's work."

"That it is," Michael agreed.

"Are you all right?" asked Mackenzie. He handed Devlin back his notebook. Several other voices expressed concern.

"We'll live, thanks," Rebecca replied.

A weak smile moved like a sine wave through the group. Everyone started talking at once, pretending nothing was wrong. "Psychic vibrations are difficult to interpret," Adele said to Dennis. "I sensed a masculine aura close to Anne, but misunderstood whose it was." Dennis brushed crumbs from his Star Trek T-shirt and glanced suspiciously at Jerry.

Tony crumbled shortbread onto a column drum, trying to entice a couple of sparrows to take the food from his hand. "I'd get the milk off the stoop and find the cream gone. So I got up early, ready to shy a brick at the neighbor's cat. But birds had learned to perch on the bottle and peck through the foil. Dead brilliant.''

Elaine looked from Adele to Rebecca to Mackenzie, her red mouth crumpled tightly.

Mark said to Hilary, ''Thousands of bats live beneath the Congress Avenue bridge in Austin. You can sit in the top floor bar at the Hyatt and watch them come swarming out at sunset. . . .'' His voice died away and he shot a sharp glance beyond Hilary to Tony and Elaine.

''Can you order garlic with your drink?'' Hilary asked, her laugh as forced as a beauty queen's smile.

Jerry walked by Elaine and muttered something under his breath. She colored and slapped a camera bag shut. Tony sent Jerry a sharp sideways glance. Nora collected the cups as though one of them was poisoned and she wasn't sure which.

By this time a gallon or so of tea was making tidal pools in Rebecca's stomach. She sat down beside Mackenzie while Michael sat beside Devlin; separated, as usual, by the police. ''The inventory may not necessarily be in the attic,'' she said. ''And just because the inventory is missing doesn't mean the treasure's still here.''

''All Pringle knew,'' added Michael, ''is that she didna have it. But that was sixty years after Anne.''

Mackenzie's eyes were charcoal, burning beneath a layer of ashes. He said quietly, ''We have a sodding efficient killer, with gumption to match.''

''Who's not reluctant to kill again,'' put in Devlin.

Jerry's bellow of ''Back to work!'' broke the silence. He charged through the transept door with all the finesse of a rhinoceros. Mark and Dennis followed. Hilary seized her drawing board, and she and Adele walked toward the infirmary. Tony hoisted his cameras, and Elaine picked up a bag.

''Who left the hotel door unlocked?'' asked Michael.

''Bob Jenkins,'' answered Mackenzie. ''He said he was properly soused last night, and judging from his sniveling this morning, he was.''

''He has an alibi at a pub in Melrose,'' Devlin added. ''Ought to do him for drunk drivin'.''

''He's about the only reporter still around,'' Rebecca said.

Mackenzie focused on Tony and Elaine as they set up a tripod by the footbridge. ''They have alibis for each other, although Tony and Jerry were on the pavement exchanging insults when

I got here. Hilary said Adele is up and down all night anyway; in other words, they can't speak for each other. Mark and Dennis swear they were both in bed when the balloon went up. And the constables, who were supposedly on guard, were chasing something white over here at the priory. I suggested they reconsider their tactics.''

Rebecca hoped the hapless bobbies had survived Mackenzie's suggestion. He was using first names, which was not a good sign. His lips were set tightly together. His burning eyes moved from the camera crew to a group of searchers returning lead-footed and empty-handed to the Craft Centre. She asked, "And where is Michael's sgian dubh? Where are the dragon brooch and the signet ring?''

"There's a lot of countryside around Rudesburn," Devlin replied.

Mackenzie got up and paced away. With a half-shrug toward Michael and Rebecca, Devlin followed. A tour bus stopped in Jedburgh Street. The whipper-in herded everyone past the perimeter wall, no doubt expounding on unsolved mysteries and spectral nuns.

By lunch time the police had once again been through the drawers, in the closets, and under the beds at the cottage. The mail was arranged on the dining room table. Rebecca glanced narrowly at it—no, it hadn't been opened.

Her letter from home came with a snapshot of a niece's birthday party. Adele had another letter from the ashram. Hilary had a note in pink paper covered with cat stickers. Michael had a postcard from Maddy, a photo of a stately home. *Saturday at Chatsworth Hall*, she wrote in a clear, rounded script. *The boys loved the ducks. Hello, Rebecca.* "Hi," Rebecca said to the card.

She sleepwalked through the afternoon, working purely on instinct, but tossed and turned all that night. She'd always thought Michael, with his bravura haircut and casual clothes, looked closer to twenty than thirty, but by Wednesday morning he looked forty, his face pleated with pain and uncertainty. She saw with a horrified glance in the mirror that she looked like her own grandmother.

Laurence brought the tea for elevenses, Mackenzie at his heels, and announced that the lock to the attic had been changed, and Mackenzie had the only key. The Chief Inspector looked narrowly at them all, firing shots across their bows. Everyone quailed, looking up, down, into the distance, anywhere but at Mackenzie. There would henceforth be a guard assigned to the hotel lobby as well as the street outside, Laurence continued. Still no one shouted, "Curses, foiled again." The news that Devlin and Mackenzie themselves were moving into the hotel was anti-climactic.

Laurence went to contend with the three tour buses expected for lunch. Tony muttered something about room service. Jerry rubbed his hands together in anticipation of such a big audience, only to have his footlights extinguished by a severe look from Mackenzie.

Judging by the door-to-door progress of the police, they were once again interrogating everyone within a mile of Rudesburn. Mackenzie himself, Devlin in tow, spent the afternoon clambering over Battle Law; Tony photographed their stockbroker suits in altercation with the odd gorse branch. Jerry and Elaine skirmished like border clans. Hilary and Adele squabbled over a plastered wall—it had arcane symbols on it, said Adele, and Hilary insisted they were leaf and bird designs. Rebecca made peace and took a hike toward the church before she gave in to the urge to spank them both.

She found that Jerry had had no choice but to assign Michael computer duty, although he made it clear that Michael had deliberately gotten himself stabbed just to slow down the pace of work. They were making headway, though; almost six feet of the cut blocks of the crypt stairwell were visible.

"How's it—" Rebecca began cheerily. Dennis dropped one of the two-by-fours they were using to shore up the ceiling, parting Jerry's moustache.

Mark arbitrated the ensuing accusations and counter-accusations, finally sending Dennis up the tower to clear away weeds. Not the ideal solution, Rebecca thought. Dennis had to squeeze up the narrow passageway, a round peg in a square hole if there ever was one. But if Mark's scowl was any indication, another snide remark and he would have used his two-by-four for attitude adjustment.

Michael was holding his injured arm tensely, bunched at his side. "Put on your sling," Rebecca directed him.

"I need both hands to type." He didn't even glance up from the screen.

"You're straining the stitches like that."

"We're behind on the data."

"Then let me bring you another painkiller."

"I'm all right," Michael said so loudly that Mark looked warily around.

"Have it your way!" *Men!* Rebecca added to herself as she stamped away. Her shoulder throbbed as she eased her way down into the infirmary trench. She gripped her left arm with her right hand, picked up her spoon left-handed, and went on scraping at a deposit of glass shards.

That night she tried a glass of warm milk and a droning BBC documentary, and actually managed a bit of sleep. Michael, too, sat up in his bed Thursday morning looking somewhat less worn. "Good mornin' to you, hen."

"Good morning to you, rooster. Sleep well?"

"I dreamed I was playin' Macbeth—'is that a dagger I see before me?' "

" 'Tomorrow and tomorrow and tomorrow,' " quoted Rebecca, " 'creeps yet in this petty pace from day to day . . .' "

" 'To the last syllable of recorded time,' " Michael finished. "I wish Mackenzie'd bring oot the thumbscrews and get it over wi'."

"We do need something to force the issue."

"Like the end of the dig? The killer's waited around this long hopin' we'll turn up the treasure. If he—she—is half as frustrated as the rest of us, we're in for a good go."

"Thanks for the encouraging prediction, Nostradamus."

"You're welcome." Michael disappeared toward the bathroom.

Rebecca sat down at the dressing table. There was her next packet of pills. She'd have to check the calendar to see when she stopped the last one. At least she now knew they didn't have pregnancy to contend with. She glanced around at Michael's crumpled bed. Frustration was an understatement.

At the breakfast table Dennis put an extra teaspoon of sugar in his coffee. "Did you hear the singing from the priory last night?"

"There's usually singing from the priory," said Hilary.

Adele folded her hands over her omelette. "Anne is getting restless. She wants something of us. What can we do?"

Mark looked as if he had a suggestion or two, but he managed to stifle them in his toast.

Through her long acquaintance with Murphy's Law, Rebecca

knew losing a contact lens was next on the agenda. New glasses were an expense she hadn't budgeted, but she might soon be cutting down on birth-control pills. Harry Devlin drove her to a one-hour optician in Edinburgh. He had no qualms about discussing the case; they reviewed the suspects, agreed there were only four viable ones remaining, commiserated over not catching one of them in the attic, and concluded that it was all a proper cock-up, and no mistake.

By the time they returned to Rudesburn, the rainy morning had been transformed into a cool, clear afternoon. Men with lawnmowers and hedge clippers were manicuring the priory grounds, various police people dancing attendance. The pearly half-circle of the moon rose in the east.

Rebecca skirted a police car just pulling up at the curb and hurried into the cottage to change. By the time she'd put out scraps for the mendicant cats and arrived at the dig, she found Michael and Jerry in the crypt door in close consultation, Tony stalking them with a camera aimed. ". . . a circle wi' side chambers, just like Kerr's map," Michael was saying.

"Are you through the collapse?" Rebecca asked.

"We certainly are," said Mark. He hammered another two-by-four into the opening and stepped back. "Most of the crypt's untouched by the collapse. Laurence has an electrician on the way to string up lights."

Dennis was sitting on the bottom step of the tower. "Michael went in with a flashlight a little while ago."

"Dust and bones," intoned Michael. "All we need is Vincent Price."

"There's one wall made of brick," Jerry went on, "not stone, that'll need to be repaired. Probably some nabob's tomb."

"Then we should open it up." Rebecca waved her trowel, ready to go.

"Let's get the lights in there first. What you need to be worrying about now is what the girls are doing at the infirmary."

Suppressing her impulse to say, "Yes, master," Rebecca walked out to the new trench. Hilary was drawing, Adele was putting bits of glass in a box, and Elaine, of all people, was on her hands and knees scraping at a tile surface. "Thank you for filling in for me," Rebecca told her.

Elaine sat back and wiped at her face, leaving a smudge of dirt on her cheek. Without her red lipstick she looked younger, almost innocent. "No problem," she said.

Rebecca stepped down to inspect the tiles. Oh, nice; their yellow and green glaze was fairly well preserved. And since such decorated floor tiles were usually confined to lowland England, here was more evidence that Rudesburn had indeed been wealthy and on the pilgrim's route.

Shadows moved across the surface. Rebecca glanced up. *Uh-oh.*

Mackenzie looked like Death with a hangover. Behind him stood Devlin, wielding his notebook, his mouth half-smirking, half-frowning. They were backed up by several stone-faced constables. Five masculine figures, a cigar and a camera at point, looked around the corner of the chapter house. "Miss Vavra," said Mackenzie.

Elaine squeaked and stepped back, bumping into Adele.

"A man from Jedburgh drove to Melrose on the night of the murder. On his way back home, about eight-thirty, he saw a silver Jaguar parked outside the priory wall. He identified you as the driver from your photograph."

8:30? Rebecca thought. Well, could be . . .

Elaine's olive complexion turned an ugly mottled green. "I was sitting and thinking, all right? Where's the 'arm in that?" A policewoman stepped forward, extending her hand. Elaine ignored her and leaped out of the trench as though she were jet-propelled. "I didn't kill the bitch!"

Mackenzie held his ground. "Scotland Yard found notes for a story in Miss Fitzgerald's London flat. About how some nightclubs are fronts for prostitution rings. There's a photo of you doing some dance with feathers." He didn't need to put neon lights around the inference.

Hilary clapped her hand to her mouth as if suddenly overcome with nausea. All color drained from Elaine's face. She swayed and would have buckled if the female constable and one of her heavier colleagues hadn't grabbed her arms and frog-marched her away. As they rounded the end of the cloister, she shrilled, "What do I 'ave to do to get some respect?"

"Act respectful," returned Adele, and went back to her glass.

"That's a bit flip," Rebecca said. "There's more to it than that."

Adele didn't reply. Hilary lowered her hand and stared unseeing at her drawing board. The male audience beside the chapter house shifted; Tony seemed exasperated and amused both, but Jerry had the gall to laugh.

Rebecca's head buzzed—that could be it, the supplemental motive—Elaine was trying to improve her lot in life. And not only monetarily—how inconvenient for Sheila to remind her of her dirty linen.

She visualized Elaine trying to kill Guinevere. Trying to kill Michael, for that matter. But Tony had been with her that night. Although, typical man, he could have been easily induced into a sound sleep. Wearily she rubbed her shoulder. Unless Elaine confessed, she would be back. Mackenzie wouldn't prosecute until he could get a conviction, and a photograph in Sheila's apartment wasn't proof of anything.

Mark and Michael came strolling toward the infirmary. "Well," said Mark, "I got off. The same guy who saw Elaine sitting in the car on his way home saw me on his way to Melrose a little before eight. He remembered the duck T-shirt."

"A vote of thanks to the T-shirt," murmured Hilary.

Michael climbed down into the trench. "Oh, tiles. Aye, you see them all over. Sgraffiato, they're called."

"Michael," Rebecca said with a short laugh, "you're losing it. They're not sgraffiato—those are incised and are really rare. Even these are unusual this far north. Why don't you stick to rondels?"

His face jerked around. He eyed her like a police surgeon considering a bullet wound. "You dinna have to patronize me, either, Dr. Reid."

"For God's sake, Michael, I was only joking . . ."

He turned and stamped away before the words were out of her mouth. The snap of her teeth sent a shock wave through her skull. Damn that tartan chip on his shoulder.

Mark sidled quickly back to the church. Hilary bent over her drawing board, engrossed in her sketch. Adele closed the box of glass shards and set it gently on the side of the trench. Michael kicked the wall, winced and clutched his arm, and disappeared into the cloister.

Profanity was inadequate. Rebecca sat down on the ground, hard, and picked up Elaine's spoon. She was shaking. No, that had been a tiny tremor in the earth. A rumbling crash echoed from the church, followed by cries of alarm. Now what? All three women leaped to their feet and ran.

Dust eddied from the transept door. Tony stood peering dubiously inside, protecting his video camera beneath his jacket. "What is it?" Rebecca demanded, shoving him aside.

"Wall's come down, I think."

Rebecca squinted through the haze. There were Michael and Mark, standing just inside the door, hands raised defensively. Jerry's strangled voice emanated from the depths, shouting something that evolved from incoherent into, ". . . blasted idiot! You don't lean on brick walls with decayed mortar!"

"You pushed me!" returned Dennis, and broke off coughing.

The dust was settling. Grant raced down the nave demanding explanations. "Give me your flashlight," Rebecca said to the bobby.

It was Michael's hand that took the flashlight from Grant's. He and Rebecca ducked through the crypt door. The beam of light illuminated curtains of swirling dust, clogging her throat with dirt and decay. Someone bumped into her, and she turned to see Mark, his eyes shining in the backspatter of light. "Can I come, too?"

They followed Michael down the steps, hollowed treads slippery with grit—right, left. . . . All Rebecca could see was a few feet of narrow passage. She didn't want to know what was crunching beneath her feet. An aperture opened into shadow. A niche held a long, dim shape surrounded by debris—a lead coffin, its wooden sheathing rotted away.

A large gray figure lunged toward them. As one they jumped. But that rotund form had to be Dennis. The whites of his eyes glinted. "Michael?" he croaked. "You and Mark went outside, Tony followed Elaine and the police, and Jerry came in here all by himself. I figured he was plotting something, so I followed him. And he deliberately pushed me against that wall."

"To break it down?" asked Rebecca.

"He could've destroyed everything behind it," Mark protested. "An archeologist wouldn't do that!"

"We're talkin' aboot Jerry," Michael said.

Like an evil genie out of a bottle, Jerry plunged from the murk. Dennis yelped and ran. "Stupid geek jumped out at me," shouted Jerry. "Ran smack into that brick wall. Down it came—broke my flashlight." He pulled off his glasses, blinked at the faces confronting him, apparently decided the view was no better without them and put them back on. Another flashlight beam wavered in the thick air, Laurence's voice calling, "Is everyone all right in there?" Still muttering, Jerry, too, shoved past.

Rebecca figured Laurence could protect Dennis and glanced

at the garishly shadowed faces beside her. "Okay. Who wants
to go see what was behind that wall?"

No one needed to answer. Michael aimed the flashlight and
pushed on ahead. One pace, two, their footsteps thudding in the
quiet. A bend in the corridor. He stumbled over a brick, and
Mark seized his arm. The injured arm. Michael gasped.
"Sorry," said Mark.

Gingerly they stepped through the still-settling pile of bricks
and found themselves facing a black void. The slow sweep of
the light revealed a room about the size of a closet. The walls
were smudged with damp, tracked with the angular marks of
writing and with sketched emblems. One was repeated over and
over—the crowned heart of the Douglases.

The floor was lumpy. . . . An electric shock quivered through
Rebecca's limbs. A skeleton lay on the flagstones, the brown
threads of a nun's habit strung like cobwebs over it. A fallen
brick crushed the right femur, but the rest was chillingly intact.

Her hand was outstretched, fingers splayed, toward the door;
her face peered upward, mouth open, empty eye sockets focused
as if in one last despairing look toward the invisible heavens.
Between the upthrust pelvic bones, swaddled in dust, lay a perfect miniature. A baby, still curled inside the body that had finally, dreadfully, failed to sustain it.

The light in Michael's hand swooped and swayed, glancing
from the bones to the arched ceiling and back. "Anne Douglas,
I presume," he whispered. Even a whisper reverberated harshly
in the terrible silence of the tomb.

But not as harshly as an agonized inhalation just behind Rebecca's shoulder. She spun around. In the dim light, Mark's face
was ashen, contorted with pain, as though a dagger had just
struck deep between his ribs. He spun, stumbling over the rubble, his body only a blotch in the gleam of the approaching light.
Voices queried, then protested as he pushed by.

"What the hell?" Michael asked.

"I'm not sure I want to know," said Rebecca.

The bones lay silently, as they had lain for over four hundred
years. Rebecca couldn't tell whether she heard in her mind or in
some subtlety of light and air the distant voices singing of a
tomb opened. Adele was right. Anne had wanted something of
them.

Chapter Twenty-Four

REBECCA FOUND MICHAEL standing in the far corner of the cloister, one foot propped on a rock, his face turned toward the distant hills as though fantasizing escape. His sharp profile looked somewhat less yielding than the—what had Colin called it, the whinstone—of the Law.

She folded her hands over her notebook like a child called upon to recite. "I'm sorry I patronized you yesterday. I picked a bad time to joke."

The blue eyes he turned on her were as bright and brittle as the warning lights of a police car. "I dinna have much of a sense of humor these days. I'm sorry, too, lass. But . . . ."

The caveat hummed in the air like an electric field. "Hey, Rebecca!" shouted Jerry from the door. "Lights, camera, action! You're on!"

So much for the only two minutes they'd had alone since the discovery of Anne's body yesterday afternoon. Once Jerry had cleaned off a layer or two of dust, he'd made a beeline for the pub and Bob Jenkins, leaving Michael and Rebecca to fend with academic necessities and media impertinences far into the night. They'd gotten to bed so late that even a polite kiss had been an effort, let alone remembering to set the alarm clock. Hilary's discreet knock had woken them up barely in time for breakfast and Adele's solemn dissertation on Anne's life, death, and supernatural proclivities.

At least they'd had no time for a pitched battle like the one they'd fought the day Sheila died. Maybe neither of them had that kind of fight left in them. "Duty calls," Rebecca said, faking a smile.

Michael's smile was no less stiff. "Right."

In the church Laurence and Bridget were making sure the electric cables were either tucked next to walls or covered with boards. "It was time to put the floodlights up for the Festival anyway," Laurence said. "We'll arrange some permanent fixtures in due course." He ran his hand across his scalp and inspected his palm as if to gauge how much hair the Rudesburn follies had cost him so far today. "I own finding the body is important enough for a news conference. But even so . . ."

That "but" Rebecca could complete. "You were picturing Rudesburn as an attraction for scholars and schoolchildren, not sensation seekers."

"Nora's already had calls this morning from two priests offering to exorcise Anne's ghost, and a parapsychologist who wants to set up cameras, tape recorders, trip wires, the lot. Sure is a good thing Mackenzie and Devlin already booked a room—I've had calls from all over the country."

"Hilary snagged her mohair sweater," Bridget said, "climbin' ower the fence to avoid Jenkins and his pals. I told her I'd set it to rights."

"Rebecca!" shouted Jerry. Nodding cautiously to the others, she and Michael headed for the crypt.

The place was, if possible, even more claustrophobic with light bulbs strung along the ceiling; the harsh light emphasized its desolation, a desert a million miles from the lush trees and flowers of Rudesburn. Tony was perched precariously on the pile of rubble taking both still and video photos of the corpse. Both corpses, to be accurate. The repeated camera flashes bleached the bones of humanity and made them sterile artifacts.

Jerry stood by the doorway; he'd be in half of Tony's photos. With nervous glances shared equally between Jerry and the skeleton, Dennis piled bricks into a wheelbarrow. Adele swept up dust, her luminous mask firmly in place. Mark held a meter stick and Jerry's trowels, his expression of calm industriousness virtually remote-controlled. He'd spent last evening alone in the attic, avoiding even Hilary; now she sent him a quick, curious look which ricocheted without effect.

"Here's your ID," said Jerry. "It must've been wedged between a couple of the bricks." Nestled in a piece of cheesecloth was a long, thin strip of lead inscribed with the angular letters of the sixteenth century. "Anne Douglas, *mater prioresse*, rest in pace."

Walled up alive, Rebecca thought. So that was the verdict. Maybe the soldiers had waited outside, at first joking and cat-calling and then in dreadful silence, waited for her to relent and tell them what they wanted to know. But she hadn't told them. Her child wasn't all that she'd taken with her to the grave.

It might have been years before one of the former nuns, after suffering heaven only knew what privation, crept back to the ruined priory and into the darkness of the crypt to leave the only epitaph Anne would ever have. Until now. Jerry folded the cheesecloth around the lead and put it in a box.

Hilary stood with her arms laced over her blouse. "I didn't think it would be so cold in here," she whispered.

"I'd have expected the lights to take some of the chill off. . . ." Rebecca's voice was swallowed by a flat, empty silence that muffled even the repeated whirr-click of Tony's cameras. She peeled off her jacket and her sweater-vest. "Wear this. I can't have my assistant catching a cold."

"But Michael gave you that."

"My mum would be pleased," said Michael, gracious if distant.

"Thanks. I'll get my jacket at noon." Hilary slipped on the vest.

"That'll do for now," said Tony, his voice, like his features, obscured by the camera.

"All right," Jerry said. "Dr. Campbell, if you please."

Michael stepped into the tomb. He affixed one more light bulb to the ceiling and pegged its cord into a crevice between stones. "They had to have left her a lamp," he said, half to himself, "or she'd have no written . . . There." He pointed to a saucer-shaped bit of pottery. "A wee bit of oil, a wick—she might've had several hours of light."

Adele started humming something under her breath, half smiling. Jerry said loudly, "Okay, there's a limit to how many people can get in there without stepping on something. A shame that brick broke her femur."

"You pushed me into the wall," muttered Dennis.

Jerry's moustache quivered like a mongoose spotting a snake. "You scared the hell out of me, jumping out of the dark like that. What did you expect me to do—say hi, come on in, have a cuppa?"

Dennis subsided. Rebecca didn't doubt Jerry had indeed taken advantage of Elaine's arrest to check the place out for himself. But surely not even Jerry would deliberately break down a wall.

Elaine. Non-essential personnel. Perfect timing on Mackenzie's part, to take her instead of . . . Well, assuming Hilary and Rebecca herself were exempt, the Chief Inspector was going to either have to take Adele next, start over again on the men, or expand his cast of characters.

Jerry bowed Rebecca and Hilary into the room. Michael extended his good hand to help them over the rubble. Tony took more pictures.

Claustrophobia wasn't the word for what Rebecca felt as she crouched in the dust, making herself as small as possible, not only not to disturb the skeleton, but also to keep the walls from closing in. She wrote methodically in her notebook, trying not to hurry. Hilary used onionskin paper to trace the more complex designs. More than once Rebecca called Tony and his cameras to zero in on a particular drawing or inscription. The crowned and winged heart of the Douglases. The diagonal bar of the Elliots. A rampant lion, the arms of Scotland—a reference to Robert the Bruce? Henry the VIII's greyhound.

"What did she write all this with?" asked Hilary. She pulled the sweater tighter around her.

"A piece of charcoal, I'd say. Grabbed out of a fireplace as they marched her away, possibly, so she could leave a testament?"

"An English soldier gave Joan of Arc a cross made out of twigs. In Shaw's play, he gets out of hell one day every year for that good deed."

"I don't think anyone did Anne any good deeds."

The smudged letters were blotches of shadow crawling across the wall, a mingling of Scots, English, French, German, Latin. "Many religious women were the intellectuals of their day," said Adele admiringly.

Some words were dark and firm, some faint, mere scratches on the wall. The drawings were clumsy but urgent. More than once Rebecca had to close her eyes, soothing the squirm of her shoulder blades and a creeping light-headedness. She kept wanting to look around at the empty eyes of the skull. The air wasn't good in here. If any place in the priory was haunted, this was it. . . .

Odd, how Anne's ghost had always been reputed to be a vengeful one, cursing lovers. And yet here, in Anne's very presence, Rebecca felt only sorrow. Not helplessness, not hopelessness, but sorrow mitigated by faith.

She copied a crucifix. Beside it were four representations of a wheel-cross and several lines from the ancient and semi-pagan poem "The Dream of the Rood." Between each two crosses was a similar pattern of straight and wavy lines, not unlike the pattern in Michael's and her own sweaters. She checked Hilary's notebook. Yes, a perfect copy. She murmured a compliment.

Rebecca's pencil was smearing as badly as the charcoal. "Mark, may I borrow your knife, please?" Silently he handed it over. She sharpened her pencil, tidied away the shavings, folded the knife and dropped it in her pocket.

The chamber was bone-chillingly cold. Each one of the press of bodies seemed to be hoarding its warmth. Everyone's voices, even Jerry's bellow, grew softer until they were all whispering. The noises of brick against brick, and the steady sweep of a broom, came from farther and farther away. At some point the flashbulbs stopped making little novas in the corners of Rebecca's eyes, but the charcoal letters still wriggled. "*Dieu et mon droit.* Henry's the Eighth's motto—'God and my right,' " she read aloud.

"In other words," Jerry said with a trace of envy, "I can do anything I want because God is on my side."

"Touchin' humility," said Michael. He started tenderly spooning dust away from Anne's feet.

"*Fortite et recte,*" Rebecca went on. "The motto of the Elliots."

"Thomas may have come to a bad end in London," said Hilary, "but he sure had something to do with Anne here."

"Just friends," Mark said with forced levity.

There was a long passage. Rebecca considered it. Enlightenment dawned—of course, the King James Bible came after Anne's time. This was in the earlier dialect. But it was the same verse from Matthew Rebecca herself had thought of the day she arrived in Scotland. "Take therefore no thought for the morrow," she said softly, "for the morrow shall take thought for the things of itself. Sufficient unto the day is the evil thereof."

"What is she trying to tell us?" asked Adele.

"She was just keeping herself busy," Jerry answered. "No ghostly memoranda. Sorry."

Rebecca scooted closer to Hilary. "I wouldn't be so sure of that. I think she knew someone would eventually find her. A resurrection of sorts—we've all heard the voices singing that Easter verse. All this might be to justify herself. Or she could be trying to leave a message."

"Thank you," said Adele, so fervently everyone looked around.

Mark told her, "It's just that we don't want to believe all of that supernatural stuff, you know, not that it's not true."

Jerry glared indignantly at them both. Tony, reloading his video camera in a dark corner, smiled with a flash of white teeth. Michael went on spooning dust, concealing an amused expression.

"Well!" said Hilary, eyeing yet another inscription. "My German is of the 'may I have mustard on that' variety, but does this say what I think it does?"

Rebecca dredged her linguistic gray matter. Again she recognized the passage. "My body is in torment. My soul in delight. As he draws her to himself, she gives herself to him. She cannot hold back."

"Wow," said Jerry. "Old Anne was hot to trot."

"God, Jerry!" Rebecca protested.

"Get oot of it," Michael told him. "That was written by a Bavarian nun aboot 'a greeting the body may not know.' The union of the soul with God, either in religious ecstasy or after death, I suppose."

"She didn't get that baby from religious ecstasy," retorted Jerry.

"Look at this." Rebecca's pencil drew yet another crowned heart. Below it were the words, "Alexander, I confess that I have failit, quhilk God have forgeuin. God have mercy on our childe. . . ."

The silence was absolute. Somewhere a brick or a stone shifted with a tiny creak. Something rustled in the darkness beyond the lights. Hilary's whisper, "Is it lunch time yet?" sounded like a shout.

"Yeah," said Jerry. "Let's get out of here."

In one multi-legged knot they trudged down the passageway and up the stairs and broke free into the clear, clean Scottish air. After the colorless crypt, the blues and greens of Rudesburn were so brilliant they burned the retina. Rebecca couldn't recall a time when she'd been so grateful to see and feel sunshine. She inhaled deeply, trying to chase away the grains of dust and decay still lingering in her lungs. But not even sunshine and air could clear the images of those charcoaled letters.

Tony and Jerry walked off, trading barbed remarks about Anne, Elaine, and women in general, the quest for publicity making strange bedfellows. Adele, deep in thought, wafted toward the cottage. Dennis followed, shaking his head. Hilary disappeared into the cloister; after a moment's hesitation, Mark followed.

"So it was Alexander and Anne, not Thomas," said Michael.

"Did Thomas kill Alexander?" Rebecca returned, rotating her injured shoulder. "It must've been right at the time of the trial—Alexander's name is on the warrant. Half-heartedly, I'll admit."

"Neither bloke testified against her?"

"I don't think so. I need to get back to the records." Rebecca snorted. "What I need is a thirty-hour day."

Grant looked into the west door. "Michael? Rebecca? Chief Inspector Mackenzie wants you in the pub."

"No," Michael said with a sigh. "Thirty hours is no enough."

After the silence of the crypt, the voices in the pub were like a barrage of artillery fire. Devlin and Mackenzie were ensconced at the table by the fireplace. Every other table was filled, and reporters were ranged elbow-to-elbow along the bar. Jerry held court in their midst, dropping hints about startling revelations at the press conference this evening. The cats ambled among the tables, scouting for dropped tidbits of food.

No sooner had Michael and Rebecca ordered ale and ploughman's lunches from a harried Bridget than Tony and Elaine slipped into the last empty booth. Elaine was so pale her red petulant lips made her look like a vampire who had just fed. Tony leaned his elbows on the table and jerked his head toward the four people sitting beside the fireplace. Elaine refused to look. Bridget took their order and headed into the kitchen.

"No luck, I take it?" Michael asked Devlin.

Today Devlin looked less like a leprechaun than a gargoyle. He deferred to Mackenzie. If Mackenzie was perturbed by having proved nothing against Elaine, he didn't betray it. His beaked face was that of an eagle perched on a high branch, watching for the subtle movement in the grass that would betray a mouse. "Yes," he said coolly, "Miss Vavra had been afraid Miss Fitzgerald would find out about her past. But Miss Fitzgerald never mentioned it."

"I don't suppose the photographer who took that picture of her was Tony?" Rebecca asked.

"No, it wasn't, more's the pity."

From somewhere in the melee a cat squawked and hissed, and bodies eddied. Michael, facing toward the disturbance, muttered something about people with big feet. The animals made their escape into the kitchen when Bridget emerged with four plates of cheese, bread, and salad. Rebecca asked herself what she was doing as a delicately frothing glass of ale appeared before her. She never drank at lunch. She swallowed the hearty liquid and was grateful to be alive.

"So you found the prioress," said Mackenzie, carefully dissecting his pickled onion.

"Jerry wants to hold a press conference," Devlin added.

Michael downed half his ale. He took off his sling to free both hands to manipulate knife and fork. "It'll make waves from Land's End to John O'Groats," he said in a wicked imitation of Jerry's American accent. "It'll be in the papers back home. Old Harry murdering a pregnant nun. Book deals, movie rights—we've got it made."

Devlin laughed. "Surely you're embroiderin' just a bit."

"Just a bit," Michael conceded. "But when I rang Graham last night, he said to script Jerry's announcement and make sure he stayed wi' it."

"And make sure he stays with archeology, not true crime fantasies." Mackenzie leaned forward. "Dr. Campbell, Dr. Reid, did King Henry really murder a pregnant nun?"

"Judicial murder," said Michael.

"The physical evidence supports the documents," Rebecca said, showing the detectives her notebook. "And so much evidence, too—Jerry's not exaggerating when he says this is a remarkable site. Anne was indubitably pregnant, by Alexander Douglas, her cousin. Why and how, I don't know."

Michael's eyes glinted over the rim of his glass. "Well, you see, lass, there're birds and there're bees . . ."

"Michael!"

Devlin blandly scooped salad onto his fork. Mackenzie said, "Go on, Dr. Reid."

"The English threw every charge they could think of against her, apparently to try and get her to give up the plate and the relics. Her being pregnant just added fuel to the fire. Or bricks to the wall. The morals charges would lend weight to those of witchcraft—she wasn't being a good little nun." Rebecca drank again. Her stomach felt like a trash compactor, squeezing her lunch into a tighter and tighter ball. "According to the superstition of the time, pregnancy resulted only if both parties—er—reached climax. So a woman couldn't claim rape if a pregnancy resulted."

"You think Anne was raped?" asked Devlin.

"All I know is that she says she forgives Alexander. Maybe it was more of a masculine power play. Coercion rather than brute force. The results are the same. The man gets his jollies, the woman pays for it."

"Alexander died for something," Michael murmured.

"Politics," said Rebecca.

Mackenzie said, "Dr. Reid, you must meet my wife. You have a great deal in common."

"I'd no be so sure that's a compliment," added Michael dryly.

Devlin, who presumably knew Amanda Fraser, choked into his glass. Rebecca shot an appraising glance at Michael, but his face was expressionless.

Mackenzie built himself a miniature sandwich of bread slice, cheese slice, and onion ring. Jerry made the expansive gestures of an orchestra conductor, all the listening faces nodding on cue. Tony walked by on his way to get refills of beer. Elaine plastered her fork with mounds of shepherd's pie. The Galashiels jail, it appeared, had yet to hire a cordon bleu chef.

"Or it could really have been a love match," Rebecca continued, deciding not to give Michael a behave-yourself pinch beneath the table. "Anne forgave Alexander for sinning against the church rather than her personally."

"She didna ask forgiveness for herself," Michael said. "No *mea culpa*."

Bridget asked if they wanted anything else. Rebecca ordered a cup of tea to try and counteract the ale. The objects on the mantelpiece blurred before her heavy-lidded eyes—the model trolly pulling up before the ceramic fisherman's cottage, the horn snuff box whispering from the side of its lid to Paddington Bear, salmon rising through the iridescent depths of the glass paperweights so that the fishing lures leaned forward in expectation.

"So," said Michael, inserting his arm back into the sling, "are you thinkin' the whereabouts of the treasure is concealed in the documentation?"

"Very clever, Dr. Campbell." Mackenzie drained his glass and looked at the foam still lacing its rim like a gypsy would consider a smear of tea leaves. "But it's not so much a matter of whether I believe it, but that the killer does. He or she is no fool—if he scarpered now, we'd be after him. And he wouldn't have the treasure."

Rebecca visualized a faceless form prowling around her bedroom the night she'd first gotten the trial records. She remem-

bered the lights in the hotel attic, and the knife striking Michael.
She poured milk into her cup. The rim of the pitcher chattered
against the china, and she stiffened her wrist. "Why can't Americans make good hot tea?" she asked parenthetically.

"You're fixated on puttin' ice in it," Michael replied, and
went on, his words clipped, "My friend Colin thought we probably knew something we didn't know we knew. Our historical
knowledge must be it. I take it we're no longer under suspicion,
that you're askin' for our help?"

"You may take that," answered Mackenzie, without so much
as a blink. "The more certain I am that the historical mystery is
tied in with the real one, the more certain I am I need your
expertise."

Rats, Rebecca thought. When she tried to get Mackenzie to
admit he needed their help, he wouldn't. Had he gotten that
much more worried? She didn't chide him for calling the historical mystery unreal.

"Time's running out on the dig and on the treasure hunt as
well," the Chief Inspector went on. "I'm bringing in more constables. Some of the groundskeepers will be my lads. Also some
of the tourists."

"Mind you have a care," added Devlin. "You have what the
killer wants—the location of the treasure. He'll be after you."

With that, the two detectives rose and threaded their way out
of the bar. "But we don't know where it is," Rebecca protested
to their backs.

Michael groaned. "How do we get oursel's into these things,
lass?"

"Providence? Astrology? Karma?"

They huddled with Laurence and Nora in the hall and explained the situation. The Bairds exchanged a worried look.
"You should leave," Laurence said. "We'll stop the dig and
send everyone home."

"Too late for that," said Michael.

Rebecca held her notebook like a shield, and considered the
concept of home. "Running away won't solve anything, won't
finish anything, and won't decide anything."

"The trial records are still in the safe," Nora said. "You'd
best put your book in there, too."

"Hilary and I will have to work on the inscriptions sometime.
Don't worry, we won't do it in any dark alleys."

Tony and Elaine appeared in the hallway. Nora jerked, startled, and backed into one of the sporting prints on the wall. Laurence grabbed it before it fell. "Do you need me in the crypt?" Elaine asked grudgingly. "You're paying me to work, and Mackenzie says I can't give in my notice."

"If you'd like to continue with the computer records," Laurence told her, "it shouldn't be necessary for you to go into the crypt."

"Right." Elaine walked on down the hall, Tony, his hands in his pockets, his shoulders slouched, just behind.

"Tony says he never saw the trial records when Sheila had them," Nora stage-whispered. "Does he want them back, now you have further evidence?"

"Elaine did try to leave last week," said Laurence.

"Equal opportunity suspects," Rebecca said with a sickly grin.

The telephone rang in the office, a tourist family appeared at reception, and Michael and Rebecca headed back to the church. *Don't think about knives in the dark*, she kept telling herself, attempting auto-hypnosis. *Don't think about it.* Judging by Michael's glum expression, he wasn't succeeding in not thinking any better than she was.

The crypt was mustier and stuffier than ever, and still as cold. Bridget wouldn't be fixing Hilary's sweater any time soon, not with the mobs of people descending on Rudesburn. Rebecca decided she'd wash her Missouri sweatshirt instead of burning it and let Hilary continue to wear the sweater. She felt vaguely hypocritical, after all, wearing the sweater Caroline had made for that mythological creature, her son's fiancée.

They copied and photographed every inch of the wall of the tomb. Quitting time didn't come a moment too soon. Rebecca emerged into the opulent afternoon light deciding that history was becoming altogether too intimate. Poor Anne, reducing her loyalties to the lowest common denominator. Her country couldn't help her, her church wouldn't, and the men in her life— Thomas and Alexander—were either unable or unwilling to testify for her. As soon as the English appeared on the Gowan Water, her fate was sealed. Giving up the relics and the plate might have saved her, but that was a compromise she wouldn't make. Compromising, she would have nothing left.

But then, Rebecca thought, putting both her and Hilary's notebooks beneath the mattress of her bed, compromising with Michael was hardly the same thing as selling out a sacred trust. With him, the vows had yet to be made.

Something knocked against her side as she stood. She still had Mark's Swiss Army knife in her pocket. Surely he wouldn't mind her keeping it for a while; not only was it handy as a pencil sharpener, but also its tiny scissors trimmed Hilary's onionskin.

Before dinner she sat down at the dining room table with Michael and Mark and outlined a script for Jerry's press conference, giving the information as straightforwardly as possible, anticipating what questions would be asked, toning down the sensation.

"What?" Jerry yelped when confronted with the script after dinner. He was already posing for photographs on the porch of the church, glad-handing the male reporters, leaning cozily on the female, reeking of sincerity and booze.

"As official representative of the Rudesburn Development Group," began Laurence, and Michael chimed in, "As official representative of the Historic Buildings and Monuments Commission . . ."

With bad grace, Jerry gave in. But even with Laurence and Grant standing as admonitory bookends on either side, Jerry wrung every bit of drama he could out of the situation. He even bore in mind that two-thirds of the reporters were themselves English, and avoided expressing opinions on the ancestry and sexual orientations of Henry's soldiery. To all the questions about Sheila's murder, he smiled knowingly and said, "No comment."

Tony stood at the periphery of the group, deep in negotiation with Jenkins. "Well," Rebecca heard Laurence comment to Grant, "I don't see any harm in him selling some of his photos."

"Just make sure the RDG gets their cut," returned the bobby.

Like the Ancient Mariner, Adele expounded to anyone who would listen—and a few who wouldn't—about the supernatural aspects of the find. Devlin and Mackenzie sauntered along the perimeter wall as though they were simply out for an evening stroll. Michael and Dennis, Mark and Hilary, stood beside the wheel-cross, expressions from scowls to jaundiced smiles moving from face to face at Jerry's pronouncements. Rebecca hovered on the footbridge with Bridget and Nora, watching the cottage, but no one beside the cats made any move toward the notebooks. And Lancelot and Guinevere and their twitching tails seemed much more interested in the human congregation across the stream.

After the tours were conducted and the statements read, Michael and Mark took a thick wooden door from a closet in the hotel, affixed new hinges to the wall, and barred the stairway into the crypt. They made sure to present the key to Laurence, to keep in the safe, in front of as many people as possible.

It was almost midnight before the students, Michael, and Rebecca returned to the cottage. They sorted themselves in and out of the bathrooms with remarkable efficiency, and by the time Rebecca checked on the notebooks and sat down at her dressing table to take out her contacts, a resonant silence had fallen over Rudesburn, as though the village itself were gently snoring. Here, with Michael, she felt safe.

At the bottom of her jewelry case was the metal ring from the cap of a wine bottle that had once been her engagement ring. She covered it with a strand of beads and looked around at Michael. He'd dozed off with Colin's notepad open on his chest.

It had been two weeks since they'd made love; Rebecca didn't count that awkward early morning scramble as lovemaking. In a way she was glad Michael wasn't breathing suggestively down her neck. In another way she wondered if he wanted her anymore.

No doubt he didn't want to risk a rebuff. And now, with his arm injured, it would be a little difficult. Although if he was really in the mood, she thought with a wry smile, he wouldn't be intimidated by a full body cast.

She took the new packet of pills, punched out the first one, and swallowed it. Another month wouldn't hurt. It was best to be prepared.

How about that? She'd actually made a decision, however small. Shaking her head, Rebecca turned out the lights, stowed the notepad in the drawer, and pulled the covers over Michael's supine body.

"Thank you, love," he muttered, and turned onto his side. He hit his arm and grimaced in his sleep.

"I do care for you," she whispered. "In spite of it all, I do care."

He couldn't hear her. From the dark silence outside came the ethereal sound of women's voices: *"Pater noster qui es in caelis . . ."*

"Hallowed by thy name," Rebecca concluded, and went to bed.

Chapter Twenty-Five

REBECCA'S BACK WAS against the sun-warmed stone of the church wall, and the cloister garth lay innocently in front of her Unless the malefactor swooped down from the tower in a hang glider, she was safe.

The trial records were no longer as disturbing; like an old wa wound, their pain was blunted by familiarity. She transcribed and translated the sixteenth-century officialese, feeling com mendably efficient and just as glad the crowded conditions in the crypt let her work out here.

A milkweed fluff of a cloud blocked the sun, casting her into shadow. The ferns and weeds on Battle Law waved fitfully in the cool breeze, like seaweed on a reef. Rebecca visualized Rob ert the Bruce's minions moving an antique wheel-cross to the courtyard of the castle on the Law—had it originally been nex to the one in front of the west end of the church? People bacl then had as finely tuned a sense of the sacred as people did now except pilgrims went to Canterbury then, and now they went to Elvis's Graceland.

Rebecca rubbed her eyes and replaced the records in the port folio. It would be Monday before Graham could send a copy o "The Dream of the Rood." She thought wistfully of her boxe: of books back in Missouri.

The sun gleamed out again. She opened her and Hilary's note books. Yesterday, in the darkness of the tomb, she'd quoted the verse from Matthew in its seventeenth-century version. Today she realized that even allowing for the haphazard spelling of the sixteenth century, it wasn't the same. She was letting pre conceptions get the best of her. She read the verse as it was written. "Take therefore thought for the morrow, for the morrow must take thought for the things of itself. Sufficient unto today is the evil thereof." A subtle difference, but enough to make Rebecca think Anne was indeed trying to leave a ghostly memoranda, as Jerry had said.

Someone sat down beside her, and she jerked in surprise. "You're as jumpy as a long-tailed cat in a roomful of rocking chairs," teased Mark.

"Catch-22," Rebecca laughed. "Either I can concentrate on my work or be on my guard. Did Jerry let you go, or are you AWOL?"

"He's letting us take breaks in turn. Wants to keep moving, he said. All those pictures in the morning papers have gone to his head."

"At least Jenkins had the decency to mention the rest of us."

Winnie Johnston shepherded half a dozen tourists across the footbridge and over the lawns. They snapped pictures of the church, the cross, the ruined buildings, Mark and Rebecca. Winnie shooed them back toward the road. The roar of two buses jockeying for position in narrow Jedburgh Street trembled in the stones of the church, and a faint odor of exhaust wrinkled Rebecca's nose. "Must be Saturday. The sightseers are out in droves."

"No accident," said Mark, "that Jerry timed his conference for a Friday night. He ought to be grateful to Anne for putting on such a good show."

The blade in his voice was complemented by his expression; his features were whetted to a fine edge. "It bothers you," she said, "working in the crypt."

"It would give anyone the creeps," he replied defensively. "Anne's not just a pile of bones. We know who she was."

"And that her child died with her?" He flinched. Before Rebecca could stop herself, she went on. "How long did your daughter live, Mark?"

His eyes bulged. "How did you know that? Mackenzie?"

"He told me about the divorce. I figured it had been a shotgun wedding. Then Devlin showed you the picture of his daughter, and you saw the baby's bones. . . . Why do you still wear that belt buckle?"

"Why do monks wear hair shirts? Mortification of the flesh." Mark slumped, his hands folded across his stomach to hide the accusing gleam of the silver buckle: "Mark and Karen Forever." "We thought we were in love. The white gown and tuxedo and fancy reception—that was fun. Our parents buried their hatchets and paid attention to us. But we were still in high school. We didn't know any better."

I've put my foot in it now, Rebecca thought. *Too late to say excuse me and slink away.* "Were you there when the baby was born?"

"Hey, I'm a certified sensitive New Age kind of guy." Bitterness spilled from his voice, and Rebecca tasted it. "Karen had a terrible time. Hours and hours. She cussed me up one side and down the other—it was all my fault she was hurting so bad. I'd ruined her life. She just wanted to go shopping with her girlfriends. She didn't want a baby. She didn't want to be married. After a while the nurses started looking at me as if I'd raped her. But I never forced anything on her. Never."

"My brother said he never felt so helpless as he did sitting there in the labor room. The delivery room was a bit better. The end was in sight."

Mark held up his hands, miming a small bundle. "Chelsea lived three days. Placentia praevia, it's called. Even if she'd lived, she'd have been profoundly retarded. . . ." His voice cracked. His hands made futile movements in the air, as though trying to repair something that was irreparably broken. "I know it's not my fault. I know it's not Karen's fault. But I can't help but think, if only we'd wanted her, maybe she'd have been all right."

"I'm sorry." Rebecca took his hand, pulling it away from its terrible pantomime. The tiny shape collapsed and disappeared.

His fingers tightened on hers. "The day after the funeral, Karen and I looked at each other and realized we'd lost the only thing we had in common. The divorce was a relief, like coming out of a fever dream. It was three years before I was able to touch another woman."

Rebecca remembered her comment about men getting their jollies and women paying, and bit her tongue. Voices echoed. Mark sat upright, smoothing his features into blandness. Rebecca released his hand. Grant ushered another group of tourists past the church and toward the Craft Centre. A couple of muscular young men started trimming weeds with scythes that looked like props from the third act of *A Christmas Carol.*

"Have you told Hilary?" asked Rebecca.

"Yeah, we've compared scar tissue. Illuminating, to have a platonic love affair." And, with a shake of his head, he deftly changed the subject. "A platonic affair isn't appropriate for y'all, is it?"

Fair's fair, Rebecca thought. "Once Michael told me he wanted me to want him. I'm not so sure he does anymore."

"And do you want him to want you?" Mark steepled his fingers and knit his brow, miming a psychiatrist's grave nod.

"My Ph.D. is like a grain of sand under his shell. I don't know whether it's going to turn out a pearl or a bit of muck."

"It irritates him because it gives you a reason to leave him."

"I haven't exactly been expressing my undying devotion, have I? But if I have to play dumb for him, I wouldn't respect either one of us." Rebecca slapped shut the notebook. Her shoulder ached against the stone.

Mark clasped his fingers together, squeezing intellect into emotion. "What if he simply doesn't want you to show him up? Y'all are confronting some important issues, but there hasn't been any time to deal with them."

"And we won't have the time to deal with them until the dig is over and the killer apprehended and the treasure found." She stopped and faced Mark's keen gray gaze. "Listen to me, making the same assumption the killer is, that there's a treasure that can be found."

Hilary and Dennis came out of the transept door. "Oh, Lord," said Mark, and called, "Jerry's not looking for me, is he?"

"Naw," said Dennis. "Bob Jenkins just offered to buy him lunch."

"Hoping to loosen his tongue, no doubt," Hilary added.

"If his tongue were any looser," concluded Dennis, "it would fall out."

Mark helped Rebecca gather her books. "Thanks," he said.

"Thank you," she returned.

Hilary hooked her arm through Mark's and led him off toward the cottage, asking his advice on a recipe for tomato-cucumber salad. "Add chile peppers," he suggested. She laughed.

It was after dinner that evening when Hilary and Rebecca returned the notebooks and the portfolio to Laurence's safe. The innkeeper showed them the key in his breast pocket and his cricket bat just behind the reception desk. Mackenzie sat in the lobby reading a newspaper. Rebecca wondered if he had cut holes in the page to peek through.

The women walked across to the Craft Centre, where they found Hilary's sweater as yet unmended. Bridget wasn't there, only a shop assistant. From the makeshift police lab came the murmur of voices and the swish of cards. Hilary asked, "Was Mark telling you about his baby?"

"Yes. I felt so sorry for him."

"And I thought men had no feelings."

"Or else they substitute ranting and raving for feelings. Men are as much the victims of gender roles as we are."

They strolled on to the toy shop. "Do you have any more postcards of the wheel-cross?" Hilary asked the middle-aged man behind the counter.

"That I do. Mr. Wright's contracted tae have some o' his photographs made into postcards, but they'll no be in until Thursday week."

And Rebecca had thought Sheila was the battery of the operation. Shrugging, she admired the wellie bears, each in its miniature tweed or tartan outfit, and saw that the row of model Guards was holding formation without its Queen. The clock ticked peacefully. Beside it was a shallow double-handled silver cup engraved with the Campbell clan crest. "Is that a quaich?" she asked.

"It is. An antique, used tae belong tae the Duke of Argyll's piper. For the piper's wee dram," the shopowner explained to Hilary.

"Hence the term, 'paying the piper,' " Rebecca added. "How much do you want for it?"

"Well noo, you're workin' wi' the RDG—would fifty pound be too much?"

Rebecca started. That would be way too much. But the cup was seductively smooth and cool in her hand, the engraved Campbell boar proudly walking on its engraved heather. "I can only afford thirty-five."

While they bargained, Hilary inspected a framed photograph on the counter, a kilted man and a woman in a wedding dress. "Is this your daughter?" she asked, when negotiations stalled at forty-two pounds.

"Oh, aye," the man replied. "A shame she married the same day the telly lady was killed. No that I was here, mind you; I had tae close the shop early that night."

Rebecca turned away from the photo and put the quaich down.

"Forty-two pounds? I'll take it. Can you keep it until I get to the bank?"

"It's for himself, is it? Take it, lass. Pay me when you can."

"Thank you," Rebecca told him, and bore the box triumphantly toward the cottage. Foolish, she thought, to get Michael something that expensive for a birthday present. Doubly foolish, to think it could serve as a wedding present as well. But it was such a lovely piece, and he would like it. . . .

"Rebecca!" She and Hilary spun around, the gravel of the driveway spurting beneath their shoes. Michael was doing a Highland fling in the door of the hotel. "I found it!"

Rebecca concealed the box beneath her jacket and ran. People converged from all over; nowadays the least outcry was like the trumpet before a race. Mackenzie and Michael were standing with Laurence in the corridor leading to the pub. Tony was already there, cameras at attention.

Whatever it was, Rebecca thought, it was worth it just to see Michael grin. "Look," he exclaimed, holding up a creased piece of parchment. "It's the missin' page—the inventory, right enough."

Rebecca snatched it from his hands. "It sure is. I'd know that clerk's handwriting if it was in Sanskrit. Where was it?"

"Elizabeth Kerr's box in the attic had several of these sportin' prints in it. So I thought, hell, take a wee keek. The third one I took doon had the parchment folded in the back of the frame."

"Those prints were here when we bought the place," said Laurence. "Kerr himself put them up."

"But why hide the inventory?" asked a voice from the crowd.

Rebecca started to say "to protect the treasure"—Kerr had found only the two coins, after all. But she wasn't sure that bit of intelligence needed to be broadcast.

Mackenzie said, clear as a bell, "To protect the treasure." He was poker-faced, probably because he was playing a hand at this very moment.

Thanks, Rebecca thought. She handed the parchment to Laurence. "Put this in the safe, would you please? I'll look at it tomorrow."

Muttering, the crowd dispersed like a theater audience at intermission, eager for the next act.

Rebecca managed to conceal the quaich throughout the celebratory drinks. Jerry had already been celebrating; his jokes about

Scottish skinflints and wayward nuns and girl historians were delivered with the brittle jocularity of a drunk. He, Jenkins, and a few other reporters became bellicose only when Bridget refused to serve them any more alcohol.

Back in the cottage, Rebecca stowed the quaich among her stockings just as Michael walked into the bedroom. He flopped down on his bed and picked up Colin's notepad. She watched in the mirror as he turned the pages, his mouth set as tight as the slit of a letter box. It was not surprising that his moment's elation had burned out so quickly. "Well done," she said.

He met her reflected eyes. "Findin' the inventory? Aboot time I did something to move us forwarder. Time's runnin' short."

Rebecca took out her contact lenses. His image in the mirror blurred. If he wanted to look at the mystery as a competition, fine. But a competition with whom? Time? The killer? Mackenzie? Or Rebecca herself?

Michael didn't want her to show him up. She didn't want him to condescend to her. But if one of them had to choose between solving the puzzle and tiptoeing around the other's ego, only one choice was possible, painful as the consequences might be. Anne Douglas had chosen death over dishonor. . . . With brisk strokes of her hairbrush Rebecca rejected death as an option.

Michael rolled off the bed, grabbed his shaving kit, and headed once again for the bathroom. By the time he returned, Rebecca was tucked into bed. They exchanged goodnights and lay silently in the darkness, too tired to sleep, too wary to talk, waiting for the night to pass. At last Rebecca's churning thoughts went into gridlock, and she dozed off.

Sunday morning was misty with impending rain. In the crypt Jerry supervised Mark and Michael as they laid out a coffin-shaped crate filled with foam rubber. "Can you get that?" he asked Tony.

Tony peered through his camera and answered, "Right on target."

Jerry produced an x-acto knife and with labored precision cut a cavity in the foam. He was trying to keep his hands from trembling, Rebecca realized. He'd really been sopping it up last night. "The bones of the left foot will fit neatly in here," he said to the camera. He picked up a metatarsal bone, flourished it, and dropped it.

Michael and Rebecca stared, appalled. Mark fell to his knees, rescued the bone, and muttered, "You'd better lay off the sauce, Jerry."

"Mind your own business, kid." Jerry's red-rimmed eyes darted from Mark's frown to the other watching faces. "You girls are just wasting time down here. Get back to the infirmary trench. Take Dennis with you."

Rebecca groped for a withering retort, found nothing, did an about-face, and led her troop up the stairs. Elaine sat in the chancel, doggedly entering data, her jacket zipped against the cold, damp wind funneled from west door to east window. "Playing up again, is he," she stated.

"Dennis," said Rebecca as they walked through the cloister, "make sure you keep on checking what Elaine's entering."

"Don't worry," Dennis replied. "I still have to clear Laurel's name."

By lunch time they'd uncovered a small cache of pilgrim's ampullae—tiny lead containers for holy water—marked with the woman and cross that had evidently symbolized Rudesburn. Adele's collection of glass fragments was expanding, and despite the rain Hilary did a lovely grease pencil sketch of a painted plaster wall. Dennis dug and sifted and carried dirt uncomplainingly.

By quitting time, Michael and Mark had finished plotting the positions of the bones, and Jerry was managing to get them to the box without breaking them. In a few more days, Rebecca told herself, Anne and her child would be on their way to join Alexander in Edinburgh. Had he tried to escape and failed, where Thomas succeeded in escaping Rudesburn but not his conscience?

Through the mist clinging to her lashes, Rebecca saw Jerry, Tony, and Elaine squeeze by Mackenzie's attenuated form in the doorway of the hotel. She found Michael undressing in the bedroom. "Are you going to stick it?" she asked.

"I begin to see how Fletcher Christian felt," he replied. "You ken Captain Bligh's goin' to do you ower, but if you do him first, then you've stranded yoursel' on a desert island for the rest of your life."

"Graham wouldn't exile you for saving the dig."

"Does the dig need to be saved? The location of the penny, and the heraldic disc, and whether or no Jerry deliberately broke doon the wall—it's our word against his, just like it was wi' Dennis's sister."

"I hate to say wait until he really fouls something up, but—"

Michael's eyes glinted. "Jerry himself was talkin' entrapment, remember? When I was at Fishbourne, the director would put a few Roman coins into the trench to see if we'd turn them in right and proper."

"An honesty test?"

"For Jerry, a pre-emptive strike. What we need is a bittie artifact, bait to catch him oot. Maybe I should talk to Graham."

"Talk to Graham," Rebecca told him.

That evening Rebecca sat down at the dining room table to transcribe the newly discovered inventory into the computer. Everyone else wandered in and out of the room until she felt like a mother with a houseful of toddlers. She couldn't tell them to go outside and play, not with the rain coming down hard on the slates of the roof. Only Adele pulled up the hood of her jacket and plunged out into the night.

"Gold noble of Henry III," Rebecca typed. "Silver chalice. Jeweled pectoral cross of Saint Benedict." It had probably never come near Saint Benedict. But a tenth-century jeweled cross would still be a valuable work of art. It would be valuable for its materials, for that matter. Maybe Jerry was waiting until she uncovered the treasure so he could steal it. Entrapping Jerry in academic skulduggery might be inadmissable in court, but academic disputes didn't usually go to court. . . . Her thought raveled, the dangling end tickling the back of her mind.

Guinevere and Lancelot materialized on the table. One left a neat tooth-puncture in the corner of her notebook. The other pawed curiously at the parchment. Rebecca was about to start defensive procedures when Dennis opened the refrigerator. They vanished, leaving behind strands of fur.

In the sitting room Mark strummed "The City of New Orleans." Michael got out his practice chanter and ran through his repertory. Footsteps skimmed down the staircase, and Hilary burst wild-eyed into the dining room. "Look!" She held out her hand. The ceiling light struck a halo from the gold signet ring in her palm.

Chanter and guitar stopped abruptly. A meow of protest followed the slam of the refrigerator door. Grasping coherence, Rebecca saved her file on the computer before she took the ring from Hilary's hand. "It's the one from the skeleton, all right. Where'd you find it?"

"My socks and Adele's got mixed up in the wash. I was putting hers in her drawer and felt something hard in the sleeve of that UCLA sweatshirt. So I looked—sorry." Hilary grimaced.

"You should've looked," Mark assured her. "But the police already have, several times."

"Adele?" asked Dennis. "You mean it's been Adele all along?"

"Dinna make any assumptions," Michael told him. "Where's Mackenzie?"

In a mad scramble, they pulled on their jackets and boots and found flashlights. Rebecca rushed back into the dining room, grabbed a plastic bag, inserted the inventory, and zipped it into her jacket.

It took only moments to reach the hotel. Mackenzie was at his post in the lobby, a tea-tray beside his chair, Devlin and his notebook in attendance. Voices and jangling glassware echoed down the hallway from the pub. Mackenzie listened to the students' babble for only two seconds before he pointed to Rebecca. "You." She told the tale. "Did you hide the ring?" he asked Hilary.

She shook her head in a vigorous negative, pony tail flying.

"Where is Adele?" Mackenzie went on. "In the church?"

"If she's not spouting philosophy in the bar," Rebecca replied.

She wasn't in the bar. Mackenzie delivered the ring to Laurence. "Adele?" the innkeeper asked queasily. Devlin dispatched his long-suffering constabulary into the night.

Raincoats and fluorescent vests glistened in the lights of the village. Flashlights pierced the dark. The soggy grass of the lawns squished. The rain hid the priory until they were almost on top of it. "Look!" said Dennis.

A pale light gleamed in the north transept door. Even as they watched it faded away, sucked into nothingness. Mackenzie led the way into the west door and down the nave. The face of Salkeld's effigy winked out of the darkness. Birds stirred uneasily in the rafters. Adele was sitting with her back to the barred crypt door, legs crossed, hands on knees, eyes closed. The same silk scarf she'd worn to the inquest lay on the tiles before her. On it, a flame amid the blue and green dyes, lay the dragon brooch.

Mackenzie went down on his haunches beside Adele. "Mrs. Garrity."

Slowly, reluctantly, she opened her eyes. "Why, Chief Inspector, how nice of you to join us."

"Us?" Mackenzie repeated. The students moved closer together. Grant stood in the doorway with the other constables. Devlin got out his notebook.

"Anne and I. It's her brooch, you see. The dragons symbolize the conquest of paganism by Christianity. She practiced the old religion, witchcraft, playing the sacred mother. Of course, in her present discorporeal form she can't wear the brooch, so I'm keeping it for her."

"She really was talking to Anne," said Rebecca. "But we have no proof the brooch was Anne's, let alone that she was anything but a Christian."

"You stole the brooch and the ring," Mackenzie stated.

"I borrowed them for my seances," Adele explained patiently. "Dr. Reid told me the artifacts were haunted. I knew I could help Anne by letting her talk out her problems." Adele's blue eyes, strangely pallid in the dim light, found Rebecca in the crowd and focused on her. Rebecca shrank back.

"Where did you hide the artifacts?"

"Oh, here and there." Adele's eyes blurred.

"Did you kill Miss Fitzgerald?"

Still the eyes didn't quite focus. "I helped her into the otherworld, yes. But I didn't deliver the mortal blow. Oh, no. I didn't do that."

"What?" Mackenzie asked. Devlin leaned forward.

"No surprise there," said Michael. "She put the coins on Sheila's eyes. A sacrament called the viaticum. Like the ancient Greeks puttin' coins in the dead person's mouth to pay the fare across the River Styx."

Adele smiled as sweetly as a baby on a jar of strained peaches. "Very good. But, of course, the leader of souls is the archangel Michael."

"Leave me oot of this," Michael muttered.

"She's round the twist," said Devlin.

Mackenzie stood up and summoned a policewoman. "Come along, Mrs. Garrity," she said soothingly. "Let's go for a little ride."

Adele snatched her arm away. "What do you think I am, a child? You're going to take me to the Galashiels police station, just like the others."

"Right on schedule," said Mark. Dennis looked down at his boots. Hilary looked up at the ceiling.

Two constables and Devlin trotted after Adele as she strode down the aisle. "Which car do I get to ride in, the one with the orange stripe?"

They disappeared. The church seemed oppressively still without the fluting of Adele's soprano voice. The only sound was that of rain dripping into the nave and through the mouths of the stone gargoyles outside.

Mackenzie said, "P.C. Johnston, would you bring the brooch, please?" And he, too, was off down the aisle, his coat flapping like a superhero's cape behind him.

With a groan, Grant bent and wrapped the brooch in the scarf. Rebecca sighed, glanced at Michael's somber face, and like a good little shepherdess shooed her flock home.

Chapter Twenty-Six

It was Monday afternoon before Adele was returned to the fold. She thanked the constables as if they'd had her in for tea, and sauntered down the driveway blithely unaware of Mackenzie's baleful gaze on her back.

Mackenzie turned and looked over at the steps of the church where Rebecca sat amid a pile of papers and books. Catching her eye, he beckoned. She waved acknowledgement. He and Devlin disappeared into the hotel.

The rain had stopped during the night. If the clouds hadn't completely dispersed, at least they admitted frequent rays of sun. Beyond the hotel, the Eildon Hills were a dark green brushed with tender strokes of purple heather. Tomorrow was August first. This week was the official end of the expedition. Rebecca's return ticket to the United States was dated for next month. She felt like a demolitions worker gauging what length of fuse would allow her to escape the inevitable explosion.

She gathered her papers, stuffed them into the portfolio, and tucked it beneath her arm. She called into the church, "Elaine, get Michael for me."

"Right-ho." Elaine shouted his name into the crypt.

He emerged dusting his arms and legs. In almost a week his sling had gone from sterile white to tattletale gray. "Aye?"

"We've been summoned. War council, I daresay. Adele's back."

They started off across the lawns, skirting a young woman meditating over a disemboweled lawnmower and two reporters in Grant's tow. Cameras leaped upward. In response to "Say whiskey!" Michael chirped, "Glenfiddich." The gaggle of tourists outside the gate eyed them with horrified fascination; they'd touched death and lived to tell about it. So far, Rebecca thought.

"Did that copy of 'The Dream of the Rood' help you?" Michael asked.

"Not really. The only verse Anne wrote that seems remotely relevant is, 'the warriors left me standing laced with blood, I was wounded unto death.' And that's either the cross itself speaking, or the sacred tree of Norse/Saxon myth. Take your pick." Rebecca glanced for the hundredth time that day at the wheel-cross sprouting from the grass before the door of the church. Its carved face revealed nothing.

"She'd no be writin' doon the location of the treasure too plainly," said Michael, "in case the soldiers came back to look."

"If she wrote it down at all. It's maddening, like trying to break a code."

They walked into the hotel and found the police inspectors closeted with Laurence in his office. The room was only a little larger than Anne's tomb. Rebecca set down the portfolio and shifted her chair so she could see out the window in the door.

"How did your lot react to Mrs. Garrity's arrest?" asked Mackenzie, without so much as a "good afternoon."

"They didna," Michael replied. "Jerry made some jokes aboot her, Tony frowned, and Elaine shrugged."

"By this time," added Rebecca, "it's like a game of musical chairs. Everyone's been out. Now what? Do we play again?"

Nora opened the door. Ceremonially she placed a tiered rack of cakes, biscuits, scones, and sandwiches on the corner of the desk. Bridget laid down a tray filled with teapots and cups and shut the door. As the only woman present, Rebecca was expected to pour. She started rattling crockery.

Devlin opened his notebook. "Adele's been shiftin' the brooch and the ring from place to place, in the cottage and on the priory grounds. Which is, I reckon, just what someone's been doin' with the murder weapon. Two sugars, please." He turned a page. "She dragged Sheila into the sarcophagus. She found the two coins beside Sheila's body, behind the chapter house."

"And didn't steal them," asked Laurence, "as she stole the ring and the brooch?" He accepted a cup and chose a scone.

"They were tainted, she said. But then, she's not always sensible. She takes pagan and Christian ideas and mucks them about together.''

Just like in "The Dream of the Rood," Rebecca thought. She poured Mackenzie's tea.

"Just milk," he said, and contemplated a wholemeal biscuit.

"When the Chief Inspector showed his displeasure at her movin' the body and destroyin' evidence, she just smiled at him. A psychiatrist had a go at her and agrees she's looney, but he couldn't say if she's dangerous. We'll have a bobby on her from now on, don't worry yourself." Devlin bit down on a miniature eclair so firmly that cream smeared his lips.

Michael took off his sling and peered into a sandwich. "So it was two different people killed her and put her in the tomb. I doot the murderer was right amazed to find she'd been moved. Adele's no grassed on anyone?''

"She claims not to know who did it. Although we're still far from sure she isn't the murderer herself.''

"She could be admitting one relatively minor point to deflect suspicion from the major one.'' Rebecca set the teapot down and stirred her tea. "What about the ring and the brooch?''

"She was released from custody on her own recognizance. She's not free to leave Rudesburn. We could still charge her with theft.''

Laurence brushed crumbs from his beard. "It'd be up to me and the RDG to press charges. But," he said and nodded toward Mackenzie, "we thought since she never tried to remove the artifacts from Rudesburn, we'd let that point go for now, and hope she'll blow the gaffe on the killer.''

"Somebody has to," Michael muttered into his sandwich.

Mackenzie bit into a biscuit, the crunch loud in the silent space between words. Two or three people strolled past the office door and glanced curiously inside. Rebecca realized she was still stirring her tea. She looked up and met Michael's eyes. They were like beacons on a distant peak. "Chief Inspector," Michael said, "is it no aboot time to set a trap?''

"Yes," said Rebecca. "If the killer thinks I know the location of the treasure, I should go sit out in the cloister after dark or something. . . .'' Her mouth went dry. She must be crazy to say such a thing and step so solidly on Michael's lines.

Mackenzie and Devlin looked at each other. Laurence stopped, his sandwich halfway to his mouth. Michael's eyes blazed. "Are you daft, woman? That'd be dangerous! I'll play the bait.''

"No, you won't. I'm a woman, Sheila was a woman—if the killer is another woman, would she attack a man? And no one would attack the both of us," she added, forestalling his next remark.

"No one will be attacking you at all," said Mackenzie. "I'll have someone behind every rock." His expression was so suddenly avuncular that Rebecca expected him to pat her on the head and give her a sweet from his pocket. He must have been hoping she'd volunteer, the rat.

"No," said Michael. "It's too dangerous. You canna . . ." His voice trailed off, and his eyes dropped to his lap where they stared at the cup and saucer and half a scone smeared with strawberry jam, red as blood.

"Michael," Rebecca said softly, "if the mystery isn't solved, then nothing is solved. You know that."

Mackenzie inspected another cookie. Devlin checked his notebook. Laurence completed his bite and shoved another one after the first.

The beacons in Michael's eyes burned to ash and went out. "You're a fine braw lass, are you noo?" was all he said. She couldn't tell if he was being sarcastic or complimentary. She tried to smile at him, but all her mouth would do was tremble. Her own heartbeat thudded like a drum in her ears.

"Right," said Mackenzie.

Michael said to Laurence, "I need to ring Graham aboot settin' a wee archeological trap for Jerry. I canna believe he'd be so unprofessional as to break doon the wall, but then, he's no been comin' to work sober, either."

Laurence gulped, swallowing his mouthful of sandwich. "If Jerry's the killer, you won't be needing an archeological trap."

"That's as may be," said Devlin. "Tell Dr. Graham, Michael, that we'll be sendin' the ring and brooch on to the museum straightaway."

"We'd best start keepin' the computer diskettes in the safe, too. I dinna trust Elaine." Michael reached for the phone.

Rebecca picked up the portfolio. "I'm putting my inventory on disk, but not my notes."

"Is the Bruce's reliquary on the inventory?" asked Devlin.

"Sure is. The English knew Anne had it."

"And what else?" Mackenzie asked.

"Just what we'd thought—coins, jeweled artifacts, lots of altar plate, mostly in silver, but with the occasional gold or latten piece. And the relics, some in fancy reliquaries, some not."

"What would you say the value of all that would be?"

Rebecca's eyes crossed slightly. "As hunks of metal? As artifacts? It would depend on who bought them, and why, and how . . ."

"Thousands of quid," said Michael, and forcefully started dialing. "Enough to make someone kill."

Laurence whistled. Everyone else squeezed out of the room. It took only a few moments' discussion to sketch out the campaign. They would set the trap tonight, they all agreed. Matters had dragged out long enough.

Laurence returned to the bar, and Mackenzie and Devlin went outside. Rebecca waited until Michael finished his phone call and fell into step beside him out the door and across the street. "Michael . . ."

"You have to do what you have to do, hen," he said. He tousled her hair in a gesture he obviously thought was affectionate, but which was so forceful it hurt. He headed back down to the crypt while she plodded out to the infirmary trench.

Adele was peacefully spooning dirt. "Glad to see you back," Rebecca told her.

"Nice to be back."

"We need every worker we can get," Rebecca went on. "We're so far behind, I'm going to have to work on the inscriptions tonight."

Adele nodded. Dennis and Hilary glanced up in alarm. Rebecca offered them a weak smile and wandered down to the crypt. There she consulted with a bleary-eyed Jerry about her notes, and keeping the records straight, and how much work had yet to be done. Finally he stood up from the foam box and its grisly cut-out shape and said, "All right, Miss Know-It-All, if you want to work overtime, be my guest!"

Michael's back, bent over the skeleton, shook as if he were either laughing or swearing. Mark glanced up skeptically. Tony said, "Scholars don't know when to leave well enough alone." He took a picture of her. Rebecca imagined it in the next day's newspaper—another victim of the Rudesburn Ripper. *Stop it,* she ordered herself.

In the church Rebecca compared notes with Elaine. "I'm typing as fast as I can," the woman said. "You lot should stop finding things."

"I'll be working late tonight," Rebecca told her. "Maybe I can get caught up."

Quitting time once again. Rebecca walked back to the hotel and called across the crowded pub to Laurence, "I'll be hanging onto the portfolio for a while yet tonight. I need to get in some extra work after supper."

Laurence nodded with wide-eyed sincerity. "No problem. Just be sure to bring back the crypt key, too." Rebecca returned along the corridor thinking she ought to go ahead and paint her face like a clown's and start doing juggling tricks. Surely everyone could hear the sham in her voice, but no one even bothered to look up.

In the office, she and Nora surreptitiously exchanged a handful of menus for the genuine papers, keeping out only the notebooks so Hilary could make her rough sketches into finished drawings. She'd be all right in the cottage since Mark would be with her, and Grant would be out on the doorstep . . . and the killer after Rebecca herself. The pulse in her throat pounded against her collar.

Adele fixed pot roast for supper. It was probably delicious, but Rebecca couldn't taste a thing. Michael shoved his food around on his plate. After dinner they waited in the bedroom until the appointed time, Michael shaking his head over Mark's sad story. Other people's problems could invariably make one's own look smaller. "Did you put Mark and Dennis and Hilary in the picture?" Rebecca asked after yet another long pause.

"Oh, aye. They'll hold the fort here. I'll be wi' Devlin."

She'd be wasting her breath to try and argue him into the cottage, too. They kissed. His lips were cold, his eyes as hooded as Mackenzie's. Gathering her portfolio and a flashlight, she went out into the evening.

Only in Scotland, she thought, could it be cool and oppressive at the same time. No wonder Adele had thrown open all the windows while she was cooking, and Hilary had wadded her ponytail into a bun. Overhead the sky was a deep prussian blue, stitched with the moving lights of an airplane. But banks of cloud massed on the horizon like soldiers gathering for an attack. She saw a flash that was either lightning or the reflected lights of traffic on the A68. She tied the sleeves of the jacket around her neck; she was hot enough already and felt a sick sweat pooling on her body. The chill breeze felt good.

The priory blushed in the last rays of the sun. Its grounds

seemed utterly deserted, not a living soul in sight. Nor a dead one, for that matter. Voices and slamming doors seemed to echo down a long tunnel from the village, the sounds compressed and distant.

Rebecca sat at the base of the wheel-cross and made a show of taking notes. Not that she expected anyone to jump her in this open area—she was merely displaying the decoy. The only attention she attracted was that of Guinevere and Lancelot, who came trotting across the grass and nuzzled her pockets like horses searching for sugar.

The sun glided along the horizon in a dazzle of pink and red. The shadows ran like molasses, engulfing the entire priory. Rebecca and her feline escort walked into the church. The beam of her flashlight picked out the sarcophagus where Sheila had lain. The back of her neck bristled. She hurried past and unlocked the crypt door. The hollowed steps looked like an optical illusion, extending upward instead of down. But it was down she went, into the crypt, the cats sliding along the wall and sniffing warily. It wasn't so much that the human reptilian brain was afraid of the dark itself, Rebecca thought; it was afraid of things that went bump in the dark.

There was the switch. The ceiling lights flared so harshly she winced. The close, musty air clogged her throat. The bristly feeling in the back of her neck spread down her spine until she felt like a porcupine. She forced herself not to look around. Mackenzie was out there somewhere. So were Devlin and Michael. She turned off her flashlight.

A faint scrabbling sound broke the silence. Rebecca spun around. Her teeth clenched, she inspected a narrow aperture. Just an empty tomb and tiny red eyes vanishing through a slit in the wall. The cats bounded forward, leaving pawprints in the dust, but the rat was gone.

The scientific coffin was draped with blue plastic that looked shockingly garish in this monochromatic landscape. Anne's tomb was almost empty, only the bones of her torso left to form hieroglyphics in the dust. "Earth to earth," Rebecca murmured, "ashes to ashes, dust to dust. In sure and certain hope of the Resurrection unto eternal life . . ."

Lancelot put his forepaws on the edge of the box and peered inquisitively back up the corridor. Guinevere looked up with an interrogative meow, her tail twitching, her eyes gleaming. *I shouldn't look around,* Rebecca told herself. *I shouldn't look.*

". . . through our Lord Jesus Christ; at whose coming in glorious majesty to judge the world, the earth and the sea shall give up their dead . . ."

There was a rustle behind her. She tensed. Her whisper died away. Lancelot growled softly. The odor of incense, sweat, ale, and onions wafted on a breath of cold air. Rebecca looked. A white shape wavered in the dark opening to a tomb.

Anne was once again probing that membrane between this world and the next. Had no one ever before prayed over her bones? Even the Protestant prayer for the dead Rebecca had learned for a term paper on comparative religion was better than nothing.

The shape glided forward. Rebecca forced herself to stand still. Every muscle shrieked with tension, every instinct tuned to fight or flee.

Then the shape was gone. The heavy odor disappeared as if sucked into another dimension. The cold abated. The cats whisked away up the corridor and into the night. Rebecca slumped against the wall—an uninscribed stretch of wall—quelling a wave of nausea. She thought suddenly, when was Sheila's funeral? Had she any friends or family to lay her to rest? The woman had been obliterated, leaving nothing but bitter memory.

The lights went out. Rebecca stared into the nothingness, utterly blind. Her trembling hand turned on her flashlight. Great. She might as well light up a neon sign saying, "Here I am." She turned it off. But she was supposed to attract someone. She turned the flashlight back on and sidled away from the wooden box—a scuffle might damage the artifacts, and that would never do. . . .

A beam of light struck her in the face. Galvanized, she jumped three feet backward. The grit of the wall snagged her jacket. She jerked free. There was the shape again, draperies billowing, advancing closer and closer. Except this time it, too, carried a flashlight. A faint scent of whiskey tickled Rebecca's distended senses. Her jaw writhed, her teeth set tightly to keep her from screaming—but she wouldn't give this apparition the satisfaction of scaring her.

The shape had no face, just a dark, smooth oval encircled by white fabric. But the shape did have a hand. It held a knife, a streak of cold flame. Rebecca clutched the portfolio and her own flashlight, directing its beam directly into the nonexistent face. Maybe there was a gleam of eyes, maybe not. The flowing draperies were looking more and more like a bedsheet. Part of Rebecca's mind stated very coolly, *I can't believe the trap worked.* The rest of her mind was all for immediate flight. *Where's Mackenzie? A man behind every rock, yeah, sure.* . . .

She threw her flashlight. Shadows cartwheeled. There was a thud, and the figure emitted an unmistakable yelp. The flashlight shattered on the floor. Visualizing herself as a three-hundred-pound linebacker, Rebecca tucked in the portfolio and charged head down past the figure and toward the stairs.

She plunged from light into dark, slipping on the stone floor. The merest suggestion of light spilled down the staircase. A brighter light came after her, and the thump of footsteps. A ghost with track shoes? She stumbled up the stairs and angled left toward the south transept door, hoping whoever her pursuer was would run on through the nave and into the arms of the law.

The church seemed positively light and airy after the crypt. The rectangle of night through the door of the cloister was as glorious as the pearly gates. Two bounding footsteps, three, magnified into a thundering stampede. . . . Someone grabbed her.

She gasped and struck out with the portfolio. "It's me, it's me," exclaimed Michael, dodging the blow.

There really were lots of footsteps. Those light streaks in her eyes weren't the implosions of her own nerves but flashlights. She sagged against Michael, his slinged arm a bar of iron pressed between them, her free hand a knotted claw in his shirt. Either her heart or his galloped in her ears.

Hordes of constables rushed forward, surrounded the white shape that ran out of the crypt, and brought it none too gently down onto the floor. The knife went skittering across the tile and bounced off Rebecca's shoe. A table knife. Not the sgian dubh. That wasn't right. . . . She bumped her nose on Michael's collarbone.

Mackenzie's lean form lifted the white figure from the floor and tore away a pair of panty hose the—the man had over his face. Devlin unwound a bedsheet, revealing jeans and a T-shirt reading, "Stratford-upon-Avon Drag Races."

It was Bob Jenkins. The culprit wasn't someone from the expedition after all. . . .

"Bluidy hell," said Michael in her ear. "Rebecca, no matter what else he did, he didna kill Sheila. He can prove he was in London."

Jenkins essayed a charming smile and said, "Can't you peelers take a joke?" With a snarl of disgust Mackenzie dropped him. "I knew you were onto something," Jenkins continued, "the way you were chatting up the American girl. Thought you could tell us sod-all, hide the treasure . . . the laws of treasure trove . . . it's our right to see those notes . . . freedom of the press . . ."

Devlin said contemptuously, "He's drunk."

"Take him away," said Mackenzie. Several constables surrounded the hapless Jenkins and dragged him down the nave.

Dennis burst through the transept door. "Inspector! Inspector, come quick! Somebody's knocked out Grant—and Hilary, too! The notes are gone, they got the notes after all!"

"Bloody hell" was mild compared to what Mackenzie replied to that. "Locate everyone with the expedition," he shouted. "Now!"

Michael and Rebecca joined the rush toward the cottage. She was surprised at how dark the night had become, the sky matted with damp clouds that absorbed light as well as sound. Only the blue lights of the police cars sparking and flashing on the driveway weren't filmed with gloom.

Several people gathered around a dark figure sprawled on the doorstep—it was Grant, with blood smearing his temple, his hat several paces away, a doctor taking his pulse. "How is he?" asked Mackenzie.

"A right smart blow with a heavy object," replied the doctor. "Concussion. I've sent for an ambulance."

Winnie and Laurence came running down the driveway. She fell to her knees beside her husband, touching his face and chest as if to reassure herself he was still alive. Laurence chewed his moustache with agitation. "Don't worry, Winnie, we'll look after the children."

"He'll be all right," the doctor said. Someone came out of the cottage with a couple of blankets; Winnie tucked them around Grant. A police car took off up Jedburgh Street, its siren howling.

Michael's face in the blue flashing light looked thin and hard, his eyes like arctic ice. "If Jenkins knew we were up to something," he muttered to Rebecca, "then so could the real culprit. Ah, damn it all, did he turn the trap back on us?"

The adrenaline that had pumped into Rebecca's system earlier was draining away. Her hurt shoulder throbbed at each slow thud of her heart. Numbly she fumbled at her jacket and put it on. The portfolio felt as if it were stuffed with bricks. "What about Hilary?"

The doctor stood up. "Now then, let me see to the lassie."

Hilary was stretched out on the dining room floor, her head cradled in Mark's lap. His face was set in a scowl of rage and terror. Hers was so pale as to be almost transparent, but she was blinking and looking around in confusion. She was wearing the sweater-vest, and her brown hair was still in a straggly bun—at first glimpse she could pass for . . . "My God," said Rebecca. "The trap worked just fine. He thought she was me, sitting here working late. He came after the notes, just as we'd intended."

Mackenzie pierced her with a sharp look. Devlin got out his notebook. The doctor gently inspected Hilary's head. "Well, aren't you the lucky one. Your hair softened the blow."

Mackenzie sat down hard on a chair and demanded, "What happened?"

"I was sitting here drawing," Hilary said.

"Don't try to talk," Mark told her.

"Talk," ordered Mackenzie, ignoring Mark's glare. "Did you hear anyone come in?"

"No. I was too intent on my work, I guess. All I know is suddenly something hit me, and I saw stars. I didn't know you literally saw stars."

"Excitation of the nerve endings," said the doctor. "Follow my pen."

Obediently Hilary's eyes followed the tip of the pen. "My back was to the window," she went on. "Someone could've climbed in. There's no screen."

"Screen?" queried Devlin, confused by her Americanism.

"Or it could've been someone in the house. I don't know." She nestled into Mark's lap. Reluctantly he gave up one of her hands to the doctor.

"Mr. Owen, where were you?" Mackenzie asked.

"Dennis and I were upstairs trying to fix his cassette player— his James Galway tape was dragging. Adele was in the kitchen defrosting the refrigerator. We didn't hear anything, not with the music going on and off."

"The lady's no in the hoose noo," said a constable from the back row.

"The fridge is all clean and dry," Dennis added. "She didn't go running out and leave it half-done."

Devlin asked, "Did Adele do Hilary over for findin' the ring?"

Rebecca looked over the papers scattered on the table. The two notebooks they'd had in the crypt were indeed gone. She dumped the portfolio and told Mackenzie about the latest theft. "How will that affect your work?" he asked.

"I've stared at those inscriptions so long I could sit down and write them all out again, even without the photographs. Even without the originals, for that matter." Mackenzie was waiting. "Losing the notes is a nuisance, sure, but the loss won't hurt us," Rebecca concluded. "More power to the jerk, if he thinks he can get any more out of those inscriptions than I have."

Another constable came in the front door. "All the expedition members are in the bar—Kleinfelter, Wright, Vavra, and Garrity. And a right mob of other people. Everyone went out to use the loo at least once, sometimes twice. No one can verify anyone else's alibi."

"It's a dark night," said Devlin. "With so many of our people watchin' the priory, any one of the folk in the pub could've slipped in here without bein' noticed."

"A lucky killer?" asked Michael, "or just a damned smart one?"

Mackenzie sat tapping his fingertips on the table. His face looked like a mask, so tight and still was its expression. Only his eyes moved, glittering obsidian blades flaying each face before him.

Rebecca stepped back so that she was squarely against Michael's chest. Her knees were weak, but she wasn't about to collapse in front of Mackenzie. Devlin opened and shut his notebook. The doctor got up and brushed off his trousers. The distant wail of a siren broke the silence.

Chapter Twenty-Seven

DESPITE THE THREATENING clouds of the night before, Tuesday morning dawned clear and innocent. "Fooled you!" the bright sunshine seemed to say. By late afternoon the students were mopping sweat from their faces and talking wistfully of iced drinks. "The pub has ice-cold Coke," Michael told Mark.

"Yeah," Mark said with a laugh, "without an ice cube in it!"

Michael looked puzzled. "But it's already cold."

Rebecca batted affectionately at his back and walked across the priory lawns toward the hotel. Not only did she need to take the day's printouts to the safe, but also she wanted to see if Laurence would cash a check for her.

"With pleasure," he said.

Rebecca leaned on the reception desk and watched Laurence count out forty-five pounds. From the pub emanated Jerry's boasts, the equivalent of a gorilla thumping its chest. "How's Grant?"

"Fit as ever. Winnie collected him at noon. She's always accused him of having a hard head."

"A Scottish trait," said Rebecca. Laurence smiled, but only with his mouth. His eyes had dark circles beneath them. She went on, "So Adele was in here last night carrying on about cosmic biorhythms?"

"Yes. I'm afraid most of the tourists and reporters either run from her or treat her like a performing monkey. Not that she notices. She could've coshed Grant and Hilary before she came in here, I suppose."

"And Tony, Elaine, and Jerry?"

"Coming and going all evening. Mackenzie's threatening to keep the lot of us under close surveillance."

"I thought he already was." Rebecca folded the money into her pocket. "The trap failed. That's all there is to it. I was hoping we'd catch Jerry and kill two birds with one stone—don't let Tony hear me talk about killing birds. . . ." Again they shared a weak smile. "If Jerry wanted to look at my notes, he could just ask me for them."

"Paranoia?" asked Laurence. "Megalomania?" He slammed the cash drawer and reached for a newspaper. "Have you seen today's *Sunburn*?"

"No. What has Jenkins—" She saw the headline, "More gold artifacts linked to Rudesburn murder." "Great. Now we'll get looters with metal detectors and backhoes. It'll make Henry's army look like it was a Sunday school class."

"The last I saw of Mackenzie," Laurence told her, dropping his voice and looking around conspiratorially, "he was ready to reinstate the death penalty. Devlin says they're charging Jenkins to the hilt."

"Making him a scapegoat? Well, he asked for it, prancing around in that sheet last night. I don't care if that table knife was only a prop."

"But he isn't the killer." The phone rang, and Laurence answered it. "No, we haven't any rooms for the Festival. May I recommend the George in Melrose?" He hung up and turned back to Rebecca. "Jenkins wanted your notes for the same reason the killer had done, to find the treasure. Except he claims he would've turned it in after he had his story."

"Sure," said Rebecca. She picked up Hilary's repaired sweater and left the hotel just as a group of tourists came in. Across the street Devlin and Mackenzie stood in the door of the Craft Centre, deep in conversation with a tight-lipped Elaine, Tony taking pictures of all three of them.

Rebecca went into the toy shop. She paid for the quaich, bought wrapping paper and ribbon, and made a face at the clock in the window. Eight o'clock, it had read the night of the murder. She'd seen Elaine, she'd seen Winnie, she'd heard voices in the Plantagenet van. . . . Maybe someone had slipped into the shop and changed the time. But why bother?

From the driveway Rebecca saw Mark and Hilary sitting on the cloister wall. She relaxed against him, her head nestled on his shoulder, his arm snug around her waist. His hand stayed contentedly in place, not using her flank as a base for territorial incursions. Rebecca smiled fondly at them, patted the bonnet of Michael's Fiat, and went inside the cottage.

Upstairs Dennis was singing "Greensleeves" to his flute tape. Water ran in the bathroom; that must be Adele. Michael was in the bedroom, sitting on the bed and considering Colin's notepad.

Rebecca shut the door, laid down Hilary's sweater, and looked at him like a child looking at a display of sweets. Shining antennae of reddish-brown hair framed his face. His chest and shoulders were a slender Greek torso above his jeans. His lashes were dark, making parentheses on his cheeks as he looked down at the book. His brows angled upward. "Will I do?" he asked.

"How are you at backrubs?" she responded, even though she already knew.

"I took a first in backrubs. Sit you doon."

Rebecca sat down. His hands rubbed her neck and shoulders, the touch of one only a bit weaker than the other. His wound was healing fast; no wonder he'd abandoned the sling today. She luxuriated in his touch, just a simple touch, nothing complicated. "Michael, will we always be friends?"

"Eh? Why not?" His hands didn't falter.

She saw him keeping the silver quaich as Mark kept the silver belt buckle, not in agony, but in dry, distant sorrow. "Why not?" she repeated.

She was tired. Her head flopped on her neck. Michael embraced her, his breath warm on her cheek. She held his arms tightly around her. Someone knocked on the door, and Dennis called, "It's your turn to cook."

They had no choice but to laugh. They got up and went about their duties, cooking, cataloging, record-keeping, locking doors. Night came. In the wee hours, shouts echoed from the priory. Rebecca looked out the window to see the police removing several trespassers whose nervous movements indicated that they'd encountered one of the resident spooks.

Wednesday morning Rebecca helped Jerry and Michael repeat Francis Kerr's survey of the crypt. They found a minor reliquary or two hidden in niches, and some coffins in doubtful preservation. Except for the broken brick wall, everything was as Kerr had seen it fifty years ago.

Mark placed the last of Anne's bones into the box. "I'll take them to the museum," Michael said, "when we're ready to close doon."

Mark wiped his hands on his jeans, eyeing the large skull and the miniature one as if he expected them to start speaking. "Jerry, I'll go on out to the infirmary trench and help with the triangulations."

"Huh?" Jerry was propped in a corner like a shop window mannequin, scrubbing at his glasses. "Oh, okay, sure."

Exchanging tight smiles with Michael, Rebecca and Mark went outside. Three men were inspecting the chapter house, measuring the cracks where tiers of stone had slumped away from each other. Or rather, two men were inspecting the stone; the other shot a keen glance toward Mark and Rebecca as they walked by, then an equally sharp look across the road to where the tents and booths, grandstands and portable toilets of the Festival were starting to sprout.

"One of Mackenzie's finest?" asked Mark under his breath.

"Looks like it. Here, have a tape measure. I'll do the soil samples."

All afternoon delivery trucks vied for space with the tour buses. Tony, with Dennis's help, maneuvered the Plantagenet van into a choice location. Laurence, Nora, and Bridget ran in and out settling disputes, signing purchase orders, giving interviews. The Johnston children and Winnie hung a banner outside the shop: "Official Borders Festival Souvenirs Here. Open Late." Grant sat in his garden, ostensibly resting and recovering, but in reality keeping an eye on the various reporters who bounced like badminton birdies from hotel to Craft Centre to Festival field and back. D-Day, Rebecca thought, had been less complicated.

After dinner she leaned on the railing of the footbridge, watching white clouds like mounds of meringue float in a sky so blue it made her heart ache. *I can't leave here,* she thought. But then, with or without Michael she wouldn't have to. It was the lack of a job that could drive her away.

A fast-food wrapper floated down the stream. She frowned. "Slob."

"Aye." Mackenzie materialized at her shoulder, carrying Lancelot in the crook of his arm. The cat was obviously torn between enjoying being chauffeured around the sights and having to act suitably disdainful of humans.

"Between the murder and Jenkins's story about the gold," Rebecca said, "half of Britain is here." A bobby escorted several young men carrying metal detectors off the lawn. They gesticulated, complaining in voluble French. "And some of the Continent," she added.

Banners snapped in the wind, the evening sun intensifying the reds and golds, the blues and whites of the Scottish flags. Mackenzie stroked Lancelot, who abandoned all pretense, closed his eyes to slits, and purred.

"Michael played at the Festival last year," Rebecca went on. "There was music, dancing, games—even sheep dog trials." Lancelot looked dubiously upward at the word "dog." "The Festival dates back to the Middle Ages, to a yearly Lammas Fair at the ford in the Gowan. Even into Victorian times young couples would try to catch a glimpse of the ghost, although I gather the object was not to see her. But she doesn't curse lovers, we curse ourselves." The burn chuckled beneath the bridge. The willow branches danced between air and water. "I wish it was over," Rebecca concluded. "Over for Anne, for us, for the killer. But no one's even tried to run away."

Mackenzie set Lancelot down and said, "Run along"—to the cat or to her, Rebecca wasn't sure.

The cat stretched, licked symbolically at the human scent on his fur, then trotted off toward the cottage where Guinevere was sitting on the back porch. On the sidewalk before the hotel Michael and Laurence conferred with a T-shirted man lugging a speaker and a coil of wire. All three heads swiveled to follow a buxom young woman dressed in eighteenth-century garb of the "saucy wench" variety. Laughing, Rebecca, too, headed for the cottage.

She used Mark's knife to cut the bright-colored paper and ribbon with which she wrapped the quaich. As she folded the knife and restored it to her jacket pocket, she resolved to wear the sweater-vest all day long tomorrow. *I owe Michael a decision,* she thought. *He owes me.* Her mouth was sour, as though her dinner salad had been dressed only with vinegar.

She lured the cats back outside with the remaining ribbon and then searched the cottage. No one was hiding under any beds. She locked both doors and walked up to the hotel, where the nightly ceilidh had spilled down the hall into the lobby. She shut herself in Laurence's office and finished transcribing the inventory—silver paten, jeweled chalice, wow—until her eyes spontaneously closed.

That night she dreamed again of silver dishes held aloft by transparent white hands. But the light failed, and hoofbeats rattled the darkness. . . . She awoke to hear rain on the windows. "The Festival!"

"All Scottish functions are waterproofed," said Michael's sleepy voice from the other bed.

"Happy Birthday," she told him. "How's it feel to be thirty?"

He groaned. "Watch oot, I'll be trippin' ower my long gray beard. If you'd hand me my cane, please. . . ."

She threw her pillow at him. The alarm rang. By the time Hilary and Adele washed the breakfast dishes, the rain had stopped, the clouds cleared, and the day was as clean and bright as a child on his first day of school.

Rebecca looked around at elevenses and realized that like Sherlock Holmes's dog that did nothing in the night, Mackenzie, Devlin, and their uniformed cohorts were conspicuous by their absence. After lunch, instead of returning to the barricading operations at the infirmary trench—all they needed was for a tourist to break a leg—she detoured to the hotel and caught Laurence between rushing upstairs with a pot of tea and downstairs with clean linen. "Mackenzie and Devlin checked out, said they'd been called to Edinburgh, some argy-bargy with a cabinet minister. . . . Nora, more loo paper, number seven!"

So we're under surveillance, are we? Rebecca thought waspishly. She wasn't even sure if any plainclothes people were still around. After Jerry called an early end to the day, she asked Michael his opinion.

He stood on the footbridge looking calculatingly from Law to priory to village to cottage. Tony and Elaine disappeared inside the Plantagenet van, Dennis on their heels. Jerry went into the hotel. Hilary stood outside the shop, clutching loaves of bread and fresh vegetables, while Mark kicked a soccer ball for the children. Adele went into the cottage, rolling up her sleeves. Grant strolled across the priory lawn amid the tourists at last allowed to roam freely there. "Look," said Rebecca, "he's wearing one of those radios on his lapel. To keep in touch with Festival security?"

They looked at each other. Mackenzie was a poker player. Right now he had most of his cards face-down. Rebecca didn't appreciate that at all.

"Why," said Michael, "do I feel as though I had a target painted between my shoulder blades?"

The sun slipped down the western sky. The air chilled. No paratroopers or tank convoys appeared with Mackenzie and swagger stick in the lead. They went inside. Michael changed into kilt and sweater.

They ate Hilary's fresh-from-the-can spaghetti dinner, minding their manners like children under the eye of a strict grandmother. Afterwards Rebecca piled the dirty dishes in the sink while Dennis and Adele cleared the table. ". . . business administration," the young man was saying.

"But don't you find history calling to you?" responded Adele.

Michael produced his pipes. "Want to hold them?" he asked Hilary. "Like this, drones on the shoulder."

"They're heavy!" she exclaimed.

Adele went on, "My son started out in political science. But when he was at Oxford, he found the cosmic biorhythms so compelling he took some courses in Roman Britain."

"The place does get to you," Dennis admitted, and added teasingly, "I could always minor in otherworldly experiences, I suppose."

Rebecca peered out the window. No, that figure striding across the priory lawn wasn't Devlin but Tony, applying his light meter to the contrast between sunshine and shadow.

"The pipes are African blackwood," Michael told Hilary. "They were my grandfather's. The older ones have much better tone."

"Aged, like wine or cheese?" asked Mark.

"Exactly."

Adele and Dennis went upstairs, she saying quite seriously, "I know an ashram in Arizona where you can study the two worlds, the seen and the unseen. I'll give you the address."

"Thanks," said Dennis, and rolled his eyes toward Rebecca.

Michael tuned his pipes, trying to play softly, but still eardrums and windows bulged. Within minutes everyone fled. Rebecca hung the towel over the cooker and went into the bedroom. Michael tucked his pipes under his arm and followed. "Are you all right, love?"

"My nerves feel like the hair bristling on Guinevere's back the night she cornered the killer in the bathroom. Sure, I'm fine."

"Come oot to the Festival. Ease your mind."

"In a little while. I want to—to be alone, to think, right now." She could feel his perceptive blue gaze scalding the back of her neck. *He thinks I'm deciding here and now. He's trying to decide here and now.*

"Be sure to lock up," Michael said.

She said, "See you later," but the front door had already shut.

Rebecca searched the house and locked the doors; if anybody wanted in, he could knock and identify himself. She prowled up and down the bedroom, six steps one way, six steps the other. *Think,* she ordered herself. This was ludicrous. There had to be a way out.

Was anyone ever going to catch Jerry cheating? That depended on whether he was also the killer. Why was Anne still around? They'd found her bones but couldn't avenge her—now what? Was she guarding the treasure? If Rebecca found it first, and the RDG gave Michael and her a cut, it would make a good nest egg. . . . She sat down on the bed, biting her lip. People had died for that treasure. It belonged to Rudesburn.

The sun set, and tenuous darkness filled the room. Through the slitted window came snatches of music and a murmur of voices that peaked with the occasional shout or good-natured scream. The shapes that roamed around the priory now were children leaping out and trying to scare each other.

Where is the treasure? Rebecca shouted silently. *Who killed Sheila for it?* The puzzles were interconnected, like an acrostic—solve one to solve the other. But the clues were too damnably subtle.

She bounced up, folded Michael's dirty clothes, and put Colin's dog-eared notepad away. She smoothed the bedspread and picked up her University of Missouri sweatshirt. Its bloodstains were muted to a faint sepia. The blue shirt Michael had been wearing the night he was stabbed was a total loss. What a shame, since sweatshirts were practical, comfortable garments. Even Adele kept one of her son's like a holy relic.

The shirt dropped from Rebecca's nerveless fingers. Christopher Garrity, Adele's son, had studied Roman Britain at Oxford. Sheila had done a television documentary on Boadicea, the scourge of Roman Britain. Chris had killed himself. Sheila was capable of driving a young man to suicide. Yes!

No. Rebecca sat abruptly down again. Adele had already been on her way to Scotland when Sheila signed on to the dig. Unlike Dennis tracking Jerry, Adele couldn't have tracked Sheila. And yet, cosmic biorhythms being what they were, a meeting wouldn't have been entirely accidental—Adele and Sheila moved in the same circle of historians and students and fringe newspapers. Not a yes, not a no. A maybe.

Rebecca pounded her temples with her fists. She felt as though her brain were carbonated, her thoughts bubbling and breaking as she tried to seize them.

Surely she had to reject Adele as the perpetrator for the same reason she'd rejected Dennis. Why on earth would either of them try to kill Guinevere? That the person who'd attacked Guinevere was the one who was after the treasure was proved by the cat's reaction to the figure in the bathroom. The treasure, not revenge, was the motive. Sure, a woman with an ultra-suede pantsuit and a Hermes scarf might want even more money. . . .

Rebecca leaped from the bed and raced upstairs. It could be—it had to be. It took her five minutes to find the letters in the bedside table. She knew she'd seen at least two from that ashram; here were two more. The most recent read, "Thank you for your contribution. Your generosity is much appreciated. Upon receipt of the rest of your pledged amount, we will name the new contemplation center the Christopher Garrity Memorial Pavilion."

Certainty cascaded through Rebecca's mind. Maybe Adele had been after Sheila. Maybe she'd found out about Sheila's search for the treasure and thought it would be poetic justice to find it herself and buy her son, Sheila's victim, a memorial. Maybe Sheila had never laid eyes on Chris Garrity. It didn't matter. It all came back to the treasure. And that came back to the clues in the tomb.

Beneath the pile of letters was a leaflet describing the Ruthwell Cross. Adele had stopped there on her way back from Whithorn. "The Dream of the Rood" was carved in runes on the Ruthwell Cross. The psychic power of stones, Adele was fond of saying.

"Come on," said Rebecca aloud. "Adele's an amateur. I'm a professional, and if I can't figure this out, I ought to be flogged with a typewriter ribbon." Swearing, she tucked the letter and the leaflet in her pocket and ran back downstairs. She pulled Michael's attaché case from under the bed, opened it, and dumped out the contents. There was the picture of him standing next to the wheel-cross. There was the extra page from Pringle's history of Rudesburn. Robert the Bruce, he of the wandering heart, had set up the second cross on the Law. Not so much as one verse from the "Dream" had ever been recorded on either cross.

And yet Anne had written the verses and drawn the pattern of crosses and wavy lines twice. Rebecca frowned—dammit, still all she could see in that drawing was a knitting pattern. It was an optical illusion. Everything was an optical illusion. She was still in that hotel room in Ayr, dreaming the entire scenario with its interlocking conspiracies and clashing personalities. Soon the phone would ring, and Colin would tell her about Sheila.

Colin. The wheel-cross. Not the poem, but its title—the rood itself. Rebecca grabbed Michael's address book and her jacket and headed for the hotel.

The spotlights at the Festival field were so bright the rest of the village was pitch-black by comparison. At least two sets of bagpipes and three electric guitars launched into "Scotland the Brave." Voices cheered. Although shadowy figures surged up and down the sidewalk, the hotel was deserted. A young waiter drummed his fingers at reception, obviously not thrilled to have been assigned guard duty.

"Come on," she said under her breath as she dialed the telephone, "be home, be sitting there admiring your Trooping of the Colors. . . ."

"Hello, MacLeod here."

"Colin? It's Rebecca, at Rudesburn."

"Well then, how's it goin'?"

"Sorry, I don't have time to even begin to explain. Just answer one question, please. Is the wheel-cross outside the west door of the church carved out of rock from Battle Law? Is the cross on Battle Law cut out of the same stuff?"

"That's two questions, lass. But aye, that they are. The Law is an igneous intrusion. Whinstone, it's called, extra hard, resists weatherin', though a right bugger to carve back then, I suppose."

Rebecca tapped the receiver against her temple. The rocks. The Law. The treasure. Anne. She couldn't quite see it. Like the case against Adele, it just wasn't all there yet.

Motive, but not opportunity. Adele had been seen in the cemetery at eight. She said she'd walked through the village at 8:15. That was hardly enough time to find Sheila and drag her into the church. If only there were a few more moments unaccounted for, time enough to kill.

Colin was talking. With an effort Rebecca tuned in. "Anjali liked the bear with the wellies—thank Michael for the advice. And the wee Queen looks a treat on the mantel. A good thing it was an important day for the shopkeeper, or I'd never have been able to afford it.'

A bubble burst in the back of Rebecca's mind. A cool spray of inspiration washed the dust of preconception from her thoughts. The shopkeeper had closed early the night of the wedding, the same night Sheila was killed. What if, in the excitement of the day, he hadn't wound the clock in his store window? What if it had stopped at eight? That would explain Bridget's thinking Rebecca had come into the Craft Centre later than eight. She had.

"Wish Michael a happy birthday for me," said Colin with a chuckle. "Ring me back when you're ready to visit."

"Sorry, Colin. I will. Soon." She hung up and sat with her hand on the phone, her eyes slightly crossed. *I saw Elaine. I saw Laurence. I saw Winnie. . . .* She ran from the office into the shop and danced impatiently while Winnie sold three cans of Citrus Spring and a roll of biscuits.

"Oh, aye," she answered Rebecca's breathless question. "I was shakin' a rug from the window when you walked by. It was eight-fifteen, right enough. The telly was just changin' programs, and I couldna decide between 'The A-Team' and 'The Brothers Karamazov,' so I turned it off."

There it was. Methodical Colin and his notepad had just missed it—Winnie Johnston hadn't attended the inquest, and none of the people who had questioned her since then had known what specific question to ask her.

An adrenaline rush, Rebecca decided, was right up there with a glass of good Scotch. She thanked Winnie and plunged back into the night. The band was playing "Maggie Lauder." Whoops emanated from the Festival grounds. A huge orange moon was a carnival mask peering over the eastern horizon. Several people stood warily along the perimeter fence, but the priory itself was still and silent, its lawns a dark velvet pall. Children ran from the safety of the lights into the darkness and back like swimmers testing cold water. *I'm a fool*, Rebecca thought. *I should've seen it all along.*

But it was an optical illusion; one had to look at it from the right angle. Even Mackenzie had never seen the angle of the letter and the leaflet that crinkled in her pocket as she strode across the New Bridge. Adele hadn't walked through the village at eight-fifteen. Rebecca had been there, and she hadn't seen so much as one of Adele's gray hairs.

With mingled rage and elation she told herself, *I have them now, motive and opportunity, and I'm going to give a damned good go at the treasure, too.* That tile floor around the broken cross, that would do nicely for a start. She was going to end this charade, once and for all. She was going to end it now.

Chapter Twenty-Eight

"TAKE THOUGHT FOR the morrow," Rebecca repeated under her breath. She liked Anne's version. Nothing happened in a vacuum.

A wave ran through the people ranged along the perimeter wall, paper cups of beer going down, heads coming up, children recalled. A white shape flicked across the streamers of light and shadow the Festival spotlights sent across the lawn. Anne, Rebecca wondered, or Adele?

The shape disappeared into the cloister. A mutter of excitement ran through the watchers, like spectators at a football game commenting on an interesting play. Adele had read the notes on the inscriptions. She might be one jump ahead. . . . *No,* Rebecca called silently to the invisible figure, *you don't deserve the relics Anne died for. I won't let you steal them.*

She plunged into the Festival, elbowed her way past a booth selling pungent meat pies and sausages, dodged around one offering cassette tapes, and darted between a couple dressed in full sixteenth-century finery. The faces of the crowd seemed to stretch and smear like balloons. There was Michael at center stage playing "Highland Laddie" to the accompaniment of two lasses with accordions. The lights were in his eyes—he'd never see her in this crowd. If she waited for him to finish, she thought, she'd lose Adele.

One part of her mind wanted to solve the mystery without him—that would serve him right. Another part of her mind knew that that would be cutting off her nose to spite her face. He had said, "I want you to make a decision you can live with." She couldn't live with playing damsel-in-distress. If she solved the mystery alone, then she'd made her decision. Her elation ebbed into a desperate resolve.

Mark and Hilary were clapping time in the front row. Grant was sauntering along with his hands folded quietly behind his back, his expression abstracted, as if he had a stomach ache. No need to disturb them yet. Rebecca fought her way to the Plantagenet van. Dennis stood on the step, two still cameras draped around his neck, the video camera on his shoulder. The whirring of sound equipment contributed to the din of music and voices, and she had to shout. "When Michael gets done playing, tell him I've gone into the priory. Do you have a flashlight in there?"

"Sure, but why—"

She leaped up the step and grabbed the flashlight from its bracket. "Adele's the killer. I'm going after her."

"But she has Michael's knife!"

"I'm only going to follow her until she does whatever she's going to do and goes back to the cottage. Then we'll call Grant. Don't worry—I'm younger than she is. Angrier, too, if not quite as crazy. I'll watch out."

Away from the crush the breeze was cleaner and cooler. Rebecca brushed by the goggle-eyed faces along the wall and hurried across the grass. Gasps of awe followed her. She turned and curtseyed to her audience. She rounded the corner of the church and stopped, blinking. Like when Jenkins turned off the lights in the crypt, the contrast between light and dark was absolute. But until she knew where Adele was, she didn't dare turn on the flashlight.

She picked her way across the cloister, into the south transept door, and up the tower's spiral staircase. The hollowed steps were treacherous in broad daylight; at night they were deadly. She braced her hands against either wall, feeling her way upward with fingertips and toes. Grit and fuzzy lichen crawled over her fingers. The chill wind, channeled through the narrow passage, raised the hair on the back of her neck.

Something white leaped out at her and with a rush knocked her backward. Strangling a cry, she fell. Her knees and elbows jarred against cold, hard stone. Her hands clawed at a projecting rock and stopped her plunge. She huddled against the wall, catching her breath.

She'd frightened the owl. That hadn't been draperies but beating wings. She laughed, as much to keep herself from screaming as because it was funny. Her leg hurt, wrenched the wrong way. Her bruised shoulder twinged. Her fingers were scraped raw. She reminded herself how angry she was; anger was stronger than fear.

Rebecca hobbled up the staircase. She strained to hear something, anything—a laugh, or steps behind her, or the elusive chanting that emanated from the stones of the priory itself. All she heard were voices and music from the field. She recognized Michael's touch on a pipe solo and mouthed the words, "Amazing grace, how sweet the sound, that saved a wretch like me . . . ."

She was at the top of the tower. Through the eastern window slit was the pallid face of the moon, riding higher now, its light tinting the clouds around it. Below her the priory grounds lay cool and mysterious, dappled with shadow. A white shape glided beside the infirmary. Was that Adele, acting out her fantasies of love and revenge? Or was it Anne?

"I once was lost, but now am found . . ." Cold spilled over her. Rebecca spun away from the window. On the staircase glimmered a swirl of draperies. "Where did you hide it, mother prioress?" she whispered. "On the Law?"

The gleam was gone. Rebecca edged back to the window. Darkness, and the white shape—Adele—moving over the lawn. The moon was so bright it would have cast a shadow, but the Festival lights swallowed its light in their own. The shadow of the tower stretched south toward Battle Law. In the summer, the sun was in the north. The English came to Rudesburn in the summer.

"Was blind, but now can see." Rebecca clutched at the windowsill. The tower, the straight line of Anne's cryptic drawing. The wavy line, the Law. The two crosses were made of stone from the Law. In Anne's time, the broken cross had been intact.

The shadow of the tower touched an outcropping of rock on the west side of the hill, a mound of stone and gorse that had once been a low barmkin wall, not far from where she and Michael had sat the day they'd found the warrant. If the tower and the crosses made a triangle, a plumb bob dropped from the apex would touch that outcropping. Anne must have been a latent archeologist. Rebecca grimaced in triumph—she knew she'd been on the right track.

But first she had to follow poor sick Adele, who was drifting toward Battle Law as slowly and ceremoniously as a priest in a religious procession. Worshipping a golden calf, no doubt. Rebecca started down the stairs. Michael began playing "The Flowers o' the Forest." The music was high and clear, bright and bittersweet.

She muffled the beam of her flashlight in her jacket and took one step at a time. Someone slow on the uptake was still singing "Amazing Grace." A rat scrabbled in the church. Once outside she turned off the light and, wincing, started around the buildings. She felt eyes watching her. She knew she felt eyes watching her. It was just the atmosphere of the priory, she told herself, and scuttled toward the inky bulk of the Law.

The priory buildings blocked the Festival lights, leaving only the moonlight to spangle the Law's rocks and leaves. Rebecca slipped behind a ruined wall and crouched, catching her breath. Where had Adele gone?

If she called everyone now, she thought, they'd come shouting and waving flashlights. Adele would do what she'd done so many times before, slip quietly into the hotel or the church and pretend she'd been there all along. No. She had to do this by herself.

Rebecca climbed toward the outcropping. She thought she heard a quick scrape above her. She stopped, willing her heart to stop pounding so loudly. Nothing. She moved on.

Each scuff of her sneakers against stone was the thud of a kettle drum. Each brush of her jeans against a branch was cymbals clashing. Her own breath was a banshee's wail. Still she climbed. The outcropping of the Law was a jagged line against the night, just above her. A cloud drifted over the moon.

The shadows were so dense she could see nothing. If Adele had worn black, instead of masquerading as the ghost—or as Sheila, her victim—now that was an interesting twist of psychology. . . .

Hands grabbed her. Involuntarily Rebecca's breath expelled itself in a scream. The sound was weak and ineffectual, absorbed by the stones and underbrush and the distant music. Damn—she was following me!

One of the hands crushed her mouth. The arm pinning hers was clothed in black. *She read my mind,* Rebecca thought. But the arm wrapping her waist and the body pressed against her back were not those of a woman.

"Bloody hell!" she shouted. The words were smothered. She twisted, jackknifing violently, but the grasp was incredibly strong. Her feet kicked backward at the man who held her, outward at the slippery rocks. Her feet struck a stone. Bracing herself, she pushed backward.

Together she and her assailant fell. She rolled to the side, crashed into a gorse bush, and clawed her way through it. Through the branches she looked back. He wore black beneath white, a Benedictine, not a Cistercian . . . What difference did that make?

His robes were floating loosely, giving him birdlike wings. The cold gleam in his hand was a knife. This one wasn't a piece of the hotel's pewter tableware. This one was razor-sharp.

Just as Rebecca regained her feet, the moon shone out again. The man's face was a puppet from a Punch and Judy show, teeth clenched, eyes dark and bulging. Tony. It was Tony. *Oh for the love of* . . . Rebecca didn't complete her oath. She lunged down the hill, tripped, and fell.

He was on top of her, one hand on her throat, the sgian dubh shining in the corner of her eye. "Stupid female," he said. His breath was foul with acid and beer. His knee ground into her stomach. "All cozy with the peelers, aren't you? Such a good girl. So clever. Women, they're only good for one thing, and thinking isn't it."

She had too little breath to waste in a retort—even if she could have thought of something more effective than, "Oh, yeah?" Something was digging into her side. A rock. No, Mark's Swiss Army knife. Slowly she edged her hand toward her pocket.

The sgian dubh glittered, blinding her. Tony's face was only a misshapen lump against the sky. "Miss-bloody-Doctor Reid. I kept waiting for you to lead me to the treasure, but no, just like a woman, ponce here, ponce there, do sod-all. You'll show me now, though, you worthless bint."

"Let me up," she gasped, trying to sound calm and quiet. "I'll show you." Either the music had stopped, or her blood cascading through her ears had blanked it out. Her hand touched the handle of Mark's knife.

Tony didn't move. "Sheila was going to do me over. She and Kleinfelter, they were going to nick the goods. She was showing him the coins. My coin."

"You stole it from the hotel?"

"I sussed out the place for her. I helped her, and there she was chatting up Kleinfelter. I don't need her. I'll have the treasure without her. Gormless female." His words seared Rebecca's face.

Between his knee in her stomach and his hand on her throat Rebecca couldn't breathe. She tried to think herself into two dimensions. Her hand drew the knife slowly from her pocket and opened it. With her luck, she'd pull out the bottle opener. "Let me up. I'll show you where the treasure is."

He didn't move. She wondered if the treasure was still his motivation, or if by now he was frustrated into wanting only revenge. . . .

Shouts echoed across the hillside, "Cruachan!" and "Remember the Alamo!" Dim shapes rushed forward, wielding lights. Tony glanced up, his grip slackening for an instant.

That was enough. Rebecca struck. The blade of the Swiss Army knife was small, but it bit deep. Tony jerked and howled. A solid thwack burst in Rebecca's head. The sgian dubh glinted. She wrenched away from it, every muscle contracting at once. The blade scraped the side of her head. Tony was plucked magically away from her, and she lay stunned, staring up at the moon. Its silvery eye stared impassively back. It was a hole in the darkness, opening to light and warmth. The night drained into that eye . . .

Another set of hands seized her. But these were familiar hands, with long fingers and slender wrists. They shook her, and her teeth rattled. "Rebecca, dinna go wi'oot me, love, never go wi'oot me again."

She focused on Michael's agonized face. No wonder she'd heard someone shout "Cruachan!"—the old Campbell war cry. And the other . . . Her hand still held the small knife, her fingers warm and wet. Mark was prying it away from her. "You scared the hell out of us. I'm sure glad you had this."

Rebecca looked at her hand. It was covered with blood. Her hair was sticky. "Don't let me bleed on your sweater," she said.

Michael emitted a barking laugh. Carefully he and Mark stood her up. She wobbled like a rag doll. Someone gently patted her head with a cloth.

People were shouting. Flashlights zigzagged like demented fireflies up and down the hill. A constable and a man in sixteenth-century doublet and hose dragged Tony to his feet. He staggered and spat, "Go ahead, knock me about, that's all you sodding police know, isn't it?" Strips of his own white robe wrapped his middle and supported his arm in a makeshift sling. Only then did Rebecca's mind resolve an after-image: She'd struck Tony with her knife just as Michael, in his kilted rage an English nightmare, brought a shovel down on Tony's arm. "You saved my life," she mumbled.

"You saved yoursel'," Michael returned. The music of pipes, flutes, and guitars made an incongruously cheerful background: "Hey Johnnie Cope are ye waukin' yet? Or are your drums a-beatin' yet? If ye were waukin' I would wait, To gang to the coals i' the mornin'."

There at long last were Mackenzie and Devlin, shining their lights in Tony's face as if they were going to give him the third degree here and now. "Bloody berks," he said, and added a few more choice descriptions. "I want a solicitor. It's my right, you have to find me a solicitor."

"I'll recommend one," Mackenzie told him in a flat voice. He turned toward Rebecca. "I must apologize, Dr. Reid. This time our trap worked altogether too well. Rest assured we had you under surveillance the entire time."

"You didna have tae use her as bait," Michael growled.

She shook her head. "The other night I volunteered to be bait. And I certainly wasn't hiding in a closet tonight."

"You went off wi'oot me," said Michael. His accusing voice was so obviously concealing sheer terror that she hugged him even tighter.

Mackenzie said, "I think the pub would be a better place for debriefing. Get the doctor to look at her head."

Several strong men hustled Tony down the hill. Caught between a shout and a sob, his voice cursed the police and the worldwide feminine conspiracy that had kept him from his just rewards. "What's so wrong about me having a few quid— everyone else gets it all—everyone else has all they want. . . ."

"Not necessarily," Rebecca whispered. In a year or so, she thought, she might begin to feel sympathy for him.

She looked over the shadowed priory and beyond it to the multicolored lamps of the Festival. The cold blue lights of police cars edged the street for the last time. She was trembling, cold, and nauseated. She apologized. Mark and Michael made soothing noises. Between them they got her down the hill and onto the smooth lawn. "I thought it was Adele," she told them.

"You're daft," said Michael. "I knew it was Tony. That's why I brought the shovel."

Indignantly, Rebecca demanded, "All right, Dr. Know-it-all, just when did you figure that out?"

"Aboot ten minutes ago," he admitted. "Dennis fetched me—

in a proper state, he was—but we had to wait for Grant to knock up Mackenzie. That was when I noticed Dennis was wearin' his Star Trek T-shirt.''

''Yes?'' said Rebecca cautiously. Mark grinned.

Michael raised an admonitory forefinger. ''You remember the episode wi' the wee purrin' fuzzballs that flyte at people they dislike? Well, a few days ago, when we were in the pub, one of the cats hissed and yowled. Then I thought Tony'd stepped on a paw or a tail. Tonight I thought, what if Guinevere'd hissed at Tony because he'd tried to drown her?''

Rebecca stopped dead, pulling both Mark and Michael around with her. ''You're the one who's daft! I could've told you Guinevere was hissing at the person who'd tried to kill her. Why else was she hissing that night we caught the killer—Tony—in the attic?''

''I was a wee bit distracted that night.'' Michael avoided a stone concealed in the grass. ''You remember Colin askin' people what other people were doin' the night of the murder, tryin' to catch someone oot? I asked Dennis aboot Tony. This time he said he went into the camera van at seven forty-five, to search for evidence against Jerry, and that he'd been there thirty minutes afore Tony got there.''

Yes, of course—with the clock stopped, Rebecca had heard their voices at eight-fifteen instead of . . . ''In Colin's notes from the inquest they both said they'd got there at eight! And I thought they had!''

''Dennis was hidin' his identity from Jerry, so he agreed wi' Tony's estimate of the time. Tony didna ken what Dennis kent. Dennis didna ken—until I told him the night. And then I told Mackenzie.''

Rats, Rebecca thought. Why didn't it ever occur to her to use the cat as a geiger counter? She said, ''Colin was right—someone did know something. Dennis. And Winnie, too—no one ever asked her what time she'd seen me from the window. Well done, Michael.''

''Thank you kindly. Noo if I'd only tumbled two weeks ago . . .''

A set of blue lights vanished toward Galashiels. The mob lining the road issued forth a solitary figure. ''Mark? Rebecca?''

''Here we are, Hilary,'' Mark called. ''She's all right.''

Hilary came running. ''Jerry's getting drunk at the beer pavilion. Dennis is filming the dancers. Nobody's seen Elaine or Adele for a couple of hours, and Grant's afraid—''

"That Tony was oot the night eliminatin' witnesses?'' Michael finished.

Rebecca's teeth were chattering. She unclenched them long enough to say, "I heard something when I was in the tower. Try the crypt.''

Michael and Rebecca, Mark and Hilary, huddled in the nave while flashlights swept dust and shadows from the stone tracery. The key gone, the police had to break the lock on the crypt door. The screech of the crowbar and the thud of the door opening echoed from the vaults like Armageddon.

Adele sat on the steps, her hands folded, waiting for rescue or death, whichever came first. Her cracked voice was still singing "Amazing Grace" as a constable walked her toward the ambulance; her eyes, drained of rationality, shone as pale and clear as though they no longer had pupils.

Elaine was carried out on a stretcher. Her fingernails were ripped and bloody from tearing at the door, and her face was swollen with terrified tears. "Hysterical claustrophobia," explained the doctor. "She'll be all right. Let me tend to you, too, Miss Reid.''

At the hotel the doctor checked her over and pronounced her alive and well, if bruised, contused, and looking like a scarecrow dripping moss and heather. At last she could wash her face and hands. Bloody hands. Self-defense. Her hands weren't as bloody as Tony's. As Tony's would have been—he'd no doubt intended to come back and finish off Elaine and Adele.

Rebecca assumed the face staring from the mirror was hers, even though she didn't quite recognize it. Her features sagged like elastic stretched to the limit. She limped into the pub, her head floating a foot or so above her shoulders as though her brain were a helium balloon.

Two tables had been shoved together in front of a roaring fire. Mackenzie presided, with Laurence and Nora anchoring the other end. Mark's and Hilary's laps were adorned by the carts, whose eager whiskers above the edge of the table gave them the air of third world countries admitted to the General Assembly. Michael seated Rebecca and gave her a glass of whiskey. Her hand was shaking so hard that the liquid almost slopped over. She drank deep, coughed, and said, "You people certainly have a way with alcohol.''

"In this climate, we need dependable anti-freeze." Michael took her free hand and chafed it between his own. Slowly her body began to relax and warm up.

"You look as if you've been dragged through a barbed-wire fence backwards," said Mark cheerfully.

"I feel like it," Rebecca returned. "But the stab wound is just a scratch; my hair covers the bandage."

Michael was cleaner, but his own face was as drained by strong emotion as hers. It might be foolish to be glad she hadn't single-handedly solved the murder, but she was. She didn't even have enough energy to be embarrassed over her hasty conclusion about Adele. She hiccuped with love and remorse, and visualized little hearts appearing above her head.

Bridget served sandwiches. Even Mackenzie claimed his fair share. Rebecca glanced at his profile, like Julius Caesar surveying the field after a hard-fought battle. What price victory?

The stolen notebooks lay on the table, their pages blotted and ripped with frustration, their message too subtle. "They were under Tony's mattress," said Mackenzie. "His light meter was outwith the crypt. He lured Elaine and Adele there with a story about photographs."

"If only he'd waited a few more days," Nora said, "he could've taken his photos and films and left with the rest of you."

"And the treasure?" Mark asked. "Surely he realized if he ran off with it he'd have to break it up—that he wouldn't get near its value."

"It was Sheila," said Laurence, "who would've been sophisticated enough to make a packet from the publicity as well as the intrinsic value of the plate and jewels. She was going to smile to our faces and stab us in the back. . . ." He looked suddenly down into his gin.

"Is there a treasure?" Mackenzie asked.

Rebecca replied, "Anne hid something. I only tonight figured out where." A log fell in the fire, sending a spray of sparks upward. Two pairs of gold feline eyes blinked gravely. Everyone else stared. "Oh! Well, you see . . ." Laboriously Rebecca went through her reasoning about Adele's guilt and the location of the treasure inextricably intertwined. "Come tomorrow," she concluded, "we'll see if I'm wrong about the treasure, too."

Michael had her hand in his lap, nestled in a warm fold of wool. She wanted to nestle her entire body into his kilt. That was not as risqué a concept as it sounded, she thought with a smile; the original kilts were made of umpty-ump yards of fabric that could serve as pup tents as well as clothing.

"The name of Christopher Garrity's girlfriend is in the records. She wasn't even British." Mackenzie picked up another quarter-sandwich and peered inside. "Mrs. Garrity was a spanner in the works, no doubt about it. We'll see she gets back to her family in the States."

Devlin walked wearily into the room. He slumped next to Mackenzie and laid a plastic bag containing Michael's sgian dubh on the table. "Will you be wantin' it back, Michael?"

"Good lord, no. I ordered it from a shop in Edinburgh—I wanted one that would take an edge . . ." He grimaced. "But it was made in England—it probably had a curse on it."

"It has a curse on it now," murmured Hilary.

After a long moment's silence, Mackenzie extended a long arm and swept the weapon away. The cats' eyes vanished below the rim of the table. They padded toward the hearth and proceeded to lick themselves down.

"Charges are murder, attempted murder, assault, theft, and cruelty to animals," Devlin said between swallows of beer. "Tony bought that white robe from a theatrical supply shop in Newcastle. It has traces of bloodstains. The lab'll find them to be Sheila's, I'm sure. He'd been hidin' the robes in his bed, or in the camera van—several places. And the dagger's been everywhere. He thought it particularly amusin' that part of the time it was in the wee trolley car on yon mantelpiece."

Every eye turned toward the fireplace. Even the cats looked up. Mackenzie swore under his breath, thinking, no doubt, that if a man wanted a search done well, he had to do it himself.

"We found blood on one of Tony's tripods," Devlin went on. "He admitted coshin' P.C. Johnston and you, Hilary." She smiled weakly. Mark gave her a reassuring hug. "He admitted stealin' the coin and the warrant from the hotel, droppin' the matchbook in the attic—Sheila'd been usin' it for a notepad—and vandalizin' the tomb. He also hid the coin and the warrant in the grave. Sheila knew they were there."

"We almost caught Tony the first day we were here," Rebecca moaned.

Michael said, "Twenty-twenty hindsight."

Devlin took the last sandwich. "The night he stabbed you, he slipped Elaine a sleepin' pill. She wasn't his accomplice, just none too bright. Neither was Jenkins—he didn't realize he was

causin' a diversion for Tony the other night. And Tony did think
it was Rebecca workin' in the cottage.''

Between Michael's ministrations and the whiskey, Rebecca
was no longer cold. Warmth rippled up her spine and onto her
cheeks, so that they burned. Her aches and pains quieted into
remote annoyances.

"It was Tony wearin' his own robes who scared Sheila that
same evenin' she was killed. He hadn't intended to kill her, he
says, but he saw her and Jerry comparin' the coin he'd stolen
with the one from the London shop. He reckoned they were
goin' to do him over, and confronted Sheila after Jerry left. She
had the sgian dubh; she told him to—well, commit an anatomi-
cally impossible act. He lost his temper and wrestled the knife
away from her.''

The fire emitted a long sigh. Voices echoed from the lobby,
overlaid by revving car and bus engines. Rebecca saw by a glance
at her watch that it was past midnight. Quietly Nora shut the
door.

"Tony hadn't even had time to realize what he'd done when
he heard footsteps,'' Devlin continued. "He retrieved the knife
but not the coins. He only found out a few days ago that it was
Adele who moved the body—and she who stole the ring and the
brooch before he could. He wondered what she knew. And what
Elaine knew, as well.''

"Adele must have been very confused,'' said Hilary, "to find
Sheila in that white habit, dead. She probably thought it was
Anne and tried to help her. You know those flowers behind the
chapter house? I bet Adele was leaving them for Anne, not
Sheila.''

Mark said, "Tony's mistake was to lose patience with Sheila.
He kept getting more and more frustrated trying to carry on by
himself. Why else attack Guinevere? And Grant and Hilary? No
matter how cool he was on top, underneath he was getting desperate.''

"He'd spent his entire life perfecting that good-natured facade,'' Nora said with a sigh.

"I canna blame him,'' said Michael, "for goin' round the
twist at last.''

"He hated women,'' Rebecca added. "Even when he used
Sheila and Elaine, even when he tried to use me, he hated us
all.''

"That he did.'' Devlin drained his glass and set it down with

a thunk. "And he said he was sick of bein' poor. I pointed out
that most of us could use a rise in income, but we don't steal
and kill and vandalize. He laughed at me, asked me what I
thought Kleinfelter was doin'."

"Oh, God," Rebecca moaned. "Jerry."

"In a way," said Michael, "Tony did kill Sheila by mistake,
like he attacked the wrong cat. If Jerry'd been perfectly honest,
Tony might never have thought he and Sheila were plannin' to
do him ower."

"I don't know whether Jerry came here for the relic heart or
the treasure," Mark said, "but I bet by the time Sheila got her
hooks into him, he wanted both, just as greedy for money as for
academic glory."

Hilary added, "A lot of successful men think they're above
the law."

"Jerry?" said Grant's voice from the door. "He's fair potted
the noo. Had to charge him wi' drunk and disorderly. He's sleepin' it off in the storeroom behind the shop."

"Closest thing Rudesburn has to a jail," Laurence explained,
and pulled out a chair for the bobby. Grant declined, and went
off yawning.

The yawn was infectious. Everyone gaped in chorus, like baby
birds begging for food. The cats climbed onto a bench and with
many pawings and stretchings went to sleep. Mackenzie pushed
back his chair. "Would it help if we charged Dr. Kleinfelter
with withholding evidence? He never did tell us Miss Fitzgerald
was showing him the coins—afraid we'd connect him with her
scheme, I imagine."

"I'm afraid Jerry is our problem," answered Rebecca.

"And one we'll be settlin' right and proper." Michael's smile
had the glint of a claymore in it.

"Right." Mackenzie offered his hand to Rebecca. "I apologize, Dr. Reid, for not taking you into our confidence. Our first
trap failed because too many people knew about it. I thought a
second trap, which no one knew about, might work. We didn't
expect you to force the issue like you did—we'd simply staked
out the grounds, hoping the killer would walk into our arms."

"And he did," Devlin added. "Between your and Michael's
work tonight, Rebecca, we now have enough evidence to con-
vict."

Rebecca returned Mackenzie's cool, dry handclasp, amused
by the satisfaction in his dark eyes. She was too glad to see the

end of the mystery to be resentful of being used—not that she was going to let him know that. "The reason I was in danger, Chief Inspector, is because you had taken me into your confidence. Tony couldn't decide which was more important, that I was a threat to him or the route to the treasure." She heard, smelled, tasted again those words spattering her face like acid, but she'd expended all her shudders.

"Thank you for your cooperation," Devlin said. The two detectives strolled away, headed back to Galashiels and the Mount Everest of paperwork awaiting them.

They all stood watching the empty doorway. It was as if Devlin and Mackenzie had been magnets raked through a pile of iron filings, pulling everyone and everything into the same pattern. But now they were gone. For a moment Rebecca was confused, uncertain in which direction to turn. Then Michael took her hand, and she knew.

Chapter Twenty-Nine

MICHAEL AND MARK opened the lobby doors for Rebecca and Hilary. They stepped out into cool, fresh darkness. Rudesburn dozed. Only the porch lights of the cottage still shone; Dennis's own exploits must have worn him out. The moonlight enchanted the priory into stone lace. A white shape glistened briefly inside the church and then vanished.

Inside the cottage, Mark and Hilary tiptoed upstairs. Michael and Rebecca stood in their bedroom looking at each other.

"I told you it was a' quite simple," he said.

"You did no such thing."

"It was no so complicated as you had it. You forgot Occam's Razor."

"We," she emphasized, "forgot to be a team. That's why it got complicated." She gathered up her toiletries and a towel. "Did you mean what you said, about my never going anywhere without you again?"

"Aye, that I did."

His brows and mouth were set in the wry, alert angle that defined Michael. His hands rested on his hips, his chin thrust forward. She reached into her dresser drawer and handed him the gift-wrapped package. "We're lucky, you know, to have almost lost each other. That kind of shock really cuts through the illusion. Happy Birthday. I love you."

She fled into the bathroom, not bothering to turn on the light. Moonlight suited her grainy eyes much better. She brushed her teeth and was gingerly soaping herself in the shower when Michael's voice asked, "Room for one more?" Before she could invite him in, he was standing with her in the warm cascade of water, clasping her tightly to himself from thorax to thigh, his toothpaste-scented breath bathing her face. Her bruises purred instead of protesting. "Thank you for the quaich, love. We'll share a dram at the weddin'."

"Our wedding?" she asked.

"Should we have a go at it? We can try tae no be so defensive, eh? A' we can do is try—naething's certain."

"No. Yes. I mean . . ." His hands stroked her back. Her nerves weren't stunned into insensibility after all, but stretched and preened like a cat's. Common sense fled, and she groped after it. "My salary runs out in September. I can cash in my plane ticket, and I have a savings account back in the States, but . . ."

"Mmm?" he asked, nibbling her neck.

"Listen to me!" She smeared suds over his chest.

Reluctantly he backed a hairsbreadth away. "Aye?"

"I don't have a job here. It's like I told you last winter, if I didn't get my Ph.D. I didn't want to blame it on you. If I end up waitressing or clerking in a department store, I don't want to blame you. I don't want to be jealous of your job."

Shadows, no longer threatening, softened his face. Water streamed down his shoulders, glistening in the silvery light. "I'll talk tae Graham the morn. Maybe we can share the same job."

"What?" She dropped the soap.

He retrieved it and put it in its dish. "He'll need two workers tae sift through the data frae this dig."

"But only one salary?"

"It's a place tae start. We've been cheese-parin' a' our lives. If we canna manage, who can?"

"You're a lunatic."

"Aye, that I am. For lovin' you." He turned off the water and started rubbing her down with the towel, gently, in deference to her collection of aches and pains. "Are you tired, lass?"

"Aren't you? You're a whole day over thirty."

"Come tae bed, and I'll show you thirty."

The house was dark and so quiet Rebecca could hear the breeze in the willow trees and the laughter of the stream. The bedsheets were cool. Michael's skin was warm. "No, it's not complicated," she murmured. "All we have to do is love each other."

"It's settled, then," he whispered against her lips.

"Yes." Like water running down a drain, fear, pain, and doubt spiraled away into the darkness and disappeared.

Rebecca swam out of unconsciousness the next morning to find herself entangled not only with the bedclothes, but also with Michael. She smiled; their reunion last night had been more tender and more clumsy than their reunion in June. Then they'd been separated only by distance.

Michael pried open an eye. Slowly reality registered. "You're a' right then? I didna hurt you?"

"Unorthodox treatment for cuts and bruises," she told him, "but effective. I feel great. Let's go get Jerry's head on a pike."

"Then, my Amazon, I'd best be gettin' mysel' and Anne to Edinburgh." And get himself to Edinburgh he did, leading the rental lorry with its macabre burden of bones and foam rubber into the clear morning light.

Rebecca went back to the infirmary trench with only part of her mind on the tile floor and connected drain. The future wasn't as simple as moonlit delirium had made it seem. If nothing happened in a vacuum, neither was anything felt in a vacuum. Living on love was a nice beginning, but all too often the wolf at the door delivered reality C.O.D. Even so, Michael was right. They had a place to start. They had to try.

It was almost noon when she carried yet another bucket of dirt to the spoil heap behind the chapter house and glanced toward the cottage. All right! The red Fiat was just turning into the driveway. Rebecca dropped the bucket and ran. Laurence appeared from the church. Grant, wearing civvies as befit his assignment as dig assistant, and Dennis carried an array of cameras around the dormitory.

"Tally-ho!" Michael called. He skirted a group of tourists and nodded to Bridget, this morning's Little Bo Peep.

"Tally-ho?" Rebecca asked. "What did you get from Graham?"

He pulled a box from his pocket. "Permission to finish this farce, and a belt buckle and chape from the dig at Berwick to flush oot the dirty fox. Sixteenth-century bronze. Jerry'll fancy these, right enough, but it's no important enough for him to get the wind up."

The metal pieces were still encrusted with dirt and their own greenish patina. "A chape?" asked Dennis. "Oh, the hunk of metal that goes on the opposite end of the belt from the buckle."

"But how . . . ?" Laurence asked.

"We put the buckle in undisturbed soil in the drain," Michael explained, "then we plant the chape in that eighteenth-century posthole a few inches away where the strata are mucked aboot. An honest man'd swear and moan and admit that no matter how much the pieces look like they belong together, he canna say they do."

"Because he disna have the stratigraphic evidence tae support a match," said Grant. "I see. Who'll be plantin' them?"

Rebecca took the box and handed it to Dennis. "I think Laurel Matheny's brother should do the honors."

First Dennis flushed, then set his jaw. "You bet. When?"

"As soon as Jerry gets his telephone call," said Laurence. He impressed his face with nonchalance and walked toward the infirmary. "Dr. Kleinfelter? You're wanted on the telephone."

Mark and Hilary looked up from the drain. Jerry removed the cigar from his mouth, bent to crush it out on a column drum, thought again, and smashed it on an insignificant rock. He slouched off toward the hotel where he would no doubt find the mysterious caller had hung up.

His complexion was subtly green, his passing stare at Grant hostile. But then, he didn't even remember the scene at the Festival last night that had forced Grant to jail him. That Tony's arrest let him off the hook of Sheila's murder barely seemed to penetrate his stegosaurus-like skull. His attitude suggested that he—the Napoleon of archeology—was insulted to be suspected of a petty crime.

As soon as Jerry was out of sight, the conspirators hurried toward the trench. Mark and Hilary stood aside. Grant photographed Dennis, buckle, chape, and the posthole clearly marked with a flag as an intrusive feature.

By the time Jerry returned sputtering, all was quiet on the infirmary front. Laurence had taken a circuitous route back to the hotel. Michael and Rebecca were dusting the infamous tile floor—"After you, Gaston," she said. "Oh no, after you, Alphonse," he returned. Dennis took a picture of Grant laying a meter stick on the surface. Mark and Hilary were back at the drain, the buckle a suggestive shape in the mud.

Jerry stopped. His moustache twitched. He said, "I'll handle this," took a dental pick from his pocket, and cleared the rest of the dirt from the buckle. He ordered photographs, drawings, an artifact record sheet, and finally a box. Delicately he poked the border where the different colored deposits of drain and post-hole met.

"It's past lunch time," commented Michael.

"Then go feed your faces," Jerry replied.

They trudged obediently toward the cottage. "I wish he'd hurry up and hang himself," muttered Mark. "I want to go treasure-hunting."

"We want him properly off the premises afore that," Grant said.

"After we get Laurel cleared," asserted Dennis.

Hilary shook her head. "I wonder how long Jerry's been an alcoholic?"

They ate some soup Adele had fixed, spared a few sighs of sympathy mitigated by aggravation for her and Elaine, and returned to the dig. Jerry was regaling Laurence with tales of scientific derring-do. Laurence rolled his eyes toward the approaching group, his forced courtesy starting to wane.

Mark and Hilary bent over the drain, which was now cleared of mud and neatly edged. Dennis glanced at the posthole. The flag fluttered above a clearly defined, apparently untouched, border. Rebecca picked up the box. The chape lay nestled next to the buckle like a calf next to its mother. "Nice," she exclaimed. "Do they go together, Jerry?"

"Sure do," he replied. "No problem working through lunch when you're on the trail of a display-quality artifact like that. That's how it's done, kids—persistence and expert knowledge."

Rebecca handed the box to Michael. God, she thought. She couldn't believe he'd really done it. But he'd gotten away with falsifying information too many times. What price glory—a Harington farthing, a silver penny, a belt buckle . . .

"Dr. Kleinfelter," said Laurence evenly, "I'm relieving you of the post of dig director. The RDG will pay you for your work, and Drs. Campbell and Reid will make sure you get credit in the official records. But your job is finished here. Please settle your bar bill at hotel registration."

"What?" Jerry looked like a fish jerked glassy-eyed and flapping onto the deck of a ship. "What did you say?"

"We put the chape in the posthole," Michael told him. "You took it out and smoothed over the deposit. You're lyin', and this time we can prove it."

"You set me up?" Jerry lurched to his feet. A fist the size of a leg of lamb lifted toward Michael's face. Michael held his ground. "This is entrapment. I'll sue. I'll go to Graham, I'll ruin your career."

"Graham knows all about it," said Michael. "He suggests you give Grant here a deposition clearin' Laurel Matheny of all your accusations. Then we can take the buckle and chape back to the museum instead of suin' you for falsifyin' the records. We'll keep the scandal under the table, so to speak. You decide."

Jerry's face went an appalling shade of puce. He spat several no-nonsense four-letter words and swung. Michael ducked. Grant seized Jerry's arm. "Noo, Dr. Kleinfelter, you dinna want charges o' assault."

"What the hell business is Matheny of yours anyway?" Jerry shouted. "She was just a cheap research assistant—"

Dennis stepped forward, shoulders back, chin up. "She's my sister. I'd take back that 'cheap' if I was you."

Jerry's moustache went limp, and his eyes behind his glasses went blank. He growled, "I have better things to do than waste my time with a rinky-dink hole in the ground!" He stamped off. His stamps were swallowed by the soft grass. Laurence and Grant turned to each other, shook hands, and went to speed Jerry on his way.

"I stood up to him." Dennis deflated onto the column drum.

"You did what you came here for," Rebecca told him. There was no need to point out that his lies had compounded Tony's; too many people had lied.

Dennis's face crinkled into a triumphant smile.

"Will Jerry still be able to work?" Hilary asked.

"Sure," Mark told her. "There are always jobs for rescue archeologists, following the bulldozer like seagulls following a plow. He won't destroy the last of his career by refusing to cooperate."

"And we were so worried about getting tarred with his brush." Rebecca sighed and stretched, feeling one more burden lifted from her shoulders.

"Graham was on my side, Nelson on yours and Laurel's," said Michael. "Take note, students; a guid reputation's like a strong kilt pin, it keeps you from embarrassment when the wind's blowin'."

He was as pleased with himself as a child with a good report card. Rebecca wondered what else Graham had said. But they couldn't discuss finances now. Later she'd sit him down and make him tell.

Soon the silver Jaguar roared off toward the neon lights of the south. Grant and Laurence, reinforced by Nora, Winnie, and Bridget, returned to the dig. "We have the deposition for your sister, Dennis," Grant reported as they started en masse toward the Law. "He admitted fiddlin' the penny that was wi' the skeleton, and plantin' the disc. But he says he didna break doon the wall in the crypt on purpose. He said that'd be unprofessional."

Amid a valedictory chorus of hoots and groans, Rebecca led the way to the low ruined wall. She looked from the wheel-cross before the church to the ruined cross higher up the hill. "I hope this is it."

They fanned out, wielding trowels and shovels, carefully turning over loose tiles and scraping at cut stones buried in moss and ferns. The sun slipped down the western sky like a drop of molten gold. The shadows lengthened. People gathered in the Festival field.

At last Rebecca burrowed under a thick growth of heather and found a flat piece of slate. "What's that?" Hilary asked.

"Too large to be the seat cover of a garderobe, a medieval loo," Rebecca replied. "That'd be higher up, anyway, in the castle walls."

Hilary laughed. "I hope Anne didn't hide her altar plate in a loo!"

Rebecca ferreted around the edge of the slate. Dirt and tiny heather needles seemed to be sucked away from her trowel. The space under the stone was hollow, and not with fairy caverns. "I need some strong arms!"

She was almost trampled in the masculine rush. Michael took charge, counting, "One, two, three!" The stone turned over with a reverberating crash. Beneath it was a hole. Dennis lifted the video camera and started filming. Grant, ever resourceful, handed Rebecca a flashlight. She flopped down on her stomach and shone the light within. An assortment of hot breaths tickled the back of her neck. "A pit dungeon," she announced. "Lower me down."

"Rebecca . . ." someone protested—Michael, she assumed. But it was his hands that grasped hers and steadied her while she slipped over the side and plopped down seven feet or so into damp, musty darkness.

"It *is* a pit dungeon," she called upward, her voice echoing.

Her outstretched arms could span the width of the chamber. Cut stone glinted in the sweep of her flashlight. A few dismal gray shapes lay heaped in a corner. She knelt and poked warily through the pile.

Old bones. Shreds of cloth. Lead papal seals—those, at least, were on the inventory. A pewter cup. A disintegrating wooden cross. "The relics are here," she called up at last. "They were valuable to Anne, but only historically interesting to us, I'm afraid."

Michael landed lightly beside her. "Look there. That's what happened to the silver plate." He guided her hand, and the flashlight lit what looked like a tortoise shell. No, it was armor, a breastplate and close helmet in the style of the seventeenth century.

"Rats." Rebecca looked up at the opening. The circle of heads almost blocked the blue of the sky. "Cromwell was here first. No wonder no one ever recorded the finding of the treasure—the soldier who looted it took off so fast he left his armor. Sheila died, and Tony will spend the rest of his life in prison for something that—well, that didn't really exist."

No one spoke. Rebecca stepped back from the armor, and something turned beneath her shoe. Michael scuffed at the floor. "Another slate." In minutes he had it up, revealing a dark cavity. Inside was a bundle about the size of a football wrapped in crumbling cloth. He lifted it out.

"Look!" Rebecca gasped. "Oh, Michael, look!"

As she had predicted, the reliquary was shaped like a small house. The leather carrying strap was only a mournful shred, but its elaborate gilt-bronze mounts, decorated with red and yellow enamel, shone through the grime. Gold plates covered the sides, stippled with interlaced animals in Celtic style. Michael pursed his lips and blew. Dust filled the air. An inscription ran along the roof edge. Rebecca read, *"Robertus Scotorum Rex."* Her whisper resonated through the vault.

Hilary said, "Robert the Bruce's heart. That, to Anne, was more important than any amount of gold or silver. It was a sacred trust."

"What do you want to bet," said Rebecca, "that the ghost Anne was talking to was Marjory Douglas, who brought the relic here to begin with? Marjory passed the trust on to Anne, who passed it on to . . ."

For a moment the dungeon was so silent she could hear the

mingled breaths of the watchers. The whir of the camera sounded like a jet airplane taxiing for take-off. Finally Michael said, "She passed it on to us."

"It'll go to the museum, where it belongs," Laurence stated. "Thank God Jerry or Sheila or Tony never got it. They would've claimed they found it off the property, that it was a treasure trove."

"It took an expert to find it," explained Michael. "Gey brilliant, she is." He swept Rebecca into an extravagant embrace. Everyone clapped and cheered. Dennis, with a fine eye for comedy, went on filming.

Rebecca was reminded forcibly of her various wounds when she started to scramble out of the pit. Michael boosted, and Laurence and Grant pulled, and with a clumsy scramble she regained the open air. She took the reliquary and its moldering cloth and stepped back so they could haul Michael out, too.

They replaced the slate slab and strolled across the lawn toward the road, Nora carrying the reliquary as carefully as a snowflake. "We have to report all finds of ancient objects to the police," Michael said.

"Consider it reported," said Grant.

Michael went on, "Noo a committee has to decide whether or no to keep the find for the national collections, and how much compensation to pay the finders—the RDG. You'll have your restoration and your museum, right enough."

Laurence and Bridget did a spontaneous dance step around the wheel-cross. The west front of the church looked on, blushing in the sunshine. For a story that had started out a Shakespearean tragedy of death and deceit, Rebecca reflected, the finale was looking like undiluted Gilbert and Sullivan. Except they weren't quite yet ready for the curtain.

Chapter Thirty

THE RUDESBURNERS CARRIED the reliquary in triumphal procession to the village. The students went grinning into the cottage. Michael pulled Rebecca into the bedroom and shut the door. "Well," he asked teasingly, "have we solved everything yet?"

"Not quite. Did Graham accept our two-fer deal?"

"No, he didna." But Michael couldn't get his face to frown; it kept curling up at the edges like tissue paper.

Rebecca pushed him down on the bed. "Out with it."

"Graham's offered you a job of your own, lass."

Her heart somersaulted. "You'd better not be kidding."

"Would I joke about something that important?" He pulled her down beside him and placed a proprietary arm around her shoulders. "The RDG has a grant from the Historic Buildings and Monuments lot to sort oot the priory, right? Part of that grant was Jerry's salary for writin' up the results. But Jerry got the chop. It's your job, if you want it."

"Do I want it? I never thought paperwork could look so good!" Rebecca exulted. "What would you have done if he hadn't taken the bait today?"

"Stuffed that buckle doon his throat and accused him of theft."

She laughed. That the problem could turn so swiftly to a benefit was a grace note on their decision made and accepted. "A dig that turned up as many surprises, not to say controversies, as this one will take all winter to write up. Maybe I can find a permanent job by then."

Michael smiled as smugly as a magician counting the rabbits

in his hat. "That you can. The woman who supervises the publications department for the museum is retirin' next spring. They'll be needin' someone to do guidebooks, press releases— what have you. You're a teacher; you'd be a natural."

"Great! I mean, yeah, I've taught—I guess I can write . . ."

"You can write. Graham wants the museum press to publish your dissertation to go wi' the Forbes exhibit this fall. And he'll be askin' you to do a popular account of the dig here. We needed the dig to be a success, love, and it is. A good thing Jerry disna realize how many merit badges his behavior earned us."

"Because we pulled it off in spite of him, and the murder, and—" Rebecca sat glued to Michael's side, dazzled. "Oh, wow."

"No one wanted to publish my dissertation," he concluded.

His face was set in exaggerated sulkiness, tempering resentment with self-mockery. She toppled him onto the pillow and kissed him. "Thank you, thank you, thank you."

When she came up for air, he said, "You've earned it, love. We'll no be gettin' rich, you ken, but we'll have enough to live on." She bore down on him again and, laughing, he succumbed.

But the afternoon was wearing into evening. Reluctantly they parted and started getting ready for the evening festivities. "We have so much to do this month already," Rebecca said around her lipstick. "Closing the infirmary trench, site mapping, soil and ceramic analysis, computer records. And we'll have to testify at Tony's trial, won't we?"

"Only one court in Scotland can try murder cases," Michael told her. He brushed his kilt and sweater and put them on. "They'll no be passin' a verdict of 'Not proven,' though."

She firmly shoved aside the matter of Tony, soon to be the Birdman of Dartmoor or some other British prison. "My family doesn't know about us. They've never even met you. And I bet there's some bureaucrat out there whose sole function is to hassle citizens of different countries who get married." She brushed at her hair a moment, then gave up; the waves were as unruly as her emotions. "I'll have to ship my things over; that'll be expensive. I don't have a dress. We don't have a place. We haven't even chosen a date."

Michael's reflection appeared behind hers, dazed but determined. "You'd no consider elopin' to the nearest registry office, would you?"

"Good heavens, no. Some things simply have to be done properly. A church wedding, no two ways about it."

"Aye, then. Dornoch Cathedral. It's a small one," he added when he saw her alarmed look, "but choice."

"Whew. I was imagining Westminster Abbey." She got up and straightened his collar. "Let's get to it, then."

"Aye," said Michael faintly, and then laughed. "Let's get to it."

In Laurence's office, they consulted a calendar, decided on August twentieth—no need to drag matters out any longer—and added another small fortune to the hotel phone bill by calling Rebecca's parents. She tried not to giggle as Michael adopted a perfect mid-Atlantic accent and charmed the Reids out of their qualms about their daughter marrying a foreigner. When at last he hung up, sighed, and said, "They decided I might almost be good enough for you," Rebecca told herself she had been wrong. She had thought her family wanted her to get married so badly they would have welcomed a toad.

Rebecca was charmed in turn when she realized Andrew Campbell's voice sounded so much like his son's. By the time she hung up, Caroline was already set to decorate their flat with Laura Ashley fabrics. "You warned them, didn't you?" Rebecca asked. "They weren't a bit surprised."

"I told them all aboot it last winter," Michael said with a shrug, as though he'd never doubted her. Rebecca tickled him, gave him a kiss, then had to wipe her lipstick from his mouth. A passing waiter did a doubletake and almost dropped his tray.

Maddy Lewis was ecstatic. August twenty was super. Geoff was on holiday that week, the boys loved the coast at Dornoch, and would Rebecca like to wear her wedding dress? By the time they walked out of the office, it was Rebecca's turn to feel dazed. She definitely had a new family, and she didn't feel a bit suffocated.

Arm in arm, Rebecca and Michael strolled to the Festival field and plunged into the delectable smells and cheerful noises. Michael swept Mark and his guitar into a Scottish jam session, pipes and flute and accordions wending their way from traditional to contemporary melodies and back again. Rebecca and Hilary sat on the edge of the stage clapping and singing along. *I could get used to this*, Rebecca thought. *I will get used to it.*

Michael dedicated solos of "Mo Nighean Donn, Gradh Mo Chridhe" and "Ferry Me Over" to his bride. Rebecca went scarlet and grinned like a deranged chipmunk. Mark gave her a similar grin and a thumbs-up sigh. Hilary hugged her. The crowd roared approval, and Dennis caught everything on videotape.

It was past midnight when the two couples walked back across the priory lawns. One by one the colored Festival lights winked out, leaving the landscape glazed with moonlight. The two cats sat on the porch of the church, heads cocked to the side, ears and whiskers pricked up like radar dishes.

"*Gloria tibi'* " sang voices from another time. "*Gloria tibi, Domine.*"

Glory be to God. A gauzy shape, its draperies formed of shimmering mist, wafted toward the altar. "*Gloria tibi, Domine,*" sang the voices, then faded until they were one with the night wind. A gust of cold air sighed through the door and then stilled. The figure spread itself upon moonlight and shadow, thinner and thinner, and was gone.

"Anne fulfilled her trust," Rebecca murmured. "She's free. Rudesburn is free. The priory seems lighter already."

The cats got up, stretched, and regarded the humans with benign contempt. Hilary picked up Guinevere who immediately voiced her contentment by purring loudly.

"Will Anne's and Alexander's and the baby's bones be brought back here?" Mark asked quietly.

"Oh, aye," replied Michael. 'If weddin's have to be done properly, then so do funerals. But I wonder if they should be buried together?"

" 'Alexander,' " Rebecca quoted, " 'I confess that I have failed, which He has forgiven, God have mercy on our child.' " She shook her head. "We'll never know the full story. At least Anne felt she was forgiven, there at the end—if it was an end—for whatever she did."

"Amazing grace," said Mark under his breath.

Lancelot curled around Hilary's ankles as she cuddled Guinevere. She said dreamily, "I made up a story for them, for what it's worth. Anne loved Alexander—she gave herself freely to him. But Thomas killed him for selling out Anne to the English. Realizing he'd lost everything, Thomas put his ring on Alexander's finger, hid the body, and ran away. He was the one who truly loved Anne. A clean, idealistic, perfect love. That's why his crest is on the wall, too. She knew."

"And Thomas knew they killed her?" Rebecca asked, playing along with the fantasy.

"Yes. That's why he became a highwayman; in his bitterness, he no longer cared whether he lived or died."

Mark looked at Hilary, his face lopsided with indulgence and rue. "That's a good story."

Hilary smiled up at him, put down the cat, and took his arm. Both couples walked on to the cottage and went inside, Mark and Hilary to their separate beds, Michael and Rebecca to anticipate a double bed in Edinburgh.

On Saturday afternoon Dr. Graham formally accepted the Bruce reliquary for Scotland, an event broadcast across Britain. Whether it was greeted with patriotic salutes or yawns of indifference, Rebecca couldn't say. When Graham reiterated his offers of employment and publication, she confounded the old gentleman by throwing her arms around his neck and kissing him. "Ah, lad," he said to a delighted Michael as he wiped steam from his glasses, "you have yourself a bonny lass. Welcome home, Rebecca."

The Festival ended Saturday night with a medieval joust, madrigal singing, and a rousing pipe and drum parade. By the early hours of Sunday, Rebecca and Michael were tipsy from whiskey and music and sex. They agreed that after the twentieth they'd style themselves "Campbell-Reid." "Because," said Michael drowsily, "we're a team."

"Yes, we are," she told him. "Just like Abbott and Costello."

The next morning Laurence said the Festival had been a roaring success, although he hoped next year to get fewer ambulance chasers. Grant reported that he and his fellow constables had not allowed one hammer, chisel, or spray can of paint to approach the priory. When it became a museum rather than a crime scene, he added, his job would be considerably simplified.

The people who were to have rented the cottage that week must have been the only people in Europe who weren't interested in the crime scene. They canceled, leaving the decimated expedition a place to stay during the extra time it took to close down the dig. Dennis's camera work had to be completed by the end of the week, when an officer from Sheila's bank would be coming to claim the van and all the equipment. On Monday morning Rebecca hopped up on the column drum and delivered an exhortatory speech modeled on that of General Patton. With assorted nationalistic shouts, they went to work.

On Monday afternoon Harry Devlin rang from Edinburgh to

say that Adele had been committed to a mental hospital back in the United States. Rebecca and Hilary packed her things, including the UCLA sweatshirt, and sent them on. No one would ever know, Rebecca thought, whether Adele even cared about the treasure, let alone knew where it was.

In the pub that night, Nora told the group that a bobby had brought Elaine round to get her things. "She didn't want to talk to us?" Dennis asked.

"No—she was on her way back to London. I imagine she's still afraid of being charged as an accomplice. All she said was that she'd thought Jerry was the murderer."

"I hope she can find herself a good job," said Hilary.

Everyone nodded into their drinks. From the bar Laurence said, "Michael, Rebecca—Nora and I want you to take whatever furniture you fancy from the attic. Just to show our appreciation for what you've done."

"But there are antiques up there!" Rebecca protested.

"A cousin of mine wants to sub-let his flat in Edinburgh," said Nora, overruling her objection. "Pleasance Street, just off the Royal Mile. Nothing posh, but larger than a bed-sitter. I told him you'd ring him."

"Thank you," said Michael. "We appreciate all you've done for us."

On Tuesday Rebecca and Michael took Dennis and Winnie into Galashiels, there to make even more depositions. On Wednesday the crew filled in the infirmary trench and collected the cache of relics from the Law. On Thursday they organized the computer records and maps and material analyses. On Friday Dennis pronounced the filming and photographing a wrap. The finished product would be a jigsaw puzzle, Rebecca told herself, but adequate for academic reference. Only Jerry's and Sheila's pretentiousness had intended it for the Academy Awards.

On Friday evening Devlin joined the end-of-dig ceilidh. He mentioned that a judge had ruled that any proceeds from the film and Tony's postcards and photos should go to the RDG, but Devlin seemed more interested in showing Bridget the pictures of his daughter.

As Mark was putting up his guitar, Rebecca noticed he wasn't wearing his silver belt buckle. "Oh," he said to her inquiring look, "I put it in the Oxfam collection box in the lobby. I decided I didn't need it anymore."

"Amazing grace?" she asked, and he nodded assent.

They spent all weekend packing the excavation supplies and their personal belongings and ferrying them to Edinburgh. It was hard leaving Rudesburn, but not nearly as hard as it would've been if Rebecca had been going back to the United States without a home and a job. Moving a walnut secretary, a Queen Anne wing chair, and an oak trestle table from the hotel to the flat in Pleasance Street was a positive pleasure.

With many promises to keep in touch, Dennis went home. Hilary went to France to interview for an art history fellowship. Mark stayed on at Rudesburn, in a garret in the hotel, to help plot the priory restoration. "See you on the twentieth," the Bairds and the Johnstons and Bridget called as Rebecca drove the red Fiat down Jedburgh Street and into a gentle Sunday rain. The last sight she and Michael had of the cats were two furry faces pressed against the damp window of the shop, whiskers angled rakishly.

Rebecca only stalled out once on the way to Edinburgh. Michael was polite enough not to laugh.

Places and people whirled like the bright flecks in a kaleidoscope, and before Rebecca quite realized it, it was August the twentieth. She stood in the window of the Dornoch Castle Hotel looking across to the cathedral. A small cathedral, yes, but the simplicity of its Norman lines and the character of its ancient stone did indeed make it choice, while the painted Victorian fountain in the grassy square out front added a note of whimsy.

"Did you want to open these letters?" Hilary asked from behind her.

"That one's from Jan in Ohio, isn't it? Let me see . . ." Paper ripped. Rebecca laughed. "She's thanking you, Hilary, for filling in for her as bridesmaid, and teasing me about moving over here."

Hilary put several checks from Rebecca's parents' friends into an envelope. "Getting married overseas is one way to make sure you don't get too many toasters."

The soft rose-pink dress Hilary had bought in Paris was probably three times as expensive as the wedding gown Rebecca wore. But Hilary had been so excited at getting her fellowship that she'd splurged. Rebecca certainly hadn't wanted her to get a dress she could wear only once.

Maddy's gown fit Rebecca perfectly. Not only did the off-white silk complement her dark eyes, but also the puffed sleeves and low ruffled neckline made her feel like a Barbara Cartland heroine. She pushed at her hair, and Hilary, ever mindful of her duties, rushed over with another hairpin for the roses and bits of organza that had been substituted for a veil. In another day or so, Rebecca told herself, she'd finally forget that scratch on her skull, just as Michael was working on forgetting the scar on his arm. No more fear. No more pain.

Outside on the green lawn, the wedding party was gathering. If Rebecca wasn't already in love with Michael, she thought, she'd develop a crush on his father, his brows animated by ironic humor and every hair of his salt and pepper beard meticulously trimmed. In their kilts and formal Prince Charlie jackets, Andrew, Colin, and Mark were birds of paradise flocking around the crow-like figure of Kevin Reid. Rebecca smiled—her brother looked just like the overgrown high school football player he was.

The first words out of his mouth when he'd stepped off the plane had been, "I don't have to wear one of those skirt things, do I?" But Mark's attitude ran more along the lines of, "If they can do it, so can I." As Rebecca watched, though, he made a dubious wriggle. She could almost hear him thinking, "These things are a little breezy, aren't they?"

The Rudesburn delegation stood talking with the dark, dramatic figure of Anjali MacLeod. Geoff Lewis, a compact, soft-spoken Yorkshireman in a three-piece suit, herded his three little boys in their tiny kilts away from the fountain. Caroline Campbell's red-gold curls nodded like a chrysanthemum, and every line on her face tilted upward, set by a lifetime of laughter.

And there was Simon Mackenzie and a strong-featured woman with assertive "Rule Brittania" teeth—Amanda Fraser, no doubt. Harry Devlin was escorting Bridget Hamilton; his Irish eyes were certainly smiling.

The door opened and admitted Maddy, her red hair flying every which way, as if electrically charged. "No, you canna see the bride before the weddin'," she called over her shoulder.

"I've seen the bride," returned Michael's plaintive voice.

Maddy shut the door on him. "Here," she said to Rebecca. "Michael asked me to give you this. A token of his affection, like the quaich you gave him." Rebecca opened the velvet jeweler's case to reveal a Scottish silver luckenbooth brooch, two hearts intricately knit together. 'It's inscribed on the back,"

Maddy went on. "Ruth 1:16. He said you'd be recognizin' the verse."

Rebecca did, and started bravely, " 'Entreat me not to leave thee, or to return from following after thee.' " She felt her throat close up and her eyes fill with tears, but plunged on, " 'Whither thou goest I will go, thy people shall be my people.' " Her voice broke, and a tear spilled down her cheek. " 'And thy God my God,' " she finished.

"That's really sweet," said Hilary, and pinned the brooch to Rebecca's shoulder.

Rebecca gulped and quelled her tears before her mascara ran. "I was doing fine," she protested to Maddy.

"That's Michael for you," Maddy replied with a comforting hug. "A thistle wi' a heart of toffee. Here're your flowers, your audience awaits."

By the time Rebecca, Hilary, and Maddy reached the square, Michael and the witnesses were already in the cathedral. A cool breeze ruffled her organza. Her stomach felt like a tropical rain forest, butterflies swooping through trembling fronds. She gritted her teeth and clutched at her tiny bouquet of roses. Their stems were threaded through the metal ring from the wine bottle; she wanted no other engagement ring.

Kevin handed his camera to Maddy. Gratefully Rebecca took her brother's arm. The Reids had agreed it wasn't right for her to be married alone and had passed the hat around the family to send Kevin to give her away—not that she liked the concept of being handed over like a parcel. But for someone who prided herself on not running away, she'd undeniably run from her family; letting Kevin walk her down the aisle was little enough restitution.

He patted her hand and took her across the square and into the cool interior of the cathedral. The soaring arches reminded her of Rudesburn. So did some of the faces turned toward her, except now the faces were smiling, and somewhere in the background a piper was piping a voluntary, and several miles away Michael and Colin stood beside a black-clad minister, bathed in the multicolored glow of a stained-glass window. Hilary paced up the aisle. Rebecca lifted her feet and put them down. The butterflies in her stomach grew to the size of condors.

Kevin levered her up a step. The minister spoke. Kevin spoke. He put her hand in Michael's. Michael winked at her and squeezed her fingers—he *would* be calm, just to show her up.

The colors of the sunlight melted and ran, and her own voice quavered, "I, Rebecca Marie, take thee, Michael Ian . . ." She fumbled handing her bouquet to Hilary, but Hilary caught it.

Michael kissed her. She was clutching his arm, following Colin and Hilary back down the aisle. Flashbulbs flared. Michael's nephews—her nephews, too, now—frisked before them like dolphins near a ship. "You're a sight," Michael stage-whispered. "Lovely."

If Rebecca's knees got any weaker, he'd have to carry her. "You're gorgeous," she replied. "I always wondered how you'd look with lace at your throat."

"Uncomfortable. It's prickly, and the tie's too tight."

"Where did you get the new sgian dubh?"

"An old relative of my mother's on Skye said I needed a proper one and gave me his. Antique bone handle, but no very sharp."

"Good."

The square flashed by, and they were in the banquet room of the hotel, facing a tiered wedding cake decorated with pink, white, and yellow roses. Champagne corks popped. Andrew started piping "Peace and Plenty," and Michael pulled Rebecca into a dance. The ring finger of her hand resting on his shoulder gleamed with a broad gold band. The corresponding ring was warm on his hand holding hers. She cried unashamedly, and as he kissed her tears away, he was ducking his head to hide his own.

Sometime that afternoon Rebecca sipped at the champagne, but her corpuscles were already sparkling. Michael played a duet with his father while Rebecca danced with Kevin. Then she danced with Grant Johnston, her hand engulfed by his. Mark led her out, and she danced again, her feet barely touching the floor, the fabric of her dress swirling lightly around her ankles. "When are you leaving?" she asked him.

"Day after tomorrow," he replied. "Fall semester in Austin."

"And Hilary's leaving for France. Do you feel cheated?"

He glanced at Hilary dancing happily with Colin. His eyes glinted as he answered, "Of course not, how could I?"

Michael and Rebecca stood by the table feeding each other bites of cake. From the corner of her eye she saw Devlin writing something in his ever present notebook. "Dr. and Dr. Campbell-

Reid, historical troubleshooters," he said. "The Chief Inspector has a file of consultants."

"Wi' all due respect—" Michael said to Mackenzie's hawk face, and Rebecca finished, "—don't call us, we'll call you." Mackenzie bared his teeth in a delighted guffaw.

Colin brought them the silver quaich, brimming with aged single-malt. Rebecca drank and handed it to Michael. Over the silver rim his eyes glistened blue, depth after depth of intellect and emotion, humor and challenge.

Mark danced by with Hilary. Rebecca overheard him say to her, "Have a nice life."

She replied, "It's getting better all the time."

Soon Rebecca was whisked by Maddy and Hilary back upstairs where she was stripped of headdress and gown and dressed in a skirt and sweater, the brooch pinned securely to the throat of her blouse. In front of the hotel, the red Fiat waited, painted with messages, bawdy and otherwise, balloons waving from its antenna and streamers from its back bumper. She hugged Kevin's beefy chest. He said, "I know Michael will take good care of you, Squirt."

"I can take care of—" she started indignantly, and over Kevin's shoulder caught Michael's jaundiced eye. "We'll take care of each other," she amended, and hugged everyone else in sight.

At last she took Michael's hand; he was back in his handknit sweater again, the intricate pattern hanging comfortably over his kilt. Confetti showered down on them, half of it going down the back of her neck. The Fiat zoomed around the square and toward Inverness. Rebecca combed confetti out of her hair and took a deep breath. "Dr. Campbell-Reid, I love you."

Michael shifted gears. His hand moved over to tickle her leg beneath the hem of her skirt. "I love you, Dr. Campbell-Reid."

"Nice of your parents to let us have their best room."

"It has a four-poster bed. We started in a four-poster."

She laughed. Rich green hillsides stroked with purple heather sped by on one side, backed by the celestial blue of distant mountains. Dornoch Firth opened on the other, the indigo of its waters sheened by the late afternoon sun.

What was the Burns song Michael had sung all those years ago in Ayr? Oh, yes. She tried another version: "A' that I have endured, laddie my dearie, here in thy arms is cured, laddie lie near me."

"I intend to," he said.

The world centered itself below the profound blue skies of home.

Glossary

a': all
aboon: over, on top of
aboot: about
ack emma: a.m.
afore: before
aggro: aggravation
airts: parts, areas
airy-fairy: head in the clouds
argy-bargy: argument
awful: very
aye: yes

bairn: child or baby
berk: stupid and disagreeable
   person
bide: stay
bint: derogatory term for a woman
bittie: smll
bloke: fellow
bluidy: bloody
bonnet: hood (of car)
bonny: pretty
boot: trunk (of car)
braw: brave
bugger: foul up
bum: buttocks
bung: throw
burn: stream

canna: can't
canny: clever
ceilidh: party
cheek: nerve
cheese-paring: thriftiness
chuff: please
claes: clothes
clap out: tired

claymore: traditional Scottish
   broadsword
cock-up: mess, in the abstract
   sense
codswallop: nonsense
cosh: hit with a club
couthy: congenial
cuppa: cup of tea

daft: stupid, crazy
dander: stroll
dead: very
dear: valuable
deil: devil
didna: didn't
dinna: don't
disna: doesn't
dogsbody: inferior laborer
doon: down
dout: suspect
dustbin: wastebasket

effing: ''f''-ing
elevenses: tea at eleven a.m.

fair: rather
fiddle: cheat
flannel: half-truths
flyte: scold

gey: very
gormless: unattractive
gowk: fool
grass: betray confederates
ground floor: first floor
guid: good
gumption: courage

haver: to talk incoherently, nonsensically
hen: term of affection for a woman
hivna: haven't

incomer: someone from elsewhere who's moved to Scotland
isna: isn't

jiggery-pokery: skulduggery
jink: bounce around, dodge

keek: peek
ken: know
knackered: tired
knock up: rouse

lead: leash
loo: toilet
loup: run quickly

moggie: pet cat
muck about: mess up
muckle: a lot of, great

nae: no
naething, naebody: nothing, nobody
nark: irritate
nervy: nervous, jumpy
nick: steal
noo: now
no: not

o': of
oot: out
outwith: outside
ower: over
own: admit

panda car: police car
pavement: sidewalk
pecker: chin
peeler: policeman
perjink: tidy and proper
petrol: gasoline

pillock: idiot
pinch: steal
pip emma: p.m.
po-faced: solemn
ponce: saunter showily
posh: ultra-smart, high-toned
post: mail

quid: pound (money)

recce: reconaissance
ring: call on the phone
row: argument

sae: so
sarkey: sarcastic
Sassenach: term of ridicule for English
scairt: frightened
scarper: run away
scunner: dislike
sgian dubh: small Scottish knife
shag: have sex with
shop: turn someone over to police
shy: throw
skelp: slap or hit
slag off: make fun of
slaistering: dirty, disgusting
snogging: necking
sod, sodding: term of abuse
sod-all: nothing
sporron: leather pouch
stravaige: stroll about aimlessly
suss out: reconnoiter

tae: to
takeaway: carry-out
telly: television
teuchter: country yokel
the day: today
the morn: tomorrow
the night: tonight
the now: now
thole: tolerate
thrawn: stubborn
toff: big shot

torch: flashlight
trunk call: long-distance
tumble: discover the truth
turf out: throw out
twig: discover the truth
twit: nerd

wallah: person concerned with
   something
wally: conspicuous fool
wean: child
wee: small

wellies: rubber boots
whilst: while
wi': with
widna: wouldn't
winkle out: pry out
wisna: wasn't

yobbo: hooligan
yon: that

zed: the letter ''z''

Printed in the United States
60866LVS00001BA/2

9 780595 094462